OCT 1 5 2018

Raven-Mocking

Amy Sumida

D1367008

WILLARD LIBRARY, BATTLE CREEK, MI

Copyright © 2015 Amy Sumida

All rights reserved.

ISBN-10: 1523958715

ISBN-13: 978-1523958719

WILLARD LIBRARY, BATTLE CREEK, MI

More Books by Amy Sumida

The Godhunter Series(in order)
Godhunter
Of Gods and Wolves
Oathbreaker
Marked by Death
Green Tea and Black Death
A Taste for Blood
The Tainted Web

Series Split:
These books can be read together or separately
Harvest of the Gods & A Fey Harvest
Into the Void & Out of the Darkness

Perchance to Die
Tracing Thunder
Light as a Feather
Rain or Monkeyshine
Blood Bound

Beyond the Godhunter:
A Darker Element

The Twilight Court Series:
Fairy-Struck
Pixie-Led
(Raven-Mocking)

Other Books

The Magic of Fabric
Feeding the Lwas: A Vodou Cookbook
There's a Goddess Too

The Vampire-Werewolf Complex
Enchantress

Pronunciation Guide

Aideen: Ay-deen

Ainsley: Ains-lee

Aodh: Ee

Balloch: Bal-lock

Baobhan sith: Baa-vahn-she

Beag: big(k)

Bean-sidhe: ban-she

Cailleach Bheur: CALL-yack Burr or COY-ick Burr

Catan: KAH-tan

Cliona: CLEE-oh-nah

Criarachan: CREE-are-rock-ahn

Cúl tóna: cool tone-ah (dickhead in Gaelic)

Dathadair: Dath-ah-dare

Dhoire: Doy-rah

Diocail: JU-kel

Duergar: Doo-ay-gahr

Each-Uisge: Ech-oosh-kee-ya

Eadan: Ae-dan

Ewan: You-win

Fir Darrig: Fear-durg

Gancanagh: Gon-cawn-ah

Ghillie-Dhu: Gill-ee-doo

Glastig: Clee-stickh

Gradh: Grah

Greer: Gree-air

Gwyllion: Gwith-lee-on

Iseabal: Ish-bal

Keir: Keer

Latharna: LA-ur-na

Lonnegawn: lonny-goon (forest dwelling plant-person)

Lorcan: Lore-cawn

Mairte: Mahrj-tah

Marcan: MOR-kawn

Moire: Moy-rah

Mór: Mo-ore

Mufasa: Moo-fah-sah

Nighean: Na-yee-in

Nuckelavee: Nuke-ah-lah-vee

Rayetayah: Rah-yay-tah-yah

Raza: Rah-zah

Ryvel: Rival

Searc: Sherk

Seelie: See-lee

Seren: Sare-rin

Sorcha: SORE-sha

Tiernan: Teer-nin

Torquil: Tore-quill

Tursa: Ture-sah (a type of fairy bear)

Uisdean: OOSH-jan

Unseelie: Un-see-lee

Chapter One

The shrill cry of a bird assaulted my ears as my boots crunched over the dry, dying grass. I winced and searched the barren sky, squinting in the glaring light of a harsh sun. Another cry came from my right and I ducked just as a crow swooped by.

"What's your problem?!" I shouted at the bird. "Why are you messing with me? I did right by Cailleach; she was pardoned." The crow dive-bombed me again. "Stupid crow!" I waved my arms insanely at it.

"It's not a crow," a voice very like my own said.

I looked towards the sound and saw myself standing against a backdrop of Native American tepees. My face was shadowed by my long, windswept, midnight hair but the stars radiating through the emerald irises of my eyes sparkled out of the darkness and the amethyst stripe in my hair caught their glimmer. I was definitely looking at an image of myself.

I was wearing a creamy beige buckskin dress, complete with rows of fringe and beautiful beadwork. There was a colorful, boldly patterned shawl around my shoulders and tall, beaded moccasins on my feet. The land stretched out behind the conical tents and me, ending in a blushing horizon. The sun was setting; twilight coming.

"Why am I talking to myself?" I asked her/me/it.

"Because there's no one else here," she/I shrugged.

"Oh okay," for some reason it made perfect sense. "What do you mean it's not a crow?"

"That's a raven," she pointed at the bird who was now circling above us. "Heads up!"

I ducked as the foul fowl took another pass at me.

I'm going to shish-kebob you, bird!" I shook my fist at it because that's what one does when ravens try to peck your eyes out.

"It's only trying to tell you something," she/I shrugged.

"That I should take up bird watching?" I huffed.

"In a way," she smiled and I wanted to wipe that grin off my face. Her face. Whatever.

"Just spit it out," I snapped. "When did we become so fey? And so native?" I waved at her tribal dress.

"Aren't you smart enough to figure it out for yourself? You're supposed to be this big sparkly Twilight Princess." Her voice turned into that annoying sing-song tone most often employed by kindergartners and psychopaths.

"Are you mocking me?" I balled my hands into fists. I was about to pull a Tyler Durden and kick my own ass.

"No," she went serious, "but they are," she pointed up to the sky, which was now full of ravens. They swirled together, the beat of their wings thrumming beneath the sound of their cries. They dove at me and I screamed.

"Seren!" Tiernan was suddenly above me, shaking me awake.

I sat up, pushing him aside as I looked around the airy bedroom. The silk comforter was rumpled around my feet, where Cat (my puka companion who was actually closer to a dog than a cat) crouched, staring at me warily. Through the web of delicate night-blooming jasmine which formed a canopy over my bed, I

2

looked up at the crystal dome set into my bedroom ceiling. Through it I could see the night sky, full of fey constellations. The stars of Fairy sparkled the same as they did in the Human Realm but they didn't look the same. Probably since Fairy was in another universe entirely.

"Seren?" Tiernan, my fairy boyfriend and Lord of the Wild Hunt (I have to add it or he'll be mad) gave me another shake.

"I'm okay," I laid my hand over his. "Stop shaking me."

"You screamed," he accused.

"It was just a bad dream," I sighed and laid back down.

"Oh, alright then," he pulled the covers up around us and snuggled in beside me.

"Damn mocking ravens," I muttered as I wiggled to get comfortable next to his firm form.

"What did you say?" Tiernan bolted upright.

"Ravens," I frowned and sat up too. "They were attacking me and then I told myself that they were actually mocking me."

"You told yourself?" Tiernan's eyes scrunched up with confusion.

"Crazy dream stuff, never mind," I waved it away. "Why does that upset you?"

"Raven mockers?" He lifted a brow. "I know you've heard of them."

"The raven mockers," I whispered. I had heard of them. Why hadn't I made the connection? "Those fairies who steal life from the dying and old?"

"Those are the ones," he grimaced.

3

"I've always wondered why they did that," I peered into his night-shadowed face. "Why steal the few years left to an elderly person or someone who's sick?"

"Easy targets," Tiernan scowled, "and no one is suspicious when they die."

"But they don't even need life," I shook my head. "They're fey, so they're immortal, aren't they?"

"Yes, they're immortal," Tiernan sighed. "It's not the extra time that they're after but the energy of the life. It gives them a boost of power and a sort of temporary bliss. That's what they crave."

"Like a drug? Are they energy addicts?"

"In a way, yes," Tiernan mused.

"But if they get caught, they'll be extinguished," I declared.

"Have *you* ever caught one?" He lifted a platinum blonde brow.

"Well no but they keep mainly to the American Northwest and I was never assigned that region," I chewed at my lip, remembering the tepees. That bit was strange. It wasn't like Native Americans lived in tepees anymore but I guess dreams like symbolism.

"No, they don't," Tiernan said softly.

"What?" I focused sharply on him.

"They have ties to the tribes. They're descended from fairies who once bred with the Native Americans and because of that, Native American shamans have learned how to spot them... and how to kill them."

"Right, there's a ritual," I bit my lip as I tried to remember

4

what I'd been taught in extinguisher school.

"Takes seven days though," he shook his head. "They don't always kill the mocker."

"So you're telling me that these fairies could be sucking the last bit of life out of people all over the Human Realm?" I clenched my hands in the comforter.

"Well, they do tend to stay in North and South America but yes," he admitted. "The Wild Hunt tries to keep an eye out for them but they're smart, they know how to fly under the radar."

"Literally," I rolled my eyes.

"You're not asking the right question, Seren," Tiernan was grim and that never boded well.

"What?" A chill coasted over my arms and I swear I heard the cry of a raven in the distance.

"Why are you dreaming about raven mockers?"

Chapter Two

If I hadn't been so damn tired and so accustomed to stress, I probably wouldn't have been able to get back to sleep. But my life had become full of weird premonitions and evil machinations. I was actually getting used to it and had no problem drifting off to sleep. In fact, I didn't want to stop sleeping. Tiernan had to coerce me out of bed in the morning by waving a cup of coffee beneath my nose.

"Maybe sharing a bedroom wasn't such a great idea," I whined as he led me to the dining table, placed off to the left of my bed.

It was actually off to the right if you happened to be stumbling out of the bed, as I was. Oh why must I leave the warm, squishy nest of pillows and silky blankets to emerge into the crisp, cold, cruel morning? Don't fairy princesses get to sleep in? I frowned into my coffee cup as Tiernan pulled out a chair for me. Then I saw that breakfast was already on the table. I gave a little happy smile and took a sip of coffee.

"You were really tired," Tiernan observed. "Normally tea does the trick but I had to resort to coffee this morning."

"Hmph," I mumbled but then he started piling food on my plate and I gave him a grudging, "Thank you."

"You're welcome," he laughed, his silver eyes sparkling in the sunlight coming in from crystal dome overhead and the balcony to our right. "Now, I think we should discuss your dream."

"Ugh," I groaned. "No. I don't want to. Just leave it be until I at least get some food in me."

6

"Alright," he sighed and set to work on his own breakfast.

"Thank you," I started to enjoy my food. Soon Cat had finished her own bowl of breakfast and came to sit beside me. She set her head on the table and eyed my steak. "Oh, I don't think so, Madam Puka," I pushed her nose away from my plate. "I will fight you for this food and guess who's gonna win that battle?"

Cat whined and sat back.

"Exactly," I nodded. "It's wise to know your limitations."

"Seren?" My father's voice came through my bedroom door.

"Seren's not here right now," I called out. "Leave a message at the beep. Be-e-e-p."

"Very amusing," Keir said as he opened the door and strode in.

He was my fairy father, my true birth father, but I'd actually been raised by a human extinguisher named Ewan Sloane. I had been merely an extinguisher once too, a sort of police officer who monitored fairies in the Human Realm. But then I'd come to the Fairy Realm and my true nature had revealed itself. It turned out that I was half fey. My mother had fallen in love with a fairy king and been unfaithful to my dad, resulting in me.

Ewan didn't take the news of my true parentage well and was kind of punishing me for the sins of my mother. I was heartbroken over the loss of the man I'd thought to be my father for the first twenty-six years of my life but Keir had won me over and now that heartache was dulled by the love I was starting to feel for my real father.

Though I wasn't feeling so loving towards him at the moment.

"Dad," I whined. "Whatever it is, it can wait. I'm starving."

"Eat. I'm sure you can listen while you do so," he waved his hand magnanimously. It was a bit annoying but he was a fairy king; those kind of affectations had been taught to him since birth.

"You'll give me indigestion," I complained.

"I'm sure you'll survive," Keir rolled his eyes.

My mother had supplemented Keir's royal deportment with human mannerisms and common sayings, in an effort to make him seem more approachable to me. Keir managed them well for the most part. But even when he did or said them appropriately, he still looked a little silly. Here was this fairy king, dressed in silk and velvet, with long, boysenberry hair fading to lavender at the tips, rolling his sparkling, star-adorned, amethyst eyes. It was surreal. Hell, he was surreal all by himself.

"Your Majesty," Tiernan looked at my father in concern. "What is it?"

"I have just received a scry from Councilman Alan Murdock, Head of the San Francisco Human Council House," Keir sighed deep. "Seren has been summoned to the Human Council House in Tulsa, Oklahoma. There's an urgent meeting being held even as we speak."

"A meeting concerning what exactly?" I asked as the food churned in my belly.

"Raven mockers," Keir said the dreaded words and Tiernan groaned. "What is it?" Keir narrowed his eyes on me.

"Seren dreamed of the raven mockers last night," Tiernan answered for me.

"What were they doing?" Keir lifted an eggplant-colored eyebrow.

"They were just ravens actually," I grumbled. "But they were mocking me."

"Not a good sign," Keir sat back in his chair and closed his eyes briefly. "And not much of a warning," he opened his eyes and set them on Tiernan. "You'll accompany the Princess, of course."

"Yes, Your Majesty," Tiernan bowed his head in acceptance.

"And you'll take Cat with you as well," Keir said to me.

"I can't take Cat," I waved my hands towards the puka who had perked up when she heard her name. "She's way too fey for the Human Realm."

"She can glamour herself to look like a big dog," Keir waved at Cat.

Cat suddenly became a Chihuahua, jumping up and down excitedly, and I gaped at her.

"Did you do that?" I asked Keir accusingly.

"No, that's all her," he chuckled.

"I don't know, Cat," I frowned at her form.

She cocked her head at me and changed into a Shar-Pei. I grimaced as she shook her head, all of her wrinkled skin wobbling with her. She looked at me askance and I shook my head. Then a massive mop head sat before us. I gave a horrified gasp and pulled back in my seat as I stared at the cotton ball-colored puff of dreadlocks.

"What the hell is that?" I pointed at Cat.

"I believe it's called a Puli," Tiernan observed. "They're Hungarian, supposed to be waterproof."

9

"No, Cat," I shook my head emphatically. "You'll attract more attention as that than you would as a puka."

She shifted back to her normal form with a whine.

"She'll figure something out," Keir waved a dismissive hand. "The point is; I want you to have all the protection possible. You'll take your Guard and a few of mine as well."

"Dad, I don't think that's necess-"

"Seren!" Keir stood abruptly and slashed his hand through the air like he was physically cutting my sentence short. "You will not disobey me in this. I want you protected from our enemies and from your own folly. My knights will report to me alone and will have orders that will supersede yours."

"What?" I gaped at him.

"I don't want you running off and signing things in my name again," he growled.

"First of all," I stood up and glared back at him, "you didn't have to honor that contract if you didn't want to. I signed my name, not yours. Second, this trip is an ambassador mission so I'll be acting as Ambassador Seren, not Princess, and therefore, I'm not obligated to you or your instructions. I have to be seen as functioning in a neutral capacity and your personal guard will screw that image up for me. Lastly, what the hell are you so pissed off about? I'm the one who has to go to freakin' Tulsa!"

Keir took a shaky breath and rubbed an elegant hand over his face. "I apologize," he sat back down and I followed suit. "I feel unsettled about this, deeply unsettled, and that translates into a desire to control everything."

"I'll be okay, Dad," I gave his hand a pat. "I can take care of myself, remember? I got that new fancy smancy firethorn magic. If someone attacks me, I'll pull a *bind and burn* on them."

10

"Don't get cocky," Keir shook his head. "Any magic can be overcome, no matter how powerful it is. And any magic can fail you unexpectedly. The first step towards downfall is believing yourself to be invincible."

"Yeah, I get that," I sighed. "I was just trying to make you feel better."

"I'd feel better if you never left Twilight again," Keir grimaced.

"Hiding isn't really my thing," I said gently.

"I know," Keir smiled indulgently. "And I'm so proud of your heroism. Still, I'd rather you be safe and alive, than a dead hero."

"Safe is boring, Dad," I grinned when he groaned.

"There's one more thing you should know about the raven mockers," Keir exchanged a circumspect look with Tiernan.

"What is it?" I sobered.

"They're ours," Keir said simply.

"Excuse me?" I blinked at him, sure that I'd misunderstood.

"They're twilight fairies, Seren," Keir sighed. "The raven mockers are our people, one of the twilight races."

Chapter Three

The Fairy Realm, isn't technically a planet, it's a solar system, as the Human Realm refers to the solar system which Earth is a part of. But Fairy and Earth are the only planets in both of those systems that are populated. So generally, when one refers to the Realm of Fairy or the Human Realm, they're referring to the planets of Fairy and Earth. That being said, Fairy is connected to Earth in several locations by pathways which can be used to travel between the planets. These paths are like wormholes through space, anchored by fairy mounds which are also known as raths. Each rath leads to a specific location and if you were to lay a map of Fairy over one of Earth, you could connect the raths with a pin shoved through the maps. That's how perfectly aligned the planets of Fairy and Earth are.

The Twilight Kingdom is connected to the United States, with exception to Hawaii and Alaska, which are in Unseelie territory. Even though raths are controlled and guarded by fairies, the Human Councils had built their Council Houses nearby, to both keep an eye on the fey and keep in communication with them. So there was a fairy mound which led directly to Tulsa. I just had to travel to the Tulsa rath in a rather medieval style; by carriage... which would take days.

I'd once suggested to my father that we create some kind of magic powered vehicle which could speed up transportation in the Fairy Realm but he'd been horrified. Frankly, after giving it some good thought, I agreed with him. A bunch of cars zipping down the roads of Fairy would kinda ruin the ambiance. Still, it would make the ride to the rath much faster.

I could have traveled the In-Between at twilight; stepping

into the dark, cold place where my magic was strongest, and then stepping out at whatever destination I could envision or name. But only twilight fey could travel in such a way, which meant that I'd have to leave Tiernan behind. Tiernan, although considered a twilight fairy through allegiance, was born seelie.

So instead of traveling the In-Between or taking the long road to the Tulsa rath, it was finally decided that we use the rath which led to Gentry Technologies (Keir's human-based company) in San Francisco and then take Keir's private plane to Tulsa. The SF rath was much closer to Castle Twilight and the plane ride in HR would be faster than traveling that same distance in Fairy by horse.

Still, the SF rath was a hard day's journey from Twilight Castle. We usually took it at a moderate pace and stopped somewhere along the way for the night but the Human Council wanted us in Tulsa as soon as possible. So we'd be riding hard, on horseback instead of in a carriage. Which meant that Cat had to shift into a horse so she could carry me; something which pleased her to no end.

I normally whined about being cooped up in a carriage but riding horseback had its own set of drawbacks. Mainly sore thighs. I was already in human clothes; a pair of bluejeans and my *Ewoking Dead* T-shirt with a picture of zombie ewoks on it. Honestly, I changed into human clothes every chance I got. As amazing as fairy dresses could be, they were annoying to someone used to having a certain amount of ease of movement. Basically, I liked being able to draw my sword and use it if I had to, and that wasn't something fairy dressmakers took into consideration when they designed clothing for fairy princesses. So I was joyous to be in my old clothes, which made for a much easier ride than if I'd been weighed down with some frilly fairy frippery. Still, with a full leather satchel on my back and my iron sword strapped to my waist, the journey exhausted more than just my lower body. By the time we reached the rath, I wanted nothing more than to curl up on the grass on go to sleep.

The meadow before the mound was idyllic. Spotted with little fey flowers, it was a lush layer of verdancy placed amid overhanging trees, which provided bits of shifting shade. The air was scented with crushed grass and the sugary berries which hung in mass clumps on bushes among the trees. I dismounted in a shaft of warm sunlight and sighed, my knees buckling with the urge to just fall to the soft ground and bury my face in the flowers. I didn't even care about bugs, I just wanted to sleep.

That wasn't happening though. On the other side of the fairy mound, my Uncle Dylan Thorn would be waiting to whisk all of us away to the airport. Dylan was the only non-psycho relative I had on the Unseelie side of my family. Actually, after the stunt my Uncle Shane had pulled, it was looking like Uncle Dylan was the only non-psycho relative I had from both the Seelie and Unseelie sides.

Who knows? Maybe I was going psycho too because I started imagining the Wicked Witch of Oz saying; *Poppies, poppies, poppies,* as I stared at the alluring meadow. At least we were traveling by private plane so I could shower and sleep on the way to Tulsa. That thought just might give me enough strength to follow Tiernan through the golden door of the rath and resist the poppies... er, fairy flowers.

Set into the side of a small hill covered in thick blanket of grass and wildflowers, the golden door, with its image of the Earth carved into it, looked out of place. But then that was pretty normal for the Fairy Realm. Fairies loved to stick bits of flashy metalwork out among nature, or bits of nature within their flashy homes. So I guess the door didn't look out of place unless you were a human. Which I still was, at least half of me was.

Tiernan opened the door and I followed him into the shadowy darkness of the In-Between, with Cat and my Star's Guard close on our heels. A couple of grooms were staying behind

14

with the horses. They'd be camping there until we returned or we sent word that we wouldn't be returning through this rath. Unfortunately, I often left people waiting outside a rath while I returned to Fairy via another route. I didn't do it on purpose, that's just how things go. So the grooms knew they might be waiting for nothing.

They didn't seem to mind though. They were all young boys, cat-sidhes as most of the stable boys were, and I think they looked on it as a camping trip. At the very least, they got out of the castle and away from most of their duties. So it wasn't surprising when one of them, Searc was his name, told me to take my time in the Human Realm.

Walking the path within the rath was always comforting to me and despite my exhaustion, I perked up once we were immersed in the darkness of the In-Between. It had once scared me; that endless emptiness which lurked beyond the solidity of the path. But now I knew I belonged there, that I was at my strongest within the dark and even were I to step off the path, I could borrow the power of the In-Between and use it to take me anywhere I wanted.

The gloom was pierced by a shaft of sunshine and I looked up to see that Tiernan had opened the door and was stepping out into the basement of Gentry Technologies. Gentry is an unusual company in that it's a research facility run by fairies. The fey generally stick to nature, the elements, and magic; science was awkward territory for them. But my father wanted to push the limits and see if science could be blended with magic. He insisted that science was a type of magic, that it was a study of the laws of Nature and as such, was closely related to our elemental magic.

It was a brilliant concept and had already proved itself to be true in numerous minor experiments but it was also terrifying. Because if my father succeeded, he would have access to a power that no one would know how to stop. Keir wasn't an evil man and in his hands, I trusted that such a skill would be wielded carefully

15

but once something like that is accomplished, it's only a matter of time before someone either duplicates the process or steals the ability for themselves. And I know of several fairies who would love to get their psychotic hands on my father's research.

So, as much as I supported my father and my Uncle Dylan, I also feared the day when they became truly successful. I hoped it would never come, that they would continue making little discoveries which benefited the lives of both the fey and the humans, without lending itself to more violent pursuits. My close friend Aideen works at Gentry and she had once posed as a whistle blower, informing the Human Council that Gentry had created a biological weapon engineered to kill only humans. This had been a ruse to get me to follow her into Fairy but it fooled us easily because it was so probable. And despite the fact that Gentry didn't research weapons of any kind, I still feared that such an application was inevitable. It stands to reason that when you research life, you will also find death.

I guess technically, my father had already succeeded in making a weapon blended of magic and science; me. My newest mór magic (a fairy's personal magic as opposed to the minor beag magics that every fairy possessed) was a blending of my psychic ability and my fairy magic. The Goddess Danu herself had told me that my magic would be special and my firethorn ability was just the beginning. So maybe I should stop worrying about my father and his experiments. Whatever happened, I'd be able to handle it... hopefully.

"Seren, it's good to see you," Dylan looked as polished as ever; in a sleek suit and a cerulean tie which matched his eyes. His dark hair was slicked back in a careless manner which nonetheless looked as if it was done precisely.

"Wow," I slid into his hug. "I don't think you've ever said that to me before."

"Well this is the first time that you haven't showed up with

16

some kind of trouble at your back," he rolled his eyes and stepped away from me. "Ah, I see that you've finally heeded your father and come with your guards. Welcome, all of you. Have you all been to the Human Realm before?"

"Only Ainsley and I have but we've prepared the others," Conri, the only non-sidhe member of my Star's Guard, gave Dylan a cocky grin. He couldn't help it, it was the nature of the beast. In Conri's case, that beast was a bargest, a type of canine shapeshifter.

"Good. Well done, Sir Conri," Dylan nodded.

Conri's eyes went wide. I don't think he expected approval or respect from my Uncle Dylan who, although he abdicated his place as heir to the unseelie throne, was still considered a royal. In fact, he was a duke, which placed him right below me on the royal scale. A very close below though, since he was the heir to a throne, just as I was.

The members of my guard who hadn't been to HR (the Human Realm), weren't spooked yet. Even with our arrival into one of the strangest rooms I'd ever seen. Gentry's basement was really just a secret room to conceal a fairy mound. The building had been built over and around the rath to protect it but the rath didn't seem to know that it was now indoors.

The door we'd come out of was set into a mound almost exactly like the one which held the door we'd gone through in Fairy. It was covered in grass and flowers; a living carpet which spread out halfway across the cement floor, and the sun shone brightly down on it from somewhere above us. If you tried to look up at that impossible sun, all you would see is blinding light; no ceiling, no sky. But my Star's Guard was used to such things and this didn't startle them in the least. It was the rest of HR that was sure to be a problem, no matter how much they had been prepped.

"My lord," Tiernan bowed to Dylan. "We appreciate the efforts you've made towards our travel arrangements."

"Not at all," Dylan handed Tiernan a black briefcase and then turned to lead us up a spiral staircase. "My assistant did all the work. In that briefcase you'll find disposable cell phones for all of you to use while you're here. I'm sure you'll find them indispensable for keeping in contact with each other... and me," he turned to cast me a stern look over his shoulder and I grimaced. "We have a van ready to transport you to the airport. The pilot of your father's private jet already has his flight plan set and approved. He's ready to leave as soon as you board."

"Wonderful," I stepped out into the second floor office space and headed through the maze of cubicles and desks.

We went through the silent, staring, fairy employees, right over to the elevators at the back of the room. I gave them all a little wave as we passed and a few even waved back. They were getting used to seeing me emerge from their basement. Dylan hit the down button and I realized that we'd have to take more than one elevator car. We wouldn't all fit. I glanced over at Conri and Torquil, who were the first to come up behind me.

"Don't worry, Princess," Conri smirked. "I'll ride down with some of the Guard. I'll keep them calm."

"When has keeping people calm ever been one of your strengths?" Torquil rolled his eyes. "I'll ride down with them."

"You can both take an elevator down with some of the Star's Guard," Tiernan declared as the elevator dinged and the doors slid apart. "Get in."

Torquil and Conri scowled at each other as they got into the elevator car. Several guardsmen followed them in until the car was full. Dylan leaned in and hit the button for the bottom floor, then got out of the way. The doors slid shut and the panel above the elevators lit to show their descent. Uncle Dylan pushed the down button again.

"Well, I don't hear any screaming, so that's a good sign," Dylan shrugged.

"They're twilight knights," Tiernan said. "Even if they're terrified, they won't scream."

"If they really are scared of the elevator, the plane will horrify them," Dylan grimaced.

"I'm kind of looking forward to seeing that," I grinned.

Chapter Four

The knights were wide-eyed for quite awhile when we first boarded the private jet but they acclimated fast. It was fun to see the magical fey clench their armrests during take-off, some even closed their eyes, while it didn't bother Cat at all. She just curled up at my feet and went to sleep. Maybe it seems childish to delight in their fear but these were the same people who teased me about gawking at the wonders of Fairy. So it was nice to see that they could be awed by simple human engineering.

Then Tiernan passed out the cell phones and explained how to use them. No fear there. Instead of being intimidated, my stalwart knights turned into children, phoning each other and then laughing at the echo of their own voices. When Conri showed them how they could choose their own ringtones, I thought we'd never get another moment's peace.

I'd recently learned that fairies were crazy about human music. Their own musical evolution seemed to have plateaued somewhere around the fey equivalent of Bach. They did orchestral music, instruments that were mostly played sitting down, and if they wanted to get really wild, they might add some vocals. So our extensive offering of music genres was mind-boggling to the fey.

Human music had become big business in Fairy. The markets had stalls offering Mp3 players full of any genre you wanted, along with solar chargers to power the devices and headphones to listen to them. It really isn't all that surprising when you consider that there is a huge fairy population in HR. Why wouldn't they bring some human culture back into the Fairy Realm? But when I first saw Mairte, my brownie personal assistant (I hated calling her my maid), wearing a pair of headphones and rocking out to Taylor Swift, I nearly had a heart attack.

Suffice it to say that my Star's Guard was delighted when they discovered that their new phones could also play music. I had a feeling that I'd be buying them all headphones before the trip was through. Either that or I'd be listening to a wide variety of music played all at once, all the time.

"So if raven mockers are twilight fairies, why haven't I ever met one?" I asked Tiernan as we headed back to the private cabin in the rear of the plane where we could hopefully escape the cacophony.

I needed a shower and then some sleep. I fully intended on letting the rest of the guard shower too but I was using my princess prerogative of going first... and of claiming the bed.

"They keep to the woods and the Human Realm," Tiernan closed the cabin door and pulled off his traveling tunic. I spared a moment to appreciate the sculpted muscles of his chest before I started taking off my own clothing.

"Not much for court?" I headed to the bathroom and started the water.

"They're a quiet group, they like to keep to themselves," Tiernan slid into the small shower stall with me and began soaping me up.

I sighed and draped my arms over his shoulders, closing my eyes to better enjoy the sensation of his expert hands kneading at my knotted muscles. I felt his lips press to mine and opened to his kiss, luxuriating even more in the moment. But I didn't have the energy for sex, so I pulled away, giving him a rueful look. He laughed and backed away as much as the tiny stall allowed him, taking those magic hands with him. Insert disappointed sigh here.

"So they like to keep to themselves, except when they're sucking the life out of dying humans," I ducked under the spray to

21

rinse off.

"They actually went out among the Native American tribes before America was settled and given its name," Tiernan went on. "They loved the ideals of the tribes and several of the mockers married natives."

"Really?" I slid out of the stall so he could rinse off easier.

"Mockers were greatly influenced by the Native American people and most of them have American Indian physical features," Tiernan paused as he rinsed and then shut the water off and came out. I handed him a towel as he continued. "It's why the raven mocker myths speak of them being witches in the tribe. The natives never knew that the mockers weren't human."

"So they still believe the raven mockers are human witches?" I lifted a brow.

"Unless they're a government official or council person who has been told the truth behind the myths," Tiernan nodded.

"I guess it doesn't make a difference," I mused. "What race your enemy is hardly matters, as long as you know how to defeat them."

"Which they can, as long as they have a clairvoyant shaman they can turn to," Tiernan grimaced and handed me my bag.

"What do you think is going on in Tulsa?" I pulled out a T-shirt and slipped it on before climbing into the small bed.

"Honestly, Seren," he said after he pulled on some cotton pants. "I haven't got a clue but if the Human Council is this insistent on your timely arrival, it must be bad."

"When is it not?" I huffed as I dropped my head back onto the pillow and finally got to sleep.

Chapter Five

The Tulsa Council House was a beautiful old home within Brady Heights; a historic neighborhood which dated back before the 1920's. It was a quiet area with elegant homes in all sorts of styles, from Victorian to Queen Anne. I'm not sure what style the Council House was but it definitely wasn't Victorian. It sprawled across a spacious yard, fronted by a wide porch which spanned the entire length of it and topped by a peaked roof. The sunshine yellow walls were complimented by white lacey woodwork along the angled roof. We walked up a set of steps and clomped over the wood porch to the delicate looking door but before I could knock, it was opened by an extinguisher in full combat gear. A total contradiction to the setting.

"Whoa," I blinked and pulled my head back in surprise. "Ready for war, are we?"

"Ambassador Seren?" The extinguisher was a woman I'd never met before; a little taller than my five-feet-five height and well muscled. She had soft cedar eyes and blonde hair pulled back in a ponytail. Her eyes went warily to Cat, who'd glamored herself to look like a Newfoundland (big but at least not ridiculous). Of course an extinguisher could see right through that illusion if she tried.

"Yep, that's me. This is Cat, she's my guard puka," I waved a hand behind me, "and this is my Star's Guard. Can we come in?"

"Oh!" She jumped back. "Yes! Come in, please come in. I'm sorry, we're all a bit on edge today."

"I see that," I stepped into the small foyer, glancing at the framed portraits of head council members and the delicate antique table that held only a large brass candle snuffer; symbol of the Extinguishers.

"I'll take you to the Council," she turned and led us up a set of stairs. At the top of the stairs, she turned right and waved her hand towards an open doorway. "Your guard can wait in here."

"Alright," I nodded and the knights started filing into the little sitting room. "But Count Tiernan and Cat go where I go."

"Oh, I see," she looked at Cat again. "Um."

Cat chose that moment to step forward and lick the extinguisher's hand. The woman jumped and then gave a nervous laugh, holding her hand out to Cat again. Cat obliged by bumping the offered hand with her head.

"Oh, she's sweet," the woman said.

"Unless you attack me, yes," I smiled and then cocked my head at her. "You never gave us your name."

"Right!" She cleared her throat. "I'm Extinguisher Kate Teagan. It's nice to meet you, Ambassador."

"Nice to meet you as well," I nodded.

"This way," she led us down a narrow hallway to a door at the back of the house. She opened it and stepped in to announce, "Ambassador Seren is here with Count Tiernan.... and her guard Cat." Then she stepped aside and let us into the room. She closed the door behind her as she left.

The room was spacious and airy, with soaring windows overlooking the backyard. The was another house in the back garden, a smaller one but still pretty large, painted in the same colors as the main house and surrounded by spindly trees. In a corner of the room itself was a large desk, some bookshelves, chairs, filing cabinets, and a lamp all clustered together as if they were in time out. Directly in front of us there was a rectangular table, oak from the look of it, polished to a high sheen. Seated at the table were the council persons of the Tulsa House. There was only one seat left open. I glanced at Tiernan.

"I'll stand, it's fine," Tiernan assured me.

"Nonsense," a man got up from the head of the table and approached us. "I'm Ted Teagan, Head of this Council House," he reached out to shake my hand. "It's a pleasure to meet you Ambassador, and you as well, Count Tiernan. Please have a seat, Ambassador Seren, while I grab the Count a chair."

I lifted a brow at *the Count* as the Head Councilman went over to the office area and grabbed the chair from behind the desk. Tiernan smiled and shrugged, going forward to pull out the empty seat at the table for me... because a princess doesn't get to do stuff like that for herself. At least not in front of others.

My seat was right beside Ted's at the end of the table but on my other side was a stern faced man around sixty. He scooted over grudgingly to make room for the chair that the Head Councilman brought over. Cat sat herself right between me and Councilman Teagan's seat, her tongue lolling out of her newfy mouth. I think she may have been playing it up a bit.

Ted Teagan looked a little like Extinguisher Kate, with short-cut blonde hair and gentle cocoa-colored eyes. He was young for a Head Councilman, probably around forty-five, with a fit build and a boyish attractiveness.

"Are you any relation to the extinguisher who showed us in?" I asked him as he came around the back of my chair.

"Yes," he beamed at me. "She's my daughter, Kate."

"Oh. Did you get to train her?" I asked.

"Yes," he leaned back on his heels and slid his hands into

his pockets to talk with me as if he had all the time in the world. "I may be a councilman but I was trained to be an extinguisher first and I've kept up with that training."

"And kept in shape," I nodded appreciatively and Tiernan cleared his throat. "It was just an observation," I grimaced at Tiernan while the Councilman laughed.

"And a welcome one," Ted smiled and slid into his seat. "I don't get a lot of compliments these days," he shot an irritated look around the table.

"Perhaps we could get down to business?" The man beside Tiernan asked.

"Yes, Councilman Murdock," the Head Councilman sighed.

"Murdock?" I looked over to the councilman.

"No, I'm not directly related to Head Councilman Murdock of San Francisco," he griped. "You know how many Murdocks there are, Extinguisher Sloane."

"It's *Ambassador*," Councilman Ted corrected Murdock.

"It's fine," I waved away the intended insult. "I am and will always be an extinguisher."

"Well said," a man across the table nodded approvingly. "Nothing wrong with being an extinguisher, especially one with scores like yours."

"You know my rating?" I lifted a brow at the brunette. He looked neither stern nor friendly, just an average sort with average Irish features and the typical pale Irish skin.

"We looked into you before we sent for you," Councilman Ted explained.

"You're a fascinating woman," the man across from me added. "The highest rated female as far as psychic abilities goes."

"I think you'd find her to be the highest rated *extinguisher* now," Tiernan added. "The block to her fey blood was hampering her psychic talent."

"Oh," the man's dark eyes widened. "Maybe you should retake the tests."

"Blast the bloody tests!" Councilman Murdock snarled. "We could be attacked by fairies at any second."

"Attacked?" I looked over to Councilman Teagan, absently laying a hand on Cat's head when she started to growl. "What does he mean by that?"

"He's exaggerating," Teagan sighed.

"Not entirely," the man across from me muttered.

"I am not exaggerating at all!" Murdock declared.

"Enough!" Ted Teagan stood and the room went silent, even Cat stared up at him respectfully. Gone was the boyish charm. Before us stood an imposing man who looked like he'd sooner kick your ass than tolerate any lip. "Thank you for your input, Councilman Murdock and Councilman Sullivan. I will take it from here."

Both men nodded contritely and Councilman Teagan took his seat. I turned expectant eyes to him.

"Ambassador Seren," Teagan began. "We called you here so expeditiously because something disturbing has come to light." Councilman Sullivan coughed and Teagan gave him a quelling look before continuing. "I'm sure you've been informed that this matter concerns the raven mockers and I'm also sure you know more about those fairies than I do."

27

I nodded but didn't offer anything, so he went on with a slightly disappointed look.

"The legend of the raven mockers is alive and well in this part of the United States," he sighed. "A local shaman went as far as to contact a ghost hunting group to come out and research the occurrences."

"A ghost hunting group?" I lifted my brows.

"*Paranormal Parameters*," Councilman Teagan made a face. "They do a television show where they scientifically research hauntings and the like. Out of all the shows about ghost hunting, theirs is probably the most respectable. Most of their time is spent debunking hauntings or monster sightings."

"But they didn't debunk this one, did they?" I asked as Tiernan tensed beside me.

"No, they caught a raven mocker on infrared camera, as it was attacking its victim," Teagan confirmed, tapping his fingers nervously on the table before him. "We managed to steal the footage but they're a rather determined bunch, especially after what they witnessed. I think they'll be back."

"They're the least of our concerns," a councilwoman said from the other end of the table.

"Councilwoman Erickson is right," Teagan gave me a grim look. "The raven mockers now know that not only are these ghost hunters after them but we are. They've gone for so long without being caught, I think this has really thrown them. We have warrants to extinguish any we catch but there's the rub; we have to catch them in the act because we don't know which individuals are actually instigating these attacks and we cannot simply extinguish a fairy for being a raven mocker."

"Well, as much as I feel your frustration, Councilman," I offered. "I have to admit that I'm relieved that you don't want to

28

simply go on a hunting spree and kill every raven mocker you can find. I've just been informed that they are twilight fey and as such, I feel both responsible for them and protective of them."

"So what do you propose we do, young lady?" Councilman Murdock asked me.

"Did you seriously just call me *young lady*?" I asked him as Tiernan's lips twitched.

"Murdock," Teagan shook his head.

"Well, if she won't kill them, how will she help?" Murdock grumbled.

"I never said I wouldn't kill them," I declared in a vicious tone, silencing the whole table. "As you've pointed out, I'm an extinguisher and our job has always been to protect the fey. We kill only when necessary and that's what I'll do. However, I'm also an ambassador and the Princess of Twilight, so that makes this situation very complicated for me. I must keep the peace between the realms as I try and remain loyal to my fey. As their ruler I am responsible to them and *for* them. So if they've broken the truce, I will extinguish them myself. But I must be certain of their guilt; so I have to make an effort to verify that this is *their* crime and to hear their defense against the charges against them before I act."

"This is what we get for contacting a diplomat," Murdock waved his hands in frustration.

"I thought I was an extinguisher to you?" I leaned forward so I could glare at Murdock across Tiernan. "Make up your mind, *old man*."

"Well I..." Murdock started to stand as Tiernan laughed outright.

"Cease!" Teagan shouted. "You deserved that, Murdock. Now please control your outbursts around Princess Seren.

Remember what she represents. It shouldn't be so hard, since she's just reminded all of us of her numerous responsibilities. Let's try and be supportive since one of those responsibilities is to us."

"Thank you, Councilman Teagan," I took a deep breath. "I apologize for my own outburst."

"It's fine, Princess," Teagan rubbed a hand over his face. "We're all a little twitchy. What I didn't get to say is that the raven mockers have harassed us already."

"What?" I went still.

"We don't know if it's the video that they're after or if they simply believe that we'll be hunting them now that we've acquired proof of their actions, and they wish to make a preemptive strike," Councilman Teagan explained. "They've yet to attack us outright but we've heard their cries circling above us at night and we're on high alert."

"Hmm," I pondered it. "Actually, that might be helpful."

"How's that?" Another councilman asked.

"I thought I'd have to search for them," I shrugged. "But now I can simply sit on your porch and wait for them to come to me."

"Yes, very convenient," Tiernan agreed.

"And what happens when they attack us?" Murdock growled but instantly quieted when Teagan gave him another sharp look.

"They wouldn't dare attack their own princess," Tiernan sounded horrified. "If they did, far worse things than death would come for them."

I swallowed hard, knowing exactly what Tiernan was referring to. The Sluagh; the monsters of Fairy. You never really saw them, they stayed hidden until the King of the Unseelie commanded them forth... or someone murdered a royal fey. Even attempted murder could call the Sluagh down upon your head and though I'd personally faced them twice and lived, that was not usually the case. Normally, once the Sluagh began to hunt you, you were as good as dead.

"What does he mean?" Teagan looked to me.

"There are laws in Fairy, just as you have laws here," I glanced at Tiernan, unsure of how much I could share with them. Tiernan nodded so I went on. "One of our laws states that royals are sacred. If any fey, royal or not, were to murder or even attempt to murder a royal fairy, the Sluagh would come for them."

The table gasped as one. When I'd been just an extinguisher, I hadn't known nearly as much about the fey as I do now but I did know about the Sluagh. Of course, now that I'd actually seen them, been up close and personal with them, I knew even more... and wished that I didn't.

"Yes," I swallowed hard. "It's a hell of a deterrent but also, fairies tend to be loyal and I'm banking on that. I will demand a meeting with their leader and then see what can be done."

"You're gonna parley with them like they're pirates?" Sullivan smiled but when I merely stared back at him, he lost the grin. "Wow, you really are."

"Did you miss the part where I said that they are my people?" I cocked my head at him. "I know the concept is still new to all of you but I am both fairy and human. As an ambassador, I'm trying my best to remain fair, if not entirely neutral."

"Then, I wish you luck, Ambassador," Teagan declared. "The raven mockers usually come after midnight, when the darkness makes it harder to see them."

"Of course they do," I chuckled. "I'm sure you've got the

house surrounded by flood lights though."

"We do," Teagan confirmed with a smile.

"Great," I nodded. "I'll need them to be kept off tonight."

The whole table looked at me in horror. All but Tiernan, who smiled at me confidently. Goddess, I love that fairy.

Chapter Six

"I'd like to take a look at that tape now, if you don't mind?" I asked Councilman Teagan as we left the council chambers.

"Of course," he nodded. "We'll use my office, I have the tapes in there."

He led us down a hallway and then up a narrow set of stairs which led to a slim door. The brass plate on the door read; Theodore Teagan, Head Councilman. He opened the door and we followed him into an attic office. It was really nice for an attic; with plush carpets laid over the wood beam floors and bookshelves built right into and out from the angled walls, making the room appear to be box-like when it was closer in shape to a pup tent. There was a large window at the far end of the room, set into a triangle shaped piece of wall, and it let in a lot of light through its wispy curtains.

"I'd thought that was your office back in the council chambers," I mused as I looked around.

"Ah, no," Teagan grinned. "We use that as a common work space for anything that needs to get done in chambers."

"Well this is much nicer," I looked towards the window.

Under the window was a heavy desk, with a chair positioned behind it, facing us. But Teagan led us over to a work table set against a side wall. There was a lot of books and paperwork covering the table, including several council published tomes on raven mockers, but Teagan pushed all of it aside to clear our view of the large TV screen placed at the back of the table. Beside it was a DVD player and Teagan pushed the play button as

Tiernan and I sat before the table.

"There were several recordings but this is the final cut," Teagan said as he took a seat beside me.

Cat sat between us and Teagan casually reached out and stroked her head. That lifted my eyebrow. I didn't expect humans to respond so well to her, much less a councilman who could see what she actually was. But then the voice coming from the TV caught my attention.

"Raven mockers," it said ominously. "I'll bet you've never heard of them. I myself was unfamiliar with the legend until we at *Paranormal Parameters* were approached by a shaman of the Cherokee Nation who told a the chilling tale."

The man was attractive, with short russet hair and a medium build, but it was the gleam in his eyes that was the most compelling. This footage must have been shot after he'd seen the raven mocker because that was the look of a man who had glimpsed something he'd always hoped to find but never actually believed he would. A look like that meant trouble.

"Shaman Kevin Chepaney spoke of witches and dark magic to us and I never for one second believed a word he said," the man went on. "I have never been so wrong in all my life."

The man was standing in front of a modest home made of wood and red bricks. He moved up the stairs and the white door opened to reveal an older Native American man. His shoulder-length hair was pulled back in a ponytail neatly and he had a crisp, sky blue, cotton shirt on, the cuffs adorned with simple cuff links and the top button open to reveal the leather cords of his medicine bag. His blue jeans looked brand new and his boots were polished. He must have dressed up for his camera debut.

But one look in his dark molasses eyes showed me that this was not about fame for him, this was a cry for help. He had a desperate, anxious expression on his face. The kind of look you see sometimes on mental patients; people tormented by their own demons. Except this man's demons were very real... and they were actually fairies.

"Hello, Shaman Chepaney," the host nodded to the man.

"Justin," the man stepped back and admitted the whole group into his home. He led them into a simple but clean living room with a rocking chair near the small fireplace and an indigo cotton couch with an Native American blanket laid over the back of it. "Please, have a seat."

"Thank you, Sir," Justin said as he sat. "Would you please tell everyone the story you first told us."

"Yes," the man swallowed hard, his lined face looking like worn leather but in an oddly attractive way. "Raven mockers, kalona ayeliski, sunnayi edahi, the night goers. There are many names for them but what they are is very simple. They are witches; evil shamans with horrible powers."

"Yes, and as I've just said to our viewers, I was very skeptical when you first told me your witch tale," the host looked contrite. "I apologize for not believing you."

"No apology necessary," the shaman held up his hand. "It's a hard thing to believe, even with Christianity so widespread in the United States. People forget that God has a counterpart, that evil does exist and at times, can be just as powerful as good."

"Yes, I see that now," Justin whispered and gave the camera a dramatic look. "If you believe in God, you must also believe in the Devil."

"But this is not the Devil, not any devil," the shaman went on and the camera focused back on him. "This is human evil; human's with magic, as I have been blessed with magic. But these people have allowed the lure of wickedness to turn their magic

35

dark."

I leaned forward to stare at this shaman. He was speaking the truth as he knew it but he was also very wrong. This wasn't human magic at all; these were fairies attacking his people, and the power he possessed was simply psychic ability.

"Please tell us about their magic," the host urged.

"They have found a way to prolong their lives by stealing life from others," the shaman went on. "And they do it in a devious manner."

"Yes, it's fascinating actually," Justin said to the camera.

"They come after dark," the shaman was speaking such theatrical words but in a stoic way that made them feel genuine... as I knew they were. Goose bumps lifted on my arms as he continued, "on wings of fire. You cannot see them unless you are a shaman and have the ability to see beyond this world. But all can hear them. They make a sound like a diving raven, which is why we call them raven mockers."

"Ahh," Justin nodded. "And Night Goers because they come at night, obviously."

"They need the shadows to hide their flight and their faces," Shaman Kevin said. "But we know what they're after and what to look for."

"What is it that they want?" The host asked as he leaned forward. "How do they steal life from people?"

"They sneak into the homes of the sick or elderly, invisible to all but shamans, and they torment their victims by strangling or throwing them about," Kevin explained. "Anyone in the room simply thinks the victim is struggling to breathe. No one knows that a witch is tormenting their loved one, wearing them down so the raven mocker can steal their victim's heart."

"What do they do with the heart?" Justin asked.

"They consume it and from it, they gain life," the shaman said with a bleak tone. "They leave no sign behind. No one can tell that the heart has been taken unless an autopsy is done."

"But luckily, the Cherokee know to look for abnormal signs of distress in their sick and elderly," Justin prompted the shaman.

"Yes," the shaman nodded. "And then they call me."

"And how do you catch the raven mocker?" The host prompted.

"There is an old ritual," he sighed. "It's basically a trap for the raven mockers. After the trap is sprung, the mocker usually dies seven days later. That's how we find the witch; when someone in the community dies on the seventh day, we know who the mocker was."

"Now let me reiterate here that I was very skeptical over Mr. Chepaney's claims," Justin spoke to the camera. "But he seemed so genuine and so sane, that I started to wonder if there could be some truth to his words. So we agreed to investigate the next incident and Shaman Chepaney promised to call us as soon as he was alerted to some suspicious activity." The camera drew in closer to Justin's face. "And he did. I must warn you that the following footage is disturbing and violent. It clearly shows that the actions taken by Mr. Chepaney were in defense of the victim and we hope that no legal action will be taken against him but that is the risk he is willing to take to expose these evil beings and save his community. Please, remove any children from the room before watching further."

I glanced at Tiernan and saw his jaw clench as the scene changed to a bedroom. There was an elderly man lying in the bed, obviously not long for this world, and a group of people huddled around him whom I could only assume to be his family. The

Paranormal Parameters crew was there, including the host, three camera men, and two more researchers manning all sorts of equipment.

"This is Mr. Hayecha," the host stood beside the bed, looking significantly less solemn than he had earlier, and indicated the man lying within it. "Thank you so much, Sir, for letting us into your home and allowing us to film this."

"Yeah," the old man nodded, closing his eyes and nodding off immediately.

"And thank you all for being here to support your loved one," Justin nodded to the man's family and they nodded back solemnly. "Now we're going to quietly make our way outside where Shaman Chepaney is preparing to defend Mr. Hayecha from supernatural forces." You could hear the almost derisive note underlying Justin's words but he kept the dramatic look on his face like any good actor.

The camera followed him out of the house and into the front yard, where the shaman was standing before a deer hide laid on the ground. On the hide were four sticks with sharpened tips, a bowl of tobacco leaves, a piece of black cloth, and a long pipe adorned with feathers. The shaman picked up the sticks with a determined look and started towards the house. The camera followed along with him as he drove a stick into the ground at each corner of the house, sharpened tips pointing upward. Then the shaman came back to the deer hide and sat upon it cross-legged.

He started to chant as he picked up the bowl of tobacco and filled the pipe with it. Sure fingers tamped the tobacco tight and then took the black piece of cloth and wrapped the pipe in it completely. Without even looking at the camera, the shaman got to his feet and walked off into the woods that bordered the backyard. The camera followed his progress for a minute and then panned back to the host.

"Shaman Chepaney has told us that he must spend the day preparing for the confrontation that will come tonight," Justin glanced down at the empty deer hide and then back at the camera. "Will this truly be a battle between good and evil? Will this night take us further than any paranormal parameter we've established so far? Or will this be yet another performance that falls short?"

The screen went black for about two seconds before showing the same house at night. The host was standing outside, staring into the camera intensely. Behind him, the house lights were on but the surrounding area was dark. Still, you could easily see the shaman approaching.

"Night has fallen and Shaman Chepaney has returned," Justin nodded towards the shaman, who walked up to them. "Are you prepared to face the raven mockers, Shaman?"

"I'm prepared," the shaman said gravely. "Please, whatever you do, do not run. Stay calm and I will do my best to save Mr. Hayecha. If you panic and disturb my focus, the mocker may escape."

"Believe me, Shaman Chepaney, we are all professionals and will not disturb your focus," Justin said with just the barest hint of disdain.

"Your beliefs will be questioned before this night is through," Shaman Chepaney said in such a sober, assured way, that it was chilling. Even the host blinked and gave the camera an unsteady look. "Now, follow me."

The shaman walked calmly up the porch steps and into the house. The host gave the camera one last baffled look before they all followed the shaman in. Through narrow hallways they went, past empty rooms, until they came to the bedroom. Shaman Chepaney motioned them over to a corner, where the rest of the crew was already set up.

"Stay there and stay quiet," Chepaney said with authority and the *Paranormal Parameters* crew did as they were told.

"Should we expect-" Justin started to ask but the shaman shot him a hostile look and he shut up.

The family was gathered in another corner and the shaman went to them, telling them gently to be calm and to please not interfere or try to help the old man in any way, no matter what they saw. They all nodded their acceptance and the shaman went to turn off the overhead light. The room fell into darkness and the cameras shifted into night vision.

Then the screen split into two, showing the room in both night vision and infrared camera views. Justin's voice came as an obvious added in voice-over to the scene.

"In order for you to clearly see what happened next, we had to split the screen into two. Please note how the entity shows clearly in infrared but not in the night vision footage. They are being played simultaneously for you. Again, I urge you to remove any young children from the room."

As his voice stopped, the cry of a raven came from somewhere outside the house. Then the old man sat up on the bed and several people gasped. Someone whispered, *What the (beep) is that?* but was immediately hushed as cameras focused on the bed. The night vision view showed only the chartreuse tinted glow of the old man, sitting up and gasping for air, his eyes bright in that creepy way all eyes under night vision appeared. But the infrared view showed a massive shape which had a cherry red center radiating out into tangerine and neon yellow blotches. It had a distinctly human shaped lime border around those core colors but it didn't stop there. The lime turned to teal and then darkened to cobalt clouds which shifted around the human shape like it was a separate entity.

The shaman stood up and shouted something in a Native

American language, which I assumed to be Cherokee. The shape on the infrared screen flinched, its head turning abruptly to look over its shoulder at the shaman. Its brightly colored hands released the old man and poor Mr. Hayecha fell to the bed, gasping for air. The shaman spoke again and the shape rose into the air; the cobalt clouds pulling in close to the teal and seeming to lift the human core up.

It launched itself at the shaman and Kevin Chepaney was thrown back into a wall. I couldn't help gasping and leaning forward to watch as the shaman struck out at the raven mocker. Chepaney shouted as he threw something into the mocker's face. A horrible screech pierced the night and several people screamed. Ruby light shot through the cobalt haze surrounding the raven mocker and fire sparked, briefly illuminating the rictus of a man's face on the night vision side of the screen. Then the mocker flew out of the doorway and the shaman chased after it. A bumpy camera shot shifted to just infrared, following the bright form of the Cherokee shaman out of the house and into the night.

The shaman motioned violently and another screech was heard. A sound like rushing wind began to grow in strength as the screen split once more. This time, one side showed a normal perspective and one was infrared. The normal view focused on a corner of the house, where one of the sticks had lifted out of the ground and was hovering in the air. The cameraman and several others from the ghost hunting team were making horrified but excited comments. I was impressed that no one ran. They just kept filming; the infrared focused on the hovering, screeching glow of the raven mocker while the normal view showed the stick shooting upwards. It hit the crimson center of the mocker, right where the heart should be. The mocker gave another screech as his invisibility glamour failed him.

People screamed as the entire screen went back to normal vision. A huge shape lifted up and hovered above the group of shocked people. Shadows shifted around it, oily black like the

41

smoke from a crematorium. A face shot out of the morphing murk, its mouth stretching open grotesquely on one last screech before the thing sped away, sparks trailing from the boiling black concealing it. The camera tried to follow but lost the trail in seconds.

"I think that's all you need to see," Councilman Teagan got up and turned off the DVD. "I'm sure you understand why we had to acquire this footage."

"It would be a horrible way for humans to find out that fairies exist," I nodded.

"Oh, this has nothing to do with fairy reputation," the councilman looked surprised. "Do you really think that your average human would view this and immediately think *fairy*?"

"They'd begin to believe in witches again," Tiernan observed. "Because that is precisely what the shaman believes."

"Sweet Danu," I breathed. "All humans with any sort of psychic gift would be in danger."

"Precisely," Teagan nodded. "Our first instinct when met with aggression is to defend ourselves against it... or anything that resembles it."

"There would be witch hunts again," I whispered, remembering my history lessons about the days when extinguishers had to be extra careful to hide their abilities. The Human Council had grown considerably in those days because they kept taking in hunted humans who were born outside of the Great Five Families.

"It would be far worse this time, Ambassador," Councilman Teagan resumed his seat. "With the type of weapons we have these days, witch hunting could turn into war. Civil war, where neighbors kill neighbors and brothers kill brothers. The military would have to be brought in and with only the higher officials knowing the truth about fairies, they would most likely attack talented humans."

"The United States would turn into Nazi Germany," I swallowed hard.

"And we, the persecuted Jews," Teagan nodded as chills coasted over my arms. "We cannot let these people investigate this any further."

"We can take care of the ghost hunters," I gave Tiernan a weighted look and he nodded.

"A simple forgetting spell, Councilman," Tiernan explained. "No one will be harmed. We can take care of the shaman too if necessary."

"But he'll still be dealing with raven mocker attacks," Teagan said. "Wouldn't he remember eventually?"

"The raven mockers are a different problem," I sighed.

"One that will require more than a forgetting spell to solve," Tiernan said grimly.

Chapter Seven

I sat on the porch between Cat and Tiernan, waiting for night to come. The rest of my Star's Guard was spread out along the wide veranda, some at the railing and some leaning against the house. Well, all but Torquil and Ian, who had been dispatched to find the crew of *Paranormal Parameters* and erase their memories.

Twilight came and I closed my eyes to the rush of power that it always brought me. Energy surged through my limbs, making me inhale sharply and jerk in response. I could feel it pressing up beneath my skin, a vibrant effervescence; champagne and electricity. My fingers tingled, eager to release the magic building inside me. I gave in to the desire and let just a few lavender sparks drift down to the wood planks beneath me.

"You can do better than that," Tiernan teased.

"What do you want; fireworks?" I laughed.

"What are fireworks?" Ainsley asked and Tiernan gave me a smug grin.

"Oh fine," I huffed and flung my hand out.

A swirl of sparkling light flew out from my fingers and coalesced in the air before the house. The energy gathered together and then burst apart in an explosion of lavender, iris, hyacinth, periwinkle, and orchid. A glittering, bursting bouquet of magic, bright against the sunset sky. The knights applauded the display.

"How would humans accomplish that?" Ainsley asked.

"With explosives," Tiernan chuckled. "Humans like things

that explode."

"No kidding," I muttered.

"Ambassador Seren," Extinguisher Kate stepped out onto the porch. "The Head Councilman wants you to know that not only will the floodlights remain off but we'll be turning off the house lights soon too, so it will be completely dark for you."

"Wonderful," I nodded.

"We will be wearing night vision goggles," she went on. "Would any of your knights or yourself, like to borrow a pair?"

"We'll be okay, thank you," I smiled at her.

"Alright then," she headed back into the house. "We were told to let you handle this but we're here if you need us, Extinguisher Seren. You're still one of us and we have your back."

"I really appreciate that, Extinguisher Teagan," I said sincerely. "I've had a bit of a mixed reaction from my fellow extinguishers. It's nice to know there are those who still support me."

"I'm sure they all still support you," she said gently. "We extinguishers can be temperamental when it comes to change but we're loyal, especially to our own."

"You're right, we are," I gave her smile.

"Good luck, Ambassador," she nodded and closed the door behind her.

"Hopefully I won't need it," I sighed as darkness fell.

It was a long wait. Hours later, some extinguishers brought dinner out to us and we ate in tense silence but no mockers arrived to ruin our meal. It wasn't till way after midnight that we finally heard the cry of a diving raven. I sat up straight in my chair and

Cat let out a low growl.

"Shhh," I hushed her and she immediately quieted.

I stood up and went to the railing, staring into the darkness expectantly. A few sparks and the whoosh of wings were the only things betraying the presence of a flock of raven mockers. I strode down the porch stairs and my Guard rushed to follow me but I held up my hand and all but Cat fell back.

"I am Princess Seren Firethorn of the Twilight Court," I called out in a commanding voice. "I demand to speak with your leader!"

A hush followed, only broken by Cat's anxious shuffle beside me. She was staring up into the sky, following movement that I couldn't see.

"Show yourselves now or be labeled traitors to your court!" I shouted and several of my knights gasped.

A form dropped suddenly before me and Tiernan rushed forward but again, I waved him back and he stopped just one foot shy of me. The mocker was merely standing there, offering me no harm, and I didn't want Tiernan's behavior mistaken for an attack. So I stepped forward, away from Tiernan and Cat, and drew close enough to the mocker to clearly see him.

He wasn't at all what I was expecting. First off, he looked young and I'd read that most raven mockers had a withered appearance. As much as it sounds impossible for a whole species to be withered and old, it sometimes happens with fairies. It was simply the form their bodies took and had nothing to do with age. Just as someone of Tiernan's unknown but certainly lengthy lifespan could appear to be no older than thirty.

This man didn't even look that old. I would have guessed maybe twenty-five if he'd been human. But he wasn't, he *so* was not human. He could have passed for it though, if not for the pair of enormous, ebony, feathered wings flowing from his back. Without them, he looked Native American, in a very old school way. As in; buckskin pants and long, pin-straight, midnight hair adorned with a single raven feather tied on with a leather strip. He was shirtless and his magnificent chest was a deep, tawny fawn; like sunlight on a rocky mountainside. He belonged in a historic painting and I realized that my dream self, dressed in leather and beads, would have looked perfect standing beside him.

The angel-like wings folded serenely behind his back as he stepped forward just barely an inch, bringing him close enough to smell. I breathed in the scent of sage smoke, leather, and cinnamon; odd but appealing. The hollows beneath his high cheekbones fluttered as his jaw clenched and he looked me over.

"*You* are the new princess?" He asked in a skeptical tone.

"Do you need proof?" I lifted my hand and an eyebrow.

His response was to lift his hand very slowly to my temple and stroke back the hair there. I held still as he pulled forward a swath of my hair and brought it into the moonlight. It was the ombré stripe of purple that faded to lavender at the ends; the coloring I'd inherited from my father. He dropped the hair and leaned his face into mine, staring me straight in the eyes. No doubt, he was searching for the stars that were the true proof of my heritage.

"You are just as he said," the mocker nodded and stood back.

"He?" I asked as Cat edged forward.

"My father," the mocker cocked his head at Cat, looked her over just as intensely as he had me, and then gave her a slight nod. "Her as well."

"I've met your father?" I blinked in surprise. "I thought most raven mockers kept to the woods or the Human Realm and

I'm sure I would have remembered meeting one."

"My father is not a mocker," he said simply.

"You're one of the first then?" I asked.

"*The* first," he bowed. "I am Rayetayah; son to Ayita, raven fey of the Seelie, and Raza, dragon-djinn of the Unseelie."

"Raza?" I whispered as Tiernan shifted forward. "You're Lord Raza's son?"

"I am," Rayetayah lifted his chin.

"Well damn," I huffed. "I'm surprised your wings aren't more leathery."

"Did you not hear me say that my mother was a raven fairy?" He smirked.

"Raven fairy," I frowned. "Oh right, the Native American animals spirits are actually types of fey."

"Yes, Princess," he chuckled.

"Hey," I wagged my finger in his face. "I'm new to this, cut me some slack."

"I know this too," he nodded. "My father told me you were still learning our ways but that your ignorance was a blessing because it made you completely unprejudiced. He spoke very highly of you and that's rare for my father."

"Oh really?" I blinked as Tiernan muttered something along the lines of; *I bet he did.*

"He believes that you will be good for Fairy," Rayetayah went on. "But why are you here, standing against me, when you should be beside me?"

"I'm also an extinguisher," I said and a sudden fluttering of wings gave away the location of several mockers circling above us. "I am half fairy and half human. Did your father not tell you that part?"

"He told me of your blood but not that you were a human murderer of fey," he ground out.

"You, of all people, should know better than to call me a murderer," I chided him. "I expect that you've lived here a long time and you should know that we are peace keepers, not murderers. We only kill when we have warrants to do so. Warrants given when fairies break the truce."

"Perhaps," he conceded.

"No perhaps about it," I growled. "Your kind have been getting away with murder for a long time, Rayetayah," I accused. "But now the humans have found a way to prove your guilt. They caught a raven mocker trying to kill an old man on tape."

"Tape?" He frowned.

"Camera," I explained. "You know what I'm talking about. You live here, so I'm sure you know the technology that's available. Some human investigators used infrared cameras to catch a raven mocker's heat signal on film. We have proof that you've been doing just what the myths accuse you of."

"You have proof that someone committed this deed," he narrowed his eyes on me. "You don't have proof that it was an actual mocker."

I frowned and glanced back at Tiernan in consternation. I hadn't expected him to take this route. He seemed like the type to go for a blatant approach. Something more like; *yeah, we did it. So what?* But this round about, *maybe we did, maybe we didn't* thing seemed silly. A waste of time at the very least. Unless...

49

"You seriously want me to believe that someone else could have done this?" I lifted a brow at him.

His jaw clenched and with a swift movement, he reached out and swept me against him. In seconds, we were in the air, flying away from the Council House with dizzying speed. I heard shouting and knew that Tiernan would try to follow us. I also knew how fast Tiernan could fly with his air manipulation magic and it wasn't nearly fast enough to catch up with this guy.

"Take me back!" I shouted over the rush of wind.

"Not yet," Rayetayah stared straight ahead and held me tight.

I could have probably made him drop me but I wasn't proficient enough with my air magic yet to be able to stop my fall and we were high enough that the fall might actually kill me. So instead of fighting him, I held on, pressing myself against his bare chest. His skin was warm, almost hot, and the heat felt good up in the cool air. I might have even enjoyed the ride under different circumstances. As it was, I was supremely irritated by the time we landed in an open field several miles away from the Council House. I jerked away from Rayetayah as soon as my feet touched ground.

"Not cool," I snapped at him as other raven mockers landed around us. I stared around me at stoic-faced men with wingspans to match Rayetayah's. This had the potential to go very bad for me.

"You weren't listening," he accused me. "And I had concerns for my people. I saw the amount of fairy knights you had with you."

"I was listening," I sighed. "I *am* listening. I just don't understand what you're saying."

"We did not try to kill anyone," he ground out. "Years ago, we discovered that we had the capability to take the last drops of life from the dying or the old but it entailed consuming the heart of our victim. Still, the energy was delicious and we gave into the lure of it for many years. But then my mother's people came to us and begged us to stop. The ravens, the beavers, the coyotes, the badgers, even the waukheon and nanabozho; the thunderbirds and trickster rabbits, came. We took very little from the humans, just the last, painful moments of their life, but still the animal spirits believed it was cruelty against the people who had taken us into their tribe. So we stopped."

"You stopped?" I frowned.

"We stopped. We never again took life from the humans," Rayetayah confirmed. "But something else did. Don't ask me what or who because I don't know. All I know is that something watched us, learned from us, and took over where we left off.

I considered his words as the other mockers drew in close. The faces on those fairies were somber, their eyes begging me to believe in them. As their princess, I found that I couldn't deny them. If anyone should believe in them, it should be me. So I did.

"I believe you," I whispered and they inhaled sharply, as one.

"You do?" Rayetayah asked dubiously.

"Why would you lie to me?" I asked him. "You're my people and I will look after you as long as you obey the truce. If you say you're innocent in this, I'll believe and back you until it is proved otherwise. However," I held up a hand. "If it *is* proved to me that one of you is responsible for this, I will do my duty as an extinguisher and hunt you down. Is that understood?"

"Yes, Your Highness," Rayetayah inclined his head in acceptance. When he lifted his face, he was smiling. "Thank you. Perhaps my father was right about you."

"Don't thank me yet," I warned. "I'll need your help in

51

proving your innocence. I need to find out who really is guilty and to do that, I'll need you to stay in Fairy for awhile."

"What?" Rayetayah cocked his head at me. "You want us to leave the Human Realm?"

"For now," I nodded. "I want all of you to go to the Twilight Court, where you will stay until I can find the impostor. With you under the watchful eyes of my father, you will have an alibi, a royal alibi. Do you understand?"

"Yes, I see your logic," he nodded. "So be it, Princess. We will go to court and submit to observation. But how will we help you find the culprit if we're in another realm?"

"*You* are going to stay here with me," I said to him and he began to smile; slow and sensuous. Just like his father. I nearly rolled my eyes. "Not that kind of stay with me," I snapped and his smile faded. "You'll stay here, in the Council House, with me and my guards. You'll be under our supervision while you help us find whomever is behind this."

"Alright, Princess Seren," he sighed and looked to his people. "But first, I will see my family safely to Fairy."

"I'll help with that too," I agreed. "I have fairies waiting for me at one of the raths in Twilight. We'll take your people there and I will escort them through with you. Then my fairies will lead the raven mockers to Twilight Castle. Is that acceptable?"

"Yes," he nodded and scooped me up, launching us into the air.

"What the hell?" I snapped.

"I'm taking you back to the Council House," he glanced down at me with a little smile. "I'll leave you there and return tomorrow evening. My family and I need a night to gather our things and prepare to leave."

"Oh, okay," I settled in against him. "I guess that works."

"It will have to," his low voice slid over me and I thought again of his father.

Raza had told me that he was one of the last of his kind and that his race would eventually go extinct. Rayetayah was proof of that. The dragon blood wouldn't continue past Raza, instead, it had helped to create a new line entirely. Which I guess, was Nature's way. One race ends and another begins.

Chapter Eight

I called Tiernan from the air, to let him know I was alright and to tell everyone to stand down; I was unharmed and on my way back. He was angry but relieved enough that it didn't matter. I made a mental note to thank my Uncle Dylan for the cell phones. Without them, Tiernan and the rest of my Guard would have been wandering around Tulsa, searching for me all night.

As it was, we returned to find the Council House all lit up, floodlights illuminating the entire yard, and were instantly surrounded by fairy knights and extinguishers when we landed. Rayetayah gave me a smirk as he let me go.

"They're still scared of me," he chuckled.

"They're afraid that you'll hurt me," I corrected. "But that brings up a good question," I waved everyone back as I turned to look up at him. "Why have you been attacking the Council House if you're innocent?"

"We never attacked them," he shook his head. "We heard about what went on with the shaman and knew we'd be blamed. So instead of just waiting for them to hunt us, I thought it would be better to try and simply scare them off. No one gets hurt that way," he shrugged.

"Except that it made you look guilty as hell," I sighed. "Alright, go do what you need to do and meet me back here tomorrow evening."

"Yes, Your Highness," he took my hand and bowed, kissing the back of it. Then he launched himself straight up into the sky.

"I know," I said to everyone as I walked towards the house. "I have a lot of explaining to do. Let's go inside first, it's cold out here."

"Ambassador, are you all right?" Councilman Teagan stood on the porch, waiting for me.

"I'm perfectly fine," I assured him. "The raven mocker leader was concerned for the safety of his people, so he flew me to a neutral location for us to speak."

"*He* was concerned," Councilman Murdock huffed.

"Let's talk in the living room," Teagan ignored Murdock and waved me inside. "I think everyone has a right to hear what you have to say."

"Absolutely," I agreed and followed him in to take a seat on an overstuffed beige couch beside him.

Tiernan sat beside me, taking my hand to give it a relieved squeeze before letting it go. Cat laid across my feet and my Star's Guard spread themselves around the room, keeping a watchful eye on everything as they listened. The extinguishers made like my Guard; standing around the room, several near windows so they could keep a watch over the perimeter of the house. The council members though, just came in and took seats.

"Now that we're all settled," Teagan nodded. "Please tell us what you've learned, Ambassador Seren."

"I believe the raven mockers are innocent," I said and the room erupted into surprised shouting; mostly from the council members.

"Enough!" Teagan yelled over everyone and got the silence he demanded. "Please go on, Princess."

"I understand how this looks," I began again. "If you had

said the same thing to me earlier today, I wouldn't have believed you."

"Why do you think they're innocent?" Tiernan asked gently.

"For one thing, they told me they are," I said simply and Councilman Murdock made a disgusted snort. "They have no reason to lie to me but I won't argue the point. Rayetayah, their leader, told me that initially they were behind the attacks but the other local fey, including his mother, asked them to stop out of love for the Native Americans."

"You're telling me that fairies asked other fairies to stop hurting humans?" Murdock scoffed.

"Councilman Murdock, are you deliberately trying to be insulting or are you just too senile to remember our history?" I said snidely.

"You-" Murdock started but was cut off by Teagan.

"Stop arguing with the Princess," Teagan said to Murdock. "Let her finish and then we'll ask our questions."

"Thank you," I nodded to him. "Fairies have a history of loving humans and vice versa. The Native Americans especially appealed to the nature-loving fey and several fairies became guardians of the tribes. The humans thought they were animal spirits or gods."

"Gods," Murdock huffed.

"Say one more word and I will remove you from this room myself," Teagan glared at the older councilman and Murdock looked away. "Go on, Ambassador."

"Rayetayah is the son of one of those spirits; a raven spirit to be exact," I explained and all of the fairies in the room nodded in understanding. It made sense that the mother's traits would influence the son. "His mother had a deep respect for the Cherokee and she felt that he was hurting them, so she asked him to stop. He says that they did but something else had been watching them and took over where they left off."

"So the monster is telling us it's another monster's fault?" Murdock huffed.

Every fairy in the room tensed, including me. Teagan started to say something but I waved him down as I stood. I had the supreme satisfaction of seeing Murdock's face go white. I admit that I relished his fear as I closed the distance between us.

"How did such a horrid racist become a councilman?" I asked him in a deceptively calm voice.

"I am not a racist," he sputtered.

"You've insulted me and now you've insulted my people," I narrowed my eyes on him. "Either you're a liar and a bigot or you're very, very stupid. Because if we truly were monsters, you should be afraid of what we might do to you," I leaned in to whisper, "without you even knowing we were doing it."

"How dare you?" Murdock drew back his hand and all of my guard reacted, moving towards us with fairy speed.

They were fast but I didn't need their help. I could protect myself, especially from some old fool. I didn't even strike him or use any of my new fey magic. I used good old fashioned human telekinesis to give his hand a small nudge. Just enough to send it into his own face instead of mine. The slap rang out and the councilman sat there in stunned silence as a red mark appeared on his cheek.

"Stop hitting yourself," I mocked him in the sing-song tone of a child.

All of my guard stopped short and with extreme effort they managed to hold in their laughter. Not so for the extinguishers and council members. They laughed at Murdock and it was a merciless, growing laughter that started out small and shocked but evolved into full out hilarity. Murdock stood and left the room without another word.

"Why is it that whenever we meet new council people, one of them always ends up leaving the room?" Tiernan mused.

I turned to smile at him and saw that Cat was still relaxed on the floor. She had never viewed Murdock as a threat. I guess after his earlier bluster and my handling of it, she thought I was good on my own. I kind of loved that about her; her ability to analyze like a human. Or a fairy, I guess.

"I have never seen anyone deal with him so brilliantly," Teagan applauded as he stood. He held his hand out to me and I walked over to shake it. "Bravo, Ambassador."

"Thank you," I sat back down. "Now that the room has been cleared of fairy-haters, I'd like to proceed."

"Please do," Teagan still had laughter around his lips.

"I believe it speaks to their innocence that Rayetayah is willing to send his people into Fairy while he remains behind to help us in our investigations," I went on. "The raven mockers will go to the Twilight Court, where my father can watch over them and Rayetayah will be here under our supervision. That way, if there is another attack, we will be certain that it isn't a raven mocker."

"But how will you know that all of his people are accounted for?" A councilwoman asked. "One of them could stay behind and do the deed."

"And then be hunted by his or her own leader?" I lifted a brow. "I don't think that would go well for them. Rayetayah knows that we won't stop searching until we have the villain in hand and I have already vowed to them that if we catch the killer and he turns out to be a raven mocker, I will extinguish him myself. Then, not only would one of his raven mockers be dead but the rest of them would be suspect and held for questioning."

"That's a rather good point," the woman conceded.

"And if that doesn't convince you," I added. "I'd like to point out that raven mockers have wings."

"What does that have to do with anything?" Teagan asked as Tiernan's eyes went wide and he gave a huff of comprehension.

"Remember the tape you showed us, Councilman," I reminded him. "The heat signature showed no hint of wings and even when the criminal was revealed, there were only shadows around it; no wings."

"And those were some significant wings," Teagan mused.

"Also, from being held by one," I went further. "I can assure you that they run very hot and those wings, although appendages, would retain some of that heat. That's what feathers are meant to do after all."

"They'd show up on infrared," Teagan nodded. "Alright, Ambassador, you've made a good case. We'll go with your plan."

"So instead of being hunted by raven mockers, we'll be assisted by one," Extinguisher Kate mused. "Isn't life funny sometimes?"

"As long as the joke's not on us," Conri observed in a low tone.

Chapter Nine

"Do you think I should notify Lord Raza of the situation with his son?" I asked Tiernan as we snuggled in bed later that night.

We had a very nice guest room in the Council House. Technically it wasn't in the Council House but in that smaller building I'd glimpsed from the council chamber windows. It was the old servants quarters and as awful as that sounds, it had been refurbished into a beautiful guest house. It fit all of my Guard comfortably, with a couple of rooms to spare, so it was perfect for our needs. I guess back in the day, rich people needed a lot of servants.

"Do you *want* to notify Lord Raza?" Tiernan tensed beside me.

"Are you getting jealous again?" I lifted up on my elbow to smile down at him.

"No," he glanced away.

"OMG, you're like a little girl," I laughed.

"*I'm* like a little girl?" He shot back. "You're the one who just used OMG."

"I obviously added it so I could relate to your teenage girl mentality," I rolled my eyes. "But seriously, is that something I should do, you know, as in proper princess procedure?" I stopped and considered. "Proper princess procedure. PPP. Triple P. Yeah, I like that, definitely one to remember."

"I suppose it would be a nice gesture to make Lord Raza aware of the situation," Tiernan conceded, completely ignoring my ramblings about acronyms.

"T-Baby," I kissed his nose. "I don't have to even talk to Raza personally. I can scry Uisdean and ask him to tell Lord Raza."

"Oh," he blinked. "Well then, that's fine."

"I'm so glad you approve," I huffed and laid back down.

"And Seren," he pulled me into his side.

"Yeah?"

"Don't call me T-Baby," he grimaced. "That's weird."

"No?" I barely contained my laughter. "Your little, jealous, teenage-girl mind doesn't like T-Baby? I thought it would be perfect for you."

"Seren," he growled.

"How about TeeTee?"

"That's one letter away from being a Native American dwelling," he said dryly.

"NanNan?" My lips were twitching so bad, I had to bite them.

"That makes me sound like someone's grandmother," he scowled.

"Tier-Pac?"

"What?" He laughed and sat up to shake his head at me.

"Well, you did tell me once that you're living the thug life," I shrugged and then gave up and chortled. "Hey, have you ever

61

noticed how similar your name is to my father's? Tier and Keir."

"First of all, it is not similar. My name is Tiernan and his is Keir," Tiernan sighed. "And second; are we really going to go from talking about Raza to talking about your father... while we lay naked in bed together?"

"Hmmm," I sat up and looked him over. "You're absolutely right. Maybe we should be talking about a nickname for little Tiernan," I pointed down into his lap.

"What?!" His beautiful silver eyes, exotically shaped (as most sidhe eyes are), rounded in horror.

"You've never named it?" I giggled.

"Why would I name it? It already has a proper name," he gaped at me.

"For pillow talk of course," I laid back on said pillow.

"Pillow talk?"

"You know, so you can say something like," I dropped my voice into an imitation of his, "Tiny Tiernan wants to play."

"Tiny?!" He nearly shouted.

"I didn't mean it was tiny," I rolled my eyes. "I meant that it was like a mini you."

"Never use the word tiny in reference to me again," he narrowed his eyes on me. "Not in bed, not out of bed, not ever and not in any way."

"Alright," I laughed. "Sensitive much?"

"Yes, it is rather sensitive," he smiled wickedly as leaned over me. "But not in the way you're implying."

"I think I'm going to need an example of its sensitivity," I slid my hand down to investigate.

Chapter Ten

The next morning, Rayetayah arrived with a flock of raven mockers. I hadn't even considered that there might be children. I don't know why, it made perfect sense that there would be. And there they were; raven mocker families. Mothers, fathers, and children; all holding hands as they stood behind their leader and all of them staring at us with grim expressions. Most of them had black, feathered wings folded behind their backs. They each held a piece of luggage, even the children, and I felt like I was staring a a group of angelic refugees.

"That's a lot of fairies," I whispered.

"He called them all in," Tiernan lifted a brow at me. "You wanted all the raven mockers and that's what you got; the entire lot living in the Human Realm."

"I don't think the plane will hold them all," I said to Tiernan.

"I had our plane prepared for you," Councilman Teagan said from his place on my right. "It's large enough to transport two-hundred-fifty people."

"Thank you. That sounds perfect," I nodded to him and then I headed down the porch steps to Rayetayah and his mockers... *our* raven mockers. "Thank you all for agreeing to do this," I said to them. "I know this is a hardship on you and your children but I promise that you will be very comfortable in Twilight Castle. You will be safe there and as soon as we discover who is behind these deaths, you'll be returned to your homes."

They all nodded their heads in acknowledgment but no one

spoke.

"We'll be driving to the airport in these," I indicated the black SUVs waiting in a row down the driveway. "But before we go, I want you to know one more thing. We don't know each other yet. You have no reason to trust me except for this; I am my father's daughter and I vow to do right by you. You are twilight fey and although most of you have lived your lives here in the Human Realm, you will always be twilight fey. In that we share common ground. I was raised here too. I know exactly how it feels to be pulled from your home and thrust into Fairy, and I can honestly tell you that you're going to be alright. The Twilight Court is different from the other courts of Fairy. We don't abandon our fey and I won't abandon you. I promise you that, as your princess."

Tense shoulders sagged and grim faces eased. Several children smiled at me and parents nodded in acceptance. Sometimes you just needed someone to tell you it was going to be okay. I was glad that I could be that person for them.

"Alright then," I waved to the cars. "Let's get going. It looks like we may have to make multiple trips."

Chapter Eleven

Raven mockers were able to appear completely human. It wasn't just a glamour, it was an ability to magically tuck away their wings. I don't know where the wings went and I didn't ask. Never look a magic horse in the mouth. Whatever the case, I was glad for it because it meant that we were able to squeeze more of them into the vehicles than we would have with their wings exposed. But even with the extra space the lack of wings provided, we still didn't have enough room in the SUVs and instead of making multiple trips, we decided to bring in a few buses to get everyone to the airport in one go.

The plane ride was an astonishing thing for the raven mockers. Unlike my guard, these were fairies who had lived in the Human Realm. They knew all about the modes of transportation available to humans and had seen planes flying overhead many times. However, none of them had ever been in an airplane.

Once we were in the air, it became very difficult to keep the mockers in their seats, especially the children. They all wanted to be near the windows, watching the clouds go by and goggling at how high we were. I hadn't occurred to me that fairies who could fly might marvel at being in a plane but there were limits to their wings and we were exceeding them. We were taking them where they'd only dreamed of going.

Several adults cried tears of joy; a sight I was totally unprepared for. Mothers hugged their children, husbands kissed their wives, and children laughed in delight. I was overwhelmed by their happiness and so grateful that I was able to provide a moment of wonder for them during such a frightening time. I told the extinguishers who had accompanied us to stand down and let the mockers roam, let them enjoy their first flight above the clouds.

"I can touch the sun," a little boy exclaimed to me.

"It feels like it, doesn't it?" I smiled at him.

"I wish I were out there," he pointed out my window and suddenly, his wings appeared, spreading wide like they were carrying him instead of the plane.

"No you don't, Samuel," Rayetayah came up behind the boy and tapped his wings down until Sam pouted and put them away. Then Raye turned him about and shooed him off down the aisle. "It's much too cold out there; even with our body heat, your wings would freeze. Now go find your mother."

"I didn't expect so many children," I stared after Samuel.

"We're a fruitful lot," Rayetayah grinned at me. "Probably because we intermarry often with the humans."

"Humans," I frowned as something occurred to me. "Are some of them human?"

"Didn't you notice that some of my people had to be flown in by others?" He countered. "Couldn't you sense their humanity?"

"No," I blinked. "I mean, I saw that some didn't have wings but I hadn't considered what that meant and I was too focused on getting everyone to the airport to sense whether they were fey or not."

"Will it be a problem?" He took a seat across the aisle from me and Tiernan.

"I don't know," I glanced at Tiernan and he shrugged. "No," I said suddenly, with complete certainty. "As long as they know what they're getting into, I think my father will be fine with it. He loved a human woman after all."

"That's very true," Rayetayah smiled. "It's been a long time since I've seen your father. I almost wish I were accompanying my people."

"You knew my father?" I lifted a brow.

"Yes, of course," he smiled. "I am the first raven mocker. Your father was the one who welcomed me to Twilight when my mother brought me to court."

"You know, I've never asked any of my fey how they felt when they had to leave their families for Twilight," I mused. "Would you mind telling me what it was like? I just want to know what my people go through to join our court."

"It wasn't a trauma," he shook his head. "Back then, it was like winning the lottery. I was one of the blessed and I felt honored to become a part of the Twilight Court. Several mothers used to bring children to Twilight at a young age, thinking it best to have them raised by twilight fey, but my mother raised me among the Cherokee and then took me to Twilight when I was sixteen."

"So it wasn't like you were leaving your family," I mused.

"Not at all," Rayetayah shrugged. "It was more like gaining family. Your father was kind to me and when I asked to return to the Human Realm, he agreed immediately."

"King Keir would never hold anyone at court against their will," Tiernan agreed.

"No," Rayetayah smiled. "Besides, other mockers had been born by then and it was determined that we were a new breed of twilight fey. So King Keir thought it was a good decision for me to return to the Human Realm, where a lot of the raven mockers were being born."

"Sweet Danu, I didn't think to ask," I huffed, a little angry at myself. "Do you have a family? If you do, you don't have to stay with-"

"No, not as you mean," he leaned forward and laid a hand on my arm. "I am unmarried. I have a human lover but she doesn't know about all of this yet. I've been waiting for the right time," he sighed and sat back in his seat.

"What did you tell her about this situation?" Tiernan asked.

"I told her I had to take care of some tribal matters," Rayetayah shrugged. "She's not Cherokee so it wasn't too hard to come up with a plausible explanation for my absence."

"Good," I nodded. "But I'm sorry you had to lie to her."

"I've been lying to her for a very long time," he shook his head ruefully. "Hopefully I'll be able to come clean soon but sometimes with humans, it's easier to just hide what you are and wait for time to take them."

"Don't they get suspicious when you don't age?" I asked.

"We have glamor for that," Rayetayah said sadly. "It's when children are born that the truth must be told."

"It seems tragic to have to hide who you are from those you love," I noted.

"It can be," Rayetayah turned somber eyes to me. "But that is the choice we make when we allow ourselves to love a human. You begin the relationship knowing that you might never be able to be completely honest with them and that you will most likely outlive them."

"Exactly, it's a tragic sort of romance," Tiernan nodded and I glanced at him in surprise. He shrugged, "I once thought you were purely human."

"You were the one trying to convince me into being with you," I huffed. "I thought I was the only one with misgivings about

69

our relationship."

"If you'll recall," Tiernan smiled wickedly. "I had plenty of misgivings but my lust for you outweighed them all. The call of Danu won out in the end, as it always does."

"Danu called you two together?" Rayetayah asked with interest.

"The Goddess herself told me to look after Seren's heart," Tiernan's smile turned sweet.

"The Goddess herself?" Rayetayah lifted a brow.

"Danu revealed herself to Seren and the Star's Guard," Tiernan nodded. "Though she spoke to and through Seren many times before that."

"The Goddess speaks again," Rayetayah whispered. "Now I'm truly jealous of the others."

"You can visit Fairy any time you wish," I shrugged. "You're a fairy, you know?"

"Maybe I will go back after this is all over," he smiled brightly. "But right now, I'm going to tell the others that Danu is among us once more. It will lighten their spirits and make this trip into something to be treasured instead of born."

He got up and headed off to speak with the other raven mockers.

"That's definitely an innocent man," Tiernan observed.

"I think so too," I agreed. "And for his sake, I hope we're right."

Chapter Twelve

I had phoned my Uncle Dylan before we left Tulsa so there was a fleet of passenger vans waiting for us when we landed in San Francisco. The few Tulsa-based extinguishers who had come along with us, waited with the plane while I headed over to Gentry Technologies with everyone else.

When we arrived at my father's company, the vans dropped us off in front of the entrance to the basement parking garage. There were a few fairies in business suits waiting to help direct everyone down into the building and then to the rath. It was quite a long process; getting all of those families up to the second floor and then downstairs to the hidden fairy mound. Uncle Dylan had given directions for his people to lead us up the stairs instead of using the elevators, so there wasn't any hold ups while people waited for the elevators to arrive. It was a good idea even though it meant that my poor tired fairies had to tromp up two flights of stairs with luggage and whining children before climbing down yet another flight of stairs to get to the rath.

My guards positioned themselves along the route to help keep everyone heading in the right direction. It was mid-day and the second floor was full of employees, so I'm sure the mockers wouldn't have had any trouble finding someone to direct them but we wanted to make sure things went as smoothly as possible. I went first, ahead of the group, to lead them through the rath so I could explain everything to the stable boys waiting on the other side.

Dylan had mirrored my father and Keir had sent a group of knights to meet the mockers but they wouldn't have been able to reach the rath in time to warn the waiting boys. So I had to go through with Rayetayah first so that they didn't panic. Panicking cat-sidhe was not a pretty sight. Cat came with me but Tiernan stayed behind to help lead the mass of mockers through the building.

"So far, you've proven yourself true to your word, Princess," Rayetayah noted as we stepped through the golden door and into the fairy mound.

"I try to always keep my word," I led the way along the dark path and opened the door on the other side.

The bright meadow around the rath now had a small tent erected in the center of it, its white walls so startling against the verdant background of the forest. Off to the side of the tent were several horses and in front of it was a cooking fire, around which the stable boys were settled. They had been relaxing in the sun, enjoying their time off when they spotted me.

All of them jumped up and came to attention. Then they spotted Rayetayah and the rest of the raven mockers. Their bodies went slack with confusion as they looked to me for answers. That's when I realized that we had no way of transporting all of the mockers to the castle.

"Oh crap," I looked to Rayetayah. "I hadn't thought about how to get everyone to Twilight Castle."

Rayetayah just started to laugh and the stable boys in front of us began to look nervous.

"It's alright guys," I said to the boys. "These are the raven mockers, they'll be staying at court for awhile. I need you to escort them back to my father. You'll be met partway by some knights and they'll take over the transport but I'm not sure how we're going to do this. They've already had a long journey and I hate to ask them to walk all the way to the castle. Why are you laughing?" I finally turned and asked Rayetayah.

Instead of answering, he revealed his wings with a whoosh of sound and a rush of air.

"Oh," I closed my eyes at my own idiocy. "Right, you guys can fly."

"It's easy to forget when our wings are enchanted," a female mocker said sympathetically as she chased her son past me. The child had given a shriek of delight upon seeing the Twilight Forest and had immediately made a beeline for the trees.

"Well, I guess, you'll be escorting them from the ground," I said to the cat-sidhe boys. "But, like I said, some twilight knights are already on their way to meet you."

"It's not a problem, Princess Seren," Searc smiled at me as he swept a golden blonde lock out of his pear-green eyes. "The horses are well rested, they can keep up with the raven mockers."

"I just don't know how I feel about leaving my people with only a few boys to guide them," Rayetayah looked over the stable lads.

"The road leads straight to Twilight Castle," Searc shrugged. "It's not like we'll have to do a lot of guiding. Plus, they'll be able to see the castle from the air. We'll have more chance of getting lost than they will."

"I don't know how reassuring that is," Rayetayah frowned at Searc.

"The twilight knights will be meeting them shortly," I offered. "And it's not like twilight fey need protection in the Twilight Kingdom. Especially when the mockers can fly. They'll be fine."

"Alright," Rayetayah sighed.

"But why don't they just go and stay in Criarachan, with the other raven mockers?" Searc asked simply.

"Criarachan?" I blinked.

"It's the raven mocker village here in Twilight," Rayetayah explained and then faced Searc. "There has been some criminal charges laid upon us in the Human Realm and we must be under watchful eyes to be exonerated."

"Ah," Searc nodded. "And the mockers living here are not under suspicion?"

I groaned, facing yet another aspect I hadn't considered.

"Perhaps, once we meet up with the knights, they should escort them to Criarachan and simply stay there to watch over them," Searc suggested.

"No, my father already expects them and I don't want to put the village out," I sighed. "Take them to court and tell the knights to see my father for instruction. I'll return to HR and scry him to discuss this."

"Yes, Princess," Searc nodded and went to help the other stable boys take down the tent and pack up camp.

"You didn't expect this to be such a huge production, did you?" Rayetayah chuckled as we stepped to the side and watched our people stream through the rath door.

"No, I didn't," I admitted. "You've got to be the largest group of twilight fey I've met."

"There are quite a lot of cat-sidhe too," Rayetayah nodded towards Searc. "It's just that they're not pack animals, so they wander about a lot. You don't see them all together at once."

"Hmm," I thought about it. "What about the bargests?"

"Well, I haven't been back to Fairy for awhile but the last

time I was here, there wasn't a whole lot of them," he cocked his head in thought. "Though they are a pack animal and I know they have a village too. I've never been there myself. Bargests can be temperamental fairies and it's best to give them their space."

"Why doesn't that surprise me?" I laughed and then suddenly sobered.

"What is it?"

"Can I call you Raye?" I diverted his question.

"Yes, I think I'm okay with that," he narrowed his eyes on me. "If you tell me what chased the laughter from your eyes so quickly."

"It's just hard for me sometimes," I shook my head. "I shouldn't complain. Here I am; this new royal fairy with an incredible magic and the Goddess backing me up."

"But?" He prompted.

"But sometimes I feel like an outsider," I shrugged. "I've spent my whole life studying the fey and I thought I knew them, when actually there was an entire kingdom I didn't know about. And it just so happened to be *my* kingdom."

"And now you must learn about your own people," Raye nodded. "You're our Princess but even I, a fairy who hasn't been home in years, knows more about your fairies than you do."

"Yes, exactly," I nodded. "I've been studying hard ever since I first got here but it still isn't enough."

"Most things about Fairy must be experienced to be learned," Raye said gently. "You need time, not education."

"And it's time for us to return," Tiernan said stiffly.

"Tiernan," I turned to see him standing near the rath door

behind us. "Is everyone through?"

"They're all here," he nodded and cast Raye a guarded look. "Are you satisfied that they're safe?"

"I am," Raye nodded. "Just give me a moment to speak with them and I'll be ready to leave."

"Of course," I nodded and watched him walk away. Then I turned sharply to Tiernan. "What is with you?"

Cat, who had been sitting calmly beside me, stared back and forth between us.

"Nothing," he sighed. "I'm just tired."

"Are you sure?" I edged closer to him. "Because that seemed more like jealousy than exhaustion. And although you're kind of cute when you're jealous, it's beginning to get old."

"I'm not jealous," he huffed.

"Uh huh," I rolled my eyes.

"Please," he crossed his arms over his chest. "The man's a bird."

"Wings can be pretty sexy," I offered innocently.

"Have you ever tried to have sex with winged fairy?" He lifted a pale blonde brow at me.

"No, of course not," I harrumphed.

"They're not so sexy when you're trying to get around them in bed," Tiernan chuckled.

"That sounds like personal experience," I smirked.

"All I have to say is that it wasn't worth the effort," Tiernan smirked back.

"Hmmm," I glanced over at Raye and his impressive wingspan. "I guess they might get in the way." Tiernan made a satisfied snort. "But then again, raven mockers can get rid of their wings whenever they want," I winked at my horrified boyfriend as I walked by.

Chapter Thirteen

I stepped out of the fairy mound and into HR, to find my Uncle Dylan waiting for me. He was leaning against the curved rail of the staircase, looking like he belonged on the cover of Esquire magazine or maybe even Forbes. His mink-dark hair was combed back from his high forehead, bringing attention down to his lapis eyes which glimmered in the sunlight. He looked completely human in his tailored suit and silk tie but if I concentrated hard enough, I could see past his glamour and the true Dylan Thorn revealed himself.

Eyes without whites, just endless blue, stared at me intensely out of a starkly angled face. His skin was actually pure white, moonlight skin; an unseelie trait. He looked almost vampiric without the illusion of humanity in place but still very beautiful. In fact, I preferred him without the glamour. He seemed more natural to me as a fairy than in his stoic human guise.

"I need to scry my father," I said to him.

"I assumed you would," he nodded.

Without another word, he turned and led me, Tiernan, Raye, and Cat up the stairs, through the second floor office cubicles, and over to the elevators. My Guard was standing there, waiting for us.

"You can bring your Cat-puka but the rest of them need to wait here," Dylan waved an elegant hand at everyone.

"Sure," I looked to Tiernan. "I'll be right back."

"No," he shook his head. "I'm going with you."

"She'll be fine with me and her guard Cat," Dylan sighed.

"I've learned that it's a bad idea to let Seren out of my sight in the Human Realm," Tiernan crossed his arms. "I'm going."

"Fine," Dylan huffed just as the elevator dinged its arrival. "I don't have time to argue with you, I've already had hours stolen from me dealing with this gargantuan gaggle of deportees you've brought me. I do have to run a company, you realize?"

"Yes, Uncle Dylan," I rolled my eyes, used to his complaints. "And we're very grateful for all of your help."

"As you should be," he nodded and tapped the button for the thirty-third floor.

It was the top floor and all it held were two offices; one for Dylan and one for my father, though my father was rarely there. Half of the floor went to Dylan and the other half to my father, with the elevators and a reception area between them. There was a single secretary sitting at a desk in this reception area, placed facing the elevators with the office doors to either side of her. So I assumed that Dylan shared her with my father as well.

The secretary smiled brightly at us as we stepped out of the elevator but didn't say a word when we walked by, just returned to her typing. Efficient and quiet; my uncle probably loved that. I gave her a little wave as we passed and she inclined her head in a bow, just as proper as my uncle was.

Dylan's office was decorated to resemble the Unseelie Forest, with a detailed mural of the forest painted over the walls. The furniture was all dark wood, carved to fit in with the theme, and several potted plants also helped with the illusion. But the large windows ruined the effect, showcasing a splendid view of San Francisco that was at odds with the fey woods.

"It's through here," Dylan placed his hand against the trunk of a painted tree and pushed. A panel in the wall pivoted and

79

revealed a hallway. We started to follow him through but he glanced back. "That's far enough, Count Tiernan. You may wait in my office. I won't allow a member of the Wild Hunt to enter my inner sanctum."

"I understand," Tiernan nodded and backed into the office but Cat stayed by my side.

The panel pivoted closed behind us and Dylan led me down the narrow passage, past several rooms furnished luxuriously. I spotted a library, a living room, and a kitchen, which confirmed my suspicion that my Uncle Dylan lived at Gentry. Then I followed him into a simple room with only a small table and a few chairs in it. The table was set in the center of the room and a large crystal ball was placed on top of it, held by an elaborate stand of gold thorny vines.

"Would you like some privacy?" Dylan offered.

"No, it's fine, you can stay," I took a seat in front of the crystal and Dylan sat beside me. "King Keir Bloodthorn of Twilight," I called out as I touched the crystal.

Crystal balls are used by fairies as a form of communication. They're kind of like Skype; you connect with someone and get to see them as you speak with them. In this case, the image appears in the center of a crystal ball and the process is called scrying.

The center of the ball filled with mist and it stayed that way for a little while. I knew that on the other side of this connection, my father's crystal ball was emitting a chiming sound in an attempt to catch his attention. It would continue to chime until he came to answer my call or until I gave up. Pretty much like a telephone except crystal balls didn't have answering machines. If he wasn't in the castle, the call would go to any crystal ball in close proximity to him. If he wasn't close to any, the ball would remain clear on my end. But he was there and he answered at last.

"Seren," his fair face came into focus. "You made a wise decision, sending the raven mockers here. Have they all crossed over safely?"

"They have," I assured him. "And I'm glad you agree with me but there's something I hadn't considered."

"Criarachan," Keir nodded. "I've sent a group of soldiers out to watch over the village. The other group that was sent to meet the raven mockers, will escort everyone to Criarachan and the mockers can remain there with their kin. I think they'll be more comfortable with family than at the castle."

"Well, never mind then," I chuckled. "You're a step ahead of me."

"I've had years of practice," Keir smirked but then sobered. "Do you truly believe they're innocent?"

"I'm almost completely sure of it," I nodded.

"Almost?" Keir lifted a deep purple brow.

"Well, there's always the possibility that I'm wrong," I shrugged as Dylan snorted. I gave him a nasty glare before continuing. "I believe Rayetayah is telling the truth as he knows it but perhaps one of his people is betraying him."

"We'll find the truth," Keir sighed. "I have faith in you and until you do discover who is behind this, I'll watch over the flock."

"Thanks, Dad," I smiled. "Oh one more thing; do you think I should scry King Uisdean and ask him to notify Lord Raza that his son is involved in this?"

"Raza," Keir mused. "He's unpredictable and may react badly but courtesy dictates that he be informed. As a father, I know I'd want to be told if you were in danger and I know I'd be enraged if someone kept the information from me. So, yes," he nodded decisively. "I think you should tell him."

"Alright, I'll scry Uisdean next," I swallowed hard.

"I love you, Seren," Keir touched the crystal and I laid my fingertips over his.

"I love you too, Dad," I closed the connection and his image faded away.

"Would you like me to scry Uisdean for you?" Dylan offered gently.

I looked over to him in surprise, "No but thank you. I'm sure that conversation would be more uncomfortable for you than for me."

Uncle Dylan was born unseelie, brother to my Uncle Uisdean and heir to Uisdean's throne. But Dylan abdicated his position and aligned himself with Twilight, choosing to work for his half-brother in HR instead of live a life of luxury as the heir of Unseelie. I think Uisdean viewed Dylan as a traitor. Yet despite all that, Dylan retained his title and was given all the respect a Duke of Fairy deserved. I assumed there was more to the story than I'd been told.

"I'm not afraid of my brother," Dylan smiled.

"I didn't think you were," I smiled back. "Still, I'm not going to add a conversation with Uisdean to your already annoying day."

"I appreciate that," he laughed and waved his hand, "though I'll stay to watch your misery."

"Thanks," I rolled my eyes. "King Uisdean Thorn of Unseelie," I called and then muttered, "and general thorn in my side."

The crystal misted once more and stayed that way much

longer than it had for my father. Finally, colors came out of the mist and formed into shapes. The shapes condensed and Uisdean's face came into focus. He stared at me with his unreadable, fully-black eyes, surrounded by a fall of sword-straight ebony hair. He had on a midnight velvet tunic, laced with silver cords at his neck, but the silver did nothing to alleviate all that darkness and his pale skin shone out from it like the moonlight it was named for.

"Ah, the serious Seren is scrying me," Uisdean's sharp lips twisted up into a smile. "What do you want, Serious Seren?"

"I'm investigating a crime in Oklahoma, Unpleasant Uncle Uisdean," I began and watched his dark eyes narrow. "It appears to be a fey crime, raven mockers to be exact, but I don't believe the mockers are actually behind it."

"What do raven mockers have to do with me?"

"Not you," I shook my head. "Lord Raza."

"Go on," Uisdean's face went still.

"Lord Raza's son is Rayetayah, head of the raven mockers," I continued. "He's helping me investigate the accusations against him and his people, and I just thought I should inform Lord Raza of the investigation."

"A wise decision," Uisdean nodded. "Was it yours or did someone counsel you to tell the dragon?"

"It was my idea," I huffed.

"You're learning, little one," Uisdean chuckled. "Well done. Fairy society is a lot more complicated than human, isn't it?"

"Not really," I grimaced. "Raza is a father and parents like to be told when their child is in trouble. It's common courtesy."

"It's *Lord* Raza," Uisdean corrected with a twitching jaw. "And this is not about common courtesy, this is about pacifying a dragon-djinn. Your instincts are smarter than your brain. Think, you idiot extinguisher. Politics between warring courts are tricky but those concerning dragons get downright dangerous."

"Yeah, okay, I get it," I snarled as Dylan chuckled low.

"Who is that?" Uisdean tried to peer around me.

"That's Cat," I waved Uncle Dylan away. "Never mind her. Will you tell Lord Raza about Rayetayah for me?"

"Of course I will," Uisdean huffed. "I'm not the stupid one. Perhaps I should have called you Simple Seren."

The crystal misted over before I could say another word and my Uncle Dylan burst out into laughter.

"Really?" I looked at him in disgust. "This is what finally gets you to laugh?"

Chapter Fourteen

"I ordered Chinese food for the trip back," Tiernan said as I stepped out of Dylan's secret hallway. "They'll deliver it to the receptionist in the lobby."

"Good idea, I'm starving," I groaned.

"Bon voyage," Dylan waved us off.

"Goodbye, Uncle Dylan," I said sweetly.

"Yes, goodbye," he sat down at his desk and didn't bother to look up as we left.

"Goodbye, Your Highness," the secretary said as we went past her.

"Goodbye," I smiled as we headed for the elevator.

By the time we'd stopped on the second floor and collected Raye and my Guard, then went down to the first floor, the Chinese food had arrived. The receptionist had paid for it with petty cash and assured us that it wasn't a problem, the company would cover it. Well, it was technically my father's money, so I didn't feel bad.

A limo drove us to the airport and within half an hour, we were back up in the air, dining on black bean shrimp and roast duck. We had plenty of room now that most of the passengers were gone and we all stretched out across the seats to get some shut-eye on the way back to Tulsa.

"You will find help where you least expect it," Raye's voice drifted over to me from a few rows down.

"What's that?" I sat up and looked across the rows of seats.

He sat up too and waved a little slip of paper at me. "It's my fortune from within the cookie," he smiled.

"Oh," I laughed. "Where you least expect it, eh?"

"The fortune is a little late," he shrugged. "It's already happened," and he laid back down.

I smiled at that and went back to lying on the firm airplane seats, fluffing the horrible pillows Flight staff had given me. Cat was already asleep on the floor beside me and Tiernan was stretched out along my same row, his head laid next to mine. He looked up at all my aggressive fluffing.

"Have you gone soft now that you're a princess?" He teased. "What happened to the hard core extinguisher I first met in Hawaii?"

"Even an extinguisher likes a good pillow," I huffed and flopped down on the little rectangles of flattened batting.

"Just close your eyes, Seren," Tiernan laughed. "I have a feeling that we're all going to need our sleep."

"At least Cat can sleep anywhere," I sighed.

"Close your eyes," Tiernan said again as he angled up to look at me.

I did as he asked and felt his fingertips brushing against my forehead, smoothing out my frown. I sighed as he gently massaged my temples and then stroked my hair until I fell asleep. I didn't wake up until we were coming to a jarring stop on the Tulsa runway.

I yawned as I braced myself and then sat up to see that everyone else was already awake and belted into their seats for the landing. Tiernan was seated beside me, smiling at me like he was entirely responsible for the length of my nap. That sneaky fairy must have worked a sleep spell on me.

"I thought I was the only one with sleep magic," I grumbled.

"I didn't place any magic on you," he laughed.

"You didn't?" I narrowed my eyes on him.

"Nope, I just used my physical talents," he smirked.

"You should have at least woke me up before we started to land. I could have fallen on Cat," I grimaced and Cat added her accusing glare to mine.

"You're reaction time is way too fast for that," Tiernan scoffed.

"Our ride is here already, Ambassador," Extinguisher Kate came up to us to say.

"Great, the sooner we can get back, the better," I stood and stretched.

"I agree," she hurried off.

We followed her off the plane and into one of three waiting SUVs. I sighed as we settled into the back and Cat gave a little whine as she spread across the floor. I knew how she felt; like the journey was endless. We had gone from car to plane to car to car to plane and now to car again.

"We'll be there soon," I promised her.

And we were. It didn't take long to get us back to the Council House. Which was a good thing because they were in a bit of a tizzy. This was a little surprising since it was now 3 AM in Tulsa; time for sleeping not tizzies. We'd been traveling for more than thirteen hours and I was grateful for that long nap on the plane because without it, I would have been beat. I was still tired from all the travel but at least I was wide awake and ready to face whatever had happened while we were away.

An extinguisher met us at the door and escorted Tiernan, Raye, Cat, and I up to the council chambers. I could hear them as we approached the door; the council members were arguing. We walked in and everyone who was not yelling into a cellphone, stopped shouting to stare at us. Those on phones toned down their voices and the room quieted significantly.

"Ambassador Seren," Councilman Teagan got up to greet us, relief evident in his voice. "Count Tiernan, please come have a seat. And... Rayetayah, is it?"

"Yes," Raye nodded. "What's happened?"

"Please join us and we'll show you," Teagan gestured to the table as he took his seat. He passed some photos to me and I looked them over as he spoke. "The shaman's spell worked and someone in their community died on the seventh day. He was found in his bed with a nasty chest wound."

The photograph showed a young Native American man, sprawled across his bed with his hand clasped to his chest and his face frozen in a grimace of pain. There was a stick lying on the floor beside the bed; a stick which looked very similar to the ones the shaman had used in his defense spell. I passed the pictures to Raye.

"Do you recognize him?" I asked Raye.

"That's Jay Hocktochee," Raye frowned. "He's human, *completely* human."

"Human?" I lifted a brow and looked to Teagan.

"We haven't been able to get in to view the body yet," Teagan shrugged. "So I can't confirm that. We were hoping that you would go in and take a look. We don't seem to be able to agree on any other course of action and we haven't been able to get any of our contacts to come through for us."

"It's 3 AM," I blinked in surprise.

"The best time to sneak into a morgue," Councilman Sullivan grinned.

"I just told you, this man is human," Raye growled.

"No one is doubting you," I held up my hand. "We need to look at the body to see if it has any clues for us, not just to verify that it's human."

"Then I'll go with you," Raye said.

"I don't think that's a good idea," Teagan shook his head. "It could cast a poor light on any evidence collected."

"What does that mean?" Raye narrowed his eyes on Teagan.

"It means that someone could suggest that you tampered with the evidence," Tiernan snapped. "You'll stay here, where you'll be held above reproach, and you'll be happy about it."

"What about you, you're a twilight fairy," Raye grumbled. "Won't they accuse you of tampering?"

"I'm also a Lord of the Wild Hunt," Tiernan stared Raye down. "As such, I'm entitled to be there."

"And we'll be sending more extinguishers with you to ensure that everything is properly collected," Teagan offered.

"We'll take two," I said decisively. "With Tiernan and me, that makes four. Which is more than enough people to be breaking into a morgue."

"I thought perhaps you could simply walk right in," Teagan lifted his brows.

"How's that?" I asked.

"You know, with that whole jedi mind trick you fairies do," Teagan smiled.

"If there's a morgue attendant, then yeah," I agreed, "we can render him fairy-struck. But if it's closed for the night, then we're out of luck."

"A morgue is like Denny's," Sullivan smirked, "it's open twenty-four hours."

Chapter Fifteen

"A morgue is like Denny's, eh?" I grumbled as we walked up to the obviously closed Tulsa Medical Examiner's Office. According to the sign on the door, the place had closed at five. Not anywhere near to being open twenty-four-seven. "What do we do now?"

"We need to look at that body," Extinguisher Kate, one of the two extinguishers sent with us, said. "The ME's office is overwhelmed and underfunded here. Autopsies can take longer than five months to get done. We can't wait that long."

"Great," I looked over the nondescript khaki cement building. It looked like a bunch of boxes laid against each other in a weird way, no doubt someone's idea of creativity. I spotted an open window near the top of one sheer wall. "How about there?"

"I can get us in there but what about them?" Tiernan nodded to the extinguishers.

"You'll have to make multiple trips, honey," I said sympathetically.

"So be it," he sighed. "Who's first?"

"I'll go," Extinguisher John Sloane said. He was our other escort. "That way I can get in there and take a look around before the Ambassador goes in."

"I like that idea," Tiernan nodded and offered his back to the extinguisher.

Extinguisher John slung his arms over Tiernan's shoulder

and Tiernan used his air magic to carry them up to the open window. John climbed in and Tiernan floated back down. We waited a few minutes for the extinguisher to check everything out until he finally popped his head out of the window and waved us up.

Kate went next and then I finally got to go in, followed by Tiernan. Someone turned on an overhead light and I blinked in the sudden glare. We were in a sad, gray room with cracked and yellowed linoleum tiles on the floor and sagging ceiling tiles held in place by numerous bolts, which looked like they'd been recent additions. Mold was seeping through the tired tiles in places and the smell of it competed with the scent of chemicals.

"Is it wise to have a light on?" Tiernan asked.

"We're high enough up that no one will notice," John shrugged. "And really, who's going to investigate a light in the morgue in the middle of the night?"

"Good point," I grimaced. "Where are the bodies?" I stared at the cluttered desk and droopy chair which took up most of the small room.

"Across the hall," John led us out of the depressing room and into an even more dismal coroner's office.

"Does that crock pot have a human bone in it?" I asked in horror.

"I told you they're underfunded," Kate sighed. "They've been trying to get the state to grant them more money for years."

"This is awful," I walked through the room, taking in the tiny broom closet which had a table covered in bones inside it. Behind the table were stacked cardboard boxes with case numbers written on them in black sharpie.

"Here we go, Ambassador," John pulled out a shelf from

the mortuary cold chamber installed in one wall.

On it was a sheet-draped body. Feet stuck out of the sheet, one with a tag tied on to its big toe. I walked over as John pulled the sheet back. Beneath it was the man from the photograph; Mr. Hocktochee. His face was no longer grimacing but that wound was the same, just a little cleaner. There were no others signs of trauma to his face or body but there was an odd tattoo on his chest, right beside the wound. It was a circle with two feathers inside it.

"Two feathers within a circle," Tiernan narrowed his eyes. "Placed like mirrored opposites, one black and one white."

"It's probably some kind of Native American thing," Sloane shrugged.

"The circle is an important symbol for a lot of cultures, often a magical one," Kate offered.

"You know, psychic gifts were once believed to be magic," Tiernan added.

"But they're not magic," I protested. "Humans don't have magic."

"Not that we know of," Tiernan raised his gaze to mine.

"Are you implying that there could be actual witches out there that none of us, not the Extinguishers, the Councils, or the Wild Hunt has ever come across?" Extinguisher John asked.

"It's called evolution," Tiernan shrugged. "Perhaps all the stories of witches, like those of fairies, are actually based on truth."

"And what; these people just hid for centuries?" John scoffed. "That's a bit of a leap from a feather tattoo."

"They could be a group of psychics who have been honing their skills for centuries, just as the extinguishers have done. Except their skills altered into magic," Tiernan said calmly.

93

"Anything is possible. Plus, there's this," he pointed towards the man's chest.

"What?" John asked as Kate inhaled sharply.

I peered at the body and focused my senses. Dead bodies don't have auras. They're dead so there's no energy there to interact with the environment. Which is why I hadn't thought to look for one. But there was an aura on this body. It was fading, clinging to the chest like it was searching for a heartbeat, but it was there. A deep murky green mist. It flared under my scrutiny and I gave a gasp too, backing away a little.

"What is that?" Extinguisher John stared at the body in morbid fascination.

"It's the remnants of powerful magic," Tiernan said. "Healing magic but with a darkness within it. I think this is the power that takes life energy from one being and transfers it to another."

"Why is it still here?" I watched the aura move sluggishly over the body. "Shouldn't it have left when its host died?"

"Some magic lingers," Tiernan was watching it too. "Especially healing or death magic. Healing magic wants to heal and death magic is attracted by death."

"And you think this is both?" I asked.

"I don't know what it is exactly," Tiernan's jaw clenched. "All I can tell from the color and its behavior is that it has healing aspects to it but has been influenced by something darker."

"Is it dangerous?" Kate asked as she eased forward.

"Honestly, I don't know," Tiernan frowned down at the body as Kate backed away again. "But it's doubtful. I imagine there would have been some sort of reaction already if it was. And it seems to be fading."

"Hold on, hold on," I held up my hands. "So what you're saying is; the Cherokee shaman was right? All those myths are true; there really are witches who can steal life from people?"

"It appears to be a distinct possibility," Tiernan looked back to the corpse grimly.

Chapter Fifteen

"This is just fantastic," I huffed. "I've gone from chasing my own fey to chasing witches. Witches! I feel like I'm in the wrong fairy tale."

"But isn't it better to chase witches than twilight fey?" Tiernan asked.

We were sitting in the back seat of the SUV as Extinguisher John drove us all back to the Tulsa Council House. My stomach was in knots, my hand clenched on the paper evidence bag that we'd stolen out of the morgue's highly secure evidence room (a small closet so stuffed full of evidence that we found the bag tossed on the floor). Inside the bag was the sharpened stick that had been used to kill the possible witch, Mr. Hocktochee.

"It's better, yes," I finally said to Tiernan. "But now I have to try and tell the Human Council that not only are humans behind this but they're probably witches."

"We'll back you, Ambassador," Kate said immediately. "We both saw that aura."

"I saw the aura alright," John agreed. "But honestly, I don't know what it means."

"But you can at least testify to what you saw," Kate smacked his arm.

"Of course," he huffed. "Why would I lie about it? I want to catch the criminals as much as anyone and I don't care if they're human or fairy; they just need to be stopped."

"I appreciate your attitude," Tiernan said. "And I don't expect you to support our theories, just stand up and tell them what you saw. We'll take it from there."

"No problem," John shrugged and then frowned, leaning forward as we drove down the driveway to the Council House. "What's all this now?"

We all stared out of the windshield at a limousine parked in front of the house. All of the lights were still on inside the Council House, even though it was so late now, it was more accurate to say it was early. Dawn would be lighting the sky soon. The in-between time that belonged to us twilight fey. We drove down the lane along the side of the house, just as the limo pulled away.

Voices filtered out to us through the open back door; anxious voices. I didn't like their tone and I jumped out of the SUV as soon as we stopped. I hurried up to the house, went in through the back door, and followed the strident voices to the foyer. I found myself standing before a crowd of extinguishers. Councilman Teagan was hovering around the edges of the group, calling for calm.

"What the hell is going on here?!" I shouted and everyone went quiet.

"I seem to have caused a bit of a stir," a sensual voice slid over me, making my throat go dry and other places go... well, the opposite.

Oh, sweet Danu, I didn't expect to see him again so soon and I certainly hadn't expected to have such a visceral reaction to the mere sound of his voice. Tiernan tensed beside me and I instantly felt guilty for my response. I'd been laughing off Tiernan's jealousy over men that I wasn't really attracted to but here was one whom I was... seriously and disturbingly attracted to. Attracted to in that dangerous way; when you know a man would be so very bad for you and yet you still can't help wanting him.

That was how I felt about Raza.

I saw Raye first, he angled his way through the crowd of extinguishers and fairies, clearing a path for his father which led straight to me. Then Raza stood in front of me; dressed in a human-made suit. It was dove gray with a sage shirt beneath, open at the collar. The color of the shirt brought out the angled swatches of crimson in his sable shoulder-length hair; one stripe at his right temple and one just below his right ear. He was a big man, bigger even than Conri (whom I've always thought of as linebacker large), and he was markedly muscled, straining at his suit in places. The suit itself enhanced the blue tones in his midnight skin. Midnight as in pure black, as black as his hair, as black as his heart if the rumors were true. His eyes gleamed gold; pirate dubloons set above dramatically ridged cheekbones.

His whole face was dramatic, more predator than human or even sidhe. Once you knew that Lord Raza was part dragon-djinn, it all became clear because that was what his face resembled; a dragon. His brow bone was slightly ridged and angled up into his hair while angling down in the center towards his long nose. It made his eyes appear deep set and intense, always on the hunt. His mouth was wide and hungry, adding to his predator presence, and his elegant hands were tipped in dangerous looking tar-colored talons.

But the most sinister aspect of his appearance was the pair of leathery wings lifting from his thick shoulders and rising above him in a display of male dominance that brooked no defiance. Those wings clearly said ; *Try it and I'll kill you slowly then eat you for dinner*. In case you didn't get the message on first glance of those wings, all you had to do was look closer at the claw tipped joints to understand that you were a step below this guy on the food chain.

"Lord Raza," I had to clear my throat before I could go on. "What are you doing here?"

"I came to support my son," his voice vibrated into my chest and I shivered a little.

Cat whined and backed away. Generally speaking, when a puka was afraid enough to whine, you should probably run.

"Now, little one, you know I won't hurt you," Raza peered down at Cat and held his hand out to her.

She went forward carefully and he placed his hand gently on her head, using his talons to give her a good scratch. She sighed and relaxed.

"Great, he's conquered Cat now too," Tiernan huffed.

My glare jumped between Raza and Tiernan, unsure whether I was more annoyed at Raza calling Cat *little* or of Tiernan implying that I'd been conquered.

"Count Tiernan," Raza stood and smiled at Tiernan.

"Relax, everyone," I finally realized that the humans in the room were still on high alert. "This is Raye's father, he's an unseelie nobleman and he's not here to do anyone harm."

"Raye?" Raza lifted a brow, making him appear even more wicked. "You call my son, *Raye?*"

"He said it was okay," I gulped, suddenly nervous.

"It's fine," Raza laughed. "As long as he's okay with it," he glanced back at Raye and they shared a secret smile.

"Alright," I get over anxiety really fast when someone teases me. "What's so funny?"

"His name means *hanging maw,*" Raza explained. "You've sliced it in half to simply mean hanging... if that," he frowned back at his son in question.

"It ends up just being nonsense," Raye shrugged. "But I'm okay with nonsensical nicknames from beautiful women."

Tiernan stepped forward with a narrow-eyed look and Raza lifted his hand to stop him, "Count Tiernan, you have nothing to fear in regard to my son and the Princess." Tiernan started to settle back when Raza added. "I've already made it clear that my interest supersedes his."

"Whoa now," I held up my hands when Tiernan started to rush forward, a look of murderous rage on his face.

Then twilight arrived and the tingling rush of it had me gasping and swaying forward. Two pairs of hands shot out to steady me and the magic that had been filling me sparked between all of us. The men inhaled sharply but held firm to me as I closed my eyes and breathed through the lure of it, the bubbling urge to set the magic free and let it do what it will. I had learned to control it months ago but it still took conscious effort and my unsettling attraction to Raza had weakened my focus.

Which wouldn't have been so bad if they hadn't touched me. My magic liked Tiernan, it always had, and we spent many a pleasurable twilight wrapped around each other enjoying that fact. But the addition of Raza had amped it up to fan girl fascination. It was practically screaming inside me, jumping up and down like a rock star had just entered the room. I wrestled down the urge to metaphorically throw my panties on Raza's stage and after a few tense minutes, finally got the crazy magic under control.

"Lord Raza," I opened my eyes the men released me. "Did you come here to help Raye or start a fight? Because if it's the latter, I'll kick your ass myself and send you packing back to Fairy, got it?" I lifted my hand and let my magic trail across my fingertips.

"Not yet but I now I definitely intend to have it," Raza's pupils had dilated so that there was only a thin rim of gold around them. Before either I or Tiernan could say anything, he went on. "Now tell me in great detail what is happening in reference to my son and these murders."

I sighed deep and looked to Tiernan for help. I don't know what was worse; Raza as an aggressive suitor or Raza as the concerned parent. Either way, this was going to require some delicate handling. Sweet Danu, whose bright idea was it to notify Raza? Yep, go ahead and call me Simple Seren.

Chapter Sixteen

Why had they seated me next to him? How had I wound up here? Why was he having this effect on me? What was Tiernan thinking? Oh Goddess help me. These were the thoughts running through my mind as I sat between Raza and Tiernan at the Tulsa Council's meeting table. Raza was sitting in Teagan's seat at the head of the table. He'd simply walked in and sat down there. No one seemed inclined to ask him to move. Especially after Raye took up a post behind his father like some kind of thug bodyguard. Not that Raza would even need a guard.

Instead, Teagan had nodded his head graciously and held out the chair beside Raza for me. He had then gone across the table and taken the seat on Raza's left. Tiernan had sat on my right stiffly and Cat had taken a seat on the floor between us. The atmosphere was tense, practically sparking, and even Murdock kept his mouth shut.

"So you think my son is a murderer and a criminal," Raza said conversationally.

"No, we don't," I leaned forward to address him. "I believe Raye is innocent and that's why I'm trying to help exonerate him and the other raven mockers. These are my fairies, Lord Raza, and I will defend them. You don't need to be here."

"Princess Seren," Raza took a deep breath, like he was trying to control his anger. "If you think that I'm the type of father who would sit by and do nothing as my son's life hangs in the balance, you have sorely misjudged me."

"I don't think that," I sighed. "I don't think anyone here thinks that but if *you* think," I hardened my voice and his eyes narrowed on me, "that I am the type of leader who allows my people to be falsely accused and sentenced for crimes they did not commit, then *you* have sorely misjudged *me*."

"My apologies," he whispered as his expression changed to one of fascination. "I know you're trying to be the best ruler you can be but I cannot remain in Fairy when my son clearly needs me here. He is my blood, my only child, and I would sooner slice my own throat than ignore a threat against him."

"There's no threat here. Your son is safe with me," I laid my hand over the clenched fist of Raza's which was set on the table between us.

His bluster was obviously hiding his fear for Raye and it was completely understandable, especially now that I knew Raye was his only child. Raza must have been panicking inside, knowing that we had the right to judge his son and if we found him guilty, we could kill him legally. For such a powerful man, feeling helpless must have been maddening.

So I had responded to his fear, as I would have to any parent's, by reaching out to comfort him. In retrospect, it was so stupid. I should never have touched him. If for no other reason than he was a volatile being. But I wasn't truly afraid of Raza. I had moments of stomach clenching terror around him but it was an instinctive reaction to what he was, not *who* he was. Like how Cat had reacted to him; she sensed the beast inside but then the man had reached out and reassured her. That was how I felt around Raza too; instinctively afraid while consciously knowing that I had nothing to fear.

Turns out, I was wrong. I did have something to fear from Raza but it wasn't the possibility of physical harm. It was something far worse. When I laid my hand over his, his fist twitched and then slowly released; his fingers spreading flat and then rolling in a sensuous slide to place his palm flat against mine. Long fingers curled up around my hand, talons going even further over the back until they just dimpled my skin. One twitch and he'd draw blood.

But I knew that wasn't his intention and I had a feeling that Raza never did anything he didn't intend to do. So it was with clear purpose that he slid my hand closer to him, pulling me along with it, until I was within whispering distance. I could smell his scent; sweet and smoky, like apple cider warmed over an open fire. His eyes caught the light, flashing gold, and his lips pushed together, as if in invitation, while he considered me.

"I told you to be careful who you give that compassion to, Princess," his words seemed to fall from his lips onto my skin.

"And I still don't believe that compassion should be given carefully or with reserve; everyone can use some kindness. Especially those who don't seem to deserve it," I leaned away, pulling my hand from his grasp, and he instantly flicked his fingers open so he wouldn't cut me. "Don't try to intimidate me into becoming my grandmother. It will never happen."

"Well thank the blessed Goddess for that," Raza smiled and it transformed his face into something gentle and sweet.

"How's Balloch?" I asked Raza as I sat back and took Tiernan's hand. I needed him to ground me and remind me what I had to lose if I continued to let Raza enchant me.

"You remember his name," Raza's smile softened further. "My friend is well, completely recovered from his time in Seelie. Thank you for asking."

"Lord Raza," Councilman Teagan interrupted bravely. "I want to assure you that we are doing our utmost best to discover the truth of this situation. We have just tonight sent out Ambassador Seren, Count Tiernan, and two of my most trusted extinguishers, one of them my own daughter, to investigate a murder which we believe is connected to the case."

"What did you discover?" Raza looked back to me and I saw Raye's intense gaze settle on me as well.

"We discovered the possibility that we have missed an evolutionary leap among humanity," Tiernan answered for me and the entire table gave various sounds of surprise.

"Do go on," Raza transferred his focus to Tiernan.

"Impossible!" Murdock burst out. "There's no way we could miss a new breed of human."

"Be silent!" Raza rumbled out and the echoes of his shout vibrated through the table. "You have all missed quite a lot in my opinion. Count Tiernan, please continue."

"This is pure theory at the moment," Tiernan shook his head. "We went to investigate the corpse of a man who appeared to be killed by a shaman. The shaman had set a trap for raven mockers, believing that they were behind several attacks. The trap included sharpened poles set at each corner of the intended victim's home and when the murderer appeared, he was struck by one of these poles. The corpse we viewed was definitely killed with the same kind of weapon," Tiernan placed the evidence bag with its sharpened stick in it, on the table. "We found this at the morgue. But the truly fascinating evidence was that the corpse was purely human but had remnants of magic lingering around it. A dark green aura."

"A human with magic," Raza mused.

"We both witnessed the aura," Extinguisher Sloane waved to indicate him and Kate. They had been brought into the meeting to give their reports.

"I'm sorry," Teagan frowned. "How does an aura prove magic use?"

"It doesn't entirely," I took over. "It's possible that there is another explanation for the remnant but honestly, Councilman, I can't think of one. After death, a fairy's magic can linger, especially healing magic. Tiernan believes, judging from the color, that this was a type of healing magic."

"An altered healing magic," Tiernan added. "The darkness could be a strain of death magic. This combination could potentially be used to take life from one person and give it to another."

"Is it possible that this was just a spell cast upon this man?" Teagan asked.

"No," Raza waved a deadly hand. "Magic applied by another would flee a dying body. What Count Tiernan has described is evidence of an innate ability. This human must have been born with magic."

"A witch," Councilman Sullivan whispered. "A real witch, not just psychic talents but actual magic."

"It's not so surprising," Tiernan mused. "Fairies have been living among humans for thousands of years. Some of us have even bred with them," Tiernan cast me a gentle look. "Some kind of transference was bound to take place."

"And my people are deeply rooted within the Cherokee," Raye added. "The magic doesn't surprise me as much as the fact that I didn't notice it."

"You were focused on your own people," Raza waved his hand, as if to negate any responsibility his son might feel. "This was not for you to find but for the Extinguishers or the Wild Hunt. Those are the ones who should have noticed magical humans."

"Witches," Sullivan said again. "They're witches. I'm not trying to be rude, it's just that we need to give them a distinctive title that separates them from us and our abilities. *Magical humans* just doesn't have the same ring to it."

"*Witches* is more succinct," I nodded. "Okay, so it looks like there may be real witches living among the humans. That is a possibility, but there was one other piece of evidence we discovered."

"What's that, Ambassador?" Teagan prompted.

"The man wore a tattoo on his chest with this symbol," I motioned Extinguisher Kate forward and she showed her father the picture of the tattoo that she'd taken on her phone. "A circle with two feathers inside it. It may be nothing but I think it's most likely some kind of signal, announcing this man's affiliation to others like him."

"Like that Death Eater's snake tattoo," Sullivan nodded and then looked around guiltily. "Sorry, I'm a Harry Potter fan."

"Evidently not enough of one if you think the dark mark was a tattoo," I gave him a wink. "But if it were a tattoo, then yes, it would be exactly like that. Let's be clear though, this is all theory, conjecture really at this point, as Tiernan said."

"Then let's get some *hard* evidence, shall we?" Raza smiled at me and I had to swallow past the dry lump in my throat.

Chapter Seventeen

"So are you going to tell me that my jealousy is irrational now?" Tiernan growled as we closed the bedroom door. Raye and Raza had been given rooms in the guest house with us, aggravating Tiernan even more.

"No, you have every right to be angry," I sighed.

"I do?" He instantly lost his steam, flopping down on the end of the bed to gape at me.

"I'm attracted to him," I held my hands out and shrugged. "I'm not going to lie to you; I think he's sexy."

"You do?" Tiernan's face was falling fast.

"But there's a big difference between being attracted to someone and acting on that attraction," I sat down beside him and took his hand. "I love you and as far as I know, we have a monogamous relationship."

"We do," Tiernan twisted towards me and squeezed my hand. "And I want to remain so."

"I want that too," I nodded and he closed his eyes in relief. "I can't help having a physical reaction to someone but I can make a conscious decision to not take things further."

"Thank you," he sighed.

"I wish you would have known that without me having to say it," I laid a hand to his cheek and kissed him.

"I did know," he leaned back to look at me. "I did. But

when I saw the way you both... Seren, it's obvious how much you want each other. That does something to a man's ego and rationality goes right out the window."

"I get it," I slid my hand onto his thigh and rubbed at his tense muscles. "I'm sorry I had such a huge response to him. I didn't expect it and it was hard for me to control. I would have felt horribly betrayed if I'd seen you react like that to another woman and I'm so sorry to make you feel that way. I don't want to be with Raza, I want to be with you."

"Are you sure?" He started to smile. "Is it the claws? Because I can grow my nails out."

"Shut up," I laughed.

"Or is it those damn wings again?" He growled as he tossed me back onto the bed. He followed, laying his body over me. "I don't need wings to fly."

He started kissing me, his hands sliding beneath my back and kneading at my flesh. His mouth was demanding, a harsh testament to his fading anger, but it was kind of thrilling. I tore at his clothes and he did the same with mine, freeing us of anything that could separate our skin. When he finally pressed against me, solid curves against my softer ones, I sighed in satisfaction.

Then he was biting at my neck, pushing apart my hips with his own, so he could slide into me with a deep-throated growl. I gave a gasp as we started to levitate off the bed, Tiernan thrusting harder and harder as we rose. My hands clenched around him and I rolled us, taking me to the top. He looked up in surprise and I leaned down to whisper.

"Remember this the next time you wonder who I want," I rolled again so that he was above me. "You're the only man, I've ever given up control to."

And he took that control. Tiernan lifted us higher into the

air, tangling our bodies in ways that would be impossible on solid ground, and our passion rose with us. We soared through ecstasy like acrobats and when I finally fell into screaming relief, he was there to catch me with hands and lips and magic. So much magic.

Chapter Eighteen

"If you cover that up, I'll spank you," Tiernan came up behind me as I was looking over my reflection in the mirror. He'd left a love bite on my neck. Not a hickey but a definite mark. He leaned in and laid a kiss right over it.

"You realize that this is childish behavior?" I turned in his arms to give him a saucy look.

"I would hope that no child has ever done what we just did," he teased.

"I guess I deserve to endure a little male marking after the way I behaved," I sighed. "But don't do it again."

"Don't pant after Raza again and I won't have to," he grinned.

"Fair enough," I sighed and pulled away from him. "Come on, we better go check on the dragon. I think we've left him alone too long; he may have eaten half the Tulsa Council by now."

"He's probably *running* the Human Council by now," Tiernan huffed as we left the room.

"You gotta admit that was kind of funny," I shook my head. "The way he sat in Teagan's chair and took over the meeting."

"I think your council friends would call it terrifying, not funny," Tiernan grimaced.

"He's not going to hurt anyone," I scoffed as we headed downstairs and then out to the backyard.

"No," Tiernan agreed and then added, "not unless they try to hurt his son. Then there will be blood, lots of blood."

"And fire probably," I nodded. "I guess we have another reason to prove Raye's innocence."

"I didn't need one, I already believed he was innocent," Tiernan huffed as he opened the back door of the Council House for me.

"I know," I took his hand as we went down the hall. "I did too but witches... Tiernan, this is huge. What if there's another secret society-"

"What the hell do you mean; there's another secret society living right beneath our noses?!" A voice screeched and we followed it into the library.

"We are fairly certain there are humans who have developed magical abilities," Teagan said calmly into a speaker set before him. He was seated at a central table in the massive library, with Councilman Murdock beside him.

"Sir," Murdock jumped in as Tiernan and I took seats at the table. "The evidence presently points to it but we cannot be one-hundred-percent certain as yet. We simply wanted to apprise you of the situation."

"If we are correct," Teagan took over, "and there are indeed witches living among us, then it would make sense that they had a society of their own, hiding in plain view. The tattoo points in that direction but I assure you that we will investigate this until we discover the complete truth."

"I'm sending my own investigators to assist you," the voice coming through the speaker box said. "You will allow them access to everything you discover."

"Yes, Sir," Teagan said immediately but he rolled his eyes

as he did so. "Just tell me when to expect them and I'll have a team meet them at the airport."

"My secretary will phone you with the details later," the line went dead.

"Well he sounded lovely," I said brightly.

"That was Reginald Murdock," Teagan grimaced, "Head of the Human High Council."

"And my Uncle," Councilman Murdock added with a grin that was part remorseful and part proud.

"Oh damn," I widened my eyes. "And he's sending his investigators? What does that mean exactly?"

"He has a team of extinguishers whose talents are geared towards investigations," Teagan explained. "Precognition, psychometry, telepathy, and advanced clairvoyance; that sort of thing. They're very good but very annoying."

"So they're literally a bunch of know-it-alls," I rolled my eyes. "What could possibly be annoying about that?"

"As long as they find out the truth, I don't care how annoying they are," Tiernan said.

"Count Tiernan," Murdock grimaced, "you may end up eating those words."

"Councilman Murdock, I have a feeling very few people *don't* annoy you," I teased him.

"That may be true," he gave me a little smile. "But I tend to get even more irritated when the annoying party can read my mind."

"Telepaths," I sighed. "Right. They are annoying... and usually crazy. I didn't think we had any sane ones left."

113

"Only a few," Teagan scowled. "And the ones on Murdock's team are barely holding onto their sanity."

"Great, crazy mind readers," I huffed. "This just keeps getting better and better."

"Well hold onto your knickers, little girl," Councilman Murdock chuckled. "Because we found that symbol."

"You found it?" I sat forward in my seat.

"Ah-yup," Murdock nodded but it was Teagan who explained.

"We Googled it," Teagan pushed a print out over to me. "Found it on a site devoted to magical symbols. Two feathers, back to back, one white and one black. It's the symbol for a group of witches known as Flight."

"Bird witches?" I asked dubiously.

"The name implies some sort of flying ability," Teagan nodded. "But we're not sure. We've had to wade through massive amounts of information."

"All the bullshit we once thought was... well... bullshit," Murdock added.

"Yes, thank you," Teagan gave him a disgruntled look. "He's right, though," Teagan looked to us. "All of this occult stuff was never interesting to us because we thought it was just a bunch of people running around naked in the dark, chasing shadows and calling on old gods. We never believed that they could hold some true power."

"And now?" I lifted a brow.

"Now we're concerned," Teagan sighed. "If there are real witches, we have no idea what they're capable of. All of the stories could be true. In which case, we'd be royally screwed."

"Alright, let's think about this rationally," Tiernan offered. "Say they are super powerful. Say all of these spells and occult knowledge you uncovered is true. Power like that would be hard to hide, why haven't we seen any evidence of it?"

"Maybe we have," Teagan offered. "Maybe we've seen lots of evidence but simply covered it up because we thought it was fairy magic."

"Oh crap," I whispered. "Just like this raven mockers thing. What if we've extinguished innocent fairies?"

"Let's not get ahead of ourselves," Teagan gave my hand a pat. "We make every effort to investigate crimes before we issue a warrant. I was thinking more of crimes that have gone unsolved."

"I see your point," Tiernan frowned. "Still, they've made no move against the Human Council. Perhaps they simply want to be left alone?"

"Left alone to kill people?" I lifted a brow at him.

"There is that," Tiernan grimaced.

"We will handle this," I said to the councilmen. "No matter what it is, we'll handle it. If we have to, we can call the Wild Hunt in to assist us."

"That's true," Tiernan nodded. "If humans have inherited some kind of magical ability from the fey, that means the abilities would most likely be weaker than their source."

"What do you mean?" Murdock narrowed his eyes on Tiernan.

"He means that no matter how powerful these witches are, the fey are more so," Teagan smiled.

"And you've dealt with the fey for a very long time," I added.

115

"So we can handle the witches," Teagan nodded.

"Unless you're wrong," Raza said from the doorway and we all turned startled eyes his way.

He strode in and took a seat beside me, sending me a sly smile. His eyes coasted over Tiernan's bite and his smiled widened. He chuckled, glancing at Tiernan and shaking his head.

"What do you mean?" I prompted.

"Princess Seren of Twilight," he drew my name out with a sexy purr. "Think of your people. What happened when seelie mixed with unseelie? Or better yet," he leaned towards me. "What happened when twilight mixed with extinguisher? Was the result less or more powerful than the originals?"

"Oh sweet firethorns," I turned my magic's name into a curse.

"Exactly," Raza waved his hands out to the sides. "It could be precisely as you've surmised and the witches are poor shadows of the fey. Or they could have compounded the magic into something greater than it was, twisted it into something new. Like a new race," he waved his hand back to the door, where Raye stood. "Or a new power," he waved his hand towards me. "Magic is so unpredictable."

"Just like you," I muttered under my breath. But Raza heard me and smiled.

"Exactly, Twilight Princess," he confirmed. "Just like me."

Chapter Nineteen

"So how do we find these witches?" Teagan asked.

It was hours later and the rest of the Council, as well as a couple of high ranking extinguishers and my Guard, had joined us in the library. Food had been brought in and then leftovers taken away, arguments had ensued and been settled, plan after plan had been proposed and shot down. We had no idea what we were going to do.

"The shaman," I whispered.

"What was that, Ambassador?" Sullivan focused on me.

"The shaman," I said louder. "Sweet Goddess, we're idiots. That man performed magic and we witnessed it. He's a witch. He may call himself a shaman, but it's just semantics; he's a magic user."

"She's right," Teagan blinked. "I had just passed it off as psychic talent when I first saw the video but in light of this new information, I believe the man might actually possess some magic."

"Might?" I lifted my brows. "What we saw on the video wasn't telekinesis or clairvoyance; it was a spell. That human cast a spell and laid a trap for a raven mocker. Only, he didn't catch a raven mocker; he caught another witch."

"Witches fighting witches," Tiernan mused. "So not only have we discovered a secret society but also a war among them."

"Sounds familiar," Raza smirked.

"Perhaps we should leave them to it," Murdock shrugged. "Let them handle their own."

"While some of them kill humans?" Teagan gaped at the other councilman.

"Our job is to monitor the fey," Murdock said grimly. "Not other humans. People murder people everyday and we do nothing about that. This is not our fight."

"It involves magic," I said before Councilman Teagan could reply. "There isn't another police force capable of handling magical criminals. We have a responsibility to the world."

"Why?" Murdock asked simply.

"Because we have the knowledge," Teagan took over for me. "Because; *When bad men combine, the good must associate; else they will fall one by one.*"

"The true Edmund Burke quote," one of the other councilmen nodded in appreciation.

"Well, you have to admit that the variant of; *All that is necessary for the triumph of evil is that good men do nothing,* is pretty catchy," Teagan grinned. "But it boils down to the same truth; we are good or at least, we try to be. But if we ignore this, I don't believe we'll be able to call ourselves the good guys anymore."

"This is a lot of debate over a simple question," Raza said in a bored tone.

"I don't believe this is simple at all, Lord Raza," Teagan argued.

"Head Councilman," Raza sat forward, "war is always simple; you kill or be killed. But first, you must decide whose side you are on. Now, I ask you; on which side do you intend to fight?

118

Are you for the witches or the humans?"

"Simple?" I huffed as the humans in the room groaned. "You just made this so much more complicated."

"I fail to see how," Raza sipped at the glass of red wine someone had brought him.

"They are *all* human," I explained. "And we cannot condemn all witches on the act of what might be a small fraction of their kind. So far, we have very little proof but what proof we do have points at only one person, and that person is dead."

"Then find the rest of these tattooed bird witches," Raza put his glass down with a thump, sloshing the liquid inside. "Get your proof, clear my son's name, and kill the guilty!"

The room went silent but something snapped in me and I got angry. I was a fairy now but I was still human too and I took exception to Raza intimidating my people.

"Enough!" I sat forward and slammed my hand down on the table, startling everyone, including Cat, who had been asleep at my feet.

"Pardon me?" Raza cocked his head at me.

"Your presence is being tolerated due to the circumstances and your title, *Lord* Raza," I growled. "But I've had enough of these barbaric displays intended to subdue us into compliance. You are not in charge of this investigation, you are a guest. We welcome your help and your insights but cut out the bad ass behavior or I'll send you packing. Understand?"

Silence. Deep, horrified silence.

"I have never," Raza leaned forward and set his intense gaze on me, "been so attracted to another being in all of my existence."

Awkward, tense silence. Then coughing. Someone cleared their throat. Actually, I think that was me.

"Yeah, that's not going to work for me either," I finally said. "Stop with the sexy," I waggled my fingers over his provocative expression, "sultry, sensuous, seduction routine you got going on. I'm with Tiernan and I'm a one-man kinda girl."

"Are you now?" Raza chuckled. "Sexy, sultry, sensuous," he laughed harder. "That's a lot of S words, Princess *Seren*. I think you're enjoying my seduction routine and I think there will come a day when you change your mind about the one man restriction you've imposed upon yourself. But," he held up his hand when I started to protest. "I can be patient and I'm a beast at heart, so I love a good chase. Go ahead and run, my sweet Seren. I'll catch you in the end."

"Holy shit that's hot," a female extinguisher breathed a half second before Tiernan stood and drew his sword.

I gaped at the shining, razor-sharp steel tip, just a half an inch from Raza's throat. Raza simply smiled and lifted a brow. His eyebrow caught the light and a single red hair was revealed among all the black. I was fascinated by it. A crazy kind of fascination, like I needed to focus on something inconsequential, anything other than the fact that my boyfriend was about to slay a dragon for me.

"We are fey and we find multiple lovers, even multiple spouses, to be socially acceptable," Tiernan said casually as his forearm flexed and the tip of his blade swung lower, to hover over Raza's heart. "So I will forgive your previous flirtations with my lover. But now she has made her intentions clear and revealed our monogamous commitment to each other. Yet you insist on pursuing her. You say you're a beast at heart. Well, persist in chasing Seren like prey and I will hunt you. We'll find out exactly what kind of heart you have."

120

"Twice in one day," Raza laughed as he stood. "It's been centuries since someone has stood up to me and now I find it done twice in one day. Thank you for adding some entertainment to this taxing business." He bowed to Tiernan. "My deepest apologies for any insult I may have offered you or the Princess. I fear I have been given my own way for far too long and have lost some manners in the process. I will try to be more courteous in the future."

I released the breath I'd been holding as Tiernan nodded stiffly and sheathed his blade. His hand slid over my shoulder comfortingly as he passed by me to take his seat. I just stared at Raza as he too sat down and gave me a wicked wink.

"But do not mistake my civility for capitulation," Raza added with a smooth smile. "I still have every intention of wooing the fair maiden but I will do so within the bounds of polite society. If you truly are committed to each other, my advances should make no difference. In fact, you should welcome the test to your love."

"I'm going to welcome your face with my-" I started but was cut off.

"I think we've come at a bad time, Brother," a woman's voice came from the doorway.

She was slim and dressed in typical extinguisher fashion; serviceable black top and pants. Her pale skin had a healthy pink glow to it and was covered in freckles, her sleek black hair was cut to just above her shoulders, and her intense dark eyes were staring right at me. The man holding her hand was nearly identical to her, just with slightly more masculine features and a thicker build. He was staring at me too.

"I think we've come at the perfect time, Is," he smiled and it sent a shiver down my spine.

"You must be Extinguishers Alexis and Alex Kavanaugh,"

Teagan recovered first and jumped up to greet the creepy twins.

"And you are Head Councilman Theodore Teagan," Alexis said confidently. "A pleasure to meet you, Councilman," she looked down at his offered hand pointedly. "You'll forgive us if we don't shake your hand? It exacerbates our talent, you see. We lose control of what we're shown."

"Oh, yes, of course," Teagan pulled his hand back as if he'd been burned. "I was beginning to get concerned. I sent someone to pick you up hours ago."

"Our flight was delayed," Alex shrugged.

"Oh, well, please come in," Teagan gestured to the room. "We were just discussing our issue with the witches."

"Now that's not entirely true," Alex smiled and looked Raza over. "We were just witnessing a lover's quarrel, I believe." He took the seat on Raza's left and Raza cocked his head at the much smaller man. "Come sit here, Is. This one is fascinating."

"A dragon-djinn," Alexis smiled. "I've never met a dragon before." She sat beside her brother and stared intently across him at Raza. "Oh, so passionate. He's in..." she looked at her twin with a surprised smile.

"Absolutely," Alex smiled back mischievously.

"I haven't seen such childish behavior in adults since I was a boy at court," Raza perused them right back. "Was your maturity somehow stunted by your telepathic abilities?"

I choked back a laugh, rubbing at my lips to conceal my smile, but Teagan looked horrified. He tried to recover by jumping into the conversation.

"Lord Raza, this is the psychic investigative team sent over to us by the Human High Council," Teagan cleared his throat.

122

"Perhaps-"

"It's alright, Councilman," Alex waved away Teagan's concern. "We're not easily offended. You develop tough skins when you delve into the minds of others for a living."

"People tend to be more offended by us than vice versa," Alexis added. "To answer your question, Lord Raza, my bond with my brother can seem childish to some but it helps us retain our sanity when so many of our kind have gone absolutely bonkers."

"We do apologize for bringing up bad memories though," Alex went on. "Childhood can be such a traumatic time to those of us who are different."

"We understand," Alexis leaned forward across her brother, and hovered her hand above Raza's as if she were patting it in commiseration, without actually touching him.

"Do you?" Raza's eyes narrowed. "I don't think you do." His hand shot up and grabbed hers. Both of the twins reacted violently.

Alexis screamed, her eyes rolling back into her head as she dropped into her brother's lap. Alex held her while taking hold of her wrist, trying to free it from the dragon. But Raza had a strong grip and his sharp talons insured that if Alexis did manage to free herself against his wishes, she'd pay for it.

"Stop!" Alex shouted at Raza, pulling a dagger from his belt and placing it at Raza's throat. "Free her now!"

"Draw one drop of my blood and your sister is dead," Raza smiled at Alex, who went deathly pale.

I had stood without even realizing what I was doing, and moved up behind Raza. I laid my hand on his left shoulder and he jerked, making Alexis scream again, but he didn't bother to look behind him. I think he already knew who was touching him.

Meanwhile, Alex's eyes shot to mine, full of shock for a brief moment, but then they cleared and he nodded, pulling his dagger away from Raza's throat. He sheathed it and went back to simply holding his sister.

I slid my hand down Raza's tense arm, over the bulging muscles, until one of my hands neared the dangerous bond he'd forged with Alexis. I wrapped my hand around his, careful not to touch her, but still she moaned and dropped limply across Alex.

"Let her go," I whispered into Raza's ear. "You've punished her enough, don't you think?" Raza's jaw clenched but he held tight to the telepath. "Raza, we need her to help prove Raye's innocence. Now, let her go."

I slid my fingers further down his hand and gently wedged them between his and Alexis'. She inhaled sharply and her eyes flew open, so wide that the whites showed all around her irises. I lifted his talons one at a time and finally pried Raza away from her. He allowed both actions; flexing his talons back and relaxing his hand into mine. I sighed in relief and wrapped my hand around his as it dropped into his lap. This had me hanging over him, my head draped across awkwardly between a wing and his neck with my arm around the wing. I could feel the buttery softness of the skin of his wings, where they pressed against my chest, and the flexing muscles along the bones of them.

I'd never thought of wings being muscular but of course they were, especially right at the juncture where they met his back. It was an odd sensation. An intimate contact of skin on skin, of that thick wing base flexing between my breasts, while we were both fully clothed. I could feel the silky weave of his suit right beside his shoulder joint, and a line of hidden buttons beneath his wing pressed into my belly. I would have smiled to have discovered the secret to a wing-friendly suit but he dropped his head and a fine tremor coursed through him, so I instinctively hugged him.

"I'm so sorry," Alexis whispered as she stared at us. She

124

had managed to sit back in her chair but her brother still held her hand. "I'm so sorry," she said again.

Raza lifted his head and set his glowing eyes on Alexis. "The minds of dragons are just as dangerous as the rest of them," he gave her a wicked grin. "Remember that in the future."

"I will," Alexis nodded. "I'm sorry I presumed to have something in common with you. You," she shook her head. "What you went through... I."

"Enough," Raza growled. "My past is not for public consumption."

"It goes no further. I promise you," Alexis nodded and swallowed hard. But then she looked up at me, her eyes terrified and awestruck at the same time. "I don't know whether to feel jealousy or pity for you," she whispered.

"What did you say?" I frowned and straightened. Raza caught my hand as I did and held it so I remained pressed to his back.

"Too many fathers and too many suitors," Alexis' stare went distant. "So much magic and so much anger. Power and prejudice, blood and fire. Don't get lost in what you lose or you'll never appreciate what you gain."

"As cryptic and vague as any precog," I sighed. "But thanks for the advice anyway."

"Thanks for the save," she nodded to Raza's hand, still clenched around mine. "Just as dangerous as the rest of him," she mused. "To all but one, it seems."

"Is, are you alright?" Alex asked his sister.

"I'm fine," she squeezed her brother's hand as I disengaged my own from Raza. "Though I will carry those memories with me to my grave."

"I should not have done that," Raza admitted, surprising us all. "I reacted poorly, please forgive me."

"It's an honor to share the burden with you, Sir Dragon," Alexis bowed her head deeply, like she was addressing a king.

"*Sir* Dragon?" I gave Raza a teasing smile as I headed back to my seat. "Is there something I should know?"

"I'm a knight of the unseelie," Raza shrugged. "I wouldn't count it among my greatest accomplishments."

My own fairy knights stirred, probably taking his statement as an insult, but I didn't bother to defend Raza. I had done enough of that already and Tiernan was looking understandably tense again. I leaned over and took his hand to reassure him and he gave me an irritated glance. I deserved it, I guess. I really needed to stop touching Raza.

"Nor would I," Alexis responded to Raza. "But I liked the way it sounded."

"Are we quite done with the dramatics?" Councilman Murdock huffed. "If so, I'd like to get back to discussing the possibility of a witch war."

"A witch war," Alexis lifted a black brow at Murdock. "Oh, I almost forgot. Councilman Murdock, your uncle sends his regards."

"Er," Murdock cleared his throat. "Thank you."

"Of course," she smiled and looked to her brother.

"We don't want a witch war," Alex winked at his sister. "Do we, Is?"

"No," she shook her head. "As much as it has a nice ring to

126

it, I don't think it would be all that fun."

"Why do you call her; *Is*?" I asked Alex.

"Oh, I thought it was obvious," he smirked. "It's the difference in our names."

"Oh," I nodded and then said dryly, "Cute."

"We have sorted through your information," Alexis got back to the subject of witches.

"And we agree with the Ambassador," Alex continued.

"What are you talking about?" Murdock grumbled. "We haven't told you anything yet."

"And I haven't offered my opinion," I added.

The twins gave us identical smirks.

"God damn telepaths," Murdock cursed.

"Send for shaman," Alex said exactly what I'd been thinking.

"You're right," I said to Murdock. "People are even more annoying when they can read your mind."

Chapter Twenty

Shaman Kevin Chepaney was frightened. He had looked desperate and anxious on the *Paranormal Parameters* video but now he was flat out scared. A group of extinguishers had grabbed him up off the street and brought him to the Council House in a very men-in-black way (the actual government men in black, not the movie, though I guess that was applicable too). Now he was sitting at a table with me, Tiernan, Cat, Councilman Teagan, and the twins.

"I hope you haven't started without me," a man walked into the room. He had Lord Raza's voice but he looked human; tawny skin, blunt fingernails instead of talons, wingless broad shoulders, and topaz eyes. The shape of his face was softer, the harsh edges muted back into human angles, but his hair was the same and so was his physique.

"Lord Raza?" I tried to peer past his glamour but it was too strong for me... and that was pretty impressive.

"Yep, that's him," Alexis grinned.

"In the flesh," he bowed and then took a seat at the table with us.

"Glamoured flesh," I muttered.

We were in the council chambers again and it seemed like a huge space without the rest of the council in it. Still, with the curtains drawn back and sunshine bombarding the room, the atmosphere was cheery. Raza's glamour was a good idea, it kept the harmless illusion going, but when you were a clairvoyant, as I'm sure Chepaney was, you could sense the unseen. So as soon as

Raza sat down, Kevin Chepaney started to tremble.

"No one is going to hurt you in any way," I promised the shaman. "We want to help you."

"Help me how?" The shaman's eyes kept straying to Raza. Raza smiled but that only seemed to make things worse.

"First off, by giving you information," Teagan took Chepaney's attention away from the dragon-djinn. "Then, hopefully, you'll feel inclined to reciprocate."

"I have no information that I feel the need to keep secret," Chepaney lifted his chin. "If you want to know something, just ask me so I can be on my way."

"Mr. Chepaney," I extended my hand across the table but didn't touch him. "We know about the raven mockers but I'm afraid our raven mockers and yours are different."

"What?" Chepaney leaned forward, completely forgetting about his fear. "What do you mean by that?"

"The true raven mockers are fairies," Councilman Teagan said gently and we all watched Chepaney for his reaction.

"Fairies?" The shaman blinked.

"They really do exist, Sir," I glanced at Tiernan and he nodded. So I dropped the glamour I had over my eyes and let the shaman see the silver spokes of the stars laid over the sparkling emerald of my irises. "I am half fey. My name is Seren Firethorn and I'm the Ambassador between the Human Realm and the Realm of Fairy. But I'm also the Princess of the Twilight Kingdom in Fairy. The raven mockers are from Twilight. They're my people and I am responsible for them."

"You're a fairy princess?" Chepaney asked dryly as he stared at my eyes. "Of Twilight?"

"Yeah, don't be an ass about it," I grimaced.

"But you're so human," he laughed. "And your skin doesn't sparkle."

"I was raised here," I nodded. "And please don't take the Twilight jokes any further."

"But now you live in a fairy realm?" He asked more seriously.

"*The* Fairy Realm," I nodded. "Look, Mr. Chepaney, you understand magic so this shouldn't be too hard for you. Fairies have magic but as far as we knew, humans only possessed psychic gifts. They can appear magical but they aren't, they're more of a mental advancement. They include things like telekinesis, pyrokinesis, and clairvoyance."

"Who are you people?" Shaman Chepaney blurted out.

"No, we're not witches," Alexis said gently, answering what must have been his unspoken question. Chepaney gawked at her.

"I apologize," Teagan took over. "We should have said right away. We are the Human Council, an organization formed to keep the peace between us and the fairies." The shaman looked even more confused, so Teagan went on. "Let me explain; for thousands of years, we have had a truce with the fey. When they come into our realm, we monitor them and if they break that truce, our military unit, the Extinguishers, apprehends or executes the law breaker depending on the seriousness of the crime. So you see, we watch over humans and you are under our protection."

"So you really aren't going to kill me?" Chepaney asked with a little surprise.

"No, Sir," Teagan vowed. "We want to help you and we hope that you will also help us."

"You're absolutely right," Alexis said to the shaman. "If we wanted you dead, you'd be dead already. Councilman Teagan is telling the truth; you're safe here."

"Extinguisher Kavanaugh, please allow me," Teagan said patiently and Alexis inclined her head.

"How could I possibly help you?" Chepaney looked stumped.

"We saw the video you made with *Paranormal Parameters*," Teagan began.

"You were the ones who stole the footage?" The shaman lifted a brow. "You know, they haven't returned any of my calls."

"The world cannot know about the fey," Teagan said gently. "It would cause a panic."

"Wait," Chepaney frowned. "You're saying that I've been battling fairies?"

"Yes and no," Teagan wavered.

"Your myths are correct, Mr. Chepaney," I took over. "It's just the label that you have wrong. Well, one of the labels at least. Originally, it was the raven mockers who were taking life from the dying but the other fey attached to your tribe begged them to stop and they did."

"The *other* fey?" Chepaney's eyes were getting bigger and bigger.

"You know them as animal spirits or gods," Teagan went on.

"Coyote, Raven, Thunderbird," Tiernan offered.

"Our gods are fairies?" Kevin Chepaney gaped at Teagan.

131

"Well, they *have* looked after you," I offered. "It was a raven fairy who gathered the others to confront the raven mockers."

"So, it's not raven mockers who are attacking people now?" He asked and I was relieved that he was following so well. Must be the shamanic training.

"No, because of you, we have been alerted to the possibility that there are witches hiding among the humans; people who have actual magic, not just psychic gifts," I leaned towards Chepaney. "Are you one of them, Mr. Chepaney. Can you do magic?"

"I work with nature," he shrugged. "I call on the ancestors and I ask the elements to share their gifts with me. If that is magic, then yes, I am one of them."

"But what exactly can you do?" I persisted. "There are psychically gifted humans who can move things with their minds and create fire but that's not magic. Are you talents similar to that or can you do more?"

"I've never created fire," he mused. "I use a combination of things; words of power, herbs, and intent. I can make plants grow, call the wind to me, communicate with animals, and you saw what I did to the mocker... or whatever it is."

We all sat back in amazement.

"There really are witches," Teagan said with just the barest breath of air.

"*You're* shocked?" The shaman laughed. "You just told me that fairies exist, that they live in another realm entirely but come over here to play, and *you're* shocked about witches?"

"You have to understand," Teagan frowned. "We have watched over the world for a very long time and we have never found proof of the existence of witches. It is a definite shock."

132

"But here's the real issue," I broke in. "Witches are behind these murders, Mr. Chepaney. We found traces of magic on the corpse of Mr. Hocktochee and he was not a fairy."

"My family has always known of the existence of witches," Chepaney sighed. "It's an accepted fact. We shamans are specifically taught to protect our people from these evil doers. But although we know of their existence, we don't know who they are. If we did, we wouldn't have to resort to these traps to kill them."

Alex nodded to Teagan; Chepaney was telling the truth.

"Mr. Hocktochee was wearing this symbol tattooed on his chest," Teagan passed Chepaney a photo of the feather symbol. "Does this mean anything to you?"

"It looks familiar," Chepaney nodded. "Is it some kind of identifier?"

"We believe so," Teagan nodded. "Our research has found that it represents an occult group called Flight."

"Well, that would be appropriate," Chepaney huffed. "Not all that original but appropriate."

"We think that this group in particular has picked up the abilities of the true raven mockers somehow," I continued.

"Raven mocker mockers?" Chepaney asked.

"Exactly," I grinned. "You know how to kill them but do you know how to hunt them?"

"I'm afraid not," Chepaney sighed.

"What about twisting the magic you use to set the trap?" Tiernan asked. "Could you set it to wound instead of kill?"

"What would be the point?" The shaman shrugged. "They take seven days to die, that's wounded in my book. Fatally

133

wounded but wounded nonetheless."

"That's a rather good point," Raza's eyes narrowed. "So all we need to do is track one after it's been wounded and we'll have seven days to question it."

"A dying man is less likely to give up his friends and loved ones," Teagan observed.

"Getting information out of the unwilling has never been a problem for me," Raza smiled.

"We must follow the laws," Teagan shook his head. "We do not employ torture as an interrogation technique."

"Even when it could mean catching mass murderers?" Raza lifted a dark brow.

I looked at Teagan, my own convictions in the matter floundering. This was dire. We needed to find these people and stop them. And then we needed to find out if there were more groups like them. Perhaps a little force wasn't such a bad thing.

"Even then," Teagan stood firm for all of us and something inside me breathed a sigh of relief.

"Well done, Councilman," Raza chuckled. "I applaud your convictions but I was merely testing you. We are fey, remember? We have no need for such deplorable techniques. We can simply render them fairy-struck."

"Your enchantment may not work on a magic user," Teagan considered it.

"Pardon me," Alexis interrupted. "But have you all forgotten about us?"

"Oh!" Teagan chuckled. "I guess we have."

"Perhaps you will be helpful," Raza sounded a little

surprised. The twins gave him matching scowls.

"Is there anyone in your community who is sick or elderly, someone we could watch over and use to lure out one of these witches, Mr. Chepaney?" I asked.

"There are always the old and dying among us," Chepaney shrugged. "It will be hard to monitor them all. I usually wait until I'm notified of suspicious behavior."

"Princess Seren," Raza sighed. "I appreciate that you were an extinguisher for many years but-"

"I am *still* an extinguisher," I corrected.

"Oh, my sweet lady," Raza shook his head. "You are so much more than that."

"Anyway," I rolled my eyes.

"You are not utilizing all the tools available to you," Raza's voice went stern. "Stop thinking like a human and think like a fairy... a fairy princess."

"The Hunt," Tiernan whispered.

"Precisely," Raza nodded. "This is really their domain and at the very least, they should be notified. Then they can find the witches for us."

"The Wild Hunt may end up killing innocents if we notify them of this," I frowned.

"If you recall," Tiernan said gently. "I mentioned how the Hunt has kept an eye on the raven mockers for years now because they knew how difficult they are for humans to catch."

"But they never caught a mocker because it wasn't the raven mockers doing the deed," I whispered in revelation. "They were watching the fairies when all along, it was humans."

135

"But now, we know the truth," Raza nodded. "And the truth makes this even more their business. No offense to the Human Council but I believe it's the duty of the fey to monitor humans. The Wild Hunt should be in charge here."

Councilman Teagan cleared his throat and the twins shared concerned looks.

"You can't ask them to back down now," I said reasonably to Raza. "But you're right, we have a responsibility to notify the Fairy Council," I chewed my lip as I considered. "Or at least a member of the Wild Hunt.... a Lord, preferably." I looked to Tiernan.

"I don't think I'd qualify," Tiernan shook his head. "I still answer to the Council but my assignment is to watch over you."

"I wasn't thinking of you," I gave him a look.

"Oh," he blinked. "You mean Eadan."

"Of whom do we speak?" Raza lifted a brow.

"Lord Eadan Gale," Tiernan clarified. "He's a Lord of the Wild Hunt assigned to the Twilight Council House."

"Yes, I'm familiar with Lord Eadan," Raza smiled. "I approve of the choice."

"Of course you do," I smirked. "He's an unseelie sidhe."

"Hold on now," Teagan lifted a hand. "We need to discuss this further."

"I'm sorry that this seems high-handed of us, Councilman," I apologized. "But notifying the fey is not up for discussion. It must be done and I think you know that. I'm just trying to find us someone fair to work with."

"A fair fairy," Alex whispered to his sister and she giggled.

136

"Alright," Teagan sighed. "Contact your hunter. But we're going to continue to play a role in this."

"I intend for you to," I nodded. "But honestly, this may go above us."

"I can be very tenacious, Ambassador," Teagan declared and then looked to the anxious shaman. "I won't abandon you, Mr. Chepaney. We'll see this through together."

"You know that Lord Eadan will have to report to the Fairy Council before he can take an assignment," Raza said casually.

"Lord Raza," I snapped.

"I'm just trying to be of service," he shrugged.

"Please don't service anyone," I said dryly but then felt my cheeks warm as everyone turned astonished eyes my way. "I mean, don't help us."

Chapter Twenty-One

It was just as Raza had predicted. Eadan couldn't do anything without the express approval of the Fairy Council. That being said, his council was the one based in Twilight and as such, the council members were all twilight fey. They were open to hearing my opinion on the matter before they made a decision.

Unfortunately, all of this communication couldn't be done without either going into Fairy or using an enchanted crystal ball, and the only balls available to us were the ones in San Francisco; one at Gentry and one with the San Francisco Council House that had been gifted to them when I first became princess. So instead of making yet another flight to SF, we called my Uncle Dylan and asked him to relay the message to Eadan.

Dylan called back and told us that Lord Eadan was on his way to the Tulsa Council House and would be bringing with him a crystal ball so we could speak directly with the Twilight Council. That meant that the Tulsa Council had two days at the most to get as much done as possible before the fey most likely took over.

Meanwhile, the twins had reported back to the Human High Council and they were loath to give up control of the investigation. They knew that the fey had jurisdiction, as it were, but felt that in such a case as this, everyone should be included. So they instructed Teagan to do as much as he could before the Wild Hunt arrived and then to make sure that they were included in any meetings discussing possible transference of control.

Basically, it had become a huge political power play.

So Teagan sent an escort of extinguishers out with Shaman Chepaney into the Cherokee Nation to search for possible victims while the rest of us stayed back to research witches and wait for the Wild Hunt to arrive. It was pretty clear that Raye and his mockers were innocent but the Human Council refused to make any final decision on the matter until all the evidence was collected. They were obviously using the mockers as leverage to keep themselves in the witch investigations. So Raye remained in limbo and Raza remained in HR.

Much to Tiernan's chagrin.

After Raza's big declaration of pursuit, Tiernan had become a vigilant companion, rarely leaving me alone. Raza in turn, observed Tiernan, usually while smirking, and I watched the both of them warily. It was an awkward love triangle which wasn't actually a love triangle, and I had no intention of making it into one. Raza was right in one aspect though; if our love was strong, his advances wouldn't matter. However, temptation is never easy to resist, especially when it pursues you so rapaciously.

Even with Tiernan's diligence, Raza still found moments to mess with my peace of mind. He had no problem flirting with me in front of others but I could deal with that, it was the rare private interludes that were difficult. I was headed back to the library from the bathroom when he struck the first time.

A hand shot out and grabbed my wrist; a hand tipped in talons. I was pulled roughly into an empty room, some kind of study, and the door was shut quietly behind me. Before I could react, my hand was lifted and a pair of sinister lips laid over the back of it, sending tingles up my arm.

"Princess Seren," Raza purred. "You shouldn't be wandering the halls alone. Your lover would be dismayed."

"Funny," I pulled away but he swung me back and pressed me into the door with his body.

I swallowed hard as the firm length of him leaned against

the length of me and I was able to feel every dip and plane, every curve and hollow, every twitching muscle on him. He sank into my softness and a groan was pulled from my throat by invisible hands. Damn but dragons were built; for speed and strength, and... other things. His wings extended out and then curved around us, blocking out everything but him; his face, his shining eyes, his descending lips.

"Whoa," I slid a hand up between us and his mouth smacked into it.

He took my hand and kissed it again, as if that had been his intention all along. Then he shifted my palm to his face, holding it there as his mouth fell on my throat. I gave a startled gasp as the heat of his tongue met my skin and my hand clenched automatically on his cheek. He growled, low in his throat, the vibration tickling my skin as he released my hand and slid his arms around me.

"Seren," he whispered in my ear. "Don't limit yourself to one man. You have only just discovered your fey blood. Its magic has yet to be truly released, it's heat has yet to be truly ignited. Let me show you how much more you could have."

"I'm happy with what I've got," my voice was breathless.

"I'm sure you are," he leaned back to look into my eyes. "But I can take you higher; straight into the heavens."

"I'm a twilight fairy, Lord Raza," I grabbed the door handle behind me and twisted. "I'm happiest in between the earth and sky." I opened the door and slid out. "Besides," I gave him a sly smile. "You aren't the only one who can fly."

Chapter Twenty-Two

"We have one!" Teagan burst into the bedroom I was sharing with Tiernan in the guest house. Cat jumped up excitedly and circled Teagan. She didn't have her glamour on and Teagan gave her a second glance when he noticed.

"We have one what?" I looked up from the book I was reading; *True Witchcraft*. I had been hoping that the title was accurate but so far, it was not.

"A possible witch attack," Teagan explained as he scratched Cat's head absently.

"Already?" I sat up straight and put the book down.

"The shaman has verified it?" Tiernan slid off the bed and approached Teagan.

"He's convinced enough that he's already beginning the spellwork," Teagan nodded. "He believes this may be a revenge attack for Mr. Hocktochee's death."

"Why does he think that?" I asked.

"Because the intended victim is a young man with Down's Syndrome, not the usual type that mockers go for," he said grimly. "I mean witches, not the usual type that witches go after."

"Great, now they're preying on the mentally challenged?" I huffed.

"He's lucid enough to testify to his treatment, giving the witches credit for the crime, while being an unreliable witness," Tiernan observed. "It's diabolical."

141

"Well, now it's certain," I sighed.

"What is?" Teagan asked.

"We're at war," Tiernan answered for me.

"Which means that we'll need to set a guard on the Council House as well as on the victim," I added. "If the mockers were able find out about our involvement, I'm sure these witches did too."

"That's a good point," Councilman Teagan nodded. "Alright, we need to be at the site in a few hours; that's when Chepaney says he'll be ready. I'll go and choose a team to accompany us and set another to guard the Council House."

"Wait," I stopped him before he could leave. "You're coming with us?"

"Yes."

"Councilman, I don't think that's a good idea," I said gently.

"I know how to defend myself, Ambassador," he smiled and flexed his bicep. "I'm in shape, remember?"

"Yes you are and I'm sure you can defend yourself but when was the last time you had to?" I shot back.

"It's been awhile," he shrugged. "But it's just like the old saying of riding a bike," he turned and left.

"Yeah, except if you fall off this bike, it's definitely fatal," I grumbled.

"We'll watch over him," Tiernan offered.

"I'd rather not have my attention divided," I grumbled.

"It's mainly going to be a chase," he went to the closet and pulled out his bag.

"I don't think so, honey," I went to grab my things as well. "You heard him; this is an act of revenge."

"Which means it's probably also a trap," he shot me a look of sudden comprehension. "Ugh, why didn't that occur to me?"

"Because you're attention is already divided," I grimaced.

"Damn Raza," Tiernan snarled. "He's got me on edge. I can barely think straight. All that talk about challenging our commitment and then those damn creepy twins!"

"They are creepy, aren't they?" I agreed.

"Like a bunch of bogles," he huffed.

"Hey," I took his bag from him and laid it on the floor before grabbing his hands. "We got this, okay? We can handle Raza, there's nothing to worry about."

"Really?" He lifted a brow. "Because I saw him pull you into the rose garden earlier today."

"You saw that?" My face fell and heated.

"Seren," Tiernan groaned.

"Sorry," I sighed. "But if you saw that, then you also saw how I jerked away from him and bitch slapped him for his efforts."

"Yeah, I did see that," Tiernan smiled. "It was the only thing that stopped me from attacking him."

"Raza is harmless as far as you and I are concerned," I pulled Tiernan's head down to mine and kissed him. "This is real, this is what's important to me, not some make-believe fantasy that he's selling."

"I love you," Tiernan whispered. "I'm sorry if it makes me act irrationally sometimes."

"I love you too," I slid my hands up beneath his shirt and smiled wickedly "And if I have to prove it to you every day, I will."

"Every day," he scoffed and yanked me against his chest. "Try every few hours."

My hands slid up his bare back as his mouth descended. I was overwhelmed by the physical sensations that came with loving Tiernan. Coffee and chocolate on his lips, the smooth marble of his muscles, warm flesh radiating the scent of amber and sandalwood into the air, the stunning shift of platinum hair deepening to midnight black like shadows turning into sunlight, and the flash of his silver eyes. Then the delicate tracery of his beautiful silver scar, running just beneath his right eye and across his cheek. Beauty and strength, honor and kindness, loyalty and love. That was Tiernan and he was mine. I wouldn't risk losing him for a thousand dragon-djinn.

He pulled away, his full lower lip pouting just a little and glistening from my kiss. I stared up at him and lifted my hand to the scar he'd learned to love through my eyes. He'd earned it while saving his mother from my grandmother and I thought it was a badge of his honor and bravery. He'd once thought it was a mark of shame but now he wore it with pride. And I was proud that my love had done that for him; changed something ugly into something beautiful.

"What are you thinking?" He asked softly.

"How lucky I am," I slid my fingers through the length of his ombré hair. "How blessed. You know, Raza keeps telling me that I should explore the diversity of fey men but I think Danu knew exactly what she was doing when she sent you my way."

"I can diversify," Tiernan smiled. "If it's a beast in bed that you'd like to experience, I won't disappoint."

144

He moved suddenly, hands going to the hem of my T-shirt, and ripped the material in half. I gaped at the falling pieces of fabric as he scooped me up and tossed me onto the bed. Before I could even lift my head, he was on me; mouth at my shoulder, teeth biting deep. I groaned as he yanked the jeans off my legs and then rose up to pull his own shirt off.

He looked down on me and smiled, more of a baring of teeth really, and then fell upon me. Beast indeed, he clawed and snarled and bit and licked his way across my flesh until I felt completely consumed. My legs shook, my head swam, and my fists clenched in his straining muscles as he barbarically brought us over the edge of ecstasy.

I guess I *had* wanted diversity after all.

Chapter Twenty-Three

The Barnett's lived in a lovely little home in Tahlequa. It was only about an hour away from the Tulsa Council House and we were a little early but when we arrived, Shaman Chepaney was already setting up on their front lawn. He had his deer hide out and the tools of his magic were spread across it. Behind him, the red brick walls of the modest home looked perfect nestled among the golden leaves of the elm trees, already celebrating Fall. It made a beautiful picture, something that belonged on a postcard or framed on a wall. You could never guess by looking at it that this was about to be the site of a supernatural battle.

Cat jumped out of the SUV first and ran across the lawn to the shaman, her Newfoundland glamour fully in place. Shaman Chepaney wasn't startled by her approach. In fact, he kept his focus on the task before him as he nudged her affectionately with his elbow. She sat down beside him and went still, watching him work.

The rest of us, which included Councilman Teagan, a slew of extinguishers, Tiernan, my Star's Guard, Raza (in human glamour), and Raye (minus his wings), climbed out of our vehicles and immediately went about our own tasks. The Kavanaugh twins had declared that they'd be needed at the Council House and so they had stayed behind. I was actually relieved to hear they wouldn't be coming. Their probing stares were so unsettling, almost as unsettling as their knowing smiles. Twins can be so eerie to begin with but when they're telepathic twins, it's ten times worse. I swear, if they started chanting *red rum*, I was going to lose my damn mind.

My Star's Guard helped the extinguishers set up a perimeter

around the house, placing lookouts at strategic points. A few climbed up into trees and a couple even went onto the roof. The remainder took up positions directly outside of the house. The Barnett's were going to be more carefully protected than the President.

I stood with Tiernan, Teagan, Raza, and Raye in front of the house, waiting for Chepaney to finish his preparations but before he did, Mrs. Barnett came down the front steps and introduced herself to us. Mr. Chepaney had explained the situation to her so she wasn't shocked to see a bunch of people dressed for war roaming her property. She *was* rightfully concerned about her family though and asked us to join her inside while the shaman finished setting his magic trap.

"My husband is with Johnny," she said to us as she showed us into her living room. "Johnny's our son. They're in the bedroom and Mark is trying to explain to Johnny about tonight but I was hoping that one of you might help. We really don't know what to expect. I mean, should I put away the breakables? Will there be fighting inside?"

"There could be," I took one of the hands she was waving about nervously. "And I'm so sorry that this has been brought to your doorstep."

She sighed, settling a little and squeezing my hand back.

"I promise you that we will do everything we can to protect your family and your property but there may be damage done," I added grimly. "If you could put away any valuables, that would help. We'll try and keep the fighting outside but it will most likely begin near your son. He's what they're after."

"Why?" She began to sob and of all people, it was Raza who came up and put an arm around her.

"Evil has no reason," he whispered as he stroked her fluffy

henna-colored hair gently. "There is no why, only what. What they will do and we will do to stop them. We are here to help you, Mrs. Barnett. Now what would *you* like to do to protect your family? What part would you like to play that would make you feel stronger, more in control of this?"

"I..." she sniffed and pulled back to look up at him. "Yes," she nodded and swiped at her eyes. She stood straighter and took a deep breath. "Thank you, I needed that. You're absolutely right; it makes no difference why. The only thing that matters is what I do about it."

I blinked in surprise. Who knew Raza could be so inspiring?

"So what would you like to do?" Raza asked her. "Would you like to fight? We can provide you with a weapon."

"We can definitely make sure that you're armed," Teagan interjected as he shot Raza a horrified look. "But perhaps you'd be more comfortable staying beside your family and protecting your son as we handle the battle."

"Yes," she seemed to think it over. "I don't think I want to leave Johnny."

"Excellent," Teagan smiled in relief.

"But I don't need a weapon," she went on. "We have three shotguns and a rifle. We'll be fine."

"Why don't you go and get them," I suggested. "Lay them out near where you'll be sitting tonight. Keep them close but out of the way until you need them."

"Alright," she walked away much more confidently than she'd approached us.

"*Would you like to fight?!*" Teagan hissed Raza's words

back at him. "What were you thinking, asking her that? We can't have civilians in the middle of a magic battle."

"She's a mother," Raza growled. "It's her right and honor to defend her child. You should never deny a parent the privilege of protecting their offspring."

"Valid," I held up a hand between the men. "And I'd say that was well handled on both your parts. Mrs. Barnett should be allowed to defend her child but she also needed some guidance as to where she'd be most effective at doing so."

"So let's not argue about it," Tiernan added. "We have bigger issues to deal with."

"I wasn't arguing," Raza huffed, "I was winning."

"I just want to be clear that certain parties are here in a voluntary capacity only," Teagan added and looked pointedly at Raza. "They are not in charge."

"I'm going to check on the rest of the family," I rolled my eyes and walked further into the house.

I found the father and son in a back bedroom. Mark, the father was telling Johnny that there may be some bad people around the house later that night and that they may try to hurt him but good people would be there to protect him and he should try to not be scared. Johnny was a teenager but he had the look of a child much younger. His face was sweet; innocent and kind... and very confused. He asked the same question his mother had.

"But why?"

"I don't know, Son," Mark sighed and then saw me. "Maybe this lady knows."

"Hello," I went into the bedroom and held my hand out to Johnny. "My name is Seren."

"I'm Johnny Barnett," the boy said and shook my hand.

"And I'm Mark," his father shook my hand next.

"May I?" I indicated a spot on the bed next to Johnny.

"Sure," Johnny shrugged.

"Do you believe in magic, Johnny?" I asked as I sat.

"Yes," he said seriously.

"And do you believe that magic can be used for good or evil?" I went on.

"Yes, I do," he sat straighter. "I can do magic and I use it for good."

"You do?" I blinked, a little surprised by the turn in the conversation.

"Yes, would you like to see?" Johnny asked eagerly.

"Johnny," Mark chided.

"I really would like to see," I waved down Johnny's father. "Go ahead."

"Okay, watch this," he began to whistle.

It was a gentle whistle, as far as whistling goes; a sort of sweet note that resonated within me. Before I could analyze why it seemed so significant, Cat came running into the room. Mark pulled back in shock but Johnny stopped whistling and leaned forward to hug her around the neck like she was a lost friend. As I gaped at that display, a pecking came from the window and we all turned to see a large black bird sitting outside on the ledge.

"Is that a raven?" I whispered.

"I think so," Mark whispered back.

"The birds really like my magic," Johnny said as he released Cat. "But your dog likes it too. She's sweet. She says she'll look after me, she won't let the witches get me."

"She said that to you?" I forgot the bird at the window to gape at Johnny. "You can understand her?"

"Yep," he smiled wide. "I told you I can do magic."

"We thought it was a fantasy," Mark said in an awed tone. "Is this possible? Do you think he really speaks to animals?"

"I speak to them," I transferred my look to the father. "They seem to understand me but I've never heard them speak back."

"You may one day," Tiernan said from the doorway. "Your magic is still growing but it appears that this young man has fully developed his."

"I like animals," Johnny said simply and the tapping came at the window again.

"This feels very Edgar Allen Poe," I stared over at the raven tap, tap, tapping on the windowpane.

"It's just a bird, Seren," Tiernan sighed and went over to open the window.

The bird flew in and settled on the foot of the bed. Johnny gave another low whistle and the raven walked across the cornflower blue comforter and squawked at Johnny. It was an aggressive, strident sound but it didn't disturb the boy. Johnny just cocked his head and concentrated. His eyes went wide and he looked over to me and then to Tiernan.

"You're fairies?" Johnny asked and my mouth fell open.

"Did the raven tell you that?" Tiernan asked.

"Yes," Johnny gave a serious nod.

"What the hell is he talking about?" Mark stood up.

"I know this is a lot to take in," I held up my hands. "You were probably just told that magic exists and here we are, about to tell you that there's another race of people. But please know that we are here to protect you and your family. Does it really matter what we are?"

"Yes, it does," Mark scowled at me. "Now, what the hell are you? And would you mind backing away from my son before you tell me?"

"Mark," Shaman Chepaney stepped into the room and I breathed a sigh of relief. "I just found out about them too. I'm sorry I didn't tell you but I felt that it might be too much for you to accept."

"You know that they're fairies?" Mark asked. "Fairies! Like Tinkerbell?! Are you all crazy?"

"More like Mab or Titania," I offered and Mark shot me a horrified look.

"They are here to help," Chepaney said calmly.

"Dad, they're the good guys," Johnny laid his hand on his father's arm. "I know it. She's even wearing a crown," he pointed to me and I found my mouth dropping open again.

"You can see that too?" I whispered, my hand automatically going to my temple, where I knew my aura held a "crown" given to me by the fairy creatures of Twilight.

"Yep," Johnny nodded. "It's real pretty. The animals gave it to you."

"Yes, they did," I smiled in amazement.

152

Mark fell back into his chair and stared up at us before looking to his son. "You're certain, huh?"

"Yes," Johnny said serenely.

"Well, I guess I should listen to the boy who can speak to animals," Mark sighed.

"He can speak to animals?" Chepaney looked over to Johnny and then finally noticed the raven. "Oh. Hello, Mr. Raven."

The bird blinked at the shaman and squawked.

"He said they're watching you," Johnny offered.

"Who's watching us?" Chepaney stepped closer.

"The men pretending to be fairies who pretend to be birds," Johnny laughed. "That's a lot of make believe."

"Yes, it is," Mrs. Barnett said as she entered the room holding two guns. "But I have some reality for them." She handed her husband a shotgun and then pulled a box of shells out of her pocket. "I don't care who they're pretending to be, if they come after my family, the only thing they'll be is dead."

Chapter Twenty-Four

Mrs. Barnett never fired a single shot. The witches didn't make it into the house at all and I will be eternally grateful for that. However, the battle outside the house was brutal, much more than I'd been expecting.

When you watch a fight scene in some movie, no matter how real it looks, it always has a feeling of flow. The moves are choreographed, the actors know what's coming, and even when things get really wild, you can always follow the action because the camera knows where to look. You know who the bad guys are and who are the good. But a real battle isn't like that at all; it's chaos. A blinding mess that leaves you floundering, hoping that your bullets are hitting the right targets.

And a magical battle is something else entirely.

It was confusing and painfully loud, with blinding flashes of light and paralyzing screams. There was fire in the sky; trailing after soaring sorcerers and erupting from the mouth of a dragon-djinn. I added to it; wrapping burning bundles of thorny vines around the shadowy shapes of diving witches. They'd fall before me, writhing in agony, and I'd feel only a moment's regret over their pain. These were people who had stolen life from others. They were thieves and murderers and now they were after a magical child for no other reason than revenge.

"Try to keep one of them alive!" Tiernan shouted to me over the roar of the mini tornado he'd summoned.

"What about him?" I pointed to the witch being tousled about in Tiernan's tornado. "Mine tend to come out on the crispy side."

154

"Alright," Tiernan waved his hand and the tornado followed his motion, bringing the witch straight to the ground.

The air magic dispersed as I strode forward and slapped some silicone lined handcuffs on the dazed man. He wasn't a fairy, so the iron handcuffs wouldn't hurt him or weaken his magic, but they were the only kind of handcuffs the extinguishers had and hunters didn't bother with handcuffs. After the iron cuffs were in place, Tiernan punched the witch in the face. Really hard. The man collapsed into a heap.

"That works," I shrugged and then screamed suddenly as someone grabbed me from behind and lifted me off the ground.

I flailed about and Tiernan followed us up into the air but it was Raza who flew up behind my assailant and simply tore the man's head from his body. I started to plummet as blood gushed over me and the arms which had been holding me tight, fell away. They were replaced by new arms; bulging sin-black biceps. One wrapped tight around my waist as the other crossed over my chest. I felt Raza's cheek nestle against mine, his scent smokier than usual.

As we gently met the ground, his hands clenched into my flesh and his lips brushed my cheek before he released me. I turned to face him and he set a talon to my temple, just barely touching me with the tip. He drug it lightly down my face as he looked me over. Then he nodded, satisfied that I was unhurt, and leaped back into the sky. Firelight caught him in its embrace, turning him from a guardian angel into a demon, and I shivered. It felt like I'd just been saved by Satan; set back upon the earth to watch as he waged war on Heaven.

"Seren!" Tiernan shouted and grabbed me. "Are you alright?"

"I'm good," I glanced at the body of the decapitated witch, which had landed nearby. The grass was turning into a bloody swamp around the corpse. How much strength would it take to behead someone with your bare hands? I shook off the morbid fascination and looked back to Tiernan, "Where's Cat?"

"Still inside guarding Johnny," Tiernan assured me.

"Good," I looked around at the battle and was grateful that she wasn't in it. "What about Teagan?"

"His own people will have to worry about him," Conri said as he ran up to us. "We've got the upper hand as far as magic goes but we're outnumbered. They just keep coming, Princess Seren."

"Then we will keep fighting," I flung my hand out and a body dropped before us, covered in firethorns and screaming in agony. "Keep fighting until they *stop* coming."

"Yes, Princess!" Conri grinned, looking a little demonic himself, with his curling ebony horns poking out of his dark curls.

Then he lifted his head and howled, long and loud, but the sound of it seemed to just coast by me. I felt the vibration of its passing but it was like he had directed it upward. I focused on the sky and saw a shadow flinch and then a horrible shrieking carried down to us. The dark shape plummeted, striking the ground with a solid thud, but what was really fascinating was what I heard as it fell; cracking. It sounded as if the body had been breaking before it even hit the earth.

Conri looked back at me and smirked, "You're not the only one with a cool mór." He bounded off in a loping run.

"What exactly is Conri's personal magic?" I asked Tiernan.

"The shatterhowl," Tiernan smiled. "He can break things with his voice and he can be very specific about it."

"Conri Shatterhowl," I mused as another howl echoed through the night. "I'm so glad I knighted that fairy."

"Yeah but can he do this?" Gradh, my only female guard, held up a hand and twisted it in the air.

Moisture condensed around her fingers and then hardened even further, freezing into lethal looking shards of ice. She lifted her hand and searched the sky but she didn't have to look long. A witch landed right in front of her, its form hidden by tentacles of darkness. Clawed hands reached out of the murk but Gradh was already prepared; she flung the blades of ice into the masked shape and the witch screamed.

The dark mist slipped away as the witch fell, clawing at the icicles embedded in her chest. As we watched, her screams faded and her arms fell to her sides. She was actually quite beautiful; with long chestnut hair and soft honey skin. But all that changed as soon as death came for her. The years she had stolen slipped away and her skin withered, her hair seeping into gray and then stringy white. Finally, an old woman laid on the ground before us.

"Nicely done, Queen Elsa," I commended Gradh.

"The witch's true age is revealed," Tiernan said from my left.

"That's one bitch," Gradh grimaced and ran off.

"Danu damn them!" Tiernan swore suddenly and ran off too.

I followed his movement and saw that the man he'd left bound and unconscious was being carried off by two witches. They made it about three feet up into the air before Tiernan reached them. He leaped up beside them and tore one of them away with an arm around his throat. The other witch fell under the heavy burden of the unconscious man. I ran towards them but before I could get close enough to help, the second witch had dropped his cargo and followed it to the ground.

Through the shadows fluttering around the crouching

witch, I caught the glint of steel. I frowned and ran faster but it was too late. The rescuer had turned into an executioner. One hand held the blade that had cut open the man's chest and the other held a heart. The shadows fell away as the heart was lifted to the witch's lips and a young man was revealed. He looked no more than sixteen, with a cherubic face and a little, pouting mouth that opened wide to take a bite of the bloody heart.

"You sick son of a bitch," I declared as I came within casting distance of him and sent a thorny vine up from the earth to encase him.

"Fuck you, fairy," he spat at me and I set the vines on fire.

His screams were horrible and I should have just let him burn after the atrocity I'd just witnessed. He deserved it but I couldn't bear it. I strode forward and pulled my iron shortsword from its sheath. With an upward thrust, I pierced his heart and ended his misery. The vines vanished but the burning body remained, still holding half a heart. The smell of cooked meat wafted up to me and I turned away in disgust. Too much more of this and I'd become a vegetarian.

"Looks like we'll need to find another prisoner," Tiernan said as he threw another corpse onto the bonfire I'd made of the boy. "They must have something worth hiding if they'd rather kill one of their own than let him be taken."

"Tell the others," I nodded to him. "As soon as anyone can secure a live prisoner, they need to take them back to the Council House."

"Right," Tiernan ran into the middle of the fray.

"You need a prisoner?" Raye landed beside me, holding a bloody man against his chest.

The man was cut in numerous places and his head hung limply with eyes closed. Raye dropped him to the ground before

158

me and the man just slumped into a heap. I lifted a brow at Raye and he gave me a cocky shrug. His pitch-black wings stretched behind him, feathers ruffling lazily, like a man stretches his shoulders after a fight.

"Perfect," I nudged the witch with my boot, turning him onto his back. "Perhaps Teagan could take him back to the Council House."

"Teagan is in the center of a circle of extinguishers," Raye scoffed. "And I would offer to fly him back to Tulsa but I don't know what kind of welcome I'd get, showing up with a wounded human and no councilman to back me."

"Right," I chewed my lip and looked him over. "Let's get him to a SUV. I'll drive him back myself."

"They're going to panic if you disappear from the battle," Raye jerked a thumb back to indicate the others but then a witch dived out of the sky, straight for him.

The casual thumb-jerk turned smoothly into a punch which went straight into the witch's face. The shadowy shape went tumbling backwards and Raye followed after it with a screeching predatory sound. He fell on his attacker, holding him down with his knees on the man's chest, and then laid a palm over the witch's heart.

I gaped as the true raven mocker ability was revealed to me. Raye didn't need a knife to cut out the witch's heart and consume his remaining years; the heart came to him. It seeped up through the witch's skin and came to rest against Raye's hand. Raye leaned his head back and lifted the beating heart above his mouth to squeeze the blood from it. When it was nothing but pulverized flesh, Rayetayah lowered his chin and tossed the leftovers into his mouth. He savored it like a man consuming an expensive steak.

Then he got up and licked off his fingers before returning to me. I stared from him to the man on the ground, who was withering into old age. With one last sensual lick of his fingertip, Raye gave me a wink and then hefted our prisoner over his shoulder.

"So, do you wanna tell someone you're leaving?" He asked me.

"You're leaving?" Torquil, my blue-haired knight, was suddenly beside me.

"We have to get at least one prisoner back to the Council House," I said to Torquil. "Can you make sure to let the others know I've left the battle?"

"I think some of your guard should accompany you," Torquil frowned at Raye.

"Hey," Raye held out a hand. "Whatever you want to do, I'm just trying to help."

"Could you tell Tiernan where I've gone?" I asked Raye.

"No problem," he tossed the witch to Torquil, who just barely caught him in time. "Consider it done," and Raye leaped back up into the sky.

"Your Highness?" Torquil lifted a brow.

"Let's go," I nodded off toward the front of the house, where we'd parked all the vehicles.

"Traitor!" A collection of shadows landed before me but soon dissipated to reveal a Native American woman. She was very curvy, with long black hair and eyes to match. "You're a witch. A bloodless but still, you should be on our side."

"I'm not a witch and I don't back murderers," I snapped as I pulled my sword.

160

"We are as Nature has made us," she narrowed her eyes on me. "You should understand that. We cannot deny the gift we've been given."

"What I understand is that your people have been preying off the weak and sick for a very long time," I took a menacing step forward. "And all along, the raven mockers have shouldered the blame."

"They *are* to blame," she hissed. "They were the ones who gave us this power. Humans bred with them and made us."

"That's a load of crap," I snapped as I waved off Torquil, who was beginning to lower the prisoner to the ground so he could help me. "I got this, Torque. Stand down."

"How can you call me a liar when you stand here before me; physical proof," she scoffed.

"I'm not a witch," I said again. "I have psychic abilities from my mother, not magic. The magic I have is from my father, who's a fairy. If my mom hadn't been gifted, I would simply be..." I frowned as I thought about it.

What would I be? I would still be a halfling but I'd only have fairy magic. Still, I wouldn't be a witch. Witches were purely human... just as some of the fey looked human but were pure fairy. They'd received human traits from their ancestors who had once bred with humans. So what if it had also worked in humans? Humans bred with fairies and then those children bred with humans instead of more fairies. Their children then bred with even more humans, so on and so on, thinning out the fey blood until the children became purely human again... with just a remnant of magic left from their fairy ancestors. What would they be?

I guess the answer was literally right before my eyes.

This wasn't an evolutionary leap, this was simple breeding. Two races had mixed and left their mark on each other. Just as

161

human traits showed up in fairies who were pure fey, so did fey traits show up in pure humans who were pure human. So, no, I wasn't a witch, but I could see how this woman might mistake me for one.

"You'd be what?" She sneered.

"A magical half-breed," I sighed. "*You* are another thing entirely; a human with a recessive fairy gene that has given you magic."

"Semantics," she shrugged. "We are the same."

"No, we're not," I lifted my blade to her throat. "If for no other reason than I would never murder innocent people."

"No one is innocent," she swept up into the air with a whoosh of darkness.

"Damn," I tried to track her but she was already gone.

"Let's just go, Princess Seren," Torquil suggested. "Before another wingless flying witch decides to have a conversation with you."

"Or worse," I cast one last look back at the fighting before I started running with Torquil for the cars. "And what the hell did she mean that I was bloodless?"

Chapter Twenty-Five

About twenty minutes down the road, something heavy landed on top of the SUV. I swerved off the road, spraying gravel as I stopped on the shoulder. The cabin lit up as Torquil filled his hands with glowing magic which, oddly enough, matched his ultramarine hair. I started to call on my own magic as I jumped out of the driver's seat and leaped away from the SUV, my eyes flashing up and out in case our attacker had jumped. Then I dropped my arms and huffed.

"What are you doing here?" I asked the smirking dragon-djinn who was sitting casually on the roof of the SUV, his legs hanging over the side along with the bottom of his wings.

"My son informed me of your rash decision to run off with only a single guard," Raza dropped down onto his feet with the grace of a cat just as Torquil rounded the back of the SUV.

"The Princess is perfectly safe under my protection," Torquil declared.

"Is she?" Raza rounded on him viciously. "Because I could have knocked you off the road, tore into that flimsy metal, sliced your throat open, and carried her away in less time than it would take you to beg me for your life."

"Hey now," I held up a hand before Torquil went and said something that would get himself killed. "That was uncalled for."

"Uncalled for?" Raza stalked over to me. "You are Princess of the Twilight Court; the only heir to the throne of our only peace-keeping kingdom, and a half-human whom many would love to remove from that throne. Your death would throw all of Fairy into

163

chaos, not to mention what it would do the relationship between us and the humans, and you have left a battle with only a single knight, carrying a hostage that our enemies will no doubt be after. Have you no brain in that beautiful head?!"

"You will not speak to the Princess like that!" Torquil shouted as his face turned red.

"And you!" Raza swirled around to face Torquil again. "You let her. You simply picked up that witch and carted him off for her. You useless baboon! You ape! You're no better than a sightless human! A magicless monkey-descended man."

"Stop harassing my knight!" I shouted at Raza and suddenly he was on me; a hand at my throat and an arm around my back, holding me pressed tight to his chest while effectively trapping my arms.

"A mere second and you are defenseless," he whispered into my ear. "A moment more and you'd be dead. You want me to stop harassing your knight? Then stop acting like a child and behave like a Princess! Command him with intelligence instead of passion. Passion should be reserved for other pursuits."

His hand went to the back of my head, pulling me forward into an enraged kiss. Hard lips slashed across mine, bruising me and forcing my mouth open. A torrid tongue slipped into my mouth, tangling with mine as his claws clenched and jerked me closer convulsively, like an animal subduing its prey. His wings unfolded with a startling crack of air and settled around us, pressing into my back like another pair of limbs.

I could barely breathe much less think; too confused and angry and really freaking turned on. There was so much to feel; to smell and taste. Rapid heartbeats pounding through skin and cloth, the scent of smoke and leather mixing with musk, and the charred sugared taste of him in my mouth. Everything about him seemed made to drive me mad.

I finally shoved him away and stared up at him in a panting fury. He set blazing gold eyes on me defiantly, his wings remaining closed around us. I glared at him for a second longer and then threw my arms around his neck and pulled him back into our kiss.

I know, I know! Stop judging me. Parts of my mind were screaming at me to stop but my body was just incapable. I was so full of adrenaline and warring emotions that needed some kind of release. Raza gave it to me; a wild, furious liberation, and I took it. I even relished it. Savored every damn second. When his hands lowered and pulled my hips into his, I rubbed into him like a sex-crazed lunatic. I groaned and pushed onward with everything I had and soon the feel of it changed from violent to sensual, very sensual.

Oddly enough, that was when I regained my senses.

I gave a gasp and pulled back, staring at Raza in horror instead of passion. One hand lifted to my mouth and my fingertips skimmed over my bruised lips. *Oh Goddess, what have I done now?*

Raza's expression went wicked. He smiled and slid his hands up the sides of my waist, resting his thumbs just beneath my breasts. The barest movement from either of us sent twinges of pleasure through me. I tried to pull back but he held me firm, the tips of two talons pressing delicately into my chest. Then he lowered his head till his lips lay against my ear.

"When you're lying in bed later tonight," he whispered to me in that sexy purr of his, "wondering why you can't sleep, know that I'll be just as restless, waiting for you to realize that we belong together. But until you come to your senses, I'll languish in this craving and use the memory of this moment to whet my appetite."

Then he folded his wings back and stepped away from me, revealing an anxious Torquil who stared at me like I'd just sprouted a tail... from my forehead. I cleared my throat and stomped back to the SUV, where I climbed into the driver's seat without another word to either of them. Torquil said something to Raza but it was too low for me to hear and all Raza did was laugh as he walked around to the passenger side of the SUV. He got in the front passenger seat, making Torquil take the one in back, and I drove us all to the Council House in tense, awkward silence.

Chapter Twenty-Six

The twins met us at the bottom of the front porch steps; standing there calmly, hand in hand. They nodded when they saw the witch, then simply turned and led us through the Council House, down a set of stairs in the kitchen, and into the basement where a line of empty cells took up most of the room. In front of the cells was a small table and two chairs. That was it.

We had just laid our prisoner down on the cement floor of one of the cells, when Tiernan came storming down the stairs. I couldn't even look at him at first, I felt so horribly guilty for what had happened between Raza and I. Raza standing beside me smirking didn't help either.

"What were you thinking?" Tiernan growled at me as Alex closed the cell door with a loud clang.

I sent a glare in Alex's direction but he only shrugged and smiled.

"I was thinking that we needed to get a witch in our custody," I lifted my face to his, anger winning out over guilt. "Just as we talked about."

"Yeah, we talked about it and I assumed you'd stay close to me until we could implement it *together*," Tiernan lowered his face into mine. "I had no idea that you'd run off with only Torquil," Tiernan glanced at Raza, "and him."

"I didn't leave with Raza, he followed us," I tried to defend myself.

"I followed you too," Tiernan snapped. "But I was rather

far behind Raza. Would you like to hazard a guess as to why?"

"Raye," I whispered and shot Raza an angry look.

"Rayetayah," Tiernan nodded. "Why would you entrust Raza's son to tell me you were leaving the battlefield? He waited until I was frantically searching for you before he came up and casually told me where you were."

"I'm sorry, T, I-"

"Don't call me T!" He shouted in my face.

"Oh, excuse me, Lord of the Wild Hunt!" I shouted back. "You know what, *Count* Tiernan? You can go fuck yourself because I ain't gonna do it tonight."

I turned and left the room but Tiernan's angry footsteps followed me all the way to our bedroom in the guest house. I could practically feel his angry breath on my neck the entire way but I refused to look back at him. In fact, I tried to slam the bedroom door in his face but he simply smacked it open with his palm and followed me inside. Then he slammed it shut and locked it.

I was about to start yelling at him again when he said, "Damn it, Seren, you scared me."

I crumpled onto the bed, losing all of my bluster.

"Do you have any idea how it felt for me to look across that battlefield and not see you there?" He sat down beside me. "I thought you were dead or taken. And that bastard Rayetayah just let me think that until I started shouting for the Guard to spread out and look for you. Then he finally sauntered up and mentioned that you went off with Torquil and Raza."

"He said I left with Raza?" I huffed. "That little son of a prick."

"Exactly," Tiernan sighed and his whole body slumped.

168

"He made it seem like you had run away with his father. I was furious. I left everyone there, to clean up blood and corpses, while I rode the air back to you."

"You flew here?" I blinked at him. "That's over seventy miles."

"I said I was scared," he huffed. "I wasn't sure what I'd find when I arrived."

"Tiernan, I told you to trust me," even as I spoke the words, I felt the wrongness in them. How could I say that to him after what I'd done? He was right to not trust me.

"I do," he said and made it all worse. "I just don't trust Raza."

"I know," I sighed. "You've said that before."

"Seren," Tiernan turned my face to his. "I don't want to share you. A lot of fey men would be okay with an open relationship but I'm not. Not with you."

"I know, and I don't want to share you either," I felt my jaw clench as I remembered kissing Raza.

The dragon was skilled, I'd give him that much. He'd made me want him in a passionate moment. But that's all it was; lust. Raza would never be faithful to me and I was too possessive to share a lover. We wouldn't work. But Tiernan and I shared so much more than lust; we loved each other. We worked... and I'd almost wrecked it all because of some post-battle adrenaline and a dragon romeo.

"So please don't trust Raza or his son anymore," Tiernan said gently.

"I won't," I vowed. "Not as far as I can throw them... tied together."

"Good," Tiernan sighed. "I don't ever want to feel that way again."

"I don't want to make you feel that way again," I kissed him.

"That's a better feeling," he said against my lips.

"Hey, don't start anything," I pulled back. "I need to know what's happening over at the Barnett's."

"The battle is over and we've won," Tiernan went serious. "At least for now. The others should be on their way back soon but why don't we go and see if the prisoner is awake?"

"Alright," I took his hand and we left the room together. Raza and Torquil were sitting at the little table in the guest house's kitchen, waiting for us while trying to look like they weren't. So I called out to them, "We're going to see the prisoner if anyone wants to join us.

Raza appeared in the hallway and with one look, I could see that he knew I hadn't been honest with Tiernan. He knew I hadn't confessed the kiss. And I knew that he was going to use that against me. Or at least against Tiernan. I'd have to tell Tiernan the truth before Raza did. I glanced up at Tiernan as we headed across the lawn to the main house, and he gave me a sideways smile.

Yep, I'd tell him everything... later.

Chapter Twenty-Seven

Our prisoner was awake but remained mute throughout the numerous questions we fired at him. Of course, that didn't matter, the questions were used to force him to focusing on what we wanted to know, so the twins could peruse his mind easier. All it took was a few seconds, then Alex gave me a nod and started writing things into a notebook. Alexis did the same until finally, they closed their books and we stopped interrogating the witch.

"So what are you going to do with the witch?" Raye asked me casually.

"Hand him over to the Hunt I guess," I frowned as Tiernan pushed the barred door back into place and locked the man into his cell.

"What did you do to me?" The witch was starting to realize that something was wrong.

"We stole your secrets, William Sehoka," Alex said simply.

"I didn't tell you anything," the prisoner growled.

"You didn't have to say anything," I explained to him, simply because I felt it was the kindest thing to do. "They're telepaths, they can read minds."

"I'm going to kill you, bitch," he growled. "I'm going to kill all of you."

"Yeah, I've heard that before," I sighed.

"So have I," Alexis commiserated.

"I'm going to eat your hearts and live the life you were meant to have," the witch went on.

"Now that's a new threat," I noted.

"You have no idea who you're talking to, scum," Torquil sneered at the man. "She's the Princess of Twilight and she could destroy you with barely any effort at all. She's loved by the Goddess herself."

"Not my Goddess," the witch spat.

"Wait," I held up a hand and focused on the witch. "You worship a goddess? Which one?"

"The only one," he huffed. "*The* Goddess, she has many names but they are only aspects of one goddess."

"Does one of her names happen to be Danu?" I lifted a brow.

"Not that I know of," he blinked, suddenly confused.

"Then you're worshiping nothing... no one," I shook my head sadly. "There are only two divine beings; one is Danu, who rules Fairy, and one is Anu, who rules Earth. They are twins, Danu is female while Anu is male."

"Like us," Alex smiled at his sister and took her hand.

"And our Danu would never consort with murdering filth like you," Torquil scoffed.

"She wouldn't be able to, even did she want to," Tiernan frowned. "This is not her realm and he's human."

"Yet she spoke to me," I lifted a brow at Tiernan.

"You are half fey," Tiernan shook his head, "and you were born in Fairy. Danu has been with you since the second of your

172

birth. She just couldn't cross over into the Human Realm with you."

"Wait... what?" I blinked in shock. "No, I was born in San Francisco."

"No, Seren," Tiernan cocked his head at me. "Didn't your father tell you? Your mother went to Fairy to give birth to you, she wanted to stay there but your father convinced her it was best to hide you in the Human Realm."

"He never told me," I huffed. "He told me what they decided but he never told me that I was born in Fairy."

"I'm surprised that the Goddess didn't tell you," Raza mused.

"You hear her?" The witch glared at me doubtfully.

"I've seen her," I took it further. "There *is* a goddess but she's not your goddess, she can't possibly know about you witches."

"That's bullshit!" The witch screamed and I flinched back. "We are children of the Goddess. She looks after us. I may never have seen her face but my ancestors have. There are records of interactions with the Goddess in several tribes."

"Could she have crossed into this realm?" I asked Tiernan but he was already shaking his head.

"Impossible," Tiernan said to both the witch and me. "Whomever your ancestors spoke with, it wasn't Danu and therefore, it wasn't a goddess."

"You lie," the witch growled. "You're liars!"

I headed upstairs, there was nothing more I could say to the witch that would help him and I saw no point in prolonging the conversation. Still, I sympathized with him. He might be a killer

173

but everyone deserved to have a religion, something to have faith in, and we'd just stolen his, along with his memories.

"Perhaps they were speaking to fairies," I heard Raza say to the witch as I reached the top step.

The man shouted insults at Raza until we closed the door on the stairway and blocked out his voice. I gave Raza an annoyed look but he only laughed and swept past me into the hall. The rest of us followed him into the library while Alex went to gather the council members, all except Teagan of course, who still hadn't returned.

We settled around the library's central table and when the council members came in, the twin's gave us their report. William Sehoka and he was a member of Flight; a clan of witches who possessed the ability to heal themselves and extend their lives through the consumption of human hearts. They believed that they inherited this ability from their raven mocker ancestors but altered it with their humanity. Unlike the mockers, they had to cut the heart from their victim's chest and then heal the wound to hide their theft.

The twins discovered a mass amount of knowledge on William's clan; who they were, where they lived, what they did for a living. We had addresses and even phone numbers for them. It was ridiculously easy but if these witches knew what we were capable of, they'd go into hiding before we could even begin to use the information we'd gained from Mr. Sehoka.

But that wasn't all the twins learned. Flight wasn't the only clan of witches. Just as the twins began to tell us about the bigger picture, Councilman Teagan entered the room with my Star's Guard, Raye, Cat, and a few extinguishers. He looked a little bruised and dirty but otherwise unharmed.

Cat came running over to me.

174

"Hey you," I scratched her head as she sat beside me, and then I looked over to Ainsley. "Is everyone alright?"

"Yes, Princess Seren," Ainsley assured me. "We are all accounted for."

"We lost two extinguishers," Extinguisher Kate said grimly. "Tim and Kent."

"I'm so sorry," I offered gently.

"Did you interrogate a witness without me?" Teagan asked as he came forward. I could tell that the deaths had unsettled him. It wasn't often that someone got the better of an extinguisher.

"What would have been the purpose of waiting?" Raza lifted a brow. "Do you not trust your own people to inform you of all that we've learned?" Raza waved a hand towards the twins, who looked at Teagan with casual curiosity.

"No, of course I trust them to..." Teagan exhaled roughly. "I would have preferred to have been here from the start."

"I'm sorry, Head Councilman," I waved him forward. "But you've arrived just in time. The Kavanaughs have just finished telling us about the witch clan called Flight, and they're about to tell us about the other clans in the Coven."

"*Other* clans? The *Coven*?" Teagan's eyes went round as he took a seat beside me, across from the table from the twins.

"Please continue," I said to the twins.

"The Coven is a collection of witch clans," Alexis began. "They consider themselves to be true witches, while those who are born outside of the clans, are not."

"Like Shaman Chepaney?" I asked her.

"Yes," Alex took over. "He is what they call bloodless, an

aberration. Most witches are born among the Coven."

"So that's what she meant," I shared a look with Torquil.

"She?" Tiernan asked.

"This witch who called me a traitor and bloodless," I explained.

"They thought you were one of them?" Raza asked. "That's interesting."

"Go on then," Murdock growled. "Tell us the rest."

"Stop snapping at us, Councilman, and we will," Alexis gave Murdock an annoyed look,

"Sorry," Murdock muttered and sat back into his chair with a huff.

"There are eight clans," Alex looked to Councilman Teagan. "They are called; Flight, Pack, Bite, Storm, Flame, Tide, Quake, and Beckoning. Each has a specific talent."

"Eight," I whispered. "So many. Start with Pack please."

"Pack witches are shapeshifters," Alexis answered. "Mostly wolves but sometimes others are born, like foxes and horses."

"Foxes and horses," I looked to Teagan and realized that I hadn't told him the most important part. "Councilman, it appears that these witches are descended from fairies. The merging took place so many generations back that the fey blood has been diluted to the point of near non-existence. In most humans, this would mean that they might inherit slanted eyes or high cheekbones, some random fey gene. But it seems that, as with most dominant genes, fairy genes can pop up several generations in the future. The fey magic returned but it altered, giving the descendants of raven mockers dark healing. And it seems that we also have shapeshifters whose ancestors could have been cu-sidhe or bargests," I gave

Conri an apologetic look. "Or even kitsune, from the sound of it."

"Dormant genes," Teagan mused. "And we never caught it."

"Don't feel so bad," Tiernan sighed. "Neither did we and it appears that we were the source."

"Okay, Extinguisher Alexis," I looked back to the telepath. "Is that the only talent of Pack? Shapeshifting?"

"No; all witches can do little spells in addition to their main talents," Alexis shrugged.

"That sounds rather familiar as well," I glanced at Tiernan and he nodded grimly. "Spells like what?"

"Little things within nature," Alex explained. "They can make plants grow, call the wind forth, protect their homes from burglary."

"Okay," Teagan frowned thoughtfully. "What about the other clans. The next is Bite, is that correct?"

"Bite," Alex nodded. "They're very similar to the legend of vampires. Bite witches drink blood and use the life force within it to prolong their own lives. It's close to the way Flight members use the energy within human hearts, except Bite witches just need the blood."

"Baobhan-sith," I whispered.

"I agree," Raza said. "They must be descendants of the white women."

"Great," someone huffed. "And here we were thinking fairies were the only monst-" he was cut off, by someone's elbow from the sound of it.

"It appears that much more than the human myths of

witches were true," I said into the awkward silence. "Now we have werewolves and vampires. What about Storm; do they have some kind of elemental magic?"

"They control the weather through condensation and temperature manipulation," Alex moved his hands about like he was swirling things together.

"Add comic book hero to your list, Ambassador," Councilman Sullivan grinned. "They even stole the name."

"They probably had the name first, Councilman," Alex smirked. "Maybe Stan Lee stole it from them."

"And then... what was the next clans?" I asked Alex before we got off on a superhero tangent.

"Flame," Alexis offered. "They create fire and can direct it. Then there's Tide; they're water witches. They can breathe underwater and some of them can control water too. Oh! And some turn into seals but they're not considered Pack because of the water thing."

"Uh huh," I grimaced and looked toward Tiernan. "Seals huh?"

"Selkies," Tiernan growled.

"Damn but you guys get around," another extinguisher commented.

"We can't help it if you humans find us irresistible," Conri smirked and then gave a female extinguisher a wink.

"Did you learn anything else?" I ignored the banter and focused on the twins. "What about the last clans?"

"Quake," Alex leaned forward eagerly, "can control the energy within soil and they can cause earthquakes or even volcanic eruptions."

"Wonderful," I rolled my eyes."

"Last there's Beckoning," Alexis swallowed hard and went a little pale. "The most powerful of them all."

"Beckoning?" I frowned, wondering what that referred to. What exactly were they beckoning?

"Necromancers," Alex whispered. "They speak to the dead and..."

"And?" I urged him.

"They can bring them back," Alexis shivered. "They bring the dead back to life. Except it's not really life, it's decay and slavery. Zombies. Rotting corpses with a soul trapped inside, doing the bidding of the witch who brought them back."

The room went silent.

"Not possible," Tiernan whispered. "No one can do that. Not any fairy or human. They didn't inherit that from us."

"We may not have fairies who can raise the dead," Raza mused, "but there are those closely connected with death. Like the bean-nighes, bean-sidhes, nuckelavees, or dullahans."

I shivered, remembering my first sight of a nuckelavee; a type of water-horse with a human torso attached to it. It did kinda resemble a zombie, with its veins and muscles exposed. They were much more gruesome than the bean-nighe; washer women who clean the bloody clothes of those fated to die. The bean-sidhe were more vocal versions of the washers, crying out to foretell death. But the dullahan was probably the closest match to zombie magic. I'd never met one but reputedly, they were the original headless horsemen, carrying their severed head under an arm. They are death bringers, calling out the name of those about to die, but they are also living monuments to death; riding around with a wagon adorned with and made out of macabre objects. Candles in skulls,

179

thigh bones for wheel spokes, that sort of thing. It wasn't a far stretch to hypothesize that their magical connection to death be altered into reanimation.

"Sweet Danu," Gradh whispered. "Who in their right mind would shag a dullahan?"

"Or a bean-nighe. I've met a few bean-sidhes I wouldn't mind spending the night with but those bean-nighe are pretty hideous," Conri shivered dramatically. "I can't stand the whole one tooth thing."

"Bean-nighes?" Ainsley huffed. "What about nuckelavees? Disgusting. And how? I mean, does anyone know how the nuckelavee reproduce? Is the working member on the human torso or the horse," he waved his hand near his crotch. "That would be fatal for a woman, wouldn't it?"

"Unless it was a human male with a female nuckelavee," Ian mused.

"Oh please stop," Teagan groaned.

"Most likely, it was not consensual," Raza said grimly.

"Sweet Danu," I whispered as my stomach lurched.

"She had nothing to do with it," Raza declared.

"Who's having sex with a female nuckelavee?" Eadan Gale, Lord of the Wild Hunt, asked as he came into the library. "Never mind, I don't want to know," he waved his hand dismissively and then gave me bow. "Greetings, Princess Seren. Greetings, Lord Raza," he bowed to Raza, "and Your Countness," Eadan smiled wide at Tiernan before leaning forward to shake Tiernan's hand.

"Lord Eadan," Tiernan stood to reach over the table towards Eadan. "It's good to see you. How was the trip?"

"Fine," Eadan nodded. "And it looks as though I've arrived
180

just in time. Anyone care to enlighten me on why you're talking about nuckelavee sex?"

"It's a long story," Tiernan sighed, "and I think it calls for a drink."

"I couldn't have said it better myself," Teagan agreed.

He started to get up but Kate put a hand to his shoulder and pushed him back into his seat, "Let me get it, Dad. I think I need a break from this discussion anyway."

Chapter Twenty-Eight

It took an hour and several bottles of wine to fill Eadan and his team of hunters in on what had been happening in Tulsa. He'd already been briefed on the general situation but by the time we were done, his gray eyes were wide with shock.

"Eight clans?" He finally asked. "Eight? That must mean thousands of witches. How did they manage to hide from us for so long?"

"In plain sight," I laughed. "We thought they were fairy tales. Myths."

"Fairies duped by fairy tales," Eadan chuckled. "There's some irony there."

"This particular clan has been difficult but nothing a trained band of hunters can't manage," Raza observed. "However, I believe there are other clans which may pose a greater threat."

"Like Beckoning," I nodded.

"Nonsense, the worst they can do to you is kill you and then bring you back to be their rotting slave," Eadan said sarcastically. "No one's going to do that. Truly, who would want a stinky servant? Can you imagine a zombie trying to polish the silver while dripping gunk all over it? Rather counterproductive if you ask me."

"Indeed," Raza laughed.

"We think they may be descended from either bean-nighes, bean-sidhes, dullahans," I cleared my throat, "or nuckelavees."

"Ah, the nuckelavee sex. Well there's a sobering thought," Eadan grimaced. "There are some very attractive bean-sidhes but the rest of that group is hideous at best."

"Just as I said," Conri smirked.

"Do you have the crystal ball with you?" I asked Eadan before he got into a conversation about bean-sidhes with Conri.

"Yes, of course," Eadan motioned to one of the other hunters and she pulled a small crystal ball out of a satchel beside her chair. She handed it to Eadan and he handed it to me. "The Twilight Council awaits your call, Princess."

"Thank you," I held the ball on the table before me, casting a concerned glance at Councilman Teagan before I called out, "Councilman Catan of Twilight."

The ball misted and cleared quite quickly, to reveal a fey face with buttery pale skin, surrounded by long, silky, light green hair. Catan smiled to me once he came into focus.

"Princess Seren, I hope you are well," he inclined his head.

"I am, thank you Head Councilman," I nodded back. "Thank you for accepting my input in this. I'd like to update you on our recent discoveries."

"By all means," he waved a hand, revealing his bright white fingertips.

I went over all the information we'd just given Eadan. When I was done, Catan looked thoughtful but not surprised. He had been informed of the witches already but he didn't know about all of the clans and I'd expected a little more of a reaction from him.

"You don't find this shocking?" I asked.

"Not at all," he shrugged. "It makes perfect sense. You

183

cannot breed with another species and think that no mutations will ever come of it. These witches are like us twilight fey; a blending of two races. And just as with us, you never know what will show up in the children... or when."

"Well said," Raza nodded.

"Who is that, Princess?" Catan tried to see around me.

"It's Lord Raza Tnyn of the Unseelie Court," I said formally.

"Ah, yes," Catan nodded. "I suppose he's there for his son."

"You knew Rayetayah was Raza's son?" I lifted a brow.

"You didn't?" Catan lifted one back at me and I chuckled.

"Yes, he's here for Rayetayah," I sighed and then asked suddenly, "Do you think you can rule on the charges against the raven mockers, now that the evidence has been presented to you?"

"Normally, I would call a council meeting for this and we would have to consult with the Human Council since I believe the crime was set before them first," Catan shrugged. "But any fool can see that the attacks were not instigated by the mockers."

I tried not to give Teagan a smug look but it was difficult. Even without my look though, he ended up grimacing. If Catan ruled on an issue that the Human Council believed was their jurisdiction, while a councilman sat by and said nothing, that councilman might get into serious trouble.

"I agree, Councilman Catan," Raza called to the crystal. "Could you please deliver a verdict in light of these circumstances?"

"Now, hold on," Teagan growled. "This is a matter for the Human Council to rule on and they've already made it clear that they won't offer a ruling until all the information is presented to them."

"Who's speaking now, Princess?" Catan asked.

"That's Councilman Teagan, Head of the Tulsa House," I introduced him.

"Councilman Teagan, that's a ridiculous statement," Catan said stiffly. "I'm sure you're aware that on matters of this magnitude, both Councils must be consulted but the Council of the defendant's race is always given final say. This is a courtesy that has been given since the truce was first signed and one which I intend to avail myself of right now. Goddess knows that you humans have done so often enough." Catan's voice went deep as he delivered the verdict, "The raven mockers are hereby found innocent of all charges and shall be allowed to return to their homes and their lives, be they in Fairy or within the Human Realm."

"Thank you, Councilman!" Rayetayah whooped and then hugged his father.

"Go," Raza nodded to Raye. "I know you want to bring them home."

"He'll need the plane," I interjected. "We'll call ahead and have my father's jet prepared for him."

"Thank you, Princess," Raye came over to me and kissed my hand. "Thank you for looking after us."

"Thank you for helping us uncover the truth," I smiled gently. "Now go get your family. I'll scry for my father after I speak with Councilman Catan, and let King Keir know to send them to meet you at the rath."

"Then you'd better send him with our plane, instead of your father's, Ambassador," Teagan offered graciously. "Remember how many there were."

"Oh, right," I gave Teagan a grateful smile. "Thank you, Councilman Teagan, that's very kind of you."

"I agree with the verdict," Teagan shrugged. "I just didn't want to be the one who disobeyed the Human High Council. Now I can blame Councilman Catan for citing truce law."

"If I could, I'd like to speak to Councilman Teagan?" Catan asked.

"Yes, of course," I gave Teagan the ball with a *Oh damn, I think he heard that* look on my face. "I'll just see Raye out as you speak," I got up and gestured to Raye. "Do you want a ride to the airport or would you rather fly?"

"I'll fly, thank you," Raye followed me out of the room, his father close behind us.

When we got to the front door, Raza hugged his son and wished him a safe journey.

"I've missed you," Raye said to his father. "Perhaps you'll return to the Human Realm more often now?"

"Or perhaps you'll come home to the realm of your birth more often," Raza countered with a grin.

"I'll make the effort if you will," Raye smiled back and then turned to me. "May I hug you, Princess Seren?"

"Absolutely," I held my arms out to him and Raye enveloped me.

"My father can seem cruel but when he loves, it's fiercely and forever," Raye whispered into my ear. "A love like that is worth a little cruelty, don't you think?"

"It depends on who is being cruel to whom," I said as I pulled away. "Goodbye, Rayetayah. May Danu fly beside you."

"Goodbye, Princess Seren," Raye stepped out onto the porch, unfolded his wings, and leaped into the sky.

"I would never be cruel to you," Raza said casually as he walked by me on his way back to the library. "Unless you asked me to."

Chapter Twenty-Nine

"Lord Raza," Tiernan was saying as I entered the room. "Your son is safe. I assume that means you'll be leaving us as well?"

"Actually," Raza shot me a sexy look, "I've found that there's more here to hold my interest than my son's plight. I intend to stay and see this situation with the witches through to its conclusion."

"There may not be a conclusion," I took my seat beside Tiernan and Teagan handed me the crystal ball. I looked down into Catan's grim face.

"I fear you may be correct, Princess Seren," Catan said. "This is a complicated issue, one which must be brought before the High Councils. Councilman Teagan and I have agreed that we should both notify our high councils of these latest developments and allow them a say in the matter. Until then, Lord Eadan's hunt will assist the extinguishers and your team in locating any remaining Flight members. You must not extinguish any of them unless you're given no choice. We may have already instigated a war with the Coven but hopefully, we'll be able to avert it through negotiations."

"You want to negotiate with the murdering witches?" I lifted a brow.

"I think they deserve a chance to at least plead their case before the High Council," Catan sighed. "Murder is a horrible thing but extinguishing an entire race is even worse. Add to that the fact that they may have thousands of witches in these other clans who may seek to avenge their deaths, and we have a complicated situation indeed. We need to tread carefully here and perhaps a truce can be reached."

"I understand," I nodded. "We'll do our best to not kill *or* be killed."

"Good," Catan declared. "The prisoner will be escorted here by one of Lord Eadan's hunters and I will then transport him to the High Fairy Council on the Isle of Danu. After I discuss this with the high council members, I will scry you and inform you of our decision."

"Yes, Sir," I agreed.

"Oh, and Princess Seren," Catan frowned. "I overheard Lord Raza's statement and I hope you'll give him every courtesy. It will take time for us to dispatch more hunters to your location and Councilman Teagan and I are concerned for the safety of his House as well as your person. You'd do well to keep Lord Raza close, he's a skilled warrior. I myself can attest to that."

"As can I," I said without making any commitments to courtesy.

A glance at Raza showed him to be smirking. I looked back to Catan and inclined my head respectfully. He in turn gave me a bow before the crystal misted over and then cleared completely.

"Well, I have my orders," Eadan stood. "We'll need the key to the cell downstairs."

"I have it," an extinguisher held it up. "I'll escort them down, Head Councilman."

"Yes, thank you," Teagan said distractedly.

"After I see Barram out," Eadan motioned to the hunter with him. "I'll be taking my team into Tulsa to scout the area. When we return, I'll report my findings to you."

"Thank you, Lord Eadan," I nodded.

"Princess," he bowed and left with Barram and the extinguisher guard.

"There's nothing left to do now but wait, I suppose," Teagan sighed.

"We could sleep," I shrugged. "I happen to be really, really tired. What time is it, anyway?"

"3 AM," Teagan noted wearily.

"Ugh," I groaned. "And I need to shower before I can get in bed." I looked to Tiernan and found him glaring at Raza. "Hey," I snapped my fingers in his face. "Do you wanna help me with that? I might drop the soap."

"Yes," Tiernan grinned, focusing on me immediately. "I'd be most happy to assist you, my lady."

Chapter Thirty

Within two days, the prison cells beneath the Tulsa Council House were full of witches. The Kavanaugh twins had interrogated most of them and we were slowly compiling files of information on the Coven and its members.

Flight and Pack were the most unified of the clans. They had groups that generally stayed together. If they moved, they moved as a whole. The others, however, spread out wherever they would, keeping touch with their clans but not necessarily living among them. Each clan did seem to have leaders with permanent locations though, so some sort of government appeared to be in place.

Just as with the Human Council, the Coven also had members placed strategically in human leadership positions. This included government officials, police, judges, and even news reporters. They knew all about the Councils, the Extinguishers, and the Wild Hunt. It looked as if they had been watching us for centuries and they were even aware of our current interactions with the Flight witches.

Which meant we could expect some visitors soon.

"We have to move them," I said to the table full of council members, hunters, and my Star's Guard. Oh, and Raza.

Unlike fairy councils which included Lords of the Wild Hunt (or LotWH as I like to call them... I pronounce it loth-wah just to be even more annoying), the human council generally didn't include extinguishers in their discussions. It never bothered me before but now that I'd been among the fey for awhile, the exclusion was starting to annoy me. The Extinguishers should at least be represented in all of the meetings, not just seriously important ones.

"Where to?" Councilman Teagan threw his hands. "And how? It would take a lot of effort to move that many people securely. It's practically concentration camp full down there."

"And that's not cool," I leveled a look on Teagan. "Both the living conditions and your using that as a reference."

Teagan made an exasperated noise.

"There may be a way to control them," Tiernan gave me a steady look. "A way that we could make them work with us. Then we could make them more comfortable too."

"What's he talking about?" Teagan frowned and Raza lifted a brow.

"I don't know if I want to do that," I said in a low *you know what I'm talking about but I don't want them to know what I'm talking about* tone to Tiernan. "Especially to so many people."

"I think the situation may call for it," Tiernan said gently.

"Call for what?" Councilman Sullivan asked.

"Alright fine," I sighed, giving up on trying to keep my star-crossing ability a secret. "You know how fairies can enchant humans?"

"Yes, but it's doubtful that these witches will be susceptible, not with fey magic in them," Murdock huffed. "We already went over this, Ambassador."

"I realize that," I rolled my eyes. "But I have a different version of fairy-struck."

"A different version?" Teagan settled back in his seat and gave me a wary look.

"Go on," Raza purred.

"It's called star-crossing," I whispered.

Raza inhaled sharply and Eadan whistled an impressed note while his hunters exchanged looks of surprise. My Guard already knew about my magic, so they didn't react at all.

"I'm unfamiliar with the term," Teagan, along with the rest of the humans, was just plain confused. "What exactly does it mean?"

"It means that she could make any man in this room do her bidding," Raza's eye gleamed. "And I'm not referring to her using her substantial feminine wiles."

"It's a powerful magic," Eadan agreed. "And a rare one."

"So you're telling me that you can walk down into those cells and magic all those witches into becoming your willing slaves?" Sullivan's eyes were going round.

"As long as none of them are wearing any anti-fey charms," Eadan nodded.

"Well," I cleared my throat and Eadan's eyes went as round as Teagan's.

"No," Eadan whispered.

"Yes," Raza leaned forward with a huge smile. "Charms don't work on you, do they, Princess? Your human blood negates them."

"I can hold iron without a problem," I gave my iron sword a pat. "It's not like I've tested myself against charms but I used to wear them all the time."

"Anyone can wear a charm," Eadan shook his head. "It only works on the fairy who is trying to enchant you."

"She can hold iron, Eadan," Tiernan sighed. "I'd say that means she's immune."

"I still disagree," Eadan shook his head. "Holding iron is a chemical reaction to our genetics. We can't touch iron but we can all wear charms. It might make us uneasy but we can still wear them. An anti-fey charm is a ward against fey magic and her star-crossing is definitely fairy magic."

"That's a good point," I conceded. "I guess we'll need to test it after all."

"It's a moot point," Raza rolled his eyes. "We're getting carried off by tangents. The important thing here is that Seren can cross those witches into doing whatever we want them to do."

The council members started muttering among themselves.

"I don't want to keep all of those people under the star-crossing," I huffed. "I don't even know if I can."

"Why not?" Raza shrugged.

I glanced around the table and found several faces who looked to be in agreement with Raza.

"It's not like you'd be physically hurting them," Tiernan joined the ranks.

"No, just stealing their free will," I huffed and looked down at Cat. She stared up at me patiently, waiting for me to come to the right conclusion. "Et tu, Brute?" She whined and laid her face on my thigh. "Next you'll all be asking me to use them as cannon fodder when their friends show up."

"That's damn brilliant!" Teagan sat up straight in his seat.

"What?!" I gaped at him.

"They're not going to attack their own people," Teagan

194

argued. "You'll simply be preventing bloodshed. At the very least, it would stop them long enough for us to speak with them."

"And we wouldn't have to worry about guarding them at all," Eadan nodded. "They'd be guarding us. Princess, you're a genius."

"I wasn't serious," I grumbled but then I thought it over.

It would be a lot easier to keep them all star-crossed instead of worrying about them escaping or being rescued. We could let them out of those cramped cells and make them more comfortable, wasn't that a good thing? And I really didn't want to lose any more of our people. We could surround the Council House with a wall of witches and if it came down to it, they'd even fight for us. There was a certain ironic justice in that.

"This can't be right," I shook my head.

"Leaders have to make difficult decisions," Raza was saying what I already knew. "Sometimes the wisest choice can appear to be evil but we both know that appearances are deceiving. Do we not, Princess Seren? Now, are you willing to appear evil if it will accomplish good?"

"Goddess forgive me," I whispered as I stood. "I'm not turning into my grandmother, I'm turning into my Uncle Uisdean."

Chapter Thirty-One

Star-crossing over sixty people was exhausting. Each one would have to be brought out of their cell and held down while I sprinkled magic in the eyes. That was the one drawback to star-crossing as opposed to good ol' fairy-striking. To strike a human, you just had to get close to them but to cross one, I had to be able to sprinkle silly sparkles in their eyes, like a damn Disney character.

We decided to remove the witches from the cells and bring them upstairs, one by one, so they wouldn't have any idea what we were doing. Of course, they all assumed that their friends were being executed because no one returned. So that started a panic and I ended up going down into the cells and using my other fey magic, the dream dusting, to put them all to sleep.

That turned out to be a really good idea because then all we had to do was lift their eyelids. It was much easier than restraining people but the magic still took its toll on me. By the time I was done, I was barely able to stand. Tiernan had to help me up to our bedroom and tuck me in. I don't even remember falling asleep, I was simply awake and then not. I didn't dream either, just sank into a blackness that was eventually pierced by the sound of shouting.

"Princess Seren!" It was Conri at my bedroom door. "They're here and we need you to command the prisoners."

"Who's here?" I asked Tiernan sleepily.

"The witches, Love," Tiernan helped me up and rubbed my temples until I came fully awake. "Do you feel up to this?"

"Yes, of course," I nodded and went to put on some

clothes. Blue jeans; check. T-shirt... now where is that *I got ninety-nine problems but a witch ain't one* shirt? I had to wear it, it was imperative. Maybe not moral but definitely imperative. "Aha!" I pulled it on as Tiernan gave me a beleaguered expression.

I threw on some combat boots, just in case there was combat, and we rushed across the damp back lawn, Cat racing ahead of us. The sound of battle wafted to us from the front of the main house, urging Tiernan and I along faster. I ran to the kitchen and down the stairs, where the witches were all sleeping soundly in sleeping bags, spread out around the basement. With a few shouts, I woke them and then I was leading my enchanted army up the stairs and out the front door like I was Snow White and they, my dumbly-named dwarves. Although there were no *hi-ho*s to be heard, the witches were calm and even happy to follow me, showing no signs of distress. Not even when I led them out into the thick of battle.

"Surround the house and if a witch tries to get past you, stop them," I said to the members of Flight.

They filed out and did as they were told, forming a living line of defense around the Council House. It was obvious that there was something wrong with them and they were a little hard to miss. So I wasn't surprised when the fighting stopped entirely, giving the fairies and extinguishers a chance to fall back behind the line of star-crossed witches and take up positions on the porch. Cat was already at my side but both Tiernan and Raza came forward to stand at my back and lend their menace to my look.

"My name is Princess Seren Firethorn of Twilight," I called out, feeling a sense of deja vu.

Hadn't I just done this? Actually, I felt a little silly calling my name out into the night, like maybe I should be holding my sword aloft and shouting *For the honor of Greyskull. I am Seren, Princess of Power!* Note to self; Never tell my best friends Abby and Karmen about this or my next nickname will be She-Ra.

"I'm the Ambassador between the Human Realm and Fairy," I continued. "And I'd like to speak with your commander."

A man stepped forward and two more joined him, flanking him from behind. They were all dressed for combat (we had matching boots) and had the look of soldiers about them. Behind them, more witches drew forward, all of them ready for war. I walked out a few steps with my honor guard, calling three of the star-crossed witches to join us. They stood before us in a line, a human shield between us and the solemn three witches who had come forward.

"I am Aidan, Alpha of the Missouri Pack," the man front and center said.

He had deep chestnut hair, short but wild, and pale blue eyes like arctic ice. He was muscular but not overly so, and his skin was a warm, honey-brown. Hands flexing into fists at his sides, he stared at me like he wanted to tear my limbs off my torso and beat me with them.

"We don't want a war, Aidan," I said calmly.

"You have a surprising way of asking for peace," he huffed and looked over the happy-faced men in front of me. "These are flighters, what did you do to them?"

"I enchanted them," I said simply. "It's a fairy thing. Basically, I'm in control of them. Just like with your Beckoning witches and their zombies, except I don't have to kill my victims."

"Release them, and then we'll speak of peace," he smiled at me but it was a vicious smile.

"That's not going to happen," Tiernan stated simply.

"Then we're at a impasse," Aidan folded his arms across his chest. "Because I came to see Flight freed and I won't leave until I do."

"Fairies have a truce with humans," I ignored his bluster. "As I'm sure you know. As humans, you are bound by the laws of that truce and under those laws, we have the right to execute any who break the truce."

"You can't hold us accountable to laws we never agreed to," Aidan growled.

"Why not?" I lifted my brows. "Aren't you born into a society which holds you accountable to certain laws that you've never agreed to? The truce has laws very similar to that of this Nation. They are basic laws of morality and Flight has broken the biggest of them; Do not commit murder."

"Flight does only what it was born to do," Aidan narrowed his eyes on me. "They can't help it if you fairies made them hungry for human hearts."

"Oh, they can't help it?" Tiernan lifted his brows. "I'm sure that would be a great defense for them in a human court."

"That's not how it was explained to us," I waved Tiernan down. "Our understanding is that the magic allows witches to prolong their lives through the consumption of a human heart but it doesn't force them into the act. Murder is a choice for them, as it is for all of us."

"Sometimes instincts are difficult to deny," Aidan growled. "So much so, that there doesn't seem to be a choice."

"I understand instincts quite well," Raza stepped forward, his metallic eyes gleaming in the floodlights streaming off the Council House. All three witches tensed, their nostrils widening as they scented a bigger predator. "I have some of the most violent instincts of them all. Right now, they're telling me that you're food." He gave a quick, deep sniff, "Prey with tender meat that would taste sweet in my mouth."

All three witches started to growl.

"But I don't have to give into my instincts because I am stronger than they are," Raza shrugged. "It's easy enough for me to deny the call of flesh and blood or bones and marrow. Easy because I am not only an animal, I am a man. I choose to let you live, just as these *mocking* birds," he waved his hand to the enchanted witches before us, "had a choice to be men instead of murderers."

"Let's not argue about what's been done in the past," I put a hand on Raza's shoulder and he eased back. "We don't have to fight. We can find a middle ground, write a new truce which you can *choose* to live by."

"Why would we want to find a middle ground with you?" One of the men behind Aidan sneered. "All you've done is attack our people without cause."

"Without cause?" I chuckled. "I don't think so. If someone came into your house at night and took out your dying grandfather's heart so they could eat it and steal his remaining time, you'd probably kill them, right?"

The man shut up but gave me a nasty glare.

"I don't think we're asking for a lot here," I went on. "Just a chance to discuss things rationally and perhaps find a peaceful way to coexist."

"Give me these three to return with," Aidan waved a hand at my witchy shield. "As a show of good faith. And I will speak to the witch elders on your behalf."

"The Coven Elders?" I cocked my head at him. "Will you give me your word that you will speak to them as a whole and convey our desire to reach a peaceful agreement?"

"I vow it," he nodded solemnly.

"Fine," I agreed and pulled my magic away from the Flight

witches.

They went stumbling to their knees, vomiting and shivering through the return of their free will. One of them turned swiftly and rushed at me. Before either Tiernan or Raza could react, I lifted a hand in automatic response. I had no intentions, I simply wanted to ward off the blow. But my magic knew better.

It rushed out, forming thick vines around the witch and sending him crashing to the ground in his own puke. He screamed as the thorns pierced his flesh and the vines continued to grow, shifting and cutting into him. I pulled back the magic enough to stop the growth and the witch whimpered as the vines settled into place.

When I looked up, I found Aidan's eyes focused on me intently. There was an odd look in them. A little shock but mostly delighted approval and maybe just a touch of fear. His icy eyes narrowed but not in anger, more like how an art critic might view a Picasso. He was impressed.

"Not just a princess then," Aidan mused.

"Hardly," Raza chuckled.

"I was an extinguisher first," I admitted.

"But that was magic," Aidan noted.

"Then I became a princess," I shrugged. "And real fairy princesses kick ass."

I called back the magic and the vines disappeared like they'd been made of smoke. The other two Flight witches rushed forward to help their friend, who was moaning and bleeding from several wounds. They gave me nasty glares as they pulled him back among the Pack witches.

"I see that they do," Aidan smiled. "I'll tell the elders about your power *and* your offer. Then I'll return here and give you their response. I don't know how long it will take but I will be back. Rest assured."

"I don't think anyone will be resting assured until we settle this but I will trust that you'll return," I smirked. "Goodbye, Aidan, Alpha of the Missouri Pack."

"Goodbye, Kick-Ass Princess of Twilight," he laughed and ran off into the darkness.

Chapter Thirty-Two

"Why didn't you tell me that I was born in Fairy?" I asked my father as soon as the crystal ball focused on his face.

"That was abrupt," Keir frowned. "Don't I get a; *Greetings, Father* before you verbally assault me?"

"Greetings, Father," I rolled my eyes. "Now why didn't you tell me that I was born in Fairy?"

"Because it's humiliating," he sighed.

"How is it humiliating?"

"Any father who can look into the eyes of his newborn child and allow it to be taken from him, much less send it away, is not worthy of fatherhood," he swallowed hard. "I did that, Seren, I was there for your birth. I welcomed you into this world; held you and felt the magic inside you. Then I sent you away from me."

"For my own good," I whispered gently.

"And to my detriment," Keir closed his eyes briefly. "I wish I'd kept you both here. I should have tried to protect you. I should have fought for you instead of hiding you away."

"That was your way of fighting for me," I touched the surface of the crystal. "I'm sorry I brought it up. I just felt a little blindsided when Tiernan told me."

"You're right. I should have been the one to tell you. Instead, I hid it from you, just as I hid you from the fey. I didn't want you to think less of me."

"I don't think less of you. In fact, I'm glad you were with Mom when I was born."

"I love you, Little Star," he touched the crystal over the place I had laid my fingers.

"I love you too, Dad."

Then Lord Eadan cleared his throat and I was reminded that there were several others in the room; including Tiernan, Councilman Teagan, Raza, and my Guard. I cleared my throat too and filled Keir in on what had been happening.

"Have you spoken to the High Council yet?" Keir asked.

"Not yet. They'll be my next scry. Who do you think I should speak to?"

"High Councilman Greer," Keir advised. "He's the most reasonable."

"Alright, thanks," I nodded.

"I'll travel to the Isle of Danu tonight," Keir looked grim. "That way, I'll be at hand to offer my assistance."

"You mean to give them your opinion," I chuckled.

"And impose it upon them," Keir nodded. "As is my right as King of Twilight."

"Give 'em hell, Dad," I said encouragingly.

"I'll do better than that," he smirked. "I'll give them no choice. Also, I want to question the witch you caught."

"You'll have to star-cross him, Mr. Sehoka doesn't give information freely," I offered.

My father was the only other fairy I knew who possessed

the star-crossing ability. In fact, a lot of people looked on my ability of star-crossing as stronger proof of parentage than my eyes.

"Thanks for the tipping."

"Tip," I whispered to him. "Thanks for the tip."

"Right," he gave me a wink.

"Bye, Dad," I shook my head and laughed.

"I'll see you soon, Seren," he said as the crystal misted over.

"High Councilman Greer," I said as soon as the mist dissipated, and the crystal filled with fog once more.

It remained blurry for awhile and then the image focused on a fairy man with ice-blue hair, so light a blue that it was almost white. His skin was just a shade darker than his hair, contrasting sharply with the heather tunic he was wearing. Piercing pine-green eyes looked me over and I suddenly remembered him from my one visit to the Isle of Danu. My father was right, Greer was the best choice. He'd been one of the few council members who had accepted the events that occurred with reason and respect.

"Princess Seren," Greer bowed.

"High Councilman," I bowed back. "I've called to give you a status report on the situation with the witches. I'm assuming that Councilman Catan has already spoken with you?"

"Yes, not with me specifically but he did contact us and I've been informed of the situation. Thank you for scrying us so quickly," Greer smoothed his tunic nervously. "The Fairy High Council is very concerned about this new human race and their capabilities."

"Councilman Catan informed you about the different

clans?"

"Yes, he did," Greer confirmed. "What have you to add to his information?"

"I've spoken with the Alpha of a group from Pack, which is the clan of shapeshifters," I reported. "I offered them peace through the signing of another truce."

"Another truce," Greer mused. "Do you think the witches will agree to that?"

"The Alpha said he would speak to the elders of the Coven and then return with their response," I recounted. "But I don't think these are a warmongering people. I believe they'll seek peace."

"The High Councils will have to convene and meet with the witches if they want to proceed towards a truce," Greer considered.

"I assumed that would be the case."

"I'll take this information to the others. Scry for me again when you've heard back from the witches."

"Yes, Sir. But before you go," I glanced at the anxious Councilman Teagan. "I believe the human council members of Tulsa would like to be assured that they'll remain a part of the process."

"We would not be so high-handed as to evict them from the conclusion of a matter they helped to bring to our attention," Greer huffed. "Assure them that they may be as much a part of the solution as they were the investigation."

"Thank you, High Councilman."

"Ambassador Seren," he smiled briefly and the crystal went hazy, then cleared.

Chapter Thirty-Three

The next evening, my dinner was interrupted by the sound of howling. I had been eating with my Guard and Raza in the guest house kitchen, a meal that Ainsley had prepared for us, and I'd been enjoying it until the spine-tingling sound had ruined the calm. Conri perked up and seemed to listen intently before looking towards me.

"The Missouri pack leader has returned with only ten wolves," he declared.

"How do you know there are only ten?" I frowned.

"I heard them."

"You can discern ten different wolf voices?" Ainsley asked in awe.

"No," Conri smirked. "I can *discern* what they're saying."

An extinguisher came into the guest house and rushed over to me. "You're wanted in the front yard, Ambassador."

"Thank you, Extinguisher Keith," I slid my seat back and everyone else at the table followed suit.

"Um," Keith cleared his throat as he looked at my Guard. "They'll only to speak with the Ambassador. They said if anyone else comes out of the house, they'll leave."

"Ridiculous," Torquil huffed.

"It's fine," I sighed. "You guys can watch over me from the windows."

"At least take Cat with you," Tiernan said in a low tone.

"Yeah, that's a good idea," I agreed. "Come on, Cat, let's go talk to some werewolf witches."

I left the guest house and everyone followed me into the main house and then to the living room. Several of my Guard set themselves up at the windows, lifting the glass panes to get an unimpeded line of fire. Extinguishers were already spread out around the house, watching the front yard warily, and Councilman Teagan was waiting in the living room.

"Ambassador," Councilman Teagan said. "We've got Extinguishers up in my office and the upper floors, armed with rifles to watch over you."

"Thank you, Sir," I gave him a quick nod; extra protection was never a bad thing.

Tiernan and Conri flanked me all the way to the front door, where they remained, to watch me through the charcoal mesh of the screen. Cat stayed with me though, scanning the shadows as we walked down the wood steps.

"What is that?" Aidan asked as he stepped forward into the light. His eyes were glued to Cat.

"This is Cat, *she* is a puka and she can understand you, so I'd be careful to not insult her."

"A puka... I've heard of them but never seen one. She's massive," he looked her over. "Is it true that they can shift into horses?"

"Yes, I met her as a horse actually," I smiled, recalling my introduction to Cat. "We bonded and have been friends ever since."

"Well, Mistress Cat," Aidan held out his hand to her. "May

208

we be friends as well?"

Cat looked up at me but I only shrugged. Sometimes she was a better judge of character than I was. She set her cognac-colored eyes on Aidan and his expression went from casual to acute. Something seemed to pass between them, some kind of understanding was reached, and Cat laid her head in his palm.

"Not one for shaking hands, eh?" Aidan laughed and stroked Cat's cheek. "Me either, to tell the truth." And with that, he leaned forward and kissed my cheek. He turned the kiss into a cheek-to-cheek face press as he whispered, "It's nice to see you again, Princess Kick-Ass."

"And you as well, Alpha Aidan," I lifted a brow at him as he withdrew. I didn't give his kiss any regard. Aidan felt like a mini Conri to me and I assumed his flirtations were just as frivolous as the bargest's. "Did you speak to your elders?"

"I did," he pulled a length of leather cord from his coat pocket. At the end of it, a small cluster of quartz crystals was tied to the leather. "Now they would like to speak to you," he began to put the necklace over my head but I stopped him.

"What is that?" I pulled back a little to look the necklace over. It really did appear to be just a chunk of crystal shards, all grown together in a group, but I knew how deceiving appearances could be. And crystals were great receptacles for magic.

"It's a cluster," he frowned at me like he couldn't understand why I'd be hesitant.

"I know it's a crystal cluster," I huffed. "Why are you trying to put it on me?"

"So you can speak to the elders," he cocked his head at me. "Don't the fey use clusters?"

"To speak to each other?" I asked and he nodded. "No, we

use crystal balls. It's called scrying."

"Scrying," he mused. "Like divination. Interesting. We've always used cluster crystals."

"And what happens when you put one on?" I took the pendant from him, holding it by its leather cord.

"You're mentally connected with the people in the cluster," he shrugged. "I've already established a cluster link with the elders. When you hang the crystal over your chest, you'll be pulled into the cluster with them."

"Fascinating," I glanced back at the house and saw the windows full of worried faces. Tiernan and Conri were still at the door, looking like grim shadows through the screen. "Alright," I set stern eyes on Aidan. "Just know that if this is some kind of a trap, Cat will tear your throat out. Isn't that right, Cat?"

She gave a low bark.

"And then all those people watching will run out here and obliterate whatever she leaves for them."

"Fair enough," Aidan held up his hands. "I give you my word as pack leader, neither the crystal nor the link will harm you."

"Fair enough," I said back and slipped the leather over my head.

The world brightened around me like someone had changed the filter on a photograph. Brighter and brighter until everything faded and was replaced by icy alabaster. A glowing fog covered the ground and I was surrounded by thick glass walls which soared up into a multi-pointed and strangely angled ceiling. No wait, it wasn't glass, it was crystal. It was like I'd been transported within the quartz. And I wasn't alone.

"Princess Seren?" A man with a British accent asked me.

He was dressed in a perfect, tailored slate-gray suit with a cardinal tie and a matching pocket square. I could tell by his lean neck that he was bit on the wiry side but the cut of the suit made him look thicker. He was what the Brits would call a ginger; with citrine hair and fair, freckled skin. Despite this anemic appearance, he exuded power and his crocodile-green eyes were sharply focused on me.

"Yes, and you are?"

"I am Crispin Arterbury, Prime Elder of Bite," he bowed as perfectly as any fairy knight. "These are the other high elders," he waved expansively to the rest of the people in the crystal room (none of whom looked old enough to be called an elder), and then gestured to a very angry and very familiar looking Native American woman. "Jennifer Wasutke, Prime Elder of Flight," he leaned in and whispered, "She's a bit peeved with you, my dear."

"Prime Elder Wasutke and I have already met," I nodded to her. "In a way."

"We've had a brief conversation," intense walnut-colored eyes narrowed on me. They were so dark, I could barely see her irises. It kind of felt like I was staring into the plastic eyes of a stuffed animal. But I'd had lots of practice staring into strange eyes and hers didn't bother me in the least.

"More of an accusation," I noted. "I believe the word you used was; traitor."

"That may have been inaccurate," she amended. "I should have recognized you for what you really are; doomed."

She launched herself at me but a man slid between us, laughing.

"Ve spoke on zis already, Jennifer," he put an almond-colored hand on her shoulder and gave her a pat. "No violence today, da?"

"Fine," Wasutke grunted and turned away to sulk in a faceted corner.

"This is Illarion Maksimov, Chief Elder of Storm," Crispin gestured to the man before me.

"Princess Seren," Illarion turned towards me with a smile that went all the way up to his slightly slanted hazel eyes. A swath of sable hair fell over his long forehead as he bowed over my hand. "It's highest pleasure to meet you."

"Nice to meet you as well," I cleared my throat as he stepped back and gave me a wink.

"And here is Jarne Vinter, Prime Elder of Pack," Crispin indicated a Nordic giant with chalky skin that looked like it would burn with the slightest hint of sun. It paired well with the deep acorn color of his hair though, and his deep indigo eyes.

"Call me Jarne," he spoke with a Scandinavian accent, lifting his words like he did his lips, with pure joy. "We have heard great things about you."

"You have?" I sent a skeptical look in Elder Wasutke's direction and Jarne laughed boisterously.

"Not from her. Our Missouri alpha has caught your scent," he nudged my shoulder with his fist, causing me to stumble.

"My what?" I gaped at him.

"It's Pack speak for; he likes you," a woman dressed in a sangria sari walked up to me with a hickory-colored hand extended. I shook it as she continued, "I'm Akhila Trivedi, Prime Elder of Flame."

"Thanks for the translation, Prime Elder," I admired her

212

amazing periwinkle eyes, so startling in her dark face.

"An you be a lucky girl to be catchin' Aidan," another woman sidled up to me, speaking with a Jamaican accent. She had deep bourbon colored skin and a voice to match. Her tortoiseshell dreadlocks were twisted into a crown around her head, her sticky toffee eyes were set on me sweetly, and her curvy body was draped in seafoam silk. "He be a grindman from what I heard tell."

"A grindman?" I asked, unsure whether I wanted to know what she meant by that.

Akhila laughed politely behind her hand but the men looked a little uncomfortable.

"Grindman, you know," the woman undulated her pelvis. "He be good in da bedroom."

"Oh, um," I cleared my throat. "I already have one of those."

"Never can have nuff of those, nuh true?" She smiled wide.

"You can when the grindman you got is the jealous type," I couldn't help laughing.

"Getcha new man, lilly girl," her full lips pursed sensually. "Ya nuh see it?"

"Oh I see a lot of it," I shook my head, "but I don't touch."

"No," she laughed. "I mean, don't you understand? We magic women must be free to love."

"I do love," I shrugged. "That's why I don't touch anyone but Tiernan." Oh okay and Raza that once. Give me a damn break. I'm going to tell Tiernan. I am.

"Ah sey one," the Jamaican nodded. "I understand. I am Chantelle Robinson, Prime Elder of Tide."

"Seren Firethorn, Princess of Twilight," I introduced myself.

"Firethorn, yes," Akhila observed. "Aidan mentioned this name. Do you have an affinity for fire?"

"You could say so," I shrugged. "I have pyrokinesis and my personal fey magic is the firethorn; a thick, thorny vine that I can set aflame."

"It sounds lovely," Akhila sighed.

"Akhila, stop monopolizing," a blonde man stepped forward. He sounded American and looked it too. His athletic build was shown off in a pair of tailored pants and a button down shirt with the cuffs rolled up. He held out a manicured, sand-colored hand to me. "I'm Jared Turner, Prime Elder of Quake."

"Nice to meet you," I shook his hand.

"And this is Gabriel Alegre," Jared indicated a swarthy man on his left. "He's the Prime Elder of Beckoning."

"Princess," Gabriel took my hand in both of his and brought it to his full lips.

He had those smoldering Spanish looks that had made Antonio Banderas a fortune. Hair like a mink, cut in careless layers, maple syrup eyes too sweet to look at for long, and those almost feminine full lips. He was stunning, except he made my skin crawl. I had to fight the urge to yank my hand away from him.

"Prime Elder," I took my hand back as soon as politely possible.

"We've asked you here because Aidan has informed us that you seek to establish a truce between us and the fey," Crispin took over again.

"And the Human Council," I nodded. "I think that would be

214

to all of our best interests."

"You don't know my interests," Flight Elder sneered.

"Hey, I get it, you have a problem with me because my people killed several of yours and now I'm holding even more of Flight hostage," I nodded. "But try to see it from my perspective; your people have been killing humans under the guise of raven mockers for centuries. How many deaths would that be, do you think? How many years have you yourself added to your lifespan by eating human hearts? Because I don't believe for a second that you're under the age of thirty."

"It's so easy for you to sneer at me and my kind while you have immortality," she snarled.

"I only recently acquired immortality," I shrugged. "Before that, I was just human."

"With psychic gifts," she huffed.

"That granted me the ability to police the fey, not stay young forever," I shook my head. "And had you offered me such magic as yours, I would have refused to use it. But this is besides the point. Your kind have killed many humans. In the eyes of the Human and Fairy Councils, you have broken the truce and should all be extinguished."

Everyone tensed.

"But we are willing to overlook those murders," I went on. "As well as any the rest of the clans have committed. A clean slate so that we can move forward."

"We are not comfortable with the thought of signing a document we had no part in creating," Crispin said.

"All humans have to abide by the truce," I shrugged. "And most don't even know it exists. But in this as well, we're willing to

215

compromise. A new truce can be made, one that you will help to write. If you're willing to work towards peace."

"And if we're not?" Jennifer Wasutke sneered.

"Then it will be war," I said simply. "I don't want to sound arrogant or spiteful here. I've heard of your abilities and I'm certain you could hold your own against either the Extinguishers or the Wild Hunt but against them both? I honestly don't think so."

"I don't think you fully comprehend how many of us there are," Gabriel said quietly.

"I don't think you fully comprehend the source of your magic," I said gently. "The power you possess is a mutation of fairy magic. I could hazard a guess as to all of your ancestors and I could also tell you that your magic is only a portion of what they possess."

The elders began muttering angrily.

"I'm not trying to be insulting," I held up my hands. "I admit that some of the magic has revealed interesting and powerful aspects in your kind but I want you to be aware of exactly what you're dealing with and what a good option peace would be for all of us. You say that I have no idea of your numbers. Well, let me remind you that the fey fill an entire planet, just as humans do Earth. We are not a portion of the population, we are all of it. If we needed numbers, we would have them but truly, I don't believe we'd have to resort to that."

"You speak the word *we* in reference to the fey but you are clearly one of us," Jared said in confusion.

"I may be what your ancestors were," I offered. "A turning point; the person whose choice of mate would determine whether her descendants became fairy or witch. But I'm not a witch. I hold both human psychic talent and fairy magic, so I am something different than you. Your fey blood has been diluted so much that all that remains of it is a trace of magic. I can't sense any fey blood in you. That being said, I view you as a new race of human and as such, you're entitled to my protection as an extinguisher and my mediation on your behalf as an ambassador."

They all shared intense looks with each other.

"We accept your offer to become our Ambassador. You may help mediate the truce when we meet with your elders," Crispin finally answered. "Whether peace will be achieved or not is yet to be seen but I think we are interested in working towards that goal and I believe that you are genuine in your desire to help us get there."

"Excellent," I wondered briefly if I had the authority to set up that meeting and then I decided to just go with it. Peace wasn't something that should be put off. "Our High Council House is located in Ireland. It's in the countryside, a nice neutral location where we can work out the details of a truce without being bothered by prying human eyes. I'll give Aidan the directions on how to reach it. Shall we set the meeting for a week from today?"

"That's acceptable," Gabriel nodded.

"Then I'll see all of you there," I started to pull the crystal off my neck when Crispin stopped me.

"One last thing, Princess," he held his hand out towards me.

"Yes?" I dropped the crystal back into place.

"The prisoners you're holding," Crispin glanced at Jennifer, who was still scowling. "I believe it would go far to swaying the clans towards peace if you released them."

"Do I have your word that Flight will not harm anymore humans, Prime Elder Wasutke?" I countered.

"They will not use their magic to take life," Wasutke grimaced. "But this promise lasts only until we establish whether there will be peace or war."

"Sounds fair to me," I shrugged. "I'll release your people."

"Thank you, Princess," Crispin smiled, revealing a set of small but sharp-looking fangs.

I blinked in surprise. I'd completely forgotten that he was the elder of Bite; the vampire witch clan. Vampires. The word conjured images at odds with Crispin's appearance. But then fairies weren't exactly a bunch of Tinkerbells either.

"Thank you for being open to a truce," I said to all of them and then removed my necklace.

Chapter Thirty-Four

I was once again standing on the lawn before the Tulsa Council House, staring into Aidan's face. Grindman; the word snuck into my mind and I nearly blushed. I'm sure he was good in bed, he had the look of a man who wouldn't be satisfied until his partner was. But I wasn't interested in the alpha wolf. I already had a Lord of the Wild Hunt... and a very determined dragon to deal with.

"They'll be meeting with our high councils in a week," I said to Aidan. "I'll get you the coordinates and directions to the Fairy High Council House in Ireland and then you can pass them on to your elders."

"Alright," he nodded as he took the cluster crystal back. "All went well, then?"

"Not as well as I would have liked but at least they're willing to try for peace," I shrugged. "And Flight Elder Watsuke gave me her word that her members wouldn't harm any humans until we got this sorted out."

"So you'll release the ones you've taken?" Aidan lifted a brow.

"I'll release them," I confirmed. "Wait here."

"Hold on," he handed me a little card. "My information, so you have a contact to call if something should happen."

"Thanks," I tucked his card into the inner pocket of my leather jacket.

"You're doing the right thing, Princess Kick-Ass," Aidan smirked.

"I hope I don't end up regretting it, Pack-Man," I shot back.

"What did you call me?" He started to smile.

"You heard what I said," I began walking to the house. "Now just accept what a brilliant play on words it is and let it go."

"I guess I do chomp on things," he chuckled.

"And grind them," I muttered.

"What was that, Princess?" He called out.

"Nothing," I sighed. "Damn wolf hearing."

"What happened?" Tiernan asked as soon as I stepped inside.

"I've set up a meeting in a week's time," I looked to Lord Eadan and then Councilman Teagan. "We'll need to contact the High Councils and let them know that the witches will be descending upon the Fairy High Council House in Ireland, expecting to have a truce summit."

"I'll go call them now," Teagan hurried off.

"I'll scry for Councilman Greer," Eadan added.

"And I'll go release the prisoners," I watched them stop in their tracks.

"Why would you give up your advantage?" Raza cocked his head at me curiously.

"Because it helped to get the Coven to agree to the summit," I explained. "And because the Prime Flight Elder gave me her word that her people wouldn't kill any humans until then."

"Until then?" Tiernan lifted a brow.

"Well I couldn't get a promise of forever from her when she didn't know if we'd end up signing a truce or not," I grimaced. "Besides, if they do step out of line, they won't be able to plead ignorance any more and we can hunt them with a clear conscious."

"That's a good point," Conri grinned. "I do love to hunt."

"I'm going to go get them," I rolled my eyes and headed to the basement.

"I don't think this is entirely your decision," Murdock grumbled. "It should be put to a vote."

"They're under my control, Councilman," I pointed out. "And as Ambassador, I don't think I need your permission. But I will ask for your support," I looked to Ted Teagan.

"Release them," Teagan sighed. "I don't feel comfortable with a basement full of witches anyway."

"Who would?" Torquil muttered.

"Witches," I said as I passed by him.

Chapter Thirty-Five

I released the witches and earned several disapproving stares from council members as I did so. I in turn felt a little disappointed in the behavior of my fellow humans. It felt morally wrong to keep the prisoners while we sought truce with their people. So I wasn't cowed at all by their criticism. I was doing my job as an Ambassador and they could kiss my half-fey fanny.

Turns out, I didn't have to deal with them for long anyway. Eadan called me in on his conversation with Councilman Greer and Greer asked me to report to the Fairy High Council House in Ireland immediately. The high council members wanted me there to handle any problems that might arise between now and the summit. A week wasn't a lot of time to prepare for such an important event and I think they were a little annoyed with me for setting such a horrible deadline. So I got to share their misery.

All of us fey packed our bags and bid adieu to the Tulsa Council House. My Star's Guard was in an exceptional mood, laughing and teasing each other as we headed for the SUVs. For most of them, this was their first trip into HR and now they were going to see the most famous fairy site outside of the Fairy Realm. It was like telling a bunch of children that you were taking them to Disneyland. I wanted to join in their cheer but I found my stomach clenching nervously as we rode to the airport. Not because of witches or the truce. My nerves were purely dragon related.

Raza was coming with us.

Things were getting tense between Tiernan, Raza, and I. Raza hadn't approached me in anything but polite interest since our searing kiss but he didn't have to; his looks said it all. He looked at me like we'd already slept together and it was ruffling my feathers a bit. The more he looked at me, the less interested in him I became... and the more furious Tiernan turned.

It was a vicious cycle that I had no idea how to break and the plane ride didn't seem the appropriate time for an intervention. So I retreated into the private cabin with Tiernan and stayed there until we landed in Ireland. Those hours of peace were just what I needed and I luxuriated in the private time it gave me with my man. Miles up in the air, encased in metal and enveloped in Tiernan, I was able to let go of my anxieties and just be Seren. Not Ambassador Seren, not Princess Seren, not even Extinguisher Seren. Just Seren in love with Tiernan.

Once we landed in Ireland, the ride up to the Fairy High Council House was much more tense but at least we were all facing forward, so I could ignore the hot looks Raza was directing at the back of my head. After the intimate time I'd spent with Tiernan on the plane, he was even able to ignore them. So we miraculously made it all the way up into the Irish countryside without a single incident.

Unfortunately, that's where my peace ended.

My father came rushing out to meet our Hummers (it's rough terrain up there) and whisked me away immediately. Tiernan and Cat followed but us my father stopped and gave Tiernan a small head shake. Tiernan's eyes widened but he nodded his compliance and went back to our group, where some council aides were directing everyone to their accommodations. Cat of course paid no mind to Keir and remained beside me. But then Keir hadn't tried to stop her.

"What is it?" I asked. "And what are you doing here? I thought you were going to stay on the Isle of Danu until the summit?"

"The raven mockers have disappeared," Keir whispered as

he rushed me down the hallway.

"What?!" I stopped and screeched.

"Seren, we must hurry," Keir grabbed my arm and started to pull me along. "Raye made it to Twilight and collected his people from Criarachan. They left Fairy through the San Francisco rath, and were transported from Gentry to the airport, where they were seen boarding the plane provided by the Human Council. The plane took off without a problem but it never landed in Tulsa. They're missing."

"A whole plane of fairies is missing?" I growled as my hands started to shake. "Damn them, I never should have trusted those witches."

"You did as your heart dictated," Keir shook his head. "And I support your decision. It was a wise mercy that you showed, an outstretched hand offered in friendship."

"And they bit it," I shook my head. "That's what I get for being kind to werewolves. No good deed goes unpunished."

"We don't know that the witches are behind this," Keir said reasonably.

"Of course they're behind this," I huffed. "Damn them, there were children among Raye's group."

"I know," Keir's face was lined with worry. "And they're our people. We will find them and if any harm has been offered them, we will return it tenfold."

"You're damn straight we will," I looked towards Cat and she started to growl. "Don't worry, Cat, I won't leave you behind. You'll get your pound of flesh too."

"Before flesh or blood, we must have the truth," Keir pushed open a large, golden oak door.

It was carved with swirling designs similar to Celtic knotwork and opened onto a vast room with a vaulted ceiling and a pristine floor the color of fine porcelain. It looked like it had never been walked upon and I did so with a small amount of trepidation over the state of my boots and what they might leave in my wake.

Windows were built into the slopes of the ceiling, letting in large shafts of light which made the polished floor gleam like it was its own light source. Besides those architectural wonders, there was only one other window in the place and it was set into the wall at the far end of the room, behind a U shaped table.

The window was massive and came to a curving point at its top center, to fit into the angles of the ceiling. It held an amazing view of a pastoral countryside; little lambs fluffs gathered together on the glistening grass of gently rolling hills. The peaceful scene was in direct opposition to the grim and anxious faces of the fairies seated at the wide table. I recognized Greer and nodded to him. He gave me a respectful head bow back.

So my father wasn't the only one to come over from the Isle of Danu early. That didn't bode well.

"My daughter has arrived," Keir indicated me with a wave of his hand as we stepped within the center of the U. "I've given her a brief report on what has occurred."

"Princess Seren," a man with flowing cornsilk hair stood at the direct center of the table and nodded to me. He looked familiar but I couldn't remember where I'd seen him before. His eyes, a bright violet, settled on me serenely and he waved an elegant, nut-brown hand towards a chair across from him. "Please join us."

"Thank you, Councilman..." I glanced at my father.

"Timberstride," Keir whispered to me. "Lorcan Timberstride, Chief High Councilman."

"Chief High Councilman Timberstride," I inclined my head

225

as I took the indicated seat. Keir took the seat beside mine and Cat settled between us.

"I assume that King Keir has told you of the missing raven mockers?" Timberstride waited for me to nod and then continued. "We have sent hunters to investigate but they've found only one clue; the remnant of powerful weather magic."

"Storm," I growled. "It must be the Storm witches."

"You met with these witches recently, is that correct, Princess?" Lorcan asked while the other high council members stared at me silently.

"I did," I confirmed. "Through the use of a crystal amulet they call a cluster. The stone allows a group of people to form a psychic connection by projecting them into a neutral location where they can converse."

"Fascinating," Lorcan shared a look with Greer, who was seated on his right. "These witches are more advanced than we thought."

"I believe their powers are muted and mutated versions of fairy magic," I said. "It's not surprising that they would learn to use crystals as communication devices, just as the fey do."

"Well said," Lorcan nodded. "You've briefed High Councilman Greer on the witch magic and he has informed us of your findings but have you learned anything new since your conversation with their elders? Any insights you may have picked up through interaction that could help us with the disappearance?"

"I thought they were honorable," I sighed. "They seemed to want peace but I did imply that we were more powerful than they and that peace would be in their best interest. Perhaps they were offended and changed their mind."

"Do you truly believe that?" Lorcan leaned forward. "From

the reports I've had on you, Princess, I've learned that you are known to be quite perceptive and I find it hard to believe that Danu's chosen one could be so easily deceived."

"It surprised me too, Councilman," I grimaced.

"But are you certain?" He pressed. "For the moment, all we have is a missing plane and a remnant of weather magic. Perhaps you were not deceived then but are being deceived *now*."

"You think this may be a trick?" I frowned. "Who would do that? Who would abduct a plane full of fairies and make it look as if the witches were responsible?"

"Someone who wants a war," Lorcan said simply. "I have been Chief High Councilman for many years, Ambassador Seren. I have witnessed many deceptions and have developed a sense for them. This feels wrong to me... this answer is too simple."

"I see your point," I frowned, a little impressed by the fairy. "It does seem a little convenient."

"We'd like you to conduct your own investigation," Lorcan went on. "Is there anyone you can contact within the Coven?"

"Yes, actually," I thought of the little white card that was tucked in my pocket. "An alpha of the Pack clan."

"Perhaps you can speak with him and get a better sense of what has occurred," Lorcan offered. "Then you will add your sense to mine and we will hopefully be able to make a more informed decision on what to do next."

"I'll go call him immediately," I nodded and started to stand.

"Princess," Lorcan stopped me.

"Yes?" I sat back down.

"I'm sure we don't need to tell you how delicate this situation is," Lorcan glanced around the table and all of the fairies nodded in agreement. "We would prefer if you withheld this information from Lord Raza... for the time being."

"Sweet Danu," I sighed. "I forgot about Raza."

"I'm sure you can see how this would be upsetting to him," Lorcan went on. "And we'd prefer not to add a hotheaded dragon-djinn to the volatility of our plight."

"I understand," I whispered as I thought of how Raza might react to the news that his son and a huge amount of Raye's people were missing. "I won't tell Raza until I absolutely have to."

"Thank you," Lorcan inhaled deep and a sense of relief went around the table.

I looked them over in surprise. I knew Raza was dangerous but damn, I didn't realize he could scare the High Council of Fairy. It made me wonder if it was him they feared or just the fact that he was a dragon-djinn. And if it were the latter, what had his people done to scare the most powerful fey alive? Had it warranted their extinction?

"Councilmen," my father nodded to the group as he got up. "Councilwomen," a bow to the ladies (because my dad was nothing if not a gentleman). "We will take our leave now."

"Thank you, King Keir," Lorcan nodded. "And thank you for leaving your kingdom to come here and lend us your support."

"My kingdom is merely part of Fairy," Keir helped me up. "It's my honor to give aid to our realm and our people."

"Just give me a few minutes," I pulled the cell phone Dylan had given me, out of my leather jacket and held it up for them to see. "I'll go out into the hall and make the phone call."

"Please," Lorcan waved to a little door set into the wall on my right. "Use the antechamber and take your time, Princess Seren. We need as much information as you can acquire."

"I'll do my best," I headed towards the door. Keir and Cat followed me.

Once we were safely shut in the comfortable sitting room, I let out a string of curses and stalked across the thick carpet to plop down on a teal velvet couch. Then I took every throw pillow on it and threw them across the room. I figured that's what they were made for and I was merely seeing to the fulfillment of their life's purpose. Keir followed me more sedately, dodging pillows with the deftness of a Shaolin monk, and then took a carved chair on my right. Cat however, bounded after me enthusiastically (after chasing a few pillows) and jumped up onto the couch beside me.

I pulled Aidan's card out of my jacket and dialed his number with angry jabs of my fingers while I cursed his name, and his Pack, and his stupid grindman ways under my breath. It rang for what seemed like an eternity before he answered gruffly. The abruptness of his voice made me scowl at the phone.

"This is Ambassador Seren," I stated with matching brusqueness.

"You!" He nearly shouted and I frowned deeper. "Why'd you even release them if you were just going to steal them back?"

"What are you talking about?" I lost my scowl to confusion.

"Don't act as if you don't know."

"I don't; I was calling to ask what you knew of the disappearance of a plane full of raven mockers."

"What?" His voice lost its ferocity.

"Raven mockers," I repeated. "They returned from Fairy and boarded a plane in San Francisco, heading home to Tulsa. But they never made it. The entire plane has vanished and left only a trace of weather magic behind."

"Weather magic?" Aidan sounded stumped. "But... Flight; they disappeared too and all that was left behind was a trace of cold... weather magic."

"Are you telling me that the Flight witches I released are missing too?" I asked calmly.

"Yes," he whispered. "We dropped them at Hunter Park, where they were supposed to be met by other flighters. But no one was there when their rides showed up."

"Aidan, we had nothing to do with their disappearance," I vowed. "Which means that your Coven most likely had nothing to do with the vanishing plane."

"Someone is setting us up!" He shouted.

"It appears so," I ground out. "Any ideas?"

"On my end?" He huffed. "I can't think of any witch who would want to start a war with the fey. Not any, except perhaps all of the members of Flight."

"Do you think the Prime Flight elder could be behind this?"

"Abduct her own people to make the fey look guilty?" He asked with scathing sarcasm. "No, of course not, she's the sweetest, most gentle- abso-freaking-lutely she could do this!" His voice shifted into anger. "She's a damn lunatic, that one."

"Coming from a wolf, that's pretty bad," I sighed.

"Ha ha, very funny," he grumbled. "What about your people? Maybe Elder Wasutke is innocent."

"I admit that it would make more sense for a fairy to want a war," I conceded. "We are almost assured of winning. But still, capability is not a reason to fight."

"Perhaps they just don't like humans," he offered.

"Well, that's a trait several fey share," I sighed. "Whittling down the suspects based on such criteria would take forever. I can think of several fairies right off the top of my head and most of them, I'm related to."

"Harsh," he sympathized. "You're half human and have human haters for relatives?"

"Yep, my family is rather complicated."

"Aren't they all?" He snorted. "You don't even want to know how about Pack interactions."

"You're right, I don't," I chuckled. "Look, I think we both need to go back to our people and let them know what's going on. Hopefully, they'll believe us and then maybe we can work together on this."

"I'd like that, Princess Kick-Ass," his voice lowered into a purr.

"Keep it in your pants, Prince Furry-Ass," I shot back. "I've already got a man."

"You married?"

"No."

"Then you ain't got a man," the phone went dead and I found myself scowling at it again.

Chapter Thirty-Six

"King Keir. Princess Seren," a man opened the door to the antechamber and poked his head in. "You're needed at the curtain wall. It appears that we're under attack."

"Excuse me?" I gaped at him. He'd delivered the news so placidly, I wasn't sure if I'd heard him correctly.

Before he could answer, the whole castle shook, sending me stumbling forward. I caught myself and ran out of the room, following after the fairy. He waved me on urgently, past the stunned high fairy council members and out into the hallway. My father and Cat chased after us.

The sound of shouting started to reach us as we neared the main hall. I heard a boom and then the castle shook again. A large painting fell free of its moorings and plummeted to the floor on my right. I lurched out of the way as it toppled forward and made huge crashing sound. Then my phone rang.

"Hello?!" I shouted into the receiver.

"The elders have declared war!" Aidan shouted back. "I contacted the clans but it was too late, they've already left. They're going to attack the Fairy Council."

"Yeah, I figured that out," I snapped.

"Are they already there?" He asked in shock.

Another boom vibrated through the castle.

"What do you think?" I yelled. "See if you can get a message through to them, I'm going to try to stop them from my end." I hung up on him and slipped the phone back into my leather jacket as I ran out of the castle.

In the courtyard, the fey were calm and organized. I was a little shocked to see how well they were handling the surprise attack. Rows of hunters formed and were given orders before running to their assigned positions. Most went atop the curtain wall but a select few went to higher points, up in the towers, and set to raining magic down upon our attackers; in some instances, quite literally.

Thunder rumbled as the sky above us darkened ominously; oily clouds churning like the hands of a maniac. Flashes of light lit up that demon sky with streaks of cinnabar, sulfur, aubergine, and arctic blue. Howls echoed off the shivering stone walls and screams of pain cried back in response. I ran up the stairs to the walk atop the curtain wall, and looked down into a mass of madness.

Funnels of water swirled by and smashed into the barred gate on my left. Groups of wolves gathered a short distance away, pawing at the earth as they waited for the water to break down the gate. Spheres of flame shot through the sky, coming down on the fairy soldiers along the wall. Most were able to protect themselves in time but a few painful shouts rang out.

"Great balls of fire," I couldn't help whispering.

But it wasn't the fire that bothered me. Nor the funnels of water. Not even the werewolves or the Quake witches moving the earth beneath us. I could deal with all of that. It was the dead that unnerved me. There was a platoon of zombies waiting to be dispatched on the far right of the field. They just stood there numbly, some more decayed than others, staring with their dead eyes directly ahead of them. What a reprehensible but morbidly fantastic skill. To be able to command an army that would feel no pain, eat no food, and need no rest... it was a hell of an advantage. But it smelled. Eadan had been right, the scent of death was

233

atrocious, even just the light whiff that was carried to me on the breeze.

"Seren," Tiernan was suddenly beside me, leaning over the crenelated stone for a better look. "Why are they attacking us?"

"They think we stole back the witches I freed," I sighed. "Look, I'll explain later. Right now, I've got to handle this."

I was about to start shouting at the witches when a monster flew over my head and breathed fire down upon that dead army. I lurched back, staring up at the magnificent form of a sparkling scarlet dragon. Its body was covered in glossy scales going from bright cherry at its underbelly to deep crimson at its shoulders. There, the color shifted into an overlay, just a sheen of ruby over the sinful black leather of the beast's wings. It roared and angled its head down to look at me, sun glinting off its gold eyes.

"Raza!" I shouted as the whiff of decay turned into roasted rotten meat. "Stop! I need to talk to them! Stop!"

The zombie militia was on fire but they didn't seem to know it. They just stood there as Beckoning witches called over their cousins in Tide to put out the flames. I didn't think the water witches would make it in time though. Raza was spewing some seriously hot flames and the zombies were already crumbling away into piles of blackened bones. I hoped that meant that their souls were freed but I noticed that some of the piles were still moving.

The dragon pulled up abruptly and circled back while the witches scrambled about in terror and panic. Wherever his shadow fell, people froze and stared up at him like deer caught in headlights. And with a wingspan wider than a semi-truck, the shadow he cast was significant. I didn't know if it was some kind of magic or just the fear felt when a dragon was overhead but even the wolves went silent when Raza passed over them. The dragon himself came to rest on the wall beside me, his enormous talons curving over and through the crenelations as his wings settled around us.

"You called?" He seemed to smile at me.

"This is a misunderstanding," I went in closer and couldn't help being stunned by the beauty of his refined face, the curves of his onyx horns which swept back from his regal forehead, and the glint of dangerous fangs sloping over his massive jaw. I refocused and said, "I need to talk to the witches. Can you take me down there?"

"Are you sure you don't want me to just kill them all?" He asked casually. "They've so thoughtfully presented themselves to me in one convenient package."

"Yes, I'm sure," I huffed.

"As you wish," he extended a leg and wrapped his thick claws around my waist before he leapt into the sky without any warning.

I gave a little screech but then the world spread out beneath me and I realized that I was flying... with a dragon. Raza could shift! I had not only seen my first dragon but I was being carried across a battlefield by one. Flying through the air supported by slick talons that could probably tear down mountains. It was exhilarating. I may have extended my arms like Superman.

Then we landed, a much softer landing than I'd anticipated. Raza had held me gently as he met the earth with only three feet. Then he placed me carefully on the ground and sat up, towering above me as his tail curved around us like a mini wall. I went to confront the wide-eyed witches coming warily forward.

"This is a mistake!" I shouted to them. "We didn't abduct the members of Flight. Our raven mockers were taken too, in the same manner as your witches. Their plane disappeared between San Francisco and Tulsa. We have a common enemy who is trying to frame both of us!"

A roar rumbled out behind me and I winced, turning to look up at the furious dragon. I'd completely forgotten that I wasn't supposed to tell Raza about his son. As fire spewed out of the dragon's maw, I did my best to hold my ground.

"We'll get them back, Raza!" I shouted as I held up placating hands. "I don't believe the witches are behind it. Please, calm down."

"Of course we're not behind it," Prime Flight Elder, Jennifer Wasutke stalked forward. "You are. I don't believe for a second that your fey are missing. That's just another lie created to trick us into trusting you."

Fire streamed past me and hit the ground directly in front of Elder Wasutke. She fell back onto the grass and then shimmied even further backward on her elbows. Two men ran forward and grabbed her beneath the arms to help her retreat.

"This is Lord Raza," I introduced the dragon. "His son is one of the missing raven mockers. You've only seen a fraction of what he is capable of, so please understand that it is not arrogance when I say to you that it doesn't matter what you believe, it only matters what *he* believes. And right now, he doesn't seem inclined to believe you're innocent."

"Lord Raza," Gabriel Alegre, Prime Elder of Beckoning, strode forward calmly. He'd gotten over his fear of dragons fast enough, even with his zombie army turning into embers. "We would not have come and attacked a fairy stronghold if we had instigated this. Wouldn't it make more sense for us to wait for you to attack us, somewhere where we had the advantage?"

The assemblage of witches went silent, everyone staring at the dragon. Except for the wolves, who whined and paced around the edges. I wasn't about to stand around waiting for Raza's volatile verdict. Instead, I stepped forward to speak with Gabriel myself, completely ignoring Raza.

"I've spoken with Aidan and we believe that a third party is at work here; trying to undermine our goal of a truce," I said calmly. "It makes no sense for me to abduct your witches after I freed them. That would be about as reasonable as your attacking our stronghold. And yet, here we are."

"Indeed," Gabriel frowned and looked back towards the other elders. It looked like they'd all banded together to bring us down. They just hadn't factored fighting a dragon into the mix. "Perhaps we've acted rashly."

"Where is my son?!" Raza's foot stomped the earth beside me and I stumbled away from the crater it made.

"I promise you, we do not have him," Gabriel held up his hands. "And we in turn would like our coven members back."

"Raza, stop thinking like a dragon and think like a man," I snapped at him; mimicking what he'd once said to me in hopes that it would get through to him. "We'll find Rayetayah but you need to help me by regaining your composure. If you attack these witches, you're playing right into our enemy's hands."

The dragon took a deep breath and let it out slowly.

"Thank you," I huffed and turned back to Gabriel. "Why don't you come inside and we can talk this over with the Fairy High Council?"

"I think we'd prefer to stay out here," Gabriel grimaced.

Alright," I nodded. "I will serve as intermediary but I already know what they'll say. The only trace left to find when the plane disappeared, was a remnant of weather magic. That's all the evidence we have."

"Nyet!" Illarion declared with a slashing motion of his hand. "Storm is no traitor to Coven. Ve are loyal."

"I'm not questioning your loyalty," I assured him.

"There was cold magic remaining at the site where the Flight members were last seen too," Crispin came forward, giving me a quick nod of greeting. "I believe the Princess. We have another player in this game; a player who wants war."

"Aidan and I came to the same conclusion," I agreed. "And before I even spoke with him, our Chief High Councilman said something similar. He voiced doubts concerning your involvement in the disappearance of the raven mockers."

"Zen he is vise man," Illarion nodded and crossed his muscled arms.

"Can we work together on this?" I asked. "We can investigate leads among our people while you investigate yours. When one of us finds the culprit, they will inform the other."

"Nyet, unacceptable," Illarion shook his head and Raza rumbled behind me. "Ve need to combine efforts. How vill ve be able to trust zat ve each are truly trying to find villain unless ve exchange people?"

"What are you talking about, Illarion?" Crispin frowned.

"I think he means that we should send some hunters with you to investigate the witches, while you send some witches with us to investigate the fey," I said.

"And Human Council," Illarion nodded.

"I agree," Gabriel declared.

"And I," Crispin said.

The ayes went around the elders but stopped at a sulking Wasutke. Crispin prodded her and she finally nodded. He gave her a hard look until she spoke.

"I agree," she said begrudgingly.

"I'll speak with the Fairy Council and return with their decision," I nodded. "But I believe they'll consent. Choose your witches while I'm gone. The faster we can investigate this, the faster we can reach a peaceful truce between our people."

Then I turned to Raza. His expression was unreadable as he wrapped his talons around me and lifted us into the air, heading back to the castle. Oddly enough, the return flight wasn't as fun as the one into battle had been.

Chapter Thirty-Seven

To say that Raza was pissed off about not being included in the discussion about his son would be like saying that Greenland was mildly chilly. Raza was furious. He held it together long enough to deposit me within the walls of the Council House (really it was a Council Castle) and then he threw a dragon tantrum.

Fairies ran for cover as Raza thrashed about; smashing everything within sight until I covered his body in thorny vines and tightened them around him. He went quiet then, laying his head down upon the courtyard stones to stare balefully up at me with huge golden dragon eyes. A single tear slipped over his scaled cheek and soaked into the solid earth. I sent the vines away so I could step forward and kneel beside his face. Then I laid my body against his cheek and hugged him as best I could.

He shifted beneath me, scales and horns changing back to skin and hair. His wings remained, though much smaller than they were, and they wrapped around us as he hugged me back desperately. For once, there was nothing sexual about his touch, he simply needed comfort. I realized that a man like him wouldn't get much of that, so I gave it freely, letting him bury his face in my shoulder and just take a moment to breathe in some empathy.

"We *will* find him," I whispered and stroked his hair. "I promise you."

"Yes, but will he be alive when we do?" Raza lifted his face to the sky. "I can't lose him. Please, take anything but him."

"I know," I sat back and took his hands. "We're going to do everything we can to prevent that."

"They should have told me," he growled suddenly.

"Because you're such a levelheaded man?" I lifted a brow at him.

"I deserved to know."

"Yes, you did," I conceded. "But try and see their perspective. You nearly destroyed the courtyard with your little temper tantrum."

"I do not have temper tantrums," he stood and put his fists to his hips to stare down at me.

Unfortunately, he was stark naked and standing put his crotch at the level of my face. I blinked at the display as he scowled down at me. It took a few seconds before he realized why I was staring. Then a slow smile spread across his face and I shot to my feet.

"Like what you see?" He smirked.

"Do you mind?" I waved at him and then looked pointedly around the courtyard. Several fey were watching us with horrified interest. "You're making a spectacle of yourself. At least wrap your wings around your body."

"Why would I do that?" He folded his wings neatly behind his back. "I have nothing to be ashamed of."

"Certainly not," an appreciative feminine voice said from the sidelines.

I looked over and saw the one person I would have never expected to find in the Fairy High Council House; Tiernan's ex-wife. I didn't even know her name, I just knew her as the bitch who treated Tiernan like crap. But I suddenly knew why I'd thought Chief High Councilman Timberstride looked so familiar. His face was very similar to hers.

"Thank you," Raza preened as the bitch strode forward.

"If I had my way," the sundae slut purred, "you'd be naked all the time."

I call her *sundae slut* because she wore her hair in this whipped cream swirl atop her head. Then there was her nut-brown skin, her icy blue eyes, and the cherry of her lips. She was a woman who looked like she wanted to be consumed and at the moment she was offering Raza the spoon.

"Wow," I shook my head. "I don't even know what to say to that besides; slut alert!" I turned and started walking away.

"Did she just call me a whore?" The woman sounded aghast.

"Seren!" Raza ignored her and chased after me.

"No, please stay with Sundae Susan over there," I waved at her. "You realize that she's Tiernan's ex-wife, don't you?"

"She is?" Raza frowned and glanced back at the pouting parfait fairy.

"She is," Tiernan confirmed as he came up beside me. "And you're welcome to her. Please, by all means, dive right into the... what did you call her; a sundae?" I nodded and he chuckled. "Dive right into the sundae."

"I've never been so happy to see you," I smiled at Tiernan and slipped my arm around his waist. "Or to see you clothed. There's a place for naked men and it's not in public. At least not this kind of public."

"I agree," Tiernan nuzzled my face and then glanced at Raza. "Seriously, put that thing away, it's going to give me nightmares."

I gave the *thing* in question another glance and silently

242

agreed with Tiernan. I hadn't given Raza's privates much thought (well maybe a little) but I never would have guessed that the sinful sable length of it would be crowned with a scarlet tip. It looked almost alien, like it might rise up and roar just like the dragon it was attached to.

"Nightmares?" Sundae Slut had caught up with us. "Dreams, more like. Or perhaps daydreams."

"Well, if we cared enough, your smutty flirting might shock us," I smiled at her. "But as it stands, neither Tiernan nor I give one little pixie poop what you think. So you can go have your daydreams somewhere else."

"Oh my, I think I've somehow offended the Princess," she gave a gasp and held one limp hand to her breast.

"You're mere presence offends me," I growled and stepped towards her.

"Seren," Tiernan set a hand to my arm but I shrugged him off.

"Your *face* offends me," I went on. "The fact that I have to breathe the same air as you, offends me."

"Seren," Tiernan growled but I continued to ignore him. I was on a roll.

"In fact, I'm so bloody offended right now that if you don't get out of my sight within the next five seconds, I'm going to kick your offensive ass all over this courtyard!"

"Princess Seren, I'd like to know what my daughter has done to upset you," a calm voice interrupted and I nearly groaned.

"I tried to tell you," Tiernan whispered as he came up beside me.

"And Lord Raza," Councilman Lorcan said gently.

243

"Perhaps you could clothe yourself and then return to this discussion?"

Raza nodded curtly, giving me one last confused look before he stalked away.

"Chief High Councilman," Tiernan bowed.

"Tiernan, please," Lorcan came forward and hugged my boyfriend. "I've missed you, Son."

Son?

"Daddy," the parfait pouted deeper. "I don't know why the Princess is so angry with me."

"Oh, I think you do," I growled.

"Princess Seren?" Lorcan stood back from Tiernan and gave me a confused look.

"You do know about your daughter abandoning Tiernan when he was cast from court, right?" I narrowed my eyes on the councilman.

"I wouldn't put it that way," Lorcan sighed. "To ask her to follow him into exile would have been dishonorable and we both know that Count Tiernan is nothing if not honorable."

"I feel that it was dishonorable to not follow him on her own," I said tersely. "But I'm not going to stand here and argue with you over your daughter. Obviously, you must remain loyal to family. Well done on your part. Your daughter could learn a lot from you."

"My daughter has behaved as is expected of any seelie noblewoman," Lorcan defended her. "Count Tiernan was named traitor, there was nothing she could do about that."

"And apparently there was nothing you could do either," I

244

narrowed my eyes on him.

"Excuse me?" He straightened in shock.

"Seren, no," Tiernan took my hand. "You don't have to do this."

"You have the nerve to come out here and call him *son*," I sneered. "You act as though nothing has happened, as though he's still married to your daughter, and you've supported him all along. When you sat here in the High Council Castle and let him be ostracized without intervening on his behalf. Do not tell me that a word from the Chief High Councilman would not have helped his case."

"It was not my place," Lorcan said stiffly.

"Then you aren't as loyal to family as I'd thought," I shrugged and turned away.

"And they *are* still married," Lorcan said, freezing me in my tracks.

"What did you say?" I asked in a low, dangerous tone as Tiernan inhaled sharply.

"They never divorced," Lorcan looked to his daughter, who looked away guiltily. "You said you were waiting for your husband to return."

"I..." she sighed.

"She declared our marriage over," Tiernan said gently to his ex-father-in-law. "I'm sorry, Councilman but we are no longer related."

"When?" Lorcan looked to his daughter. "Tell me, Cliona!"

"Before he left," she shrugged. "I couldn't be the wife of a traitor."

"He's not a traitor," I growled and she paled to an ugly ocher color.

"You knew how I felt about Tiernan," Lorcan shook his head sadly. "How I felt about his defense of Sorcha. It was nobly done and though he was labeled a traitor, it was an honorable exile. Everyone knew it. How could you abandon your husband so easily? And such a man as he? You didn't have to follow him but you should have at least remained true to him."

"I didn't abandon him," she cried. "He abandoned me when he chose to stand against our queen."

"Your queen is a fucking psychopath," I snarled.

"She's your grandmother!" Cliona (what a stupid name) gasped.

"That doesn't blind me to the fact that she's as crazy as Caligula," I huffed.

"It's nice to see you too, Granddaughter," Caligula herself walked up and joined the conversation.

"Oh, this just keeps getting better and better," I groaned and then pasted a huge, fake smile on my face as I turned to confront Queen Iseabal, my grandmother, whom I secretly called Insane Izzy. "Hello, Grandmother."

"Still upset over that whole silly misunderstanding?" She asked sweetly.

"See what I mean?" I asked Lorcan as I swirled my fingers near my temple. "She's loo loo."

Lorcan cleared his throat but I caught his lips twitching.

"Please don't start any rumors questioning my sanity," Iseabal sighed. "They're so boring."

"What are you doing here?" I asked her baldly. There was no sense in arguing about sanity with a crazy person.

"I was informed that I'd be needed here for a summit to discuss a truce to be signed between us and some human mutants," she said derisively.

"They're witches and you don't need to be here until next week," I glared at her.

"But then I heard that my son was here, supporting his daughter and I thought that I too, should be here for my family," she added sweetly.

"And bring my boyfriend's ex-wife with you?" I lifted a brow.

"Lady Cliona wanted to visit her father," Iseabal said innocently.

"Of course she did and I'm sure she had no idea that her gorgeous, valiant ex-husband whom she foolishly abandoned would be here as well," I huffed. "I don't have time for this." I turned and started walking away again.

"Mother?" I heard Keir's voice and froze... again.

"Ah, my son," Iseabal purred as I turned on my heel and lunged for Keir.

Iseabal pulled back in shock as I pushed my father away from her.

"Dad, remember what we talked about?" I gave him a harsh look. "Do you have your amulets?"

"No," he whispered in horror and I knew then that she had already begun to influence him.

My evil, psychotic grandmother had been enchanting my

247

father for years, making him complacent to her wicked ways. But whatever juju she did, it didn't work on me and I had seen the obvious changes in Keir. We'd finally decided that he needed to wear anti-fey charms if he was ever around his mother again.

"Here," I pulled a John the Conqueror root out of my pocket and slid it into the pouch at his waist. I'd started carrying it just in case of a situation like this and I was suddenly glad that I tended toward paranoia. Instantly, Keir looked calmer and saner.

"Thank you," he sighed and then turned his angry eyes on his mother. "Did you really think that I'd never figure it out?"

"What?" Iseabal looked completely innocent but then she'd had centuries to practice her acting skills.

"The enchantment, Mother," Keir growled. "Seren discovered it; how peculiar I act around you. How long have you been using magic to make me indifferent to your insanity?"

"I am not insane," she ground out.

"If you're not insane," Keir lowered his voice, "then you're evil and I want nothing to do with you."

He turned and started to walk into the castle. Tiernan, Cat, and I followed after him. I was hoping to make it further than a few feet this time.

"Keir," Iseabal called consolingly. "Sweetheart. Keir!"

"You were the one who told me to send Catriona and Seren back to the Human Realm," Keir stopped and turned to face his mother again. "I wanted them with me. I thought I could protect them but you convinced me that I couldn't. Was that enchantment too? Did you force me to send my family away?"

I gaped at him, my throat closing in denial, and then looked towards my grandmother in stark accusation.

"It was for the best," Iseabal whispered.

"Sweet Danu, you did," Keir breathed in horror. "You killed Catriona."

"Hardly," she huffed. "We all know that was your brother's doing."

"Goddess, what a family I have," I muttered.

"You killed her!" Keir shouted as he bared his teeth at his mother.

"Keir," she paled.

"Maybe it was not your words that directed the pukas but you *are* responsible," Keir lifted his face to the sky and released a shriek of pure agony. "All of this time and I have blamed myself! I have lied awake in bed going over and over it in my head. *What if I had just kept her with me? Why didn't I? Why did I send her away?* When all along, it was you who sent her away. You made me betray the only woman I have ever loved!"

"You love *me*," Iseabal glared at Keir. "I'm your mother. You *must* love me first and foremost."

"You're dead to me," he said, suddenly very calm, and the whole courtyard went silent in shock. "Let all here witness the death of my mother!" He shouted. "You are a phantom to me. I shall not hear your voice."

"Keir, no!" Iseabal screeched and threw herself at him.

"I shall not see your face," he shoved her away from him and the Queen of Seelie fell to the ground in a froth of frosty silk. "I shall know you nevermore!"

Keir flung a hand towards her as if to strike her down, and an acidic amethyst shimmer fluttered through the air. It fell over Iseabal like misty rain and she screamed as if it had burned her.

Hands over her face, she crumpled in upon herself and wept.

"Come, Daughter," Keir turned to me soberly. "We are needed elsewhere."

I took his arm and we walked into the castle, no one daring to stop us this time. His whole body was trembling but I helped steady him and I don't think anyone was able to see how deeply affected the King of Twilight had been by his mother's death.

Chapter Thirty-Eight

"Why do I feel like that was more of a battle than the one we just experienced with the witches?" I sighed as we walked into the council chambers.

"Family can wound you far deeper than any arrow," Tiernan said grimly.

"Well, my mother can wound me no longer," Keir said somberly.

"I'm so sorry, Dad," I stopped and hugged him.

"She betrayed me," he whispered. "In so many ways. But forcing me to send you and your mother away was more than I could forgive."

"What did you do to her?" I dropped my voice so the high council members at the other end of the room wouldn't hear.

"I'll go inform them of the witches' request," Tiernan said politely and walked away to give us some privacy.

"I killed her," he sighed. "At least to me."

"I don't understand."

"It's a sort of psychic death," he explained. "It severs all ties between two people. On my side, I won't be able to see her, even should she stand directly before me. I won't be able to hear her either, even should she scream in my face."

"That can be bad," I started to get worried. "You wouldn't even see her coming. She could enchant you at any time."

"Yes, it puts me at a bit of a disadvantage," he nodded. "But only should she try to physically attack me. As far as magic is concerned, she will not be able to cast any upon me. She does not exist for me, so my essence will not acknowledge any spell she tries to inflict upon me."

"So she's invisible to you in all ways," I mused. "She can see you but can't reach you."

"If she were to grab me, I'd feel her touch," he shrugged. "But I have my King's Guard to keep her away."

"I can't imagine what this feels like for you," I swallowed hard.

"No, your mother was wonderful," he looked melancholy for a moment. "I had thought mine was too. Instead, I find that she's more monster than mother."

"Well, you slayed that dragon," I squeezed his hand.

"This one, however, still lives," Raza said as he came through the door.

"Lord Raza," Keir nodded.

"King Keir," Raza nodded back.

"That was quite a display you put on in the courtyard," Keir noted.

"I just heard that you were rather entrancing yourself," Raza shot back.

"No," I held my hand up to Raza. "Please don't. Joking about your nudity is not the same as joking about what happened with Queen Iseabal."

"Of course it isn't," Raza inclined his head. "My apologies, King Keir."

"It's forgotten," Keir waved it away. "I suppose I started it. But then again, I did just witness you waving your member in my daughter's face. That required a comment from me at the very least."

I didn't think it was possible but Raza blushed.

"That was not how I meant..." Raza cleared his throat. "I should not have... it was entirely inappropriate when viewed in such a manner."

"It's alright," Keir laughed and laid a hand on Raza's shoulder. "But please keep that unusual appendage hidden when you're in public. It will haunt me."

I clasped a hand to my mouth to keep from bursting into shocked laughter as my father walked past me. I glanced pointedly at Raza's crotch before I followed after my father. It took a few moments before Raza recovered enough to follow us down the hall and I enjoyed every second of his discomfort. We were already seated by the time he joined us.

"Lord Raza," Councilman Greer greeted him and I realized that Lorcan must still be with his daughter. "Thank you for joining us. On behalf of the Fairy Council, I'd like to offer my sincerest apologies concerning your son. We will do everything we can to find him and bring him home safely."

"Yes, I've had assurances from your ambassador already," Raza shot me a look that I couldn't interpret.

"We are just waiting... ah, here he is," Greer waved towards the door and we all turned to see the Chief Councilman Lorcan come walking in. "Councilman Lorcan, I was just offering our apologies to Lord Raza."

"Yes, well, I think we've all behaved badly today," Lorcan took his seat and gave Raza a measuring look.

I chuckled and slid a smirk in Raza's direction. I knew the look on Lorcan's face. It was the expression of a father facing off with an unsuitable suitor for his daughter. Raza was the bad boy in leather and Lorcan was the redneck daddy with a shotgun. Raza gave me an annoyed grimace.

"If we could get to the business at hand?" Tiernan asked and several council members muttered in agreement.

"Of course," Lorcan sighed. "Princess Seren, what did the witches have to say?"

"They agree that there must be a third party at work and would like to conduct separate investigations to discover the truth," I began. "They would also like to offer us an exchange of people, some witches for some hunters. So that the investigation cannot be compromised."

"I think we should call the Human High Council and alert them to the situation," Lorcan mused. "I believe they'll want to be included as well."

"I'm sure the Coven would be fine with that," I agreed.

"Good," Lorcan looked down the table and the other council members nodded. "I shall contact the Human High Council immediately. Please wait here for my return," he stood up and turned to exit the room through a small door to the left.

While we waited, refreshments were brought in and I downed two glasses before I even realized that I was drinking wine. I was so exhausted, my hands were starting to shake. I just wanted to get this settled and then sleep for two days straight. But I knew that wasn't going to happen.

"They're sending a team of extinguishers over now," Lorcan said as he walked back in. "Princess Seren, please notify the Coven that we'll have ten people to exchange with them."

"Yes, Councilman," I stood up.

"And, Princess," Lorcan added. "Please don't kick my daughter's ass all over the courtyard."

"No, Chief Councilman, I won't," I agreed but then muttered beneath my breath, "As long as she doesn't piss me off again."

Chapter Thirty-Nine

The exchange went smoothly. I personally delivered our ten people; five hunters and five extinguishers, into the Coven's keeping. Lord Eadan Gale was among the hunters and Extinguisher Kate Teagan had flown in to be one of the extinguishers. Her father and the Kavanaugh twins had come with her but they would be assisting us on our end.

It wasn't like I had to deliver them far, the Coven had set up camp right outside the castle walls. So I basically walked them outside and then walked the ten chosen witches back in with me. Among the witches was Alpha Aidan and Prime Elder Jennifer Wasutke. Ms. Wasutke evidently felt the need to keep a close eye on us but Aidan just wanted to add to my already monumental male drama.

Other than the two I already knew, there were representatives from each of the remaining clans and an extra one from Flight and Beckoning. All I could think was; great, two necromancers running loose in a fairy castle, that's not asking for trouble at all.

As soon as I had everyone settled into their quarters, I set up a meeting for all of us within one of the libraries (fairies liked their books and there were three libraries in the High Council Castle). The High Councils were leaving the grunt work to my team, which included my Star's Guard, Raza, Councilman Teagan, the telepath twins, a few extinguishers, a handful of hunters, and the ten witches. It was a pretty big team but this was a weighty matter and even though the Councils were giving us free rein, they'd be expecting frequent reports.

The Coven was already packing up and heading to the airport, to follow whatever leads they could find. We would have to find our own angle. You may think I'd leap right into something magical to help us or even try some psychic means but sometimes the best investigative work is done through the simplest ways. Or maybe I just couldn't think of any helpful magic at the moment.

"Councilman Teagan," I said after we'd all settled at one of the study tables in the library. "Did you or any of your group happen to bring a laptop with you?"

"Of course," Teagan pulled a little laptop out of his briefcase and placed it on the table. "What do you need to look up?"

"Do we have access to the US Air Traffic Control's record of the flight of our missing plane?" I asked.

"I can get access," Teagan nodded and started tapping away at the keys. After a few minutes he declared, "I have it," and spun the laptop to face me. "As you can see, the plane made it all the way to New Mexico before it simply disappeared."

"New Mexico," I mused. "Can you get an exact location?"

"Ummm," he turned the laptop back around and frowned at the screen."

"Sir?" One of the extinguishers leaned in and tapped a few things. "There you go."

"Thank you," Teagan smiled at the man and then looked up at me. "It was... um," he cleared his throat.

"What?" I frowned and everyone else went still, focused on the fumbling councilman.

"Roswell," Teagan cleared his throat again. "It disappeared right over Roswell, New Mexico."

"Shut up," I gave a disbelieving chuckle and reached for the laptop. He pushed it over to me and I stared at the screen in disbelief. "Well, I'll be damned. It looks like aliens stole our plane."

"Aliens?" Raza frowned at me.

"Roswell is home to the site of a famous UFO crash and has been the location of numerous UFO sightings over the years," I explained. "It's like a Mecca for alien enthusiasts."

"What is an alien enthusiast?" Raza asked like he wasn't sure if he wanted to know.

"Someone who not only believes in the existence of extra-terrestrials but who is obsessed by them," I shrugged.

"Do you believe in extra-terrestrials?" Raza lifted a brow at me.

"Well yeah, obviously," I huffed and he gaped at me. I lifted an eyebrow and smiled wide. "I'm looking at one."

"Extra-terrestrial... something from another land," he nodded. "Yes, I guess that's what we are."

"But UFO sightings are not fey," Teagan protested. "We're speaking of other entities entirely."

"And do you think there are other entities?" I asked him. "I mean, what do you think of UFOs?"

"Honestly," he shrugged. "I'm not sure. As you said yourself, fairies are aliens so how could they be the only ones?"

"I don't think it's a question of whether we're the only ones or not," Tiernan mused. "More of a question of why these other aliens would travel so far to come to Earth and how would they accomplish this feat? We have raths to make travel easy for us. Our planets have been connected from the beginning but other aliens would have to travel through galaxies to reach Earth."

"That's why they need spaceships, duh," I grinned at him and laughed when he rolled his eyes.

"Perhaps a little less levity when we're trying to find my son, Princess Seren?" Raza set a stoic stare on me.

"I'm sorry," I sobered. "You're right. So lets get back to the fact that the plane went missing right over this area where UFOs have been seen frequently."

"Back to the aliens?" Aidan asked with a lifted brow.

"I'm not saying aliens are involved," I shook my head. "But I think the location and what it's known for could be relevant."

"I agree," Teagan nodded.

"Perhaps," Elder Wasutke muttered. "Or perhaps it's just a way of leading us off course. Or of telling us, in a round about manner, who they are... aliens from Fairy."

I shot her a glance, wondering if she intended on making the investigation difficult for us, but she didn't say any more. She just sat and watched me with her beady black eyes. Okay, maybe that was a little unfair. Her eyes were creepy, not beady.

"Do any of you know of a witch who could make an entire plane invisible?" I asked the witches.

"You aren't supposed to be investigating witches," Wasutke pointed at me accusingly. "So never mind what we can or cannot do."

"I understand but we're collaborating because we're not sure who is behind this," I said reasonably. "If we can rule out that a witch could do something like this, then I can move on."

"The Coven will rule it out," she crossed her arms.

259

"No witch that I know of can do such a thing," one of the Beckoning witches stated.

Her name was Sarah Jacobson and she was a tiny thing; very pretty, catching the eye of several of my Guard already. Though once they found out what she could do and whom her ancestors most likely were, she became less attractive to them. Still, she had a calm and intelligent face, with sober sepia eyes and round cheeks like pearly peaches. She was quiet until she had something important to say and she listened to everything people around her said. I liked her immediately.

Wasutke shot Sarah an annoyed glance but didn't say anything. In fact, when Sarah stared back, Wasutke lowered her gaze. That widened my eyes. So a common member of Beckoning was more powerful than a Prime Elder of Flight? Interesting.

"Thank you, Sarah," I smiled at her. "Now, a question for all the fey in the room; could a fairy do it?"

"It's a type of glamour," Conri shrugged. "I would imagine that it's possible but you'd have to be very powerful and I'm not sure it would erase the plane from the sight of human machines."

"Hmmm, good point," Tiernan nodded. "Glamour magic tricks the eye but not radar and such."

"Like the heat sensors the paranormal team used," I agreed.

"Okay, let's think about this rationally," Extinguisher Mark Sloane, the one who had helped Teagan locate the exact place the plane went missing, had inherited the dark Sloane looks; sooty hair, fair skin, and mossy eyes. He was also quite intelligent, as evidenced by his next words, "ATC tracks planes using two types of radar; primary and secondary. Primary radar will find an object using projected radio signals but secondary radar relies on a transponder inside the plane itself. Every commercial plane is equipped with a transponder; it's how they keep in contact with

ATC when they're more than a hundred-fifty miles out over the sea, where primary radar signals get lost."

"Okay," I gaped at Extinguisher Sloane and then glanced at Teagan, who gave me a huge grin. "But they weren't over the ocean, so even if the secondary radar went out, the primary should have still picked them up."

"You weren't following close enough," Sloane winked at me. "Primary radar picks up objects, I didn't say planes specifically."

"Yes but in this case, it's a plane," Wasutke grumbled.

"Is it?" Sloane lifted a brow and my jaw dropped.

"You're saying that if someone had the capability to manifest an object, something solid, beneath the plane, they could then remove the plane without anyone knowing?" I frowned, not even sure if I understood it.

"This is all hypothesis," Sloane held out his hands. "But going on what I know of the fey and their magic, I believe that a fairy could form a chunk of ice from the moisture in the air."

"We could," Tiernan whispered and looked at me in horror. "Weather magic."

"Cold weather magic," Sarah added. "That's the trace we found, remember?"

"Cold like ice," Sloane nodded. "So say this person, we won't blame a fairy just yet because there are weather witches, are there not?" He looked to the Storm witch and the man grudgingly nodded. "This *person* could form a block of ice beneath the plane, holding it aloft with magic while the plane was diverted. ATC would most likely see the diversion but when they saw the ice keeping on course, they'd probably think it was a glitch. Then the ice could be melted and turned into rain, making the plane appear

261

to disappear."

"Holy river hags!" I exclaimed. "We're not just looking for one person, this has got to be the work of a team."

"Yes, Ambassador," Sloane smiled. "I believe you're right. I think one individual pulled off the ice maneuver while the second averted the plane."

"But how would you do that?" Teagan mused.

"The only way I can imagine, would be the easiest," Sloane shrugged.

"It was the pilot," I whispered and Sloane smiled wider at me. "Sweet Goddess, our pilot stole the plane, didn't he?"

"It would make sense," Sloane gave me an apologetic look. "The pilot would be able to turn off the transponder and fly the plane a short distance away, where he could land it and no one would be the wiser."

"Why are you looking at me like that?" I asked him. "It wasn't a fairy-manned plane, the pilot was an extinguisher."

Shouting erupted all around me but I just sat back and let them vent. I was just as horrified as the humans were. To think that an extinguisher would turn traitor was... well it was unthinkable. About as unthinkable as a hunter betraying the fey. But then, they wouldn't have the word traitor if no one ever betrayed anyone.

"Silence!" Teagan stood and pounded the table with his fist. The extinguishers quieted and since they were the only ones making a fuss, the room went silent. "Ambassador Seren is right. The plane was one I lent her to transport the raven mockers. They were flying it back to Tulsa and so, the pilot would have been an extinguisher."

"No," Extinguisher Jason Murdock shook his head. "He

had to have been taken. Someone killed him or captured him and took his place."

"That is completely possible," I said and Murdock gave me a grateful look. "All I'm saying is that the scheduled pilot would have been human... and if he were replaced, it would have to be with another human or the raven mockers would have known and been suspicious."

"True," Teagan nodded. "So it's definitely a human group that we're after, be it extinguisher or witch."

"We should probably share this information with the Coven," I looked to Sarah because she seemed like the most reasonable one there and it also seemed like she was in charge."

"Tristan," she looked to her left, where the other member of Beckoning sat. "Call Gabriel, please."

He nodded and stood, going into a corner to make the call.

"If it's a human, it must be one of yours," Wasutke sneered. "A witch wouldn't go against the Coven's wishes."

"The Coven has made no decree concerning this matter," Aidan stared down Wasutke. "There is no order to disobey, if say, a person or group were trying to fulfill a vendetta."

"How dare you?" Wasutke stood, her face stretching into a horrifying mask.

"Sit down, Jennifer," Sarah said calmly.

Jennifer Wasutke, Elder of Flight, sat down as she was told.

"Who are you?" I asked Sarah. "I mean, as far as rank goes?"

"I am Vex of Eastern America," she smiled sweetly.

"What does that mean?" I asked.

"Allow me," Aidan said to Sarah and she nodded. "A Vex is like an extinguisher really, a sort of military enforcer of our laws."

"So you do have laws?" Teagan asked.

"Of course we have laws," Sarah laughed. "And anyone who breaks them shall be vexed."

"Not hexed?" I joked.

"Being vexed is far worse, believe me," she waggled her brows at me.

"So you're kinda like the Bogeyman of witches?" I waggled my brows back.

"I can be scary to lawbreakers," she shrugged. "But I pose no threat to those who obey the Coven."

"And you're from the East?" My lips started to twitch.

"Don't say it," she grimaced.

"I have to," I said apologetically. "You're the Wicked Witch of the East!"

"Oh, Seren," Tiernan groaned but Sarah laughed.

"That's not at all what I thought you were going to say," Sarah shook her head. "I thought it was going to be a *Practical Magic* quote and you were gonna do the; *witch, witch, you're a bitch*, chant."

"Oh, that's a good one too," I commended her, "but it seems more offensive."

"Yes, very," Sarah laughed harder. "Thus my warning."

"The Coven has been notified," Tristan said as he resumed his seat. "The investigation team is still en route to San Francisco but they'll be informed as soon as they land."

"Excellent," Sarah nodded. "Perhaps now we should look into the original pilot of the plane?"

Another angry extinguisher muttering went around the table.

"It has to be done," I declared. "This way we can rule him out and we need to make sure he's not dead in a ditch somewhere. But beyond that, I think we need to establish a search zone around the last know position of the plane. How far do you think someone with weather magic could carry a massive piece of ice, Fred?" I asked Storm witch.

"Please," Fred sighed, pushing back a lock of dirty blonde hair. "My name is Frederick."

"Okay," I rolled my eyes. "Frederick."

"Perhaps forty meters," Frederick, the Storm witch huffed.

"And how far do you think a plane could fly before it wouldn't be able to pass as a glitch?" I asked Extinguisher Mark.

"Perhaps fifty miles," Mark offered.

"Alright," I looked around the table. "So we go back forty meters from where the plane was last spotted and then make a search radius of fifty miles out from that spot."

"I'll call the Albuquerque House and ask them to send a team there," Teagan pulled his phone out.

"Good, meanwhile, let's look into that pilot," I said to Mark.

"Would you mind if I used your laptop, Councilman?"

Extinguisher Mark asked Teagan.

"By all means," Councilman Teagan got up to make his phone call. "You seem to get more out of it than I do."

"And if the pilot is alive when we find him," Alexis added.

"We'll get more out of him too," Alex finished for her.

"I'm going to go see if I can round up some refreshments for us," I said as I stood. "I think it's going to be a long night." I waved Alexis over to me as I headed for the door. Before I even asked her my question, she answered.

"No, Elder Watsuke is not behind this."

Chapter Forty

The pilot's name was Extinguisher Nolan Kavanaugh, no direct relation to the twins, and he had an exemplary record. He had scored high in all his psychic and physical tests, had completed twenty-eight warrants, had mentored young extinguishers who had lost their immediate family units, and had earned his pilot license at age twenty-six. Since then, he had flown exclusively, leaving fairy chasing to the other extinguishers. There had never been an issue with his flying and on the one occasion that he experienced a mechanical malfunction, he heroically landed the plane in a cornfield, saving the lives of all aboard as well as those upon the ground.

It was hard to see him as a traitor.

His body had not been found, nor were any unidentified remains found in the area. So if he wasn't a traitor, he must have been taken aboard the plane. Which meant that he was probably dead since a hostage would have looked suspicious to the raven mockers. That alone had me stressed. Not just because we may have lost an excellent extinguisher but because it meant that whomever was behind this found killing to be an easy option.

"Do you think my son is still alive?" Raza seemed to echo my thoughts.

"I don't know but I sincerely hope so," I whispered as I looked around the quiet room.

People had formed groups to conduct research and talk things over in. Unsurprisingly, the groups were defined by race and this stressed me even more. It was like no matter what realm I was in, I was constantly trying to overcome segregation. First between the Seelie and Unseelie, and now in HR it was between the Fey, the Humans, and the Witches.

"I can be monstrous," Raza lowered his voice too. "I can be horribly cruel. But never would I hurt a child and there were children with my son."

"I know," I swallowed hard. "Whomever is behind this, they're far more monstrous than we are."

"You think you're monstrous?" His face went blank with surprise.

"I think I could be," my whisper went even lower. "I think at times, I want to be."

"Like when you hear that your grandmother forced you and your mother to be sent from Fairy?" His metallic eyes warmed and softened.

"Yes," I admitted. "But is vengeance upon her worth the price of becoming her?"

"You will never become your grandmother," he said with deep sincerity. "She has always been as she is, even when she was a child. You have a kinder heart, one that can conquer any monster."

I blinked, unsure which monster he was referring to; mine or his. The warmth in his eyes turned into heat and I cleared my throat, looking away from it before I caught fire.

"It cannot be a fairy," Raza went back to our original conversation blithely. "At least not one of the old ones. No one who has ever been in a magical war would want to start another."

"I get that," I sighed. "Just that little glimpse of fighting between us and the Coven was horrible."

"Now imagine battles like that a hundred times larger,

going on for years," Raza's jaw clenched. "No, they can't possibly know what they're trying to bring about. If they do, they are more evil than even child killers."

"So you fought in the Human-Fey war?" I asked him.

"We both did," Tiernan said as he placed a cup of coffee down before me and resumed his seat beside mine.

"Really?" I looked over to my boyfriend. "You've never talked about it."

"It's not something one wants to speak of," Raza answered for him.

"So you *are* pretty old," I teased Tiernan, trying to get the frown off his face.

"I'm still not telling you," he gave me a little grin.

"Well, if you fought in the war, you're older than my father," I mused and then frowned. "That's kind of gross."

"It would be if I *looked* older than your father," Tiernan chuckled.

"They found the plane!" Councilman Teagan stood and shouted.

"They what?" I sat forward, dislodging Cat, who had been fast asleep across my feet.

"What about the raven mockers?" Raza asked immediately.

"No, I'm sorry," Teagan tucked his phone away. "It's just the empty plane but at least we have a lead to investigate. Now who wants to go to New Mexico?"

"As long as the plane isn't piloted by an extinguisher, I'm in," Sarah smirked.

Chapter Forty-One

The Human Council's plane was found in a dry stretch of land between Roswell and Artesia, New Mexico. Artesia had an airport so we were able to arrive pretty close to our destination. We were met by an extinguisher team who then drove us to the abandoned plane.

It crouched in the dry grass like an injured animal, left to die by a cruel master. The main windows stared mournfully at us as our SUV pulled in front of the plane. I jumped out of the vehicle and made my way over to it, cocking my head to look at the deflated ramp hanging forlornly from the open door like the tongue of an overheated hound dog.

"I sense no weather magic here," Tiernan stared around the bleak place.

"Which lends credence to the theory that this was a team," Teagan narrowed his eyes on the plane and then turned to the extinguishers who had discovered it. "What did you find on board?"

"We haven't gone inside yet," one of the men said. "Orders were to wait for you, Councilman."

"Right," Teagan sighed. "I suppose we'll need to send someone for a ladder then."

"Not necessary," Tiernan said as he escorted me forward.

I knew exactly what he was about, so I put my arms over his shoulders and hugged him tight as he used air magic to lift us up to the level of the door. I climbed aboard and Tiernan motioned to Ainsley. Sir Ainsley went over to Councilman Teagan and motioned towards the plane.

"Uh, that's alright," Teagan smiled nervously. "I think I'll let the Ambassador handle this."

"I would like to see the plane," Sarah stepped forward. Ainsley straightened and then bowed before offering her his arm. "Oh, how sweet," Sarah laughed and took the offered arm.

He escorted her to the plane but when she reached for his shoulders, he swept her up into his arms instead of merely holding her by the waist. I shook my head at the antiquated advances of my knight and went further into the plane as Ainsley lifted Sarah up into the cabin. A few seconds later, Jennifer Wasutke joined us as well.

Inside, the plane was eerily quiet and nearly empty. I say nearly because there was still one passenger on board. The pilot. Extinguisher Nolan Kavanaugh was belted into a seat, his arms hanging limp at his sides and his sightless eyes staring straight ahead. His face was set in a rictus of fear, so chilling that goosebumps lifted on my arms.

"Well that's interesting," Sarah said from behind me.

"Interesting?" Ainsley asked in horror.

"Sir Ainsley, can you notify Councilman Teagan that we've found the body of Extinguisher Kavanaugh?" I asked gently.

"Yes, Princess," Ainsley headed back to the door in obvious relief.

"There's not a mark on him," Sarah said as she looked over the body. "I believe this man was scared to death."

"It takes a lot to scare an extinguisher," I narrowed my eyes on the body. "Are you sure there are no wounds?"

"Absolutely," Sarah stood, setting her hands to her hips.

"Lack of wounds can mean several things," Elder Wasutke shook her head. "They could have healed him, as we do our victims after we take a heart."

I set wide eyes on her, surprised that she would say something that might incriminate her own people.

"What?" She huffed at me. "Flight didn't do this, I can feel that his heart remains."

"Something scared him so deeply that it stopped his heart," Sarah reasserted. "Believe me, I'm familiar with the situation and the results of it."

"I'll bet you are," Tiernan muttered and headed away from the body.

I followed after him, looking over the rest of the plane. Every overhead bin I opened was empty and nothing was to be found beneath the seats. Had the kidnappers allowed the raven mockers to take their luggage with them? That seemed unusually considerate for a bunch of abducting murderers. I frowned and went further down the aisle, stopping to stare at an abandoned teddy bear. I swallowed hard and then took a deep, calming breath. But my calm was shattered when a thud echoed through the cabin. Startled, I turned and saw that Raza had come aboard.

"I can't even scent him here," Raza stared at the nearly empty plane like it could confess its secrets to him. "Where is my son?"

With heavy footfalls he made his way over to us and looked down at the item I'd been staring at. One elegant ebony hand reached out, catching the fluffy terracotta teddy within its claws. Raza put the stuffed animal to his nose and inhaled. He closed his eyes briefly and when he opened them, they were glowing.

"I have them," he declared triumphantly.

"What?" I gaped at him.

"He has the scent," Tiernan smiled.

"This way," Raza cast the bear aside and rushed from the plane. At the cabin door he spread his wings and jumped.

"Raza stop!" I called. "We can't all follow you like that and this is HR, you'll be seen!"

"You can follow," Raza shouted to Tiernan. "Can't you, Count?"

"If you keep it to a slow pace," Tiernan agreed.

"Then glamour yourself and follow the birdie," Raza smiled and a haze covered him. In seconds he was gone and a large black bird hovered before us.

"I am so sick of ravens," I muttered. Then I called down to Teagan, "We've caught their trail. Raza is leading us to them, I'll call you when we arrive."

"Wait!" Teagan cried but the bird was already flying away and Tiernan had launched us after it, using as much speed as he could.

"Glamour yourself, Seren," he said.

"Oh!" I hurried to conceal myself as Tiernan chased after Raza.

"You're not going anywhere without me," Wasutke cried as she too launched herself into the air.

Shadows immediately enveloped her, turning her shape into a sooty fog. Sparks streaked behind her as she flew, like she was a mass of smoking tar. I didn't see any wings but then it was hard to see much of anything within that nebulous shape. As I stared, a head turned to me from within the angry cloud, its face was shrouded but I could still make out a gaping mouth, stretched open to emit a sound like the call of a diving raven.

I looked away in annoyance.

We flew for at least twenty minutes before the bird descended in front of an old warehouse. It was clearly abandoned, with rusted metal walls and dirty broken windows. Grass had grown up around it like the beard on a homeless man; unkempt and scraggly. The raven disappeared as Raza's glamour fell and Tiernan set us down in patch of packed earth beside him. Then Raza went to the warehouse door and tore it from its hinges. He threw it aside and strode into the dark interior as Tiernan and I chased after him.

Then we stopped short. The place was empty, emptier than the plane had been. There was nothing inside except a single chair set in the center of the room. On the rusty metal seat was a black feather. Raza ran over to the chair and picked the feather up. He lifted it to his nose and inhaled. His exhale became a roar as he crushed the feather within his hand.

"I don't understand," I whispered. "Where are they?"

"Not here," Elder Wasutke's jaw clenched.

"I will incinerate them!" Raza shouted. "Whomever is behind this is already dead."

"They most certainly are," the witch agreed.

"The trail just ends here?" I asked Raza gently.

"Right here," he opened his palm and released the crushed remains of the feather.

"This makes no sense," I looked around at the oil stained

cement floors and the pitted metal beams spanning the ceiling. "How could it just end?"

"They must have removed the raven mockers from the plane in another location and then left the plane where we found it to throw us off," Tiernan surmised. "They could have taken the feather from a child at any time and then used it to pixie-lead us in the wrong direction."

Raza roared again, long and loud, and rust rained down on us from the ceiling.

Chapter Forty-Two

"We'll continue to search the area," Teagan was saying to a disconcertingly silent Raza.

He'd been quiet ever since we'd returned from that warehouse. Now we stood in front of the plane again and Raza just stared off into the distance, occasionally smiling maliciously like he was envisioning ripping someone's heart from their chest. Or entrails from their abdomen; I'm not sure what dragons preferred. He gave Teagan one of those smiles and the Councilman hurried away.

"They must have taken them somewhere nearby," I put a hand on Raza's shoulder and he jerked away from me, his head whipping around so he could give me a nasty glare. "Raza, I need your help here and you're no good to anyone like this." He started to growl at me, bringing his face down into mine, and I slapped him. Hard. "Snap out of it!"

Everyone stopped what they were doing to stare at me in horror... Raza included.

"Don't you dare pull this shit on me," I growled and stuck my face up into his. "I'm trying my best to help you. And I don't care who you are or what you can turn into, you will give me the respect I deserve as an ambassador, as an extinguisher, as a princess, and as your friend! Are we clear, dragon?"

"We're clear," Raza's eyes mellowed and he took a deep breath. "My apologies, Princess Seren. There are very few people brave enough to be my friend and I would hate to lose one of them."

"I have no idea what you're going through but I do know what it's like to lose someone you love, so I understand what grief can do to you," I took his hand, weaving my fingers through his. "You're son may still be alive and if he is, he needs you. He needs you rational and he needs you to use all the help you have available to you. So you can find him."

"Of course," Raza nodded and then dropped his voice so that only I could hear him. "Thank you. I've never known anyone who can calm my rage as you do, Seren."

"I'm good with beasts. Sometimes they make more sense to me than people," I smiled and slipped my hand from his to place it on Cat's head. She'd been standing beside me the whole time, confident in the both of us. She, like I, had seen what lurked beneath Raza's surface and now she wasn't afraid of him anymore.

"Animals are simple," Raza nodded. "They have simple needs; to eat, sleep, love, and live. All of their actions stem from those needs. Right now, my son's life is in danger and my love for him consumes me in a horrible aching way. I feel the instincts of an animal to protect its young. But you're right, I can't save him with the ferocity of a dragon, I must use the wits of a man."

"So what do those wits tell you?"

"That my son was never on that plane," he blinked, surprised at his own words.

"What?" I blinked back.

"I couldn't sense him, Seren," Raza's eyes cleared with sudden comprehension. "I couldn't sense *my own son*. Scents can't just be erased. They can covered by using something really strong, like a chemical that would confuse my senses, but there was nothing like that on the plane. Which means that my son hasn't been on that plane for significant amount of time, long enough for his scent to fade naturally."

"So if he didn't get on that plane in San Francisco," Tiernan said as he joined us, "then who did?"

"Now that is an excellent question, Count Shadowcall," Raza's eyes narrowed.

Chapter Forty-Three

"So..." I turned and smirked at Aidan over the back of my seat.

He had jumped into my SUV without asking, saying that he couldn't stand another minute with Jennifer Wasutke.

"Yes?" Aidan gave me a sexy look.

"Show us your dark mark," I waggled my eyebrows at him.

"My what?" He lost the come hither expression and just went hither, leaning towards me in confusion.

Tiernan and our extinguisher driver were laughing.

"Your clan tattoo," I explained. "You do have one, don't you?"

"Oh," he sat back with a chuckle. "Yeah, we all do but mine is in a rather inaccessible spot at the moment."

"I thought it was meant to identify you to other witches," Tiernan frowned.

"It is," Aidan shrugged. "But around the time I came of age to get the dark mark," he shot me a wink. "I was in a rebellious period and I didn't like the idea of *having* to do anything."

"You tattooed your ass, didn't you?" I said dryly.

"I absolutely did," Aidan confirmed and our driver let out a burst of laughter. "That way, whenever anyone asks me to prove my connection to my clan..."

"You can tell them to kiss your ass," the driver hooted.

"Precisely," Aidan nodded, very pleased with himself.

"At least tell us what it looks like," I huffed.

"Why? So you can add it to your files on the Coven?"

"Yeah," I said in my *duh* tone. "And if you could tell us about the other clan tattoos, that would be very helpful."

"I'm not..." he started to get upset but then stopped. "You know what? Fuck it, why not? It's not like knowing will do much for you."

"So what are they?" Tiernan slid his arm over the back of our seat and set his silver eyes on the Alpha.

"Well, they're not all that original, I'm afraid," Aidan sighed.

"A howling wolf?" The driver asked.

"No, even worse," Aidan rolled his eyes. "A crescent moon."

"Crescent?" I frowned. "Why not full?"

"Because when you draw a full moon simply, it's just a circle," Raza smirked.

"You got it, dragon-dude," Aidan nodded toward Raza. "They toyed with the idea of having just an empty circle but it didn't pass. So I've got a circle with a crescent moon in it, tattooed on my butt. At least it's not as bad as Bite; they have two free-standing fangs in their circle."

"Just a couple of floating fangs?" I chuckled.

"You got it."

"What does Beckoning have?" Tiernan asked.

"What else?" Aidan rolled his eyes (he was really good at it). "They have a skull."

"I wouldn't mind a skull," Conri mused from his seat beside Aidan.

"Yeah, the bastards get the best of everything," Aidan growled. "Tide has a wave, again so unoriginal I want to puke. Flame has.... anyone? Anyone?"

"A flame?" I offered.

"Ding, ding, ding, we have a winner," Aidan pointed at me.

"What does Storm have; a picture of one of the X-Men?" Conri asked.

"How the hell do you know the X-Men, Dude?" Aidan looked to Conri in surprise.

"I like the Human Realm," Conri shrugged. "I visit a lot."

"Yeah, I see that," Aidan flicked the sleeve of Conri's leather jacket.

"So is it a picture of Storm or what?" Conri smirked.

"No but good call," Aidan gave a huffing laugh. "They have a lightning bolt.

"Who do they think they are; Thor?" I laughed.

"Yeah, probably," Aidan grimaced. "Stormers are almost as uppity as Beckoners."

"Wait one second," Conri sat forward. "Stormers... Beckoners... Does that mean you call Flame witches flamers?"

"Yep," Aidan's grin stretched wide. "Isn't that fantastic?

They don't even get the joke."

"And Quake witches are quakers?" I smirked.

"Right again," Aidan pointed at me.

"That is hilarious," I shook my head. "Hey, what's their symbol; a rock?"

"No, a mountain," Aidan hooted.

I was about to respond when the Imperial March(aka Darth Vader's theme music) started playing from my phone. I gave a start as Aidan and our driver laughed.

"Everyone shush," I growled. "It's my Uncle Dylan. Hello?"

"Seren?"

"Yes?"

"The witches have been here, I assisted them as your father asked me to," he reported.

"Good but why are you calling me?"

"Because I wanted to make sure that you knew about what they found," he said grimly. "They asked me to pull the surveillance tapes from the day the raven mockers came through Gentry on their way to the airport."

"And?" I shot a look at Raza and he leaned forward eagerly. I held up my hand, "Hold on , Uncle Dylan, I need to put you on speaker."

"If you must," he huffed.

I pressed the button, "Alright, go ahead; Lord Raza and Tiernan are with me."

"I pulled the surveillance," Dylan started again. "And stood to the side as the witches watched. We only have cameras in the business areas, not down near the rath, so all we caught was their walk towards the elevators, but it was enough."

"Did you see my son?" Raza asked urgently.

"No, Lord Raza," Dylan said gently. "In fact, I didn't see any raven mockers at all."

"Repeat that please?" Tiernan asked.

"We have a very advanced surveillance system at Gentry. It's infused with magic to see through any glamour. We need to be sure of our employees and our guests," Dylan explained.

"Your cameras can see through fairy glamour?" I asked, impressed.

"Yes, so I'm absolutely certain when I tell you that not a single raven mocker came through the San Francisco Rath that day," Dylan said firmly. "It was a massive group of dullahans."

"Dullahans?" I whispered in horror.

"Yes," Dylan's voice had dropped too. "Suffice it to say that the witches were disturbed by the sight... as was I. You will probably be hearing from the witches soon. I just wanted to give you a heads up."

"Dullahans?" I whispered again, not quite believing that I'd heard correctly.

"Yes, Seren," Dylan sighed. "I've already called your father. He wants you back in Ireland immediately. Get on a plane and get out of New Mexico. You don't want to go up against an army of dullahans."

"An *army*?" I blinked. "We'd thought maybe a small group was behind this but an army?"

"The substitute pilot didn't need to be human," Tiernan said in bitter deduction, "because he didn't have to fool anyone. There were no mockers on the plane."

"Which means that your son is still in Fairy," I said to Raza.

"Yes, I surmised as much," Dylan added. "When I spoke to King Keir he told me that his men escorted the raven mockers to the rath but then left them there, thinking they could cross over at their own convenience. The raven mockers were free from suspicion and as such, the twilight knights felt no need to guard them. They left them to their own devices, as they would have any free fairy."

"So somewhere between the time the twilight knights rode away and the time the raven mockers lined up to enter the rath, something happened to them," I concluded.

"It would seem so and it would appear that dullahans had something to do with it," Dylan agreed. "King Keir has already dispatched knights to search the area. If they don't find any trace of the mockers, they'll expand their search until they do. We will find your son, Lord Raza. If for no other reason than he is one of ours."

"He's alive," I whispered to Raza and took his hand. "I know it. In Fairy, Danu can help him and I don't believe for one second that she would let a bunch of dullahans murder innocent fey."

"I'd like to believe that too but terrible things happen in Fairy all the time," Raza said grimly. "Thank you for the information, Duke Dylan."

"You're very welcome, Lord Raza," Dylan said sincerely. "Goodbye, Seren... go get on a plane."

"Yes, Uncle Dylan," I disconnected the call.

284

Chapter Forty-Four

Our group was traveling in six SUVs since there were close to forty of us when you included the team who picked us up from the airport. My SUV was in the middle so I didn't immediately see the ambush. All I knew was that our vehicle braked suddenly and I was thrown forward, jerking against my seatbelt strap. Cat slid into the back of the driver's seat, paws outstretched and clawing at the floor for purchase.

Then there was shouting, a lot of shouting, and everyone in my SUV jumped out onto the road to see what the ruckus was about. Tiernan was in front of me and I barreled into his back when he stopped suddenly. Cat started growling, setting herself to the side of me and staring at the thick treeline next to the road.

"Dullahans!" Tiernan shouted back to me and the rest of our team. "Only a heart shot will kill them! And if you have any gold, bring it out for them to see."

"Gold?" I asked.

"Dullahans are afraid of gold," Raza growled as he came up beside me and smiled savagely, his gold eyes beginning to glow.

"That's a strange thing to be afraid of," I remarked.

"It burns them, like iron does the rest of us," Tiernan's hands filled with light as he stared around us steadily.

"Well damn," I huffed sarcastically. "I left my solid gold dagger at home."

Aidan started to head off toward the other SUVs but Tiernan stopped him.

"We stay with the Princess," Tiernan looked over to Conri and the extinguisher who'd been driving our SUV, they both nodded.

"I need to help them," Aidan protested.

"Everyone here can handle themselves," Tiernan shook his head. "If we move, we'll play into our enemy's hands. We have to remain solid in our center or they'll break our group up."

"Right. Okay," Aidan nodded. "Then I'll watch our backs," he shifted to the front of the SUV, where he could watch the other side of the road.

Even as he moved, the rest of my Star's Guard rushed over to us, abandoning both extinguishers and witches in favor of protecting me. Well, it was kind of their job. They formed a circle around me and Cat, Sir Ian completing it beside Tiernan. Tiernan huffed, his plan shot to hell.

The witches in the last SUVs started shouting and bursts of light outlined their vehicles. Aidan looked over to his people in concern.

"Go," Tiernan said. "Do what you need to do. I guess it doesn't matter now."

"Good luck," Aidan said to us as he ran off towards the witches.

"Princess Seren," a raspy voice drew my attention to the treeline.

There stood a group of some of the most disturbing looking fairies I'd ever seen. I'd read about them both as an extinguisher in training and after I'd become princess. I knew that if you were close to death, a dullahan could call your name and kill you early. I knew they usually traveled with a wagon made of bones and skin, and if you stared at them too long, you'd be liable to get a bucket of blood thrown on you for your curiosity. I also knew they were the original headless horsemen.

Except these guys had left their wagons at home and they didn't seem to be headless at all, nor were they riding their famous black horses. They were afoot and when I looked closer, I realized that they had fastened their heads onto their necks with wide metal collars. I guess you didn't want to have to carry your head around when you went to war. It could get exhausting. Which made me wonder; how would their magic work in war? Wasn't everyone technically close to death when they went to battle? Did that mean these guys could just stand there and call out our names to kill us? Evidently not because one of them had just said my name, hadn't he?

"And who are you?" I called out over the sounds of battle surrounding us.

"My name is Malvin but you may call me Mal," the dullahan bowed, his stringy hair, the color of sun-bleached driftwood, slipped over his beady coal eyes for a second.

He pushed his hair back with a pallid hand and I swallowed hard, noting how his skin was both the color and consistency of moldy mozzarella. He was grinning so wide that the corners of his mouth reached the sides of his face... and he never stopped smiling. Nor did his eyes stop moving, flitting about to each of us and back again.

Cat growled and my Star's Guard lifted their swords.

"We know you're behind the abductions," I said to him as more dullahans exited the woods and spread out before us. "I am both Ambassador and Extinguisher and I'm in my right to extinguish all of you if you don't stand down."

287

"Oh, you can try," Mal spoke through the grin. "We outnumber you greatly and your companions are already being subdued."

I glanced to the side and saw that he was right, even though magic sparked and shouts filled the air, our side was being overcome by sheer numbers.

"But you made a fatal mistake, dullahan," Raza stepped forward and the dullahans paused, staring at his eyes like hypnotized snakes. "You stole my son."

"Lord Raza," Mal stuttered. "We had no idea you'd be with the Princess."

"Why would you try to kill me?" I shook my head. "Don't you realize that the Sluagh will be after you now?"

"We are not trying to kill or harm you in any way, Princess Seren," Mal held up his hands. "We merely need you to come with us, where you're comfort will be seen to until we release you at a later time."

"So that my father backs a war against the witches?" I lifted a brow.

"Exactly," Mal pulled a strange looking item from his belt.

It was golden cream in color, like old dice, and laced with silver wire. He flung it out and it draped beside him, clicking eerily together. My eyes widened as I realized what it was; his whip. All dullahans carried a whip made from a human spine. The protrusions of the spine were dipped in metal and were sharpened to razor-sharp edges.

"You may have succeeded," Raza mused and the darting eyes of every dullahan once more settled on him. "Had you not taken Rayetayah. Now you will all die."

"Lord Raza, your son is well cared for, as is all of his people," Mal held up a conciliatory hand. "They are safe within our village of Dathadair. They are comfortable and none are mistreated. I promise you that."

"I'm happy to hear that he lives," Raza said and the dullahans started to look relieved... until Raza continued. "So you will die quickly instead of being tortured slowly. You may thank me now."

"Lord Raza," Mal shrank back from Raza's glowing stare. "Please, we are only doing what we believe is right! You've seen the witches, our offspring. We created monsters and we must correct our mistake."

"Monsters?" I mused. It was funny how perception worked. Eye of the beholder and all that.

"Yes, we may appear monstrous to you," Mal's eyes were back to darting about. "But we are as the Goddess intended us to be and we serve our purpose. The children we fathered on humans were not meant to be born, nor were the children which followed them. The magic has mutated and become truly monstrous. They are unnatural creatures."

"Perhaps they were a mistake," I pushed Conri a little to the side so I could face Mal better. "But they are here now. They live and it's not for you to say who has that right."

"Isn't it?" Mal cocked his head. "We know death, Princess. We *live* death. We hear its call and help it along its way. We know exactly who must or must not die."

"I care not for your reasons," Raza spread his wings and stepped forward, causing the dullahans to take a step back out of the significant shadow he cast. "You are unseelie. You know better than to offend me. There is no excuse for what you've done."

"I promise you, Lord Raza," Mal whined. "We had no

289

intentions of harming your son. He's alive and well. We simply want war with the witches so we may kill these abominations."

"*You* are an abomination," Raza took another step and started to shift, "to want a war after you've seen what magic can do in battle. And I intend to stop you before you get your wish."

Yet, instead of running, as I'd thought they would, the dullahans pulled back their whips and attacked Raza before he could finish his transformation. It was a bold move and perhaps a brilliant one; kill the dragon-djinn before he becomes a dragon. It was probably their only shot at survival. But my knights didn't even pause, they instantly went to Raza's defense, launching magic into the fray as they simultaneously slashed with steel. Everything became louder; the clang of weapons, the shouts of men, and the roar of magic. But then I lifted myself off the ground, hovering between earth and sky, and spread my arms out wide.

The world went quiet, the chaos fading into the heartbeat that filled my ears. Magic rushed up my limbs and out of my hands, not bothering to fill my fingertips first. It simply flared bright and powerful, out into the twirling mass of friends and foes. I didn't worry for one second about striking the wrong person. My magic was an extension of myself and I knew that it knew who to hit.

Dullahans screamed as they were wrapped in thick vines, black as a witch's cat, and pierced by thorns the size of spear heads. Flames coasted along the swirling lengths like ballet dancers across a stage, beautiful really. And like most beautiful things, they were deadly; two dullahans fell to the ground to writhe and scream until their hearts caught fire. Once those organs burned, the dullahans went silent.

Raza pulled free of the slicing whips and completed his shift behind the wall of my Guard. Then he launched himself up into the air. It was hard to look away from the magnificent sight of a blood-red dragon against the cool New Mexico sky. Even more difficult when he made a dramatic turn and swooped down to scoop up two dullahans. A cracking sound echoed over the roar of battle as Raza broke dullahan backs and then pierced each chest with a long talon. The bodies were thrown carelessly to the ground as he dove for more victims like a heron diving for fish.

The dullahans who had been battling the rest of our group, abandoned their fight to come to the aid of their floundering brothers. Every element raged in the air around us as fairy fought fairy; shards of ice flying like spears, whirlwinds picking up victims and throwing them yards away, rocks rumbling underfoot, and of course fire blasting through it all.

This was why Danu desperately wanted peace between her children and why Raza thought these fairies were abominations to seek war. We were never meant to fight each other. When humans battle, they leave corpses behind. Sometimes they may burn buildings or tear down cities. That is horrible, yes. But when fairies fight, they destroy the very earth. They bring down the heavens and scoop up the sea. They tear down mountains and level forests. They can lay waste to the world with their fury.

The only weapon humanity that matched the level of destruction the fey could produce, was the atomic bomb... and that was originally a fairy design. Don't believe me? That quote which Oppenheimer (father of the atomic bomb) used from the Bhagavad-Gita; *Now I am become death, the destroyer of worlds*, was ironically documentation of the previous version of the atomic bomb; the fairy version which used magic to split atoms instead of science. It had been used in the Fey-Human Wars and was one of the reasons we plead for peace in the end. Yes, I hate to admit it, but it was us humans who ended up waving the white flag.

Actually, the fey were responsible for several catastrophes that history has either labeled myth or Nature. Look up Mohenjo-daro; an ancient city in Pakistan, and you'll see proof of the fey-atom bomb being used. Pompeii was actually fey fire magic, used to cause a volcanic eruption and the Antioch earthquake was fey earth magic. Floods, heatwaves, hurricanes, they brought the forces of Nature against us. So in the end, we had asked for a truce and the fey had given in. Why? Because even though it's much better to be the cause of such destruction than the victim of it; war isn't fun for anyone and the fey didn't really want to rule the Earth, just be allowed to visit it.

So we signed a truce and the fey buried that nightmarish fey-A-bomb in some fairy vault, vowing never to use it again. And by the way, referring to it as the F-bomb is not appropriate. At least that's what my councilman history teacher told me. Unfortunately, the image of that fairy weapon had already been planted in our genetic memory and several years after the Fey-Human truce had been signed, a scientist hypothesized that an atom could be split and our own version of the atomic bomb was created. I was told that the fairies had wept for us.

Tears now poured down my own cheeks as I slaughtered dullahans. Yes, they were hard to look at but they were still children of Danu and their deaths were like brands upon my soul. Still, they were already doomed. They had signed their own warrants of extinguishment the moment they abducted the raven mockers. Even if I allowed them to live, the Councils would surely find them guilty and sentence them to death. Unless...

"Stop!" I called out but the battle waged on. "I said cease!" My voice rumbled out of me, amped up by my magic, and everyone froze. "Dullahans, you are guilty of breaking the truce. You are guilty of treason against your court and against Fairy. But I will offer you leniency if you return those you've stolen and confess to the Councils as you have made confession to me."

"We have broken no truce," Mal, who miraculously still lived, called out to me. "We plot against witches, not humans."

"Witches are human but even were they not, you have murdered an extinguisher," I declared and Mal went silent. "His name was Nolan Kavanaugh and he had no part in your evil. You have broken the truce."

"One of us has committed murder but there he lies," Mal pointed to a blackened tangle of vines. "You have already extinguished him, Princess. And as far as treason; we are not traitors. The fey we abducted are twilight, not unseelie. There is no law against that."

"But one of them is my son," Raza growled. "And so you have betrayed your fellow fey after all. And I am not as lenient as the Council."

"Neither is Flight," Elder Wasutke added as she joined us.

"Raza," I floated back to the ground and stepped over to the dragon. One wing came down over my head as I laid a hand on his massive leg. "Will you let go of your vengeance if they release the raven mockers?"

Raza growled.

"I understand your anger but Raye is safe," I slid my hand over the glassy scales sympathetically.

"And I know exactly where he is," Raza's long neck curved so he could look down at me. "As soon as I'm done killing these dullahans, I'll return to Fairy and kill the rest of them."

"I'd be happy to join you, dragon," Jennifer Wasutke offered.

The dullahans muttered, drawing back and together.

"And extinguish an entire race?" I asked Raza gently.

"They were going to extinguish us," Sarah walked up and stared hard at Mal. "So you are my ancestors? I would have thanked you for the dark gift of my magic, if you hadn't tried to kill me. As it stands, I'm inclined to use it against you."

"And so here we are," I sighed and left the shadow of Raza's wing. "Facing death and extinction. All because some fairies bred with humans centuries ago."

"No one should be able to bring back the dead," Mal hissed, losing his grin for a moment. "The soul leaves and the flesh rots. To bring it back into a decaying prison is evil. We cannot bear to know that we have birthed such blasphemy." Mal shook his head at Sarah. "Such a pretty face and a little body, to hold such a malignant magic. But that is the point, isn't it? We are honest in what we are, we dullahans. We look like death and we bring death. But you deceive. You are not true to who you are. You disgust me; you foul, villainous creature. You're an affront to Nature and the Goddess!"

"Alright, easy now," I held up my hands as Sarah's eyes narrowed. "We get it, you don't like your children. Well, whose fault is that? You should have used protection." I grimaced as Conri burst into laughter. "But this is not a typo you can just erase. These are people. You helped to birth a new race and that cannot be evil. A person cannot be evil, not innately. I don't believe that. Sarah and her kind have a choice, as do all of us. They can use their magic in whichever way they wish but they will have to accept the consequences of their choices. If we killed everyone with a dark power, most of Fairy would be dead, you included," I pointed to Mal.

"We are on the verge of negotiating a truce with the witches," Tiernan added. "This truce will help to prevent the evil you speak of."

"But that's all they are," Mal spat. "What will she do, if she can't raise the dead?"

"I can speak to them," Sarah said calmly. "I can bring peace to families whose loved ones have died unexpectantly. I can end disputes and give hope. There is more to my magic than death. There is more to *me* than death."

294

"I have never raised the dead," Tristan added, turning Mal's grin into a gape. "I don't believe it's right. I divert the energy into spellwork. There is much more that we can do, just as there is more that you can do besides bring death."

"Such sorrow," Alexis came up behind me holding her brother's hand. In their other hands they held bloody, iron swords.

"Such integrity," Alex added. "You gave your children that," he said to Mal. "I see your true intentions, Malvin Skinner."

The dullahan looked sharply at the telepath.

"And they are good," Alexis added, "if misguided. You act in the name of your Goddess but is this what she'd truly want?"

"Shouldn't you trust that your children received more than just magic from you?" Alex went on. "They know death like you do and they understand the heavy responsibility that has been laid upon them."

The dullahans looked to each other in silence, smiles frozen on their grotesque faces. Then finally, Mal spoke.

"Perhaps we have been rash."

"Seriously?" Conri huffed. "Rash, he says."

"You will have to face the Council for your crimes," I said gently. "But it would go a long way in your favor if you would release your prisoners and come to the High Council of your own free will."

"I think I have a better idea," Mal shared a secret look with his fellow dullahans. "We'll hold onto our guests until the Councils issue a pardon to all dullahans."

"What?" I gaped as Raza growled.

"Harm us, Lord Raza, and your son will be killed," Mal's

voice was regretful. "If we don't report back to the others, they'll know that we are compromised and they will kill all of the prisoners."

"Now you shall die slowly," Raza rumbled.

"The dullahan speaks the truth," Alex confirmed.

"Do you really want to risk your son?" Mal shot back. "Get us a pardon and all of the prisoners will be released; alive and well. We'll give you a week to speak to the Councils on our behalf and scry us with their decisions. After that, I can't guarantee the safety of our guests."

"You're blackmailing both Councils?" I asked in shock. "Taking hostages like bank robbers?"

"I'll do whatever I have to do to ensure my people's safety," Mal sighed. "And I don't believe the Councils will pardon us any other way."

"I know where Dathadair is," Raza growled. "You're making a very poor decision."

"The Coven will find you, wherever you hide, and we will destroy you!" Wasutke added her shout to Raza's. "You cannot hold my people hostage without paying a price."

"Come anywhere near our village and your son shall be the first to die, Lord Raza," Mal declared. "Followed shortly by one of your witches," he sneered at Wasutke and then waved to his men. They disappeared into the forest as Raza roared.

Chapter Forty-Five

Fire shot out in curling streams of citrine and diamond to blast the trees in front of me down to cinders. My body started to shake as Raza literally lost his cool. I wasn't sure if I could talk him down this time but luckily, I didn't have to. He regained control himself; shifting back to man form and dropping to his knees to wail as he pounded the earth with his fists.

Everyone just gaped as the monster became simply a father, tormented by the possibility of his child's death. I rushed over and laid my hand to his bent head as I knelt beside him. He didn't look at me, just lowered his wings around us and used them to pull me in closer. I slid my hand across his shoulders and just held him as he breathed hard, trying to get his emotions under control.

Finally, he sighed and looked up at me. We didn't say anything, just stared at each other. He knew what I would have said, I saw that in his eyes, so I knew that I didn't have to say it. We would get them back, at any price. Neither of us would stop until all of those people were safe again. I wiped the tears from his face swiftly and smoothed his hair back into place before nodding curtly.

He squared his shoulders, stood, and took a deep breath, then held his hand down to me. I took it and let him help me stand. Then I gave him a little grin and waved at his nudity. He shrugged and folded his wings so that the tips angled in front of his most personal parts.

"Does anyone have an extra pair of pants?" I called back to the others before I smirked at Raza. "Why do you keep getting naked?"

"Why do you keep trying to clothe me?" He shot back.

"Because you're much less intimidating when you have clothes on," I shook my head and walked the few steps back to where everyone had gathered.

Tiernan pulled me off to the side,"I understand, I do. But if I have to watch you comfort that dragon one more time, I just may end up smashing my fist into his forlorn face."

"Noted," I nodded with a smile.

"So what now?" Sarah asked everyone in general. "Do you think your Councils will issue the pardons?"

"I don't know," I sighed. "They may, in light of the lives it would save."

"Or they may decide they don't want to negotiate with terrorists," Councilman Teagan added.

"They're not going to help us," Wasutke scoffed. "We're on our own."

"If we attack them, we put my son at risk," Raza joined us and accepted a pair of pants from Ainsley. "Thank you," he nodded to my knight.

"Anything to get you covered," Ainsley chuckled.

"I am a perfectly normal looking dragon-djinn," Raza huffed. "The weapon between my legs is nothing compared to what the rest of me can do."

"And on that note," I blinked wide eyes at the others. "Let's get back to deciding on a course of action."

"I'd like to bring the Coven team in on this," Sarah said. "They'll ask to be included as soon as we update them anyway."

"I'm alright with that," I nodded. "Councilman Teagan?"

"Yes, that's fine," Teagan agreed.

"Well of course we're bringing them in on it," Jennifer Wasutke huffed. "We found the culprits and we know where our people are."

"Thank you, Elder Wasutke," Sarah said snidely and then gave Tristan a look.

Tristan walked away as he pulled out his cell phone.

"Would you rather wait till we rejoin them before we make a decision?" I asked Sarah.

"That would probably be best or we might end up making the same arguments twice," she sighed. "They should still be in San Francisco and that's where we were headed anyway, correct?"

"Yes, there's a rath there which we can use to get to Twilight," I looked to Tiernan.

"I don't know how you're father will feel about it," he answered my unspoken question.

"We might need to bring them with us," I argued.

"Into Fairy?" Frederick, the Storm witch, asked. "Are you discussing taking us into the Fairy Realm?"

"It may be a possibility," I admitted. "But I'd have to speak to my father before I bring any witches into our kingdom."

"I would like to volunteer to go, if you do decide to allow us in," Frederick's eyes flashed eagerly.

"Why, Frederick," I teased. "This is the most animated I've seen you so far, and that includes the glimpse I had of you fighting dullahans."

"I would very much like to learn who my ancestors were," Frederick confessed. "Beckoning now is certain they are descended from dullahans. Storm would be very excited to learn whom we are descended from as well and I believe I may be able to trace our roots in Fairy."

"I don't know about that," I frowned. "Your magic isn't one so easily traced. It's an elemental power and most fey have such abilities."

"We would have to learn more about the nuances of your magic," Tiernan offered when Frederick's shoulders slumped. "But honestly, this isn't the time. Perhaps after we sign a truce."

"Of course," Frederick brightened. "Do you think they'll allow us into Fairy if we sign?"

"Uh," I gaped at Tiernan, totally unprepared for that question.

"Most likely, they'll allow chaperoned visits," Tiernan took over. "Like they do with human council members and extinguishers."

"Wonderful," Frederick nodded. "I would like to see Fairy for purely aesthetic reasons as well."

"That's fantastic," Wasutke snarled. "I'm so happy that you're excited about going into Fairy when my people are being held hostage by a bunch of death-loving freaks!"

"My apologies, Elder," Frederick cleared his throat and settled back into his boring self.

"The Coven team will meet us in San Francisco," Tristan announced as he returned. "They want us to call them when we land."

"Very well," Raza growled. "Let's be on our way. I'm tired

of wasting time on trivialities."

"Well said," Sarah smiled at Raza and he stopped, cocked his head at her, and smiled back.

Internally, I sighed in relief. Maybe the dragon would find another maiden to eat... er... to be his sacrifice... uh, to ah... oh whatever. Maybe he'd lay off me for awhile.

Chapter Forty-Six

Councilman Alan Murdock, Head of the San Francisco Council House, was in a bit of a tizzy. He hadn't expected a slew of hunters, out of town extinguishers (including the telepath twins), witches, a Head Councilman, a dragon djinn, and a puka to show up on his doorstep. I'd given him only the briefest of warnings when I called him from the Artesia airport before we took off. Murdock was a little relieved when I told him that none of us would need to be put up for the night but he was concerned that his meeting room wouldn't be large enough to hold all of us.

His fears were warranted. With the addition of the witch group who was already in SF (including the fairies and humans we'd sent with their party), along with the SF council members who wanted to sit in on the meeting, we had close to a hundred people who wished to be included in our discussion. Well, that just wasn't going to happen so we had to whittle it down to those who were integral. Even with the whittling, the room was packed. I was of course included and my title even warranted me a seat at the table, but due to the lack of space, I asked Gradh to take Cat for a walk, disguised in her Newfoundland glamour of course.

On the table before me was the San Francisco House's crystal ball (they were the only Human Council House with one), a telephone speaker with the combined Human and Fairy High Councils on the other end of the line, and Sarah's cellphone connected to yet another large speaker with the Coven Elders on that line. All groups were as fairly represented as possible.

The Councils and Coven had all been informed of the dullahan's deception and their ultimatum. Now they were arguing with each other while I sat back and listened, hoping for a solution to fall into my lap. Or barring that, for everyone to just agree on a plan of action.

I looked over my shoulder to Tiernan, who was standing directly behind me. He was concentrating on the conversation but as soon as I set my focus on him, he seemed to sense it and looked down to me. He lifted a brow in question.

"I'm starving," I whispered to him and his lips twitched.

He turned, waved Conri forward, and whispered something to him. Conri looked over to me and gave me a sexy wink before he turned and left the room. I just shook my head and sighed. Conri's flirtations had become so commonplace that I hardly noticed them anymore. It was just a normal part of interaction for him.

I went back to dejectedly staring out the windows as I waited for Conri to return with sustenance. I was one of those people who found it hard to think on an empty stomach. So what was the point in paying attention to the discussion if I couldn't contribute anything until my food arrived?

"What do you think, Princess Seren?" Someone asked, startling me out of my dining daydreams.

"Um," I cleared my throat. "About what now?" I guess the point of paying attention was to not look stupid when someone asked me a question.

"Are we boring you?" Elder Wasutke asked snidely.

I ignored her like she was a playground bully.

"You've freed prisoners from both the Seelie and Unseelie dungeons," a voice came out of the speaker box on my left, the one connected to the High Councils. "Do you think you could free these prisoners from Dathadair?"

"First off, I don't know what you're talking about," I said innocently. We'd decided that it would be best for me to never admit to the crime of infiltrating the courts and freeing their prisoners. Deny, deny, deny, just like Bill Clinton. "Second, if I were going to attempt a rescue, I would think that new tactics would have to be employed. The fairies previously freed were done so from open courts, not a secure site expecting such an attempt."

"So that's a no?" I realized it was Councilman Greer asking.

"That's a maybe," I corrected with a grin. "As I said, I've never done such a thing before but I'd be willing to try with the Council's approval."

Greer chuckled, "Can anyone assist the Princess in coming up with a plan to rescue prisoners, since she's so ill-equipped to do so?"

"Hey now," I grumbled as Conri placed a plate with a sandwich down in front of me. A glass of lemonade followed. "Thank you, Sir Conri. You're a kind and beautiful man."

"You're welcome, Princess," he chuckled.

"Does Sir Conri have a plan?" Greer asked. "If so, we weren't able to hear it."

I started to say; *No, he didn't have a plan, he had a sandwich*, when Conri spoke.

"Well, if it were up to me," Conri smirked. "I'd just walk in through the front gate."

"Explain, if you will," Greer prompted.

"I'd set something on fire nearby," Conri shrugged. "Make it look like our Lord Dragon here is closing in," he waved a hand at Raza. "Then I'd wait for the dullahans to come out to investigate. When they did, I'd sneak in under glamour. I doubt any of them will be focused enough to spot fairies under a cloak of invisibility when they're worried about a dragon attack."

"Well look who isn't just a pretty face," I smiled proudly.

"Sir Conri," Greer said crisply.

"Yes, Councilman?" Conri straightened as if the fairy was in the room.

"Well done, the Princess is lucky to have you on her Guard."

"Thank you, Councilman," Conri swallowed hard, looking a little shook up by the praise, and went to stand back beside Tiernan.

We hadn't been able to bring more guards into the room and frankly, my Guard deserved a break anyway. It wasn't like I was in any danger in the basement council chambers. So it was just Conri and Tiernan watching over me. I looked back at Conri, caught his eye, and winked. His serious expression disappeared and he smiled brightly.

"Is everyone else in agreement with Sir Conri's plan?" Greer asked and received complete approval. "Excellent. Now we just need to decide who will be on the rescue mission."

"Besides myself, you mean," Lord Raza said.

"Yes, Lord Raza," Greer's voice had an undercurrent of sarcasm. "Besides yourself."

"And me," Wasutke added.

"I would like to volunteer as well," Sarah said and I looked over to her with a bemused smile.

305

Was she volunteering because of Raza, because she wanted to see Fairy, or just because she wanted to see this thing through? She looked over and smiled back at me. I chuckled; maybe it was all of the above.

"Are witches able to glamour themselves into invisibility?" Greer asked.

"Since I was a little girl," Sarah grinned.

"It's not a problem," Wasutke huffed.

"Then you're both most welcome," Councilman Lorcan declared. "All of us here in the High Councils hope that this mission will help to forge a bond between our people so that we may move forward with establishing a truce."

"We in the Coven understand that what the dullahans did was beyond your control and we hold no grudges for it," Elder Gabriel's voice came from the speaker attached to Sarah's cellphone. "We too hope that this will go far in establishing common ground between us."

"Great," Tiernan whispered. "Now, it's not just about rescuing people, it's about fighting a common enemy to establish a bond."

"The dullahans are screwed," I sighed.

Chapter Forty-Seven

The rescue team was to consist of Lord Raza, myself, Tiernan, Sarah, my Star's Guard, Frederick, Aidan, Elder Wasutke, Tristan, Lord Eadan, and his team of hunters. The other witches would return to Ireland to await the results of the rescue mission and hopefully witness the signing of a truce. As far as the extinguishers, they couldn't use glamour, so it was decided that it would be better for them to remain behind.

When I told the Fairy Council that I needed to speak to my father before I brought fairies into our kingdom, the Council informed me that I wouldn't be taking them into Twilight at all. Dathadair, the dullahan village, was in the Unseelie Kingdom, and King Uisdean, the Unseelie monarch, had been contacted as soon as we'd come to a decision. He had freely given his consent to our mission.

Part of me was grateful that Uisdean had given his consent but another part of me wondered why he'd acquiesced so easily. My Uncle could be nefarious and it wouldn't surprise me in the least to find that he'd allowed us to enter his kingdom just so he could set us up with the dullahans. He couldn't kill me himself but he could trick a dullahan into doing it, thus keeping himself out of the path of the Sluagh.

But my evil Uncle Uisdean wasn't my only concern.

"We're going where?" I blinked at the speaker box.

"Dathadair is alligned with Papa New Guinea but there are no raths which lead directly to the island. So you will have to fly to Australia and then use the Australian rath to cross into Unseelie, where you will have a days journey to the village."

"Yeah, that's what I thought you said," I sighed.

"Quake has a large group in Australia," Elder Jared Turner's voice came through the other speaker. "Perhaps you should go along, Al. Just in case they need some help down under."

Al was Albert Fremond, Quake witch and all around timid guy. He had sad, lackluster hair, even sadder gray eyes, and pale skin prone to blotchy redness. He was thin-limbed, weak-chinned, and had a tendency to address the ground when he spoke. He was not my first choice in a team mate.

"Yes, Sir," Al's milquetoast monotone had everyone staring at him dubiously but he didn't notice since he kept his gaze fastened on the floor.

"Excellent," Jared declared like he'd just given us the key to defeating the dullahans. "May the Goddess guide you."

I couldn't help rolling my eyes a little. I was someone who had never put a lot of stock in religion until I had heard the Goddess' voice. But there was no way these witches had ever spoken to Danu, much less seen her, and it annoyed me that they would presume to have relationships with her when I knew it was impossible. On top of that, it shocked me a little that a race who was so familiar with magic, who saw the proof of it constantly, would believe in a divine being whom they had no evidence of.

But perhaps I was being too harsh on them. People needed something to believe in. Even witches. Who was I to dispute their claims and destroy their faith? It wasn't my place or my concern. They had the right to believe in whatever divinity they chose. I'd do something smart for once and keep my big mouth shut.

"Did he just say *Goddess*?" A hushed tone came through the speaker box connected to the Councils and I nearly laughed.

"So, when do we leave?" I asked before someone could

308

acknowledge the awkwardness.

"As soon as possible," Lorcan said through the speaker.

"Immediately," Raza added.

"I'm ready whenever all of you are," Elder Wasutke nodded.

"I think we need a little time to freshen up; change our clothes, take a shower, get some food, stuff like that." I held up my sandwich, which I had yet to be able to take a bite of. "And then we can head to the airport."

"Fine," Raza sighed.

"Perfectly understandable," Lorcan added.

Elder Wasutke just glared at me.

The high council members and witch elders called the meeting to a close and I stood up, intending on getting out while I had the chance. I took my sandwich with me.

"Uh, Princess Seren?" Councilman Murdock stopped me.

"Yes?" I gave him a weary and wary look.

"I have some rooms available for your use but not enough for everyone," Murdock looked concerned.

"Oh," I said in relief. "Don't worry, we'll work it out. Some of us will eat while others wash up and change."

"Great," Murdock nodded. "I'll go have the chefs prepare something and lay out a buffet in the dining room."

"Thank you, Sir," I smiled. "I'm sorry to have descended upon you like this but you're handling it admirably."

"No problem," Murdock smiled back. "And one more

thing, Ambassador."

"Yes?"

"Your father's in Ireland."

Chapter Forty-Eight

"I beg your pardon?" I asked Murdock as I followed him out of the meeting room and into the hallway, where a long line was forming in front of the elevator.

"Why don't we speak in here?" Murdock led us into his office. I say us because Tiernan followed me. Murdock shut the door and turned to face us. "Extinguisher Ewan Sloane has been sent to Ireland to witness the signing of the truce."

"Who sent him?" I asked, a little surprised that I wasn't happy with the news.

I'd been trying to get my human father to forgive the fact that I wasn't his biological offspring ever since the news about my fey heritage had first come out. Ewan had remained steadfast in his decision to boot me from his life, even going as far as to say that I wasn't his daughter. I knew better; I would always be his daughter. He had raised me and he was my father. But our last meeting had been traumatic for both of us and I found that I wasn't ready for a repeat quite yet.

"The High Council asked for his presence," Murdock sighed. "I had nothing to do with it. And there's more; his mother went with him."

"Grandma is there?" I felt my eyes go wide. "Wonderful, both of my grandmothers under the same roof. One is psychotic and the other is indifferent. I don't know which is worse." Then I frowned, shared a look with Tiernan, and together we said; "Psychotic."

"Your family sounds lovely," Murdock grimaced.

"I *have* told you about my Uncle Uisdean, right?" I shot back.

"You have my deepest sympathies," Murdock gave my shoulder a pat. "Now why don't you go upstairs while I phone the kitchens. There will at least be coffee to be had immediately."

"Thanks but I have my sandwich," I lifted the plate, getting a good look at the sandwich for the first time.

"What kind of sandwich is that?" Murdock asked as he peered at the strange colors oozing out from between the bread.

"I'm not sure," I sniffed it and then made a face. "I think Conri might have made it himself."

"Yes, well, like I said," Murdock chuckled. "There should be coffee soon which will hold you until the food is prepared."

"I think I'd prefer a real drink," I muttered as I left the office.

"You and me both," Tiernan groaned as we got in line. "Why aren't there stairs in this place?"

"Oh, there are stairs but using them would set off alarms and I'm unwilling to climb them anyway," I shrugged and searched for someplace inconspicuous to throw my sandwich.

The ding of the elevator had me lifting my head hopefully. Maybe this wouldn't take too long. I dove back down again though when I saw who walked out of the elevator car.

"What is it?" Tiernan looked down the hallway. "Oh, not him again."

Yep, it was him. Brandon Murdock, Councilman Murdock's son and general pain in my tukhus. He was of course heading in our direction because of three reasons. First, his Dad's office was right behind me. Second, the hallway was a straight shot to the meeting room and the only options were other offices. And third, it was just my luck.

I tried to slide behind some witches but Tiernan was pretty hard to miss and tended to attract attention with his shiny hair, so it was only to be expected that Brandon would notice him and then look for me.

"Seren," he spat my name out like it tasted foul.

"Brandon," I sighed as I remembered the last time I'd seen him. I believe the conversation had ended with me saying; *Namaste motherfucker*. Not exactly the best way to leave things.

"I took your advice and started meditating," he said to my utter shock. "It's really helped me."

"You have?" I blinked at him.

"No I haven't started fucking meditating," he growled. "Who do I look like, the Dalai Lama?"

"Well, no, I think he wears glasses," I looked to Tiernan for help.

"And has better fashion sense," Tiernan agreed.

"Fuck you, you fairy fag," Brandon said, making my eyes widen further.

"Pardon me but I couldn't help but overhear you insult my friend, Count Tiernan," Raza purred.

Brandon looked over, ready to snap at whomever was stupid enough to interfere, and then froze. His mouth dropped open as he looked over Raza's wings, the clicking talons in his maniacally folded hands, and the gleam in his predator eyes. He had to stare up a bit since Raza topped his own considerable height. Extinguisher Brandon Murdock swallowed hard and then pushed past us, retreating into his father's office without another word.

"I don't know whether to resent the fact that you have that affect on him while I don't," Tiernan mused. "Or just enjoy the pleasure of watching that cúl tóna shit himself."

"Cúl tóna?" I lifted my brow at Tiernan.

"I believe the closest English translation is *man with a penis on his head*," Raza explained for Tiernan.

"You just called Brandon a dickhead in Gaelic?"

"Yes," Tiernan looked at me like he was confused as to why it was such a big deal.

"You're my hero," I laughed and gave him a one-armed hug.

"Um, I believe I was the one who sent the *cúl tóna* running," Raza huffed. "Shouldn't I get a hug?"

"No," Tiernan and I said together.

"Here, have a sandwich," I handed Raza the plate and he stared down at it dubiously before lifting the sandwich and taking a bite.

"Not bad," he noted and started scoffing the sandwich down as Tiernan and I exchanged disgusted looks.

Chapter Forty-Nine

"What's up, Princess Tinkerbell?"

"Abby!" I shouted as I ran through the crowded living room, elbowing extinguishers out of my way, to hug my friend.

"Hey, Count Tightass," Abby chucked Tiernan in the shoulder after she got free of me. "How's it hanging?"

"Everything hangs as it should, thank you," Tiernan smiled at her. "Torquil is around- ah," Tiernan smiled wider as Torquil came up and handed Abby a can of soda. "And here he is now."

"I was getting the lady a drink," Torquil said stiffly.

"Thanks, Torque," Abby kissed his cheek.

"Extinguisher Abby," Torquil sighed. "How many times do I have to ask you to call me by my whole name?"

"Two-thousand-five-hundred-sixty-eightand a half," she said with stone-faced sincerity.

"What?" Torquil gaped at her.

"She's joking," I whispered to Torquil as Tiernan chuckled.

"Oh, I'm a joke to you," he said to Abby as he straightened. "I understand," he turned on his heel and tried to leave but Abby wasn't having any of that.

"Relax, I only tease men who I like," she huffed as she grabbed his arm and swung him around.

He started to protest again but then she took his face in her hands and laid one on him. Tiernan and I gaped, in fact most of the room stopped to stare as Abby committed social suicide in front of us. What was so wrong with kissing Torquil? Well nothing, if you were anyone other than an extinguisher. Extinguishers married other extinguishers. Period. You didn't date anyone outside the group, you didn't sleep with anyone outside the group, you didn't even kiss anyone outside the group. To do so was a declaration of dissent against centuries of tradition. It was a slap in the face of our ancestors. An act of insubordination that could get you into serious trouble. And Abby had just done it at the worst possible moment.

The thing was; nobody did anything. No one shouted for justice or cursed her for being a traitor. Nothing happened except a lot of staring and the most aggressive response I'd ever seen from Torquil. He picked Abby up, tossed her over his shoulder, and headed for the elevator.

My mouth dropped further.

"I don't know what surprises me more," I finally said. "Torquil running off with Abby like he's Conan the Barbarian, or Abby letting him do it."

"Yes," was all Tiernan could get out.

"I definitely need a drink now," I headed for the bar in the corner of the room.

"Make mine a double," Tiernan said.

"She's been waiting months to do that," Councilman Karmen Simmel sidled over to us and started pouring the drinks. "And she stole the name I was gonna call you," he pouted.

"You're still here?" I grinned, unbelievably happy to see a familiar face that wasn't kissing a fairy, grim with anxiety, or spewing venomous words at me.

"I asked to stay," he shrugged. "I know it's cliché, a gay

316

man in SF, but I'm happy to be home. And how are you, you silver-eyed fox?" He asked Tiernan.

"Tired but otherwise fine," Tiernan smiled and accepted the drink Karmen handed him. "Thank you."

"Anytime, Sweetie," Karmen purred.

"Brandon just called him a fairy fag," I blabbed.

"Oooh a fairy fag?" Karmen straightened. "Do you know where I could find one of those?"

"What the hell is going on here?" I gaped at him. "Did Murdock decree that extinguishers should now date fairies?"

"Not exactly," Karmen shrugged. "But after you became princess, people started to talk, saying that mixing our blood might be a good idea. Look what it did for you after all."

"So that's why no one has commented on Abby's ardent display?" Tiernan asked.

"Yep," Karmen came around to the front of the bar and leaned against it casually. He batted his long lashes up at Tiernan and flicked a thick lock of dark hair over an ear. "No one's come out and made a statement but the whole *marry an extinguisher thing* was never really a law anyway. Not that it's ever mattered to me, being a councilman, and a Simmel, and a *gay*," he said the last word with a flourish.

"Why do your friends flirt with me?" Tiernan asked me dryly.

"Because you're sexy," I said back in the same tone. "Would you prefer to be ugly and have no one flirt with you?"

"No, I'm fine with the flirting," he took another sip of his drink.

"I need to have a word with Brandon," Karmen pursed his lips. "He shouldn't be using the word fag. Not in reference to gay men and certainly not in reference to straight. It's an offensive word."

"Oh," I blinked, surprised that he was so sensitive about it. "Yeah, you're absolutely right. It's a horrible word."

"I mean there's so much more creative words for gays," Karmen mused. "There's; puff, queer, jobby-jabber, butt pirate, lemon, Peter puffer, nellie, poofter, chickenhawk, bear, and my favorite... Twinkie. That's what I am," he ran a hand down his slim physique, "a Twinkie."

"I'm sorry," Tiernan was staring at Karmen like he'd started speaking Chinese. "Did you just say that you're a Twinkie?"

"Yep," Karmen smiled proudly.

"I think my understanding of what a Twinkie is must be incorrect," Tiernan frowned.

"If you think it's a golden spongecake filled with cream, then you're not mistaken," I said to Tiernan.

"Oh, then I fail to see the correlation," he looked over Karmen.

"I'm slim, beautiful, and full of-"

"Okay, we get it," I interrupted before Karmen could finish.

"So, about these witches..." Karmen's voice fell away as he stared at something over my shoulder.

I turned and saw Raza coming towards us with Cat. Cat bounded across the room, people parting for her like the sea for Moses. She had dropped her glamour and appeared as she was; a giant puka. Having a dragon-djinn in tow didn't help either. Karmen's hand shot out before I could stop him and the next thing

318

I knew, Cat was levitating off the ground, her legs still pumping but getting her absolutely nowhere.

"Who the hell let a puka in here?" Karmen's voice lost it's gay melodic quality and dropped into commanding councilman tone. "And who is that?" He pointed to Raza.

"I let the puka in, you schmuck," I smacked Karmen. "Can you put Cat down please?"

"Cat?" He gaped at me while Cat just gave up running and started to enjoy floating. She plopped herself down but ended up in a slow spin.

"My *twilight* puka," I waved towards her. "She protects me."

"You named a puka Cat?" He asked in horror.

"After my mother," I nodded.

"You named a *puka* after your *mother*?!" He nearly shrieked.

"You wanna tone it down? We're already attracting a lot of attention with your floating fairy dog trick," I waved a hand towards Cat.

"Oh, sorry," he let Cat down and she ran over to us and sat beside me. "Hello," he said to her.

She nodded.

"She just nodded at me," Karmen gaped at Cat.

"She's a fey animal," I gave his shoulder a pat.

"But, Seren, a puka?"

"She's a twilight puka," I said again. "A blend, like me.

She's a little less violent than her cousins. Notice that she has gray fur instead of black."

"Twilight?" Karmen lifted a brow. "So like a hybrid? Like a zebra?"

"Wait, what?" I frowned. "Zebra's aren't hybrids."

"Of course they are," Karmen frowned back. "Like mules; they're made when you mate a donkey with a horse."

"Karmen," I asked carefully, "what do you think they crossbreed to get zebras?"

"A black horse and a white horse," he said simply.

"Um, no," I gave a little giggle.

"No?" Karmen asked.

"No," Tiernan assured him. "They are their own breed."

"Oh," Karmen looked back to Cat. "So; not like a zebra."

"A zebra has nothing to do with it," Raza declared as he stepped up to us. "Let go of the zebra."

"Done; I've let it go," Karmen looked Raza up and down. "Which leaves my hands free to grab other things. So why don't you tell me what breed you are? Besides smokin' hot, that is," he gave Raza a dramatic wink.

"Well you got the smokin' part right," I chuckled.

"And the hot part," Raza cast an indignant look my way.

"He's a dragon-djinn," Tiernan said to Karmen with a smirk.

"No," Karmen breathed in wonder. "Stop, I'm going to faint," he started to fan himself.

"And I'm a perfectly formed dragon-djinn," Raza nodded as he reached for his pants. "Would you care to see?"

"Absolutely!" Karmen's eyes went wide, like a kid on Christmas morning.

"No!" Tiernan and I shouted together as we lunged for Raza's pants.

"I'm teasing you," Raza chuckled and pushed our hands away. "I think I'm getting quite good at drollery."

"What's drollery?" I whispered to Karmen.

"Who cares? He's gorgeous; just smile and nod," Karmen advised as he did that very thing.

Chapter Fifty

Later that night, our team boarded a plane for Brisbane, Australia. It was a seventeen hour flight so I was once again grateful that we had my dad's private jet. Boy was he going to have a hell of a fuel bill when this was all done.

I was able to get some sleep on the plane and we were even served another meal by our thoughtful stewards. So by the time we touched down in Brisbane, I was feeling much better. The fairy watcher for the Australian rath met us at the airport and gave us a ride out to Samford Valley, just a little ways outside of Brisbane.

His name was Bambam. I'm not kidding, it was Bambam, which is evidently an Aboriginal name. Who knew the Flintstones were Aboriginals? Anyway, Bambam was a bunyip. I bet you didn't know that there were Australian fairies. Well there are. Most of them are shapeshifters, like Bambam, and with all the strange creatures roaming Australia, no one pays them any mind.

Bunyips are water-dwellers, similar to kelpies. They have horse tails but aren't really horses. In fact, they look more like skinny walruses when they're in their animal forms. They have thick tusks, wide flippers, and huge dark eyes like a seal. In his man form, Bambam retained only the eyes and a trace of the flippers in his webbed hands.

Otherwise, he looked like an aboriginal; skin the color of an acorn, matching hair that hung in lustrous waves to his shoulders, a wide nose, and an equally generous mouth. He looked sweet, kind even, but I knew that bunyips had a taste for tender human flesh; usually small children or women. Of course, they weren't supposed to indulge anymore but the way Bambam kept

322

looking at my thighs had me worried.

He drove us into a lush valley, something I didn't expect to find in Australia. This was my first trip to the previous penal colony and I'd thought to find more of an African type of landscape. What Bambam drove us through was closer to something you'd find in California. The valley was surrounded by curving mountains, spotted with wide-armed trees, and covered in foliage in every shade of green. Lavish lakes adorned the valley floor, one edged up against the property that Bambam drove us to.

"Here we are," Bambam got out of the van and took a deep breath of the eucalyptus scented air. "Home sweet home."

"Beautiful," I admired as Cat went bounding off into the open field bordering the sprawling ranch style home.

"The rath is within those trees there," Bambam pointed to a copse of trees behind the house. "Did you want to come in for some tea before you leave?"

"Tea?" I blinked. What was with watchers offering us tea?

"He means food," Sarah explained before she said to Bambam. "No thank you, we ate on the plane."

"Ace!" Bambam smiled. "I'll leave you to it, then. Watch out for the bities," with that, he disappeared into the house.

"Please tell me *bities* is not another word for crocodiles," Frederick begged Sarah.

"No," she laughed. "He means insects, like mosquitoes." She started heading for the rath excitedly. "Come on, Fairy awaits."

"I think I'd rather deal with crocodiles," Conri grumbled as he slapped a bitie on his arm.

"How can I be descended from such a wuss," Aidan teased

Conri. They had bonded on the plane and Conri had confessed that bargests were most likely the ancestors of the Pack witches.

"Maybe I'm wrong," Conri shrugged. "You could be descended from pukas."

"Hey," Aidan growled.

"Yeah," I added my scowl. "Don't insult Cat."

"Hey!" Aidan transferred his angry look to me but I was already off, chasing down Sarah so I could catch her before she walked into the rath all by herself.

"Cease your shenanigans," Raza growled. "Walking the rath is sacred and should be done with respect."

"Yes, Lord Raza," Aidan and Conri said together like a couple of chastised children.

The fairy mound was similar to every other fairy mound I'd seen; a small hill with a door set into its side. This door was gold, embellished with a scene of a silver moon hanging over a carved onyx castle and forest. It was symbolic, a way for us to know where we were headed. In this instance, to the Unseelie Kingdom.

Cat came running over and then settled into place beside me, showing a reverence for the rath that the other hounds had failed to. Raza smiled down at her approvingly, then stepped forward and slid in front of Sarah, who had been first in line for the door.

"You need to be warned of what lies through this door," Raza announced.

"Shall I abandon all hope?" She teased him.

"Not yet. But soon perhaps," he smiled maliciously but instead of intimidating her, it only encouraged her.

"Bring it on, Bonfire-breath," Sarah stuck her hands on her hips.

"The path is narrow," Raza went on, ignoring her nickname for him, and looked up at the rest of the witches. "Do not step from it or you shall be lost to the Between forever."

"The Between?" Sarah finally lost her smile.

"The In-Between to be exact," I took over. "Don't worry, as long as you stay on the path, you'll be fine."

"Oh, okay then," Sarah didn't look reassured.

"Respect the rath and it will respect you," Raza said ominously and then opened the door.

Nothing could be seen beyond the door, just inky darkness, and Sarah hesitated to enter it after Raza forged ahead. So I slid in front of her and offered her my hand. She shook her head at holding hands like schoolgirls but smiled at me gratefully and stepped in behind me. I glanced back and saw that my knights were interspersing themselves between the witches and I nodded to them in approval. Eadan and his hunters were bringing up the rear.

I walked the path Between. Cat ran ahead of me and burst out into the sunlight of an idyllic meadow, to chase the jewel toned fairy butterflies through the berry laden bushes. I called to her as I stepped out of the door but when she stopped and looked back, it was to stare at something behind me. Her ears laid back as she focused intently and something about her stance made my blood run cold. I turned just as the screaming began.

Sarah was on the ground, along with Aidan and Frederick. Then Albert came through the door, followed by Tristan, and finally Jennifer Wasutke. All of them dropped as soon as their feet touched Fairy, shrieking as if they'd been set on fire.

"Oh, sweet Goddess," I breathed as I rushed over to them. I

knew exactly what was happening to them because it had happened to me. "Why didn't I think of this?"

"Because it was virtually impossible," Tiernan shook his head, his eyes gone wide. "They have no traceable fey blood in them. How could they awaken something they don't have?"

"They obviously have it," Raza growled as he held Sarah's head in his lap. "They wouldn't have magic if they didn't."

"But they register as human," Tiernan argued. "And they were born in the Human Realm. Fairy should have no hold over them."

"It doesn't matter! Just shut up!" I screeched and took Aidan's head into my lap. "Aidan, I'm doing this to help you, I'm so sorry."

Aidan's eyes shot open and locked on mine. I blew lavender dust from my fingertips, covering him in the sparkling magic, and his body instantly relaxed as he fell asleep. I laid him down and went to the others, flinging dream-dust over them until all the witches were sleeping soundly.

"Well, now what?" I ran my hands through my hair wearily.

"Now we set up camp," Tiernan pulled me into a hug. "Well done, Seren," he whispered in my ear. "You saved them a lot of pain."

"And don't I know it," I said as I eased away from him. "Alright, everyone, let's try and make the witches as comfortable as possible while we get camp set up."

"Yes, Princess," came a chorus of replies.

"Thank you," I sighed and looked down at Jennifer Wasutke. "Goddess help us when you wake up. You're the last one

I wanted to have more magic."

"You think they'll become more powerful?" Ainsley stopped, bent halfway over Aidan.

"Why wouldn't they?" I shrugged. "I did."

"Magic is a mystery," Gradh offered. She was helping Torquil carry Frederick to a shaded spot and as she walked through the sunlight, her sunset skin glimmered a rosy-bronze. She glanced over to us with her sky-blue eyes and smiled grimly. "Who knows what path it will take with them?"

"Who indeed," I frowned, wondering if I should try speaking to Danu. I decided that she already knew what we were going through and if she wanted to offer her insight, she would have done so already. "For now, we'll just have to wait and see."

Chapter Fifty-One

We brought the witches closer to the fire as night fell. Raza paced anxiously, worried about the delay and what it might mean for Raye. I didn't know what to say to help him so I just kept watch over our sleeping witches and prayed silently to Danu that they would live through whatever transformation was happening within them.

I don't know when I fell asleep but I woke suddenly to screaming. I jumped up and found Prime Elder Wasutke standing in the middle of the meadow, holding the edges of her new feathered wings as if they were vicious snakes that might, at any moment, strike out at her.

I rushed forward and took her arms as everyone else closed in. Jennifer stared at me with eyes like a spooked horse, and then she looked beyond me and screamed some more. I slapped her and she refocused on me, blinked, then fell to the ground and wept. I turned to see what she'd been staring at and felt my eyes widen as far as they could.

"What?" Sarah frowned at me, then looked at the other shocked faces and lifted her hands to her face. "What's wrong? What happened to me?"

I ran to her and grabbed her hands, pulling them away from her gaunt cheeks. "Sarah," I said calmly. "Take a deep breath."

"Tell me what's going on!" She shouted.

"When you crossed into Fairy, your fey blood was awakened," I said gently as the other witches started to gather behind me.

"Tristan," Sarah moaned as she looked over my shoulder.

I looked back and saw that Tristan had gone through a similar transformation to Sarah's. His face was deathly pale, his cheeks sunken, as were his eyes. And those eyes... they were shrunken, as beady as any dullahan's, and they started darting around uncontrollably. Beneath those crazy orbs, his mouth had widened and even as I watched, it began to smile.

Sarah screamed.

"Sarah!" I shook her. "You can fix it with glamour. It will be okay, I promise."

"Okay?" She screeched as she held her hands up to her smiling mouth. "Do I look okay to you? Because I don't feel okay," she fell to the ground and began to laugh hysterically. Then she looked up suddenly, setting her gaze on Raza. "Is this what you meant when you said; *soon perhaps?*"

"No," Raza whispered. "I had no idea that this would happen to you. None of us did. You have my deepest condolences."

"I'm so sorry, Sarah," I started to reach for her again but but then Frederick started shouting.

"There's something on my back!" Frederick pulled off his jacket and started yanking at the buttons on his shirt. "Get it off me! Oh Goddess, what is it? Get it off me!"

He yanked his shirt off and turned in a circle, trying to see what was attacking him. Jennifer, who was still crouched amid her raven-black wings, started cackling along with Sarah. The rest of us just stared in shock as a pair of delicate dragonfly wings unfurled from Frederick's shoulder blades.

"What are they?" Frederick screamed.

"Wings," I said gently and laid a hand on his arm, stilling his movement. "Their smaller than usual but clearly sylph. I know some sylphs and they have wings very similar to those."

"Sylphs?" He stared at me blankly.

"Air elementals," Tiernan added. "I don't think those are big enough to allow you to fly but at least you have your answer now. Storm is descended from sylphs."

"At least I have my answer," Frederick said blandly and then huffed. "Useless wings. Be careful what you ask for."

"And what about me?" Aidan asked. "Do I look any different? How's my face?"

"Still ugly," Ainsley smirked.

"You haven't changed at all," Conri chuckled as Aidan punched Ainsley's shoulder. "But then if you're from my line, you wouldn't; we are as we are. You lucky bastard."

"I think I must have been lucky too," Albert said over the fading cackles of Sarah and Jennifer. "I don't feel any different."

We all just gaped at him.

"Uh, you might want to take a look down," Conri advised.

"Oh!" Al declared. "Well, I think that's a bit of an improvement, don't you agree?"

"I do," Conri nodded. "You look good, man."

And he did. Albert had gained about fifty pounds and it appeared to all be muscle. His arms and legs bulged, tearing through his clothes in places, and his chest had widened. His features were thicker too, more manlier, and his voice had deepened.

"What do you suppose I'm descended from?" He mused as I headed back to Tristan and Sarah, who were now huddled together and moaning.

"*Who*, not what," Gradh corrected him as she eased up to the now-buff man. "I'd guess trolls or dwarves."

"Trolls," Ian decreed. "Look at his teeth."

"My teeth?" Albert bared his teeth and revealed a pair of thick fangs. He poked at them. "Oh wow."

"They look good on you," Gradh grinned.

"Seriously?" I asked her. "You're gonna flirt with a troll witch while I'm trying to help Beckoning witches?"

"You mean the dullahan witches," Jennifer smirked and stood. She was done cackling but I wasn't sure if this was an improvement.

"Shut up, you feathered whore!" Sarah screeched.

"No, I won't shut up," Jennifer strode over to Sarah, spreading her wings aggressively as she went. "I've taken enough of your bullshit, Vex. As far as I'm concerned, this is payback for all the witches you've ever tormented or abused. Fuck you, you dullahan monster."

"Damn you to hell Jennifer Wasutke!" Sarah shouted as she stood and the shockwaves of her voice seemed to radiate visibly through the air.

"Oh no," I whispered as Jennifer's face went blank and the life faded from her eyes.

Prime Elder Jennifer Wasutke fell to the ground; dead.

The whole meadow went silent, all of us staring at the winged corpse. Honestly, I wasn't too upset to see the Flight Elder

331

expire but I was concerned about the fact that Sarah had inherited the dullahan ability to hasten someone's death through simply calling their name. Except she shouldn't have been able to kill Jennifer unless Jennifer was fated to die. Which meant that either these witches were going to soon die from their transformations, or Sarah had just developed another mutated magic.

"What did I do?" Sarah whispered.

"It's not your fault," Tristan hugged her against him. "You didn't know. It was an accident."

"And now, I truly am a monster," Sarah cried. "Oh Goddess, kill me!" She started to bawl pathetically and then pulled away from Tristan to scream at the sky. "Kill me! Do you hear me, bitch? You've never done anything for me, you've never answered a single prayer, but if you do exist, I'll forgive all of your silence if you just kill me now!" She dropped to her knees and placed her face to the grass, weeping.

We all stood around her in a mournful circle, silent and grim. I was about to head over to give her as much comfort as I could, when a vibrant energy rushed through me, straightening my spine and lifting my head. I inhaled sharply as my body came alive with more magic than it was meant to hold.

"I have never answered your prayers because you were born too far away for me to hear you," I said with the powerful voice of Danu. All of the fairies dropped to their knees, even Raza knelt, wide eyed and reverent. Cat though, yipped happily and bounded over to sit by my side.

"Hello, Sweetling," I said and stroked Cat's muzzle gently.

Sarah stopped crying and looked up at me in shock. I don't know what she saw in my eyes but it was enough to convince her that her goddess stood before her at last. The witches gathered close, staring at me like I was their savior. Then they got to their knees as Sarah lifted to hers.

"Goddess?" She asked.

"I am Danu, sister of Anu, Goddess of the Fey," I intoned in a voice that seemed to vibrate out through the world, touching everything as it went. "I am bonded to this realm, unable to cross into my brother's domain, or I would have answered your call. I would have answered all of you."

"Danu," Aidan whispered in wonder.

"Ah, the bargest magic runs true," I said, I mean *she* said through me. "You are a miracle to me. All of you are. I am overwhelmed with joy to meet you, little lost ones. Even as I mourn the death of my raven mocker daughter."

All I could think was; well damn, the witches were right. They did have a goddess, they just didn't know how to reach her. Danu continued, speaking over my internal dialogue.

"You were born in the world of humans, the world of Anu," she went on. "So it is to be expected that you don't appreciate fey features, as we do here," she/we reached down and stroked Sarah's sunken cheek. "You are still beautiful to me; a dangerous beauty. But I feel your pain. Both for what you've done and who you've become. So I will give you a choice. Both of you," I/she looked to Tristan. "You may stay here, with me in Fairy, and I will take you to live on my sacred isle. Or I will reverse the changes in you and you may become what you were. You will go home to the realm of humans, never to return to Fairy."

"And never to see you again," Sarah concluded and Danu nodded.

"If you were ever to return, the change would occur again and it would be permanent," Danu said.

Sarah looked down at herself, pensively stroking a finger

333

over her mottled skin. Then she looked over to Tristan, who was staring at me/Danu like he never wanted to stop. Sarah sighed and closed her eyes tight. Then she took a deep breath and opened them.

"I'll stay," Tristan said before Sarah could speak.

"Tristan," Sarah gasped. "You'll never see your family again. You'll stay this way forever," she waved a hand at him.

"I don't care how I look," he shrugged. His eyes, like little glass marbles, remained focused on Danu/me. "You can tell my family that I've devoted myself to the Goddess. How could I possibly go back when she stands before me and offers me a place at her side?"

"I will return for you when you finish your mission," Danu smiled at Tristan. "Now, Sarah. What is your decision?"

"I can't stay here," Sarah said sadly. "I can't be this," she held her arms out. "I'm a Vex. I must protect my people. I have to think of them. And myself. I'm sorry."

"Can you accept what you've done here?" Danu waved a hand towards the body of Jennifer Wasutke.

"I will take responsibility for it but that's another reason why I must return," Sarah said calmly. "Please, change me back."

"I will," Danu promised her. "But first, I want you to understand where you come from, *who* you come from, and you need to learn to control the magic that has birthed you. This new body will help you do that."

Sarah bowed her head in acceptance.

"When I return for Tristan, I will change you back," we laid a hand on Sarah's head. "Until then, know that I watch over you and you are loved, for all of your strengths and all of your weaknesses," we looked to the other witches and laid a hand on each of them. "Go with my blessing and free those who have been stolen from you." Then we turned to Raza and went to him, holding our hands out to him. He took our hands tightly, staring up at us like we were something miraculous. "My son," Danu whispered and caressed the angles of his face. "So beautiful, so proud, and so sad. But I felt hope return to your heart when you first spoke to Seren."

"She told me you had returned," Raza smiled. "And I prayed that she was right."

"I know," Danu smirked. "I heard you but you weren't ready to hear me."

"I was listening," he swore adamantly.

"Action and acceptance are very different things," Danu said gently. "You were ready here," we tapped his forehead, "but not here," we laid a hand over his heart. "Now you are ready."

"Danu," Raza whispered. "You have made my heart beat again."

"It will always beat," we smiled and lowered our lips to his cheek to whisper, "and it will always be mine." Then we straightened to say louder. "But I'm willing to share it. Just be wary of giving it away too soon. Time is a tricky thing and must be handled carefully. One step in the right direction but placed at the wrong time, will only bring chaos. Be patient."

"I will," he breathed. "But, Danu, my son..."

"Is safe," we smiled brightly and Raza's shoulders dropped in relief. "I have looked after the wild birds who have finally come home to roost. *All* of them," we glanced at the witches. "But I can only do so much. You must free them and I will help you where I can. Know that I am with you always."

335

Thank you for bringing them home, Seren... she whispered in my head as she faded away from me.

I inhaled deep, closing my eyes as my body became fully my own once more. When I opened my eyes, I found Raza staring up at me with an unreadable expression, his hands still clasped in mine. Then the look was replaced with a smile as he stood and hugged me.

"Thank you for bringing her to us, Seren," he whispered, unknowingly mimicking Danu's own words.

Cat yipped again, alerting me to the fact that she had followed the Goddess around the meadow. I bent to give her a hug and then straightened to look over the awed faces around me. Everyone stood, Tiernan coming over to hold my hand supportively. But it was Sarah who I was concerned with.

"I'm okay, Ambassador," she whispered when she met my eyes.

"Alright," I sighed. "We need to get to Dathadair and rescue our friends but first, let's bury Prime Elder Jennifer Wasutke. I wish we could take her back to her people but I don't think that's an option. So instead, let's lay her within the arms of Fairy and pray that she finds peace here."

"And that her family will understand," Tiernan said under his breath.

Chapter Fifty-Two

"What does Dathadair mean?" I asked Tiernan as we laid atop a hill, surveying the dullahan village below us.

"Death Omen," Tiernan said dryly.

"Of course it does."

"Well what did you expect a bunch of dullahans to name their home; Sunnydale?" He shot back.

I choked on my laughter.

"It wasn't that funny," Tiernan cast a dark look my way.

"Oh damn, for a moment there I thought you were purposefully referencing *Buffy the Vampire Slayer,*" I chuckled.

"Buffy is the name of a vampire slayer?" He lifted his brows.

"It's meant to be funny," I slid a smile his way. "But what's really funny is that Sunnydale was the name of the town Buffy lived in and it happened to be built over a portal to Hell."

"Hmph," Tiernan huffed. "Maybe it would have been an appropriate choice after all."

The village actually looked closer to a Sunnydale then it did a Dathadair. There was a collection of cottages, each with its own little garden, painted in cheerful colors. At the center of town, there appeared to be a bubbling fountain in a courtyard, and at the far end was a huge castle keep. Castle walls encircled the entire town and guards were posted along it. But even with the presence of the guards and the shadows of the night, Dathadair had more of a homey look than a foreboding one.

"Are you ready?" Raza asked us.

"Yes, this is a good vantage point," Tiernan agreed. "Go ahead and set the fire, then join us back here. We'll sneak down the cliff and hopefully through an open gate."

"Excellent," Raza turned and rushed away.

"Okay, everyone, here we go," I said to the others. "Cat, you stay here and watch our backs." Cat whined. "You can't glamour yourself to be invisible," I chided her. Then she disappeared. "Cat?" I gaped at the empty space and suddenly she was back again, panting happily like a puppy. "Well, you told me."

"She's Goddess-touched, remember?" Tiernan whispered. "She glamoured herself into a dog, why wouldn't she be able to go invisible?"

"Pretty soon she'll be running Twilight," I chuckled. "Alright, you're in too, Cat. Just stay close and don't go running off anywhere."

Cat looked at me like I was being silly.

"Done," Raza said as he joined us and suddenly shouting was heard from below.

I angled my head to see flames blazing in the distance and dullahans gathering on the city walls.

"I hope you were careful with that fire," it suddenly occurred to me that starting a forest fire in Fairy wasn't such a good idea.

"It's a collection of logs I cast out into a lake," Raza smirked at me. "The fire won't spread."

"Well done, you," I grinned.

"Get ready," Tiernan said back to us. "They're taking the bait."

And they sure were. A large group of dullahans rode out of the gate on huge black steeds. They brandished their whips in their hands and had their heads attached with the collars we'd seen in HR. The gate was left wide open behind them and all of us snatched the opportunity to slide down the hill and sneak into the unsuspecting village.

Glamours firmly in place, we crept down the streets of Dathadair like a gaggle of ghosts. Not even Cat made a sound. The lanes were cobbled and uneven but that worked in our favor, dampening the noise of our boots. The open layout helped as well, with only cottages set back from the road, no steep walls nearby to echo sound. I glanced over as we neared the first cottage and then looked back for a longer perusal.

This was no quaint cottage of wood and plaster. This was a building made of bones. I swallowed hard and took a deep breath, reminding myself that there was a purpose to every fey and that it wasn't for me to judge the way they lived. But as I passed the fourth bone house, it became harder for me to remain neutral. Everything in me rebelled against the thought of living within the dead. How could you raise children inside walls made of people?

With morbid curiosity I stared at the dullahan homes. Fences were made of thigh bones latched together with sinew, paths were strewn with crushed bone, and I don't even want to guess what they were using for plaster; it was a putrid gray-green in the moonlight. Skulls stared back at me balefully from the corners of the roofs, mouths hanging open to serve as downspouts for the rain gutters. I shivered, my hand twitching in Tiernan's grip.

"It's just illusion," Tiernan whispered to me. "They aren't really made of bones and flesh."

339

"They aren't?" I whispered back and then looked closer, focusing hard enough to see past the glamour and view the real homes beneath; cottages of mundane wood and stone. I sighed in relief.

"Illusion can be just as important as truth," Raza whispered behind us. "Sometimes even more so. We fey, love our illusions."

"Alright, we need to stay silent, we've reached the keep," Tiernan whispered back to everyone.

The door for the keep wasn't open or unguarded but we subdued the guards easily enough and set them on the ground around the corner. We rushed inside but we didn't know where to go. If the prisoners were being held in cells, they'd most likely be in a basement level but if they were being treated as well as Mal had implied, they'd be placed in rooms above ground.

"I smell him," Raza whispered exultantly. "This way," he pushed ahead of me and we were left to follow his footsteps since Raza's glamour was strong enough to withstand my clairvoyance.

So down the dank hallways we went, chasing the sound of soft thuds on the bare stone floor. I could tell when we were getting closer because those footsteps came faster and I had to increase my pace to keep up with them.

The dullahan had been telling the truth. Raza led us to the top floor of the keep and we ended up racing down a long corridor to a guarded door. The guard could hear us coming and was able to focus long enough to see some of us. Though I don't think he ever saw Raza because he didn't even glance at the dragon-djinn before Raza knocked him unconscious. Unfortunately, that was where our momentum stopped. Raza's glamour fell as he growled and slammed his fist into the door.

"What is it?" I dropped my invisibility too.

"It's barred by magic," he searched the edges of the door

340

for some kind of weakness.

"Can't we break the spell?" Sarah asked.

"It's keyed to the dullah-" Raza stopped mid-word as he stared at Sarah. "Come here," he grabbed her hand and pulled her forward. Then he placed her palm on the door handle. The door swung open and Raza smiled. "You're handy to have around, Sarah."

"Handy," I laughed and everyone looked at me. "Because he used her hand to- oh never mind. Let's go, the door's open."

"Dad?" Rayetayah stood within the open door, gaping at all of us.

"Son," Raza pulled Raye into a hug. "You're alright."

"I've been waiting for you," Raye said with the trusting assurance of a child. "I knew you'd free us."

"I had a little help," Raza nodded back at us. "Is everyone with you?"

"Yeah, we're all fine," Raye turned and waved his hand back into the room. I had a brief glance of a huge crowd.

"Flight members too?" Sarah asked as she tried to peer around Raye's wings.

Raye flinched just slightly when he saw Sarah and I noticed that her shoulders tensed. But then he went on casually, "They're all fine. We were comfortable enough, considering."

"Great, that's great," I interrupted. "But we gotta go. It might not be as easy to get out of Dathadair as it was to get in."

"Right," Raye turned. "Come on, everyone, we're going home!" The people behind him started to cheer and he shushed them quickly. "We need to be fast and as quiet as possible."

Then they started filing out; witches and raven mockers alike. Parents held somber children and tried to keep them quiet as we rushed them through the corridor and down to the stairwell at the end. I went along the line urging anyone who could glamour themselves to do so but some of the children weren't able to work the magic yet and their parents stayed visible with them.

I took a deep breath and looked to Tiernan. How were we going to get them all through the keep and then out of the village in full view. If the riders returned and started searching the village, it would be difficult to hide even with all of us using glamour but with some of them visible, it would be impossible.

"I need you two to look within and search for the magic inside you," Raza said to Tristan and Sarah. "Try and bring it forth, glamour yourselves to look like a normal dullahan."

"Why would that help?" Sarah's gruesome dullahan smile was set in place firmly now and it kind of creeped me out a bit to see it on her when she was being so serious.

"Because then you can act like guards escorting some prisoners through town," Tiernan caught the idea. "Now that your dullahan magic is enhanced, a small glamour should fool anyone into believing that you're pure bloods, even another dullahan."

"Oh," Tristan nodded. "Okay. Let me try."

Within moments, Tristan looked like a full fledged dullahan, metal collar around his neck and everything. Sarah pulled back a little in horror, shaking her head in denial.

"It's just an illusion, Sarah," I laid my hand on her arm and she flinched. "Dullahans are obviously good at illusion. You can do this and remember, Danu promised to change you back when we're done. This is only temporary."

"Right," she took a shaky breath. "Just an illusion. Temporary."

Then she closed her eyes and concentrated. Just as with Tristan, a glamour settled over Sarah in a low shimmer, changing her into a full dullahan. She opened her darting dark eyes and grinned her dullahan grin, and I couldn't help giving a small shiver.

"Alright," I looked over the visible raven mockers. "Can all of the parents with children who aren't able to glamour come here and stand with Sarah and Tristan?" I asked. "They'll be your make-believe guards," I said to the children. "I need you to be brave for just a little bit longer and then we can get you home, okay?"

They looked scared but most gave me nods. The others were given pep talks by their parents, who then nodded to me. We were as ready as we could get.

"Let's go," I said to Tiernan as I glamoured myself invisible. "Cat?" I felt her nudge my side.

We filed down the stairs; hundreds of invisible people and a group of twenty parents with their children, being led by two dullahans. I honestly didn't have high hopes for us and as we descended past the lower levels of the keep, I began to pray. I knew Danu said she'd be with us but it never hurt to make sure. Then a hand touched my cheek and I was sure. She was there, guiding us, and we were going to make it.

We passed by a few dullahans but they simply nodded to Tristan and Sarah, who nodded back. We kept walking out of the keep, going at a modest pace so we wouldn't attract too much attention. One dullahan approached us as we headed down the steps but Sarah said something to him about giving the children some fresh air and amazingly, he bought it.

My heart started to slow down to its normal beat when we made it out into the village. I had faith now. I trusted that Danu would see us out, and when we reached the happy little fountain in the middle of Dathadair, I started to smile. I looked back at Sarah and her group and saw that the raven mocker parents were starting to relax as well, hugging their children and whispering encouragement.

That's when the riders flooded the courtyard.

We all froze as they surrounded Sarah and Tristan's group, one of the riders approaching the witches. The rest of us eased towards the side and I felt the soft nudge of Cat leaning against my leg. She was panting in dismay, her body tensing in preparation for a fight. Then a hand gripped my upper arm and a face pressed against mine.

"Get my son out of here," Raza whispered urgently. "I'll stay behind and make sure the rest of them get out safely."

"No," I started to protest but he shoved me into someone and I felt warm hands grip me, feathers brushing my skin. Cat gave a soft whine and one of the dullahan riders looked in our direction.

"Get out of this village *now*," Raza hissed at us and I felt myself pushed along.

We all pressed together, silently shuffling away from the group of terrified parents and children, and it was all I could do to set one foot in front of the other. Raza was with them, I told myself. Danu was with them. If a goddess and a dragon couldn't save the mockers, than no one could. But every bone in my body rebelled against leaving people behind... leaving children behind.

A child's wail froze me for a second but we were nearly to the gate and I felt a hand slip into mine and pull me along urgently. I almost jerked away anyway but then a roar rumbled through the night, booming out like thunder to urge me on faster. And then the screams of grown men rose above those of the children.

My group ran out of the open gates of Dathadair and clambered up the hill into the concealing arms of the Unseelie Forest. At the apex, I turned back and dropped my glamour, looking anxiously toward the village. The sky was lightening and I

344

could see the central square clearly, though most of it was blocked by the massive body of a dragon.

The dragon tossed its head and a dullahan went flying; head and body separating to land in two different places. The body got up and instantly started searching for its head. I might have laughed if things hadn't been so dire. But then I saw the fleeing mockers led through the streets by two dullahan impostors and I did laugh. I laughed in relief and thanked Danu as twilight coasted over Fairy and rushed through my veins.

"We're not safe yet," Tiernan said as his glamour fell and I looked down to see lavender sparks dripping from our joined hands. "We've got a long way to go, even if most of us can fly."

"Right," I looked over my shoulder to the mass of mockers and witches, all staring at me solemnly, and wondered what the hell we'd been thinking when we made this plan.

"They're out of the village!" Raye rushed to the slope and started down it to meet the families halfway. He helped them up the hill, Sarah and Tristan bringing up the rear.

Just as they crested the ridge, Cat gave a little bark and I looked down at her where she had pressed in tight beside me. She ran off into the forest, weaving through the dense foliage as if she'd caught the scent of some small prey. I cursed and chased after her, the twilight energy still riding high in my blood. I found my feet leaving the ground as I ran, magic coating the soles of my boots.

"Cat, this is not the time," I growled as I pushed aside obstacles with a wave of my fingers. I was leaving a glittering trail of lavender behind me but I didn't care. I needed to grab that stupid puka and get back to the others. "Damn it, Catriona, I'm leaving you at home next time. Now get your furry ass back here, we have people... we.."

I stopped in the middle of a dirt road and looked up into the molasses colored eyes of a very large horse. No, it was a puka in horse form. My heartbeat sped up and I started to lift my magic-filled fingers but then I realized that the trappings it wore bore the royal crest of Unseelie and it was hitched to three other pukas which were pulling a gleaming sin-black and silver coach.

Cat was running towards the door of the coach, yipping happily as it opened. I stepped back to watch one shiny, black boot hit the dusty road and then another. A head lifted above the barrier of the coach door but all I could see was a midnight velvet hood. Still, I knew who it was even before he spoke.

"Catriona," my Uncle Uisdean purred to my puka. "How lovely to see you again."

"Uncle Uisdean?" I blinked at him in shock as he closed the coach door and oozed up to me.

"King Uisdean," Tiernan, who had evidently been behind me the whole way, was already recovered from the shock of seeing the Unseelie King on some random backwoods road, and was bowing like he was in the middle of court.

"Hello, my darling niece," Uisdean aimed his sharp smile at me and then nodded to Tiernan, "Count Tiernan."

"What are you doing here?" I blurted as more fairies broke through the treeline behind us.

"The Goddess called upon me," for a moment, Uisdean's face glowed with wonder and worship, and then his expression cleared and his usual smirk settled in. "She said you needed transportation," he waved a hand backwards and behind his coach I saw a line of wagons waiting for us.

"Sweet Danu," I breathed. "I never would have thought she'd use you to save us."

"I admit that I see the irony in it as well," he strode forward

346

and peered at the group behind me. "But one must not ignore a request from our Goddess."

"No, one must not," I huffed as a dragon roar echoed, coming closer and closer until Raza circled overhead.

I waved Raza down and he settled on the road nearby. The pukas immediately went crazy, rearing and crying until Raza shifted into man form. Cat just watched the show with casual curiosity, glancing at the unseelie pukas in what appeared to be amusement. The pukas settled as Raza joined us and Uisdean immediately removed his cloak and handed it to the dragon-djinn.

"Lord Raza," Uisdean smiled. "I'm relieved to see that you're unharmed."

"As if my death would pain you," Raza chuckled as he accepted the cloak.

Then a horn sounded and Uisdean lifted a brow, "Should we wait for them? It may prove entertaining."

"I'm rather surprised that they're brave enough to give chase after the roasting I just gave them," Raza looked back towards the village with a perturbed glare.

"I guess you're losing your touch, old friend," Uisdean laughed and gave Raza a pat on the shoulder.

"Wait," I blinked at the two of them. "You're *friends?*"

"Why does that shock you?" Uisdean lifted one wicked, black brow.

"I didn't think you had any friends," I grimaced at my uncle.

"And I didn't think you could think," Uisdean smiled sweetly back at me.

347

"What are you; five?" I huffed.

"You threw the first glove," he gave me a sassy look.

"Punch," I growled. "I threw the first punch."

"Hardly," Uisdean scoffed. "You couldn't land a punch on me, little Seren," he swept by me and I rolled my eyes. "Now are we fighting or leaving?"

"Leaving," I started waving our people forward. "I'm not risking the children."

"Fine," Uisdean sighed and nodded to his unseelie knights.

The men rushed forward to help our fairies and witches onto the wagons. I started to join one of the groups but Uisdean took my arm and escorted me back to his coach. I got in grudgingly, simply because we didn't have time to waste arguing, and Cat jumped in after me. Before Tiernan could climb in with us, Uisdean shut the coach door in his face.

"I need a moment with my niece," he called out to Tiernan and I heard Tiernan race off to one of the wagons, cursing in Gaelic as he went.

Soon we were rumbling down the road, headed away from Dathadair and its unsettling occupants. Unfortunately I was left alone in a coach with a new unsettling occupant. I frowned at Uisdean as Cat settled on the floor between us.

"Thanks for the lift," I said warily.

"I am obeying the Goddess, that is all," he waved his hands out to the sides.

"Uh huh," I narrowed my eyes on him. "What do you want?"

"Nothing but to speak with you," he flicked one long length

348

of silky onyx hair over his shoulder and set his stare on me. At least, I was pretty sure he was staring at me, it could get hard to tell, what with his eyes being completely black; no whites or irises to speak of.

"Alright," I sighed and sat back. "What do you want to talk about?"

A screech echoed in the distance and my eyes shot to the window.

"They've realized their prey has escaped," Uisdean smiled. "And that their fate is sealed. They'll be taken before the court for this. Or simply hunted."

"They seemed to think that they did nothing wrong," I offered.

"If they hadn't knowingly attempted to impede a truce, they wouldn't have," Uisdean shrugged. "But laws of war dictate that once a truce is in the making, none shall interfere with it until it is settled or abandoned."

"I feel a little sorry for them," I admitted softly.

"Hmph," Uisdean made a disgusted face. "Pity is a waste of time. The dullahans orchestrated their own destruction. They should count themselves lucky that Raza didn't slaughter them all in recompense for his son's abduction. Honestly, it's not at all like him to be merciful," he stopped and glared at me accusingly. "Did you do something to him?"

"Of course not," I huffed but Uisdean continued to stare at me until I felt my cheeks warm. His eyes widened in shocked comprehension and I shouted, "I didn't do anything!"

"You mated a dragon?!" Uisdean shouted back.

"No, and please keep your voice down," I hissed.

"But you did do something to him," Uisdean insisted. "If you didn't bed the beast, then what?"

"We haven't done anything really," I huffed. "And don't call him a beast. I thought you were his friend?"

"Oh no, it's even worse than I'd assumed," Uisdean inhaled sharply. "You haven't seduced his loins, you've seduced his heart. You wicked, wily wench!"

"First off; you sound ridiculous. And second; I didn't do anything to Raza! Not his loins or his heart. Can we stop talking about him now?"

"Fine," Uisdean sniffed. "Keep your sluttish secrets. I merely want to give you some advice; one royal to another."

"Advice about Raza?" I gave him an incredulous look.

"Now who won't stop talking about the dragon-djinn?" Uisdean smirked. "No, not Lord Raza, about the complications and intricacies of ruling."

"Oh," I lamented, "here it comes."

"Sometimes, it is necessary to deal with those you find... distasteful," he offered.

"If you're referring to yourself, a better word would be detestable," I smiled snidely.

"It is necessary to be diplomatic when dealing with other monarchs on occasion," he went on. "And when one offers you a boon, it would do you well to remember it."

"Oh, I get it," I smirked. "The Goddess may have asked you to help us but that won't stop you from trying to profit from this."

"I must think of my kingdom first," he shrugged.

"So again, I ask you; what do you want?" I glared at him.

"I want you to remember the aid I've offered you today," he shrugged.

"And?"

"And I want you to do your Ambassadorial duty and act as mediator between the Court of the Nine Sons and Unseelie."

"Pardon?"

"I'm having some issues with the dragons," he sighed. "They refuse to come out of their watery wonderland and speak with me so I must journey into the Básmhor Sea myself."

"Why do you need me?"

"Because you, with your new untouchable, undefined, ambassador status, will confuse them into being more agreeable and will hopefully prevent bloodshed," he grimaced.

"You think I can stop the dragons from attacking you?" I scoffed.

"No, I think you can confound them as you do me and stop them from fighting with each other long enough for us to conclude our business," Uisdean huffed. "Getting the dragons to agree on anything is like pulling weeds."

"Pulling teeth," I sighed as I corrected him again.

"Pulling teeth?" Uisdean scowled. "But that's rather fun while pulling weeds is a ghastly business."

Chapter Fifty-Three

The journey back to Ireland was long and gratefully uneventful. Uisdean took us all to the rath which connected Unseelie to Samford Valley in Australia. He had already chartered planes and buses for our transport, having been warned by Danu what would be required. So a line of buses took us back to the Brisbane airport, where one large plane waited to carry the rescued Flight witches and the raven mockers home to Tulsa while the smaller plane which we'd flown to Australia, was ready to take the rest of us to Ireland... the rest of us including my Uncle Uisdean. He was coming along since he had to attend the truce summit anyway.

Sarah had been anxious when we boarded the plane, wondering why Danu hadn't kept her word and come to change her back. But Tristan was confident in our goddess and assured the Vex that Danu would surely carry out her promise as soon as they reached Ireland. I added to this, promising to take both of them through the rath within the High Fairy Council House and over to the Isle of Danu. There, I was certain that Danu would fulfill her promise. This seemed to relax Sarah and she fell into a thoughtful silence for the rest of the journey.

Raza had gone with his son, wanting to see Raye settled in Tulsa before he headed back to Unseelie. He seemed to have lost interest in the truce now that his son was safe and I didn't blame him in the least. I had hugged him goodbye, wishing him and Raye well. Raza had kissed my cheek and told me that he'd see me soon but I just shrugged it off. There was too much going on to worry about what Raza might or might not do in the future.

Tiernan was openly thrilled to see Raza boarding a

different plane than ours and even went so far as to shake Raza's hand. It seemed that the further away we got from the dragon, the happier Tiernan became and by the time we reached Ireland, my fairy boyfriend was beaming in delight. He lost that beautiful smile as soon as we pulled into the courtyard of the High Fairy Council House. There, standing on the steps to the main keep, was my human father, Extinguisher Ewan Sloane, talking to an older woman.

I sighed when I saw them. The woman had her back to us but I knew immediately who she was. Her gray hair was braided back neatly, as always, and her linen dress was pressed into obedience, falling in straight lines around her trim frame. She wore serviceable brown leather boots and wore no jewelry except for a slim gold band around her left ring finger. Even though Grandpa had died years ago.

She turned as our line of SUVs stopped in front of the stairs, and set her sharp sea-blue stare on me. Her eyes were almost exact replicas of Ewan's except they never filled with warmth. I had to hand it to Queen Iseabal, at least she had tried to be nice to me. Ewan's mother had never given me a kind word, much less a sweet look. Now that the truth of my parentage was out, I expected even less from her.

She didn't disappoint.

I took a deep breath and walked up the steps, Cat padding along beside me. I wasn't sure what I should do but I knew I had to at least be civil to them. So when I reached the stair they stood on, I paused and opened my mouth to issue a polite greeting. Grandma beat me to it.

"Keep walking, fairy spawn," she spat at me.

"What did you call me?" I gaped at her while Ewan closed his eyes as if he were in pain.

353

"You heard me," Head Councilwoman Briana Sloane sneered. "Take your bastard self away."

Twelve swords pulled free of their hilts and filled the air around my grandmother, making her blink in surprise. I looked back and saw my entire guard, Tiernan included, threatening the Head Councilwoman of New York. Then Cat started to growl, adding her teeth to the sharp weapons on display.

"Sheath your swords or I'll have you all extinguished," Briana snapped.

The sword tips angled higher and Cat growled deeper.

"A puka, Seren?" Briana spat. "You have a puka for a pet? Can you not even be faithful to that whore who birthed you?"

"Mother," Ewan ground out.

"You have given grave insult to a princess of Fairy," Tiernan intoned. "As her guard, we have a responsibility to protect her from all harm. Speak one more harsh word, Councilwoman and I will slice your head from your body."

I gaped in horror at my boyfriend as the entire courtyard went quiet. Witches, humans, and fairies all stared at us in rapt fascination, waiting to see who would back down... or die.

"Tiernan," I whispered. "It's alright, stand down."

Tiernan glanced at me and then nodded crisply. He lowered his sword and gave the rest of my guard a look so that they lowered theirs as well. I saw my Uncle Uisdean and his guard come up behind us on the stairs and stop to watch the show with obvious glee. I rolled my eyes and looked back to my grandmother.

"That's the smartest thing you could have done," she said to Tiernan. "Your bastard princess has saved you."

Tiernan lifted his sword once more and with a swirling, dance-like movement, swung it straight for my grandmother's throat. I reacted automatically, pulling my own sword and lifting it to block his. The clang of metal echoed through the courtyard as Briana's face went white.

"I said stand down," I growled in a low tone and glared at Tiernan.

"I vowed to behead her if she issued one more insult," Tiernan shrugged casually and pulled his sword from mine with a long hiss of metal. "I could not break my vow," he sheathed his sword.

"Tiernan, whatever kind of point you're trying to make, I think she got it," I whispered as I sheathed my own sword. When I looked up, Ewan was staring at me with a strange look. "Dad," I reached a hand toward him but his mother slapped it away.

"You're no kin to us," Briana said in a shaky voice.

"Mom, please," Ewan sighed. "You're taking this too far."

"You just renounced her to me," Councilwoman Sloane frowned at her son. "Now you want to take her side?"

"Denying that she's my daughter and calling her a bastard are two different things," Ewan growled. "She had no control over her own birth. Leave her be."

"You need to cut all ties with this changeling child, Ewan," Briana scolded. "Emotional ties included."

"But I don't need to insult her to do it," Ewan shook his head. "You've always had a mean streak, Mother but it's never horrified me till now."

"So you want to side with the bastard of your slut of a wife against your own mother?" Briana huffed. "You're a disappointment, Ewan."

I was about to stand up for my mother when Ewan did it for me.

"Call my wife a whore one more time, Mother and it'll be the last thing you say," Ewan's eyes lit with life, giving me a glimpse of the man he used to be before my mother's death.

"You ungrateful brat," she slapped him but it barely nudged his face and he just continued to stare hard at her. "Now you threaten my life? My own son?"

"I didn't threaten to kill you," Ewan shifted so that he stood beside me. "Just to cut out your poisonous tongue." Then he offered me his hand. I gaped at it for one brief moment before I snatched it up like the gift it was. "Now if you'll excuse me, I'm heading inside with the woman I raised."

So maybe he hadn't reclaimed me as his daughter but it was enough for me. I smiled brightly as he escorted me inside the castle, my Star's Guard and puka following us closely as my Uncle Uisdean laughed his ass off.

Chapter Fifty-Four

"Thanks, Dad," I said when we came to a stop in the main hall.

"I'm not your father, Seren," Ewan said sadly. "I wish it weren't true but you belong to another family now. I've accepted that and I think I can at least be civil to you but that's the most you can expect from me. We're done. Goodbye, Princess Seren," he held his hand out to me.

"Goodbye, Extinguisher Ewan," I said brokenly as I shook his hand. I watched a blurry Ewan Sloane walk away from me.

"You've got one screwed up family," Sarah observed as she stepped up beside me.

I blinked away the tears and squeezed Tiernan's hand, which had somehow made its way into mine.

"Yeah, you have no idea," I sighed. "I need to get everyone settled and then I'll take you and Tristan over to Fairy."

"Alright," Sarah nodded. "We'll wait down here. I could use a drink anyway." She headed towards the dining hall.

"Are you alright?" Tiernan whispered as he eased in closer to me.

"Yeah, I'm good," I whispered back. "Thanks for that ridiculous display out there."

"No problem," he grinned. "It's not like you haven't made similar displays of ridiculousness for me."

"You weren't actually going to kill her, right?" I lifted a brow. "You knew I'd stop you."

"Sure," he looked away and cleared his throat.

"Tiernan," I gaped at him but before I could say anything more, one of the house attendants came over to help us find rooms for everyone.

It took hours to get us all rooms and then another hour for me to get showered and changed. It must have been around 8 PM when I finally made it downstairs to look for Sarah and Tristan. Tiernan, Conri, and Cat would be joining us on our short trip to Fairy, so they walked with me to the dining hall. We found Tristan sleeping on a wooden bench and Sarah sitting next to him, staring woodenly at the ceiling.

She perked up when she saw us though and woke Tristan with a violent shake. Tristan slipped from the bench and came rolling up to wave his arms about, looking for his attacker. His obsidian dullahan eyes shot about the room, his wide mouth grinning as usual.

"It's time to go," Sarah stood and slapped his shoulder. "Isn't it?" She asked me.

"Yes, it's time," I agreed. "Were you able to speak to the Coven elders and inform them of what's happened?"

"Yes," she cleared her throat. "They're a bit shocked by our transformations and even more shocked to hear that we've spoken with the Goddess. In light of all of that, they've decided to pardon the murder of Elder Wasutke. I won't be punished for it but they're anxious to see me transformed back into what I once was. If for no other reason than to see proof of the Goddess."

"I imagine that there are now mixed feelings about witches visiting Fairy," I offered.

"You could say that," she grimaced. "Beckoning was not pleased to hear about our origins, nor were they happy to see what we could turn into by simply stepping foot into the Fairy Realm. But the other clans were satisfied with the discoveries, even Frederick's become a celebrity with his silly wings. The Coven elders are discussing sending representatives from the other clans into Fairy if the truce is signed."

"That'll be interesting," I blinked. "I'm glad I won't have to make that decision."

"So am I," Tristan agreed.

"For now, let's get you two back into Fairy," I offered and they both nodded excitedly. Or maybe that was just their faces, damn those dullahan grins.

I led them through the halls of the castle, then up to a tall wooden door, bound with metal hinges. There were guards standing to either side of the door, each with a spear in one hand. They came to attention when we approached.

"Princess, Seren," they spoke as one and bowed to me. Then one of them opened the door and let us through.

I had been to the Isle of Danu once before but I'd never gone through the rath which connected it to Ireland and so I wasn't prepared for the sight of the fairy mound nor of the room which contained it. The Isle rath of Ireland wasn't hidden in a basement or camouflaged by trees. It stood proudly in the middle of a flourishing garden, which the castle had obviously been built around. It was much larger than any of the other raths I'd seen. But then, this had been the very first rath, the one made by Anu himself, not the fey.

This was a rath built by a god.

Instead of a simple mound of earth, there was a large hill covered in blossoming olive trees. Creamy bunches of little

359

flowers nestled among the silvery leaves and lay scattered across the vibrant grass that covered the mound. Gnarled, smokey-quartz roots spread out from the thick, twisted trunks, curling over each other and angling down around a huge gate set into the earth. There was an image of the Isle of Danu carved into the golden door. Over the gold island hung a silver star, to the right was a silver moon, and on its left was a gold sun.

I walked forward over a pristine stone path and stood before the door, staring up at the grove of olive trees. What a strange thing to find in Ireland. I looked around me at the garden full of fruit trees and fragrant blooms. Colors abounded everywhere; in the flowers, butterflies, and exotic birds which flew about without fear. The rath almost seemed muted amid all that vibrancy, only the gleam of precious metals made it stand out.

"Olive trees?" I turned to Tiernan as he approached.

"They are indigenous to Fairy," he smiled as he explained. "A symbol of peace and plenty."

"Of course they are."

"The oil made from these olives is sacred," Tiernan went on as Sarah, Tristan, Conri, and Cat joined us. "It can be used to heal almost any wound and just a single olive can fill an empty belly. If the Fairy Council had to withstand a siege, they could survive indefinitely on the olives alone."

"Whoa," Tristan breathed as he stared up into the trees.

"Are you ready to return to Fairy?" I asked him and he transferred his gaze to me, nodding vigorously. "Alright, you guys know the drill; stay on the path."

"Right," Sarah sighed. "Stay on the path. Like that helped so much before."

"You'll be back to normal in no time," I laid a hand on her

shoulder and this time she didn't flinch, just nodded. "Alright then," I looked down at Cat. "You ready to see Danu?"

She yipped excitedly and I stepped forward. The giant door of the gate swung inward before I could lay a hand on it but I didn't hesitate. I walked confidently into the darkness of the In-Between and straight down the short path which went through it. At the end, another gargantuan door swung open for us and we all emerged into a garden very similar to the one we'd left. Nearly identical actually. I glanced over my shoulder and saw the same blossoming olive trees covering the hill.

Then the gate swung closed behind us.

I gave the witches an encouraging smile and headed for the only door in the circular enclosure. The walls around us were just like those in the last garden; smooth all the way up to the open ceiling. Here, the sky was slightly lighter and littered with fluffy clouds as opposed to the deep, clear blue of Ireland.

I opened the door and two startled guards angled their spears towards me. Then they saw my face and lifted the weapons so they could bow. I nodded to them and passed into the halls of the High Council House of Fairy, Cat striding along happily beside me. Tiernan came up on my left and took my hand. I smiled at him, feeling better than I had in weeks.

We were so close to an end. I just had to take these witches to Danu and then we could return and hopefully witness the signing of the first truce between the Coven and the Councils. I even knew where I'd find Danu; in her temple, just outside the Council House. She had once assured me that it was the only place in Fairy where you could be certain to hear her voice.

Several fairies roamed the halls and all of them gave us surprised looks when we passed. But none tried to stop us. Generally, if you made it through the gates of Anu's rath, you were meant to be there. So we walked out of the castle and down the flower-bordered path to the towering crystal temple of Danu without any issues.

I heard the witches gasp and shared a smile with Tiernan. Danu's temple was something out of a dream, beyond even a fairy tale. Crystal spires towered so high into the sky that you couldn't see the end to them. They were connected by delicate crystal arches, angled upward in places so that you kept wanting to look higher and higher.

The pale path we were on led right into the heart of the temple, where it circled a central pillar of crystal before it went on to bisect the temple completely. The heart was where I was headed; to the spirit crystal that sparkled with violet light. Set around the circular path that surrounded this crystal, were four more columns which stood guard like fairy knights; one column for each of the remaining elements.

The fire column was filled with a carnelian-crimson light and the base of it was surrounded by flames. Water held cerulean shimmers within its facets while rain fell steadily around it. Air was known by its buttery golden glow and the swirl of wind which constantly circled it. Then there was Earth; full of a mossy oak illumination and adorned with the curling clutch of vines.

I glanced at these elemental crystals but spared them only a moment before I went straight to the center one which represented Spirit; the fifth element. I placed my palms to the stone and prayed for Danu to come to us and fulfill her promise to the witches.

Tristan and Sarah were still staring about them in wonder when Danu appeared; a hazy feminine shape with a blurry face. She formed within the central pillar first and then stepped free of the crystal to stand before us. I saw my eyes in her shifting face but I knew it would be different for the others. Danu's eyes always became her viewer's. It was her way of showing how connected she was to her children.

Conri, Tiernan, and I were already on our knees when the Beckoning witches realized that Danu was among us. Then they knelt too, staring at Danu like they couldn't truly believe she was there. Cat ran up to the goddess and sat beside her, just happy to be near her, and Danu laid her glittering hand upon Cat's head.

"Hello, Catriona," the Goddess spoke and Cat gave her a joyful yip in response. "Hello, Tristan," Danu lifted her gaze and smiled at the male witch. "Are you ready to claim your place?"

"I am," he said immediately.

"Then come here," she held her hand out to him.

Tristan stood and rushed over to Danu. She placed her hands to Tristan's temples and a blinding light poured from her palms and into him. He went rigid as the light filled him and then began to shine through him, casting a glow over the ground like a halo. The Goddess remained serene; her hazy mouth smiling sweetly.

When she pulled her hands away, the light faded and we all gaped at what remained. Tristan no longer looked like a dullahan. He had grown several inches and his muscles had thickened slightly, giving him the sleek physique of an Olympic swimmer. His shoulder-length hair had darkened from oak to ebony and his skin had paled to a pearly sheen. His face was healthy again but a little longer; with a regal nose and high cheekbones. Beneath his noble brow were a pair of glittering violet eyes; the exact same color as the light within the Spirit column.

"Welcome, Councilman Tristan Lightheart," Danu said solemnly. "Your trust in me has served you well and so I reward it with the dream you most desired. I've made you into a sidhe of Fairy."

"I'm a sidhe?" Tristan lifted his hands to his beautiful face.

"Your spirit has chosen your mór magic for you," Danu

363

went on. "You were not born to be a warrior but a scholar and a healer. So you shall be. You bear a new magic; the lightheart. With it you will heal the most damaged of hearts and lighten the heaviest souls. You'll bring comfort to those without hope and peace to those who know only rage. You will be my vessel of compassion for my children."

"I'm honored," Tristan knelt and Danu laid her hand on him gently.

"But, I didn't know I could choose this," Sarah whispered.

"Faith must be rewarded," Danu said simply. "You chose duty to your people instead of love for me," she held up a hand when Sarah started to protest. "I'm not judging you, Sarah. You made a valid choice and an honorable one. I will uphold our bargain and grant you the return of your old form."

Danu held her hand out to Sarah. The witch stood slowly and moved forward as Tristan stood and moved back. Sarah knelt and looked up into Danu's face, all of her fear and anxiety leaving her as she gazed upon the Goddess. Then Danu put her hands on Sarah's head and light once more emanated from the Goddess' fingers. Sarah was filled as Tristan had been and when Danu stepped back, the magic faded from Sarah and revealed her to be as she once was.

Sarah bowed her head, "Thank you, Danu."

"I will miss you, Daughter," Danu laid her hand on Sarah's head and a brief glow lit Sarah's temples. "But I send you away with a little gift to remember me by."

Then Danu turned to me.

"Goddess," I bowed my head briefly. "Thank you for helping us. For sending Uisdean to see us safely out of Fairy."

"He was a little reluctant," she laughed and it echoed off

the crystals like tinkling glass. "I saw that in his heart. But he agreed immediately anyway. He has always been a good son, loyal to me and Fairy. I hope that someday he will show you the softer aspects of his nature."

"That's okay," I shook my head. "I'm good without knowing his softer side."

Danu laughed again. "You have put limits on your love, Seren," she chided. "Let your heart grow and go where it wills."

"Well, some places its gone are a little restrictive about where else I let it wander," I shot a teasing look in Tiernan's direction but he was staring at the Goddess like she was giving him his results from a STD test.

"There are many paths to love," Danu gave Tiernan a wink. "And many ways to experience it. Trust that Seren knows which paths to take to strengthen her heart without breaking yours."

"Thank you," I said, still feeling a bit guilty for kissing Raza.

"And, Seren," Danu set her penetrating stare on me, which just so happened to be my own stare. "Watch your step. Navigating love and life can be dangerous and you are heading into rough waters."

"I'll try my best," I grimaced.

"Don't look so worried," her blurry lips lifted in a smile. "I'll be walking the path beside you."

"When the path leads into a bedroom, would you mind waiting outside?"

Danu laughed as she stepped back into the central crystal column. Her laughter lingered as she faded into the light.

"That wasn't an answer," I called after her.

Chapter Fifty-Five

Tristan took his place among the High Council of Fairy with very little difficulty. Most of the council members were actually on the other side of the rath, in Ireland for the summit. Even William Sehoka, the imprisoned Flight witch, had been taken back to HR to be released into the Coven's care. There was only one high council member left on the Isle, the rest of the inhabitants were trainees or household staff, so there was no one to protest the witch-turned-sidhe taking his place in the High Council. The one councilman left had originally given us shocked looks but when it was all explained, he simply nodded and declared that Danu's wishes must be obeyed. Tristan was given a room and that was that.

After we saw him settled, the rest of us returned through the rath to the High Fairy Council House in Ireland. We stepped out of the garden to find my father waiting for us. My true father; King Keir. He smiled when he saw me and came forward to give me a hug and a quick kiss on the cheek, before taking my hand and wrapping it around his arm.

"The summit has been scheduled for tomorrow afternoon," he said with supreme satisfaction.

"Wonderful," I sighed. "Then I'm going to get something to eat and go to bed."

"I'm afraid you aren't," Keir laughed. "I came to collect you because you're needed immediately in the ballroom. There's a pre-summit party going on as we speak, meant to provide us with an opportunity to get to know each other."

"Oh," I ran a hand through my hair and looked down at the

velvet fairy dress I'd worn to see the Goddess. "I guess it's a good thing I dressed up for Danu."

"Indeed," Keir laughed and looked back to the others. "All of you are welcome to join. There will be refreshments and entertainment."

"I'm in," Conri smirked and then turned to Sarah. "What about you, witchy lady?"

"I think I'm gonna get some rest before the summit," she rubbed at her temple distractedly and broke away from our group, heading towards the stairs.

"Looks like you're losing your touch," I teased Conri.

"Impossible," he scoffed. "And if I'd actually touched her, she would have invited me to join her upstairs."

"Bargest, you need to learn some humility," Gradh said as she rounded a corner. "I could hear your ego coming all the way down the hall."

Conri just stopped and smiled, looking over the amazing vision Gradh made in her fey evening gown. Her lustrous cobalt hair was piled high on her head in intricate braids, showing off the graceful curve of her bronzed neck, and the pistachio dress complimented her periwinkle eyes.

"I'm open to any suggestions you'd like to give me," Conri bowed to Gradh and offered her his arm.

"If you touch anything you're not asked to," she took his arm and narrowed her eyes on him, "I'll make those suggestions with my dagger." She shifted aside her split skirt and revealed the gold dagger strapped to her thigh.

"Danu help me," Conri groaned as he led Gradh away. "I think I'm in love."

"You wouldn't know love if it bit you on the ass," Gradh huffed.

"Was that an offer?" Conri asked hopefully.

"I think we'll just let them go into the ballroom first," Keir grimaced.

"Don't want to be associated with the bargest and his female knight?" I teased my father as Tiernan came up beside us and Cat ran ahead with Conri.

"No, I don't want to be within the blast radius when Gradh decides she's had enough of Conri's flirtations," Keir rolled his eyes.

"Blast radius," I nodded approvingly. "Well said, Dad."

"Thank you," Keir beamed, proud to have got a human saying right. "Now, smile big and stay close. These witches have a dangerous aura about them."

"Dangerous, eh?" I frowned, thinking of Danu's warning.

"Not as dangerous as us, of course," Keir gave me a sideways grin. "But you might need to look after our human friends."

"Right," I slid a glance at Tiernan and he gave me a little nod.

Then we were entering the ballroom of the High Council of Fairy. Muted conversations melded with the strains of string instruments as my sight filled with fluttering gowns on dancing women and the gleam of jeweled sword hilts on dashing men. I was a little taken aback at how very many people were in the room. With all of the clans of the Coven represented, both Councils, the Extinguishers, the Wild Hunt, and every fairy noble who felt the need to be included in such a momentous affair, the room was near to bursting.

Everyone was dressed as if to show the others how important they were. I actually felt a little underdressed in my simple ruby velvet. I pulled self-consciously at the ombré aubergine stripe in my hair, twirling the lavender tip around my finger. The only jewelry I had on was my star pendant; a gift from my parents... all of them, in a way.

Keir, who was dressed as a king of Fairy with crown and all, smiled down at me and waved someone forward. It was Ainsley and he held a purple cushion with my crown on it. My crown was a daintier version of my father's; a platinum circle of thin spires topped with diamond stars. It was tall, as far as crowns go, and I generally tried not to wear it. But amidst this group, it seemed imperative that I did.

"Princess," Ainsley smiled at me as he offered the crown to my father.

"Sir Ainsley," I smiled back. "Thank you for playing the role of crown bearer."

"My pleasure," Ainsley bowed after Keir took the crown and then removed himself and the pillow discreetly.

"Daughter," Keir lifted the crown and I edged forward enough to indicate that he could place it on me. He settled it firmly on my head, the thin layer of padding within the rim helping it to stay in place. "Beautiful."

"Yes, indeed," Uisdean agreed as he sidled up to us. "Brother," he nodded to my father.

"Brother," my father gave Uisdean a measured look. "I've heard of what you did for Seren. Thank you."

"The Goddess called," Uisdean shrugged but his pride was obvious and I wouldn't be surprised to hear him repeat that phrase

369

throughout the night. *Yes, well the Goddess called me herself blah, blah, blah.*

"And he exacted payment," I added.

"You made my daughter pay for your assistance?" My father narrowed his eyes on Uisdean and Tiernan tensed beside me.

I'd forgotten to tell Tiernan about the dragons. He was just going to love this, we'd gotten rid of one only to have a whole court of them thrown in my lap.

"Merely a request for her help in an ambassadorial matter," Uisdean waved his hands out expansively. "That's her job, is it not?"

"What matter?" My father leaned toward his brother aggressively and the conversations around us ceased.

When two kings of Fairy argued, you paid attention. If for no other reason than to know when to run and in which direction.

"I have a meeting with the Court of the Nine Sons, nothing too dangerous," Uisdean's eyes were like pits of darkness but his lips smiled wide, reminding me a little of a dullahan grin.

"Nothing *too dangerous*?!" My father let go of my hand and edged into Uisdean's personal space. "You want her to accompany you into a dragon court and you say it's nothing dangerous? Fairies have died from merely standing too close to a dragon argument."

"Or an argument of kings," I muttered. "Perhaps this isn't the best place for this? Or time?"

"Perhaps not," Keir clenched his jaw as he breathed heavily through his anger.

"This is your daughter's duty," Uisdean went serious. "She's our Ambassador, that means helping to keep the peace... in

370

every kingdom. You cannot hoard her to yourself, Keir."

"We'll discuss this later, Uisdean," Keir growled and turned away, right into his sister, Moire.

"Awkward," I groaned as we faced my aunt. The last time I'd seen Moire was when she'd come to ask for her son's release from our dungeon. It hadn't gone so well.

"Keir," she hissed.

She looked fully recovered from the bloodthorns my father had inflicted upon her when she tried to attack me. But recovered didn't mean healthy for Moire. Her emaciated frame was enveloped in pallid skin, as white as bleached bone, and her hair matched it perfectly. It made her look like she didn't have eyebrows, a very creepy visual in my opinion. In fact, she was almost colorless, the only hint of life was within the barest blush of blood on her lips and in the gray of her eyes.

"Moire," Keir barely glanced at his sister before brushing past her. He did stop to speak with her son though. "Bress, how are you?"

"I'm well, Uncle," my cousin nodded politely but there were shadows under his eyes as well as within them. His slate-blue hair puffed around him like angry clouds as he bowed to me. "Cousin Seren."

"Cousin Bress," I found myself leaning forward to kiss his cheek and whisper, "The offer still stands. You'll always be welcome in Twilight."

When I pulled back, I found him staring at me in shock, a thin film of moisture over his steel-swirled, sapphire eyes. He quickly blinked it away though and recovered his composure, giving me a jerky nod before turning away to attend his monstrous mother.

I don't know why I felt pity for Bress. He'd once tried to do horrible things to me. But then I'd seen how abused he was, how broken his mind was, and I'd felt bad for him. Danu had just spoken to me about keeping myself open to love. Maybe she had meant Bress... and the Goddess must not be ignored. Besides, I didn't have a lot of family left. If I could bring Bress back from the dark side, it would feel like a huge win for me.

"Princess Seren," the rolling Spanish accent alerted me to Gabriel Alegre's presence before I turned to see him. "I would be honored if you would introduce me to your father."

"Prime Elder Gabriel Alegre of the Beckoning clan," I said politely, "this is my father, King Keir Bloodthorn, First King of Twilight."

"Your Majesty," Gabriel bowed.

"Prime Elder Alegre," Keir inclined his head and held out a hand.

"It's a pleasure to meet you," Gabriel shook the offered hand with a warm smile. "I'm looking forward to cementing a truce between our people."

"I as well," Keir nodded. "I'm sorry to hear about the difficulties that arose for your people when they entered Fairy."

"Ah, yes," Gabriel frowned. "I had wanted to visit but now I don't believe I shall."

"Sarah is fully recovered," I offered. "Danu has returned her to her previous form. But there was a very unusual turn of events as far as Tristan is concerned."

"More unusual than what had already happened to him?" Alegre lifted a thick brow.

"Tristan has been changed into a sidhe and now holds a

place in the High Fairy Council," I just put it out there.

Both Gabriel and my father looked at me in shock.

"The Princess is trying to say that the Goddess has blessed Tristan's faith in her by giving him the form he secretly desired and placing him in a position which lies close to her heart," Tiernan explained tactfully. "He resides on the holy Isle of Danu now. I'm sorry but he won't be returning to the Human Realm."

"One of our own has been changed into a full fairy by the Goddess?" Gabriel blinked. "That's wonderful news. Hopefully he can become a symbol of our unity for our future."

"Yes, hopefully," Keir agreed but he was staring at someone off to his left, giving him a warning look. I glanced over and saw High Councilman Lorcan, who must have overheard our conversation and didn't seem to feel as positive about Tristan's transition as we did.

"Some may find his rapid advance unsettling," I said to Gabriel, though I was actually speaking to Lorcan. "But when the Goddess speaks... or acts, we must obey her wishes and accept what she has done."

Lorcan gave me a bitter look but nodded and moved away.

"Unfortunately," Elder Alegre said, "we cannot count on the Goddess returning all of us to our previous forms if we should happen to be changed by Fairy too. So I think I'll remain in this realm and deny myself the pleasure of speaking with her."

"I think that's the wisest course," Keir agreed. "Besides, we don't yet know if the Councils will agree to visitation."

"You're right," Alegre inclined his head. "I shouldn't lament things which may not even be within my reach."

"But perhaps they are within *my* reach," Elder Crispin

Arterbury came forward to bow to me. "Princess Seren."

"Prime Elder Crispin," I nodded. "This is my father, King Keir Bloodthorn of Twilight. Dad, this is Prime Elder Crispin Arterbury of the Bite clan."

"Yes," my father shook Crispin's hand. "We met earlier. How are you enjoying the party, Elder Arterbury?"

"Well, I'd enjoy it better if I had the pleasure of dancing with a fairy princess," he lifted a brow at me.

"And you'd have a better chance of that happening if you didn't call me a fairy princess to my face," I teased him.

"Oh, I should have known better but the crown threw me off," he recovered immediately. "A modern woman like you must prefer those titles that you have won rather than been given. I beg your forgiveness, Ambassador."

"That's better," I laughed. "But the first dance is always reserved for my boyfriend," I nodded towards Tiernan. "Perhaps the second?"

"I'll wait with bated breath," he vowed dramatically.

"On that note, gentlemen," Tiernan nodded to the men and then offered me his arm. "Would you like to dance, Twilight Star?"

"Lead the way, Lord Hunter," I took his hand.

Tiernan whisked me into the middle of the dance floor and pulled me close. I looked up into his gleaming silver eyes and knew there was no other man I wanted to be there with. Raza's kiss might have been hot and exciting but Tiernan could keep the heat going beyond the initial flutterings of desire. Tiernan could make love to me with a look and touch me deeper than any mere physical connection would allow. That was something to be

374

treasured.

"We need to speak to your father before he goes into the summit," Tiernan also knew how to ruin a mood.

"About what?"

"We can't allow any more witches into Fairy," he lowered his voice.

"Why not? Danu didn't seem to mind."

"But what if every witch who goes into Fairy gets altered," he leaned in close so only I could hear. "They're more powerful now, Seren. Each of them with enhanced power that may even be like yours; a blending of psychic abilities and fairy magic."

"The witches don't have psychic abilities," I shook my head.

"We don't know that for sure," he shook his head. "Look at what happened to Tristan."

"Danu helped to create that new magic," I argued.

"Seren, think about all of the members of the Coven pouring into Fairy to gain magical power," Tiernan growled. "They could grow more powerful than us. What would happen if they decided they didn't want to leave Fairy? Or that they wanted to rule it?"

"War in Fairy," I whispered.

"Yes," he sighed. "The best way to keep peace is by retaining the upper hand."

"We can't let them in, can we?" I stared up at him.

"No, not ever," he looked over to a group of council members. "I'm going to speak to the Councils. Do you think you can make your rounds with the royals?"

"You mean my Evil Uncle Uisdean and Psychotic Grandmother?" I lifted a brow.

"You'll get further with them than I will," he grimaced.

"Point taken," I grimaced back. "Fine, swirl me over to Iseabal," I gestured to where my fairy grandmother stood, just a few feet from the edge of the dance space.

"Good luck," he whispered and gave me a kiss before he angled us through the other dancers and over to my fairy grandmother.

"I'm gonna need it," I huffed as I stepped up to my grandmother and her husband, King Marcan. Tiernan wandered off towards the council members with a determined expression on his beautiful face. "King Marcan," I nodded to the shiny King of the Seelie. "Queen Iseabal," another nod to my grandmother.

They made a stunning couple; her with her gold curls piled atop her head like a Rumpelstiltskin masterpiece and her sunlight skin gleaming as if she'd been dusted with even more of the stuff, and him with his crystal hair which lit up like light bulbs when he used his magic. He was tall and regal, she was dainty and beautiful. They were the perfect fairy couple. Too bad one of them was bat shit crazy.

"Seren," King Marcan took my hand and gave me a kiss on the cheek. "How lovely you look."

"Thank you, Your Majesty," I inclined my head respectfully. I actually liked Marcan, it was his choice in women I didn't approve of. "How's my Uncle Shane? Is he here?"

"No, Shane stayed in Seelie to watch over the kingdom while we're away," Marcan said sadly. "I'll tell him you asked after him."

"Please do," I smiled sweetly, knowing that it would send Shane into a tizzy, wondering if the message had some secret, malicious meaning.

My Uncle Shane wasn't exactly insane like his mother but we'd had a misunderstanding recently. He'd tried to wipe out the human race and I, failing to understand why that would be a good thing, stopped him. It appeared that he'd kept our little argument from his parents. Probably because he'd been in league with an unseelie hag. Or maybe it was because he failed.

"Seren," Iseabal stared grimly at me. "You're still speaking to me, despite your father's enchantment?"

"We need to discuss this summit," I lowered my voice and saw that their attention was piqued. So I leaned in closer and explained our concerns to them.

"Humans growing stronger than fairies," Iseabal scoffed but Marcan looked worried.

"Either way, my love," Marcan said diplomatically, "I don't want them in our realm if we can prevent it."

"Agreed," Iseabal said grudgingly. "Fear not, Seren, your grandmother won't allow Fairy to be invaded by mutant humans."

"Maybe refrain from calling them that during the summit," I suggested and then gave King Marcan a look.

He sighed, pulling his wife into a corner to speak to her and hopefully explain why tact would be needed, as I headed towards my Uncle Uisdean.

Uisdean took even less convincing, nodding his agreement before I'd even finished a single sentence. It was my father who I had to spend some time persuading. But by the end of the evening, Tiernan and I had convinced both Councils and all of the royals to withhold visitation rights from the witches. It felt a little underhanded and wrong, especially when I thought of how happy Danu had been to see the witches, but in the end, fear for Fairy won out over love for the Goddess.

"One more day and this will all be over," I sighed as Tiernan shut the bedroom door behind us.

"I admit, I won't be sad to see the witches leave," Tiernan started unbuckling his sword belt. "Being assigned to you has brought me more headaches than any duty I've ever performed for the Council."

"Thanks a lot," I made a face at him while I kicked off my shoes. "Well I'll just go take a bath by myself so you can get some relief from your headache."

I turned but he was too fast for me, sweeping me up and carrying me into the bathroom. I laughed as he set me down but then he began kissing me and the comedy ended abruptly. Hot hands on cool flesh, hot tongues twirling together. I leaned into the fiery love he offered and soon we were moaning beneath a spray of warm water, heading towards the best headache remedy ever.

As I dug my fingers into Tiernan's muscled back and moaned his name, I wondered if we'd be like this forever. Could love as passionate as ours keep burning or would it eventually cool down to mere embers? I guess it didn't really matter. This was the only path I wanted to walk, whether the Goddess walked it with me or not.

Epilogue

The truce was signed.

It took three days for all involved to agree on terms but in the end, everyone did and the very long document was signed by quite a lot of people and then magically sealed. Visitation to Fairy was denied the Coven and the reason given for the denial; that the witches had proved unstable to possible alterations which Fairy would impose upon them, left little room for argument.

They were granted information rights though. This means that they are to be allowed access to all documents that the Human Council has on themselves and fairies. A select few of them would even be allowed to attend council classes and then take that knowledge back to share it with the Coven. In return, the Coven was to allow us access to their records and libraries.

In regards to the fey, this meant that we'd be working on establishing an exchange of magical information. The Fairy Council was interested in the possibility that witch magic could be supplemented to the elemental magic that fairies already possessed. The witches hoped that we would help them use their abilities to their fullest potential. Of course, this meant additional laws which the Human Council especially insisted upon.

The witches already had their own police to enforce these new laws; the Vexes. But there was about to be a huge change for them; they wouldn't be policing their own anymore. The Vexes would be trained by the Extinguishers to watch over the fey and then by the Wild Hunt to watch over the humans. In return, they would train hunters and extinguishers in the ways of policing witches.

As with anything of this nature, compromises were made but I believe that most were happy with the outcome. Even Shaman Kevin Chepaney, who was notified of the truce and what it entailed, expressed relief over the signing. He was given Councilman Teagan's direct number and was encouraged to call should he ever experience anything negatively supernatural. I think that alone, having someone he could turn to for help, made a huge difference in his life.

A few weeks after we returned to Twilight, we received the news that the dullahans had been judged by the High Councils and several had been found guilty of treason but surprisingly, most were spared execution, and punishment was meted out to just a few leaders. Malvin Skinner was not among them because he'd already been killed by Raza during our wild rescue of the witches and raven mockers.

Things are peaceful for now. I guess everyone is just too busy to cause trouble. Whatever the reason for the calm, I just pray that it continues. But as I look down at the letter in my lap, I know that my prayers are probably pointless. I'm sure that Danu can hear me but I'm also pretty sure that she never intended for my life to be peaceful. Danu wanted me to unite her people; all of them.

Dearest Niece,

I have received word from the Court of the Nine Sons. The meeting is set for two weeks hence. Please make preparations to be here at least one day in advance so we may set the magic upon you which you'll need to visit the underwater kingdom. You may bring your Count with you if you wish but please leave the rest of your Guard behind, including the lovely Catriona. I fear that the dragons might mistake her for an appetizer. Rest assured that I will provide protection for us both.

Sincerely,

King Uisdean Thorn of Unseelie

-Your Evil Uncle

Keep reading for a sneak peek into the next book in the Twilight Court Series:

Here there be Dragons

Chapter One

"I'm actually a little excited about seeing the dragon court," I said to Tiernan.

Tiernan looked up from the book he'd been reading in a chair near our bedroom's fireplace, and frowned. He closed the leather-clad tome and placed it on the small table beside him. I knew that look, a lecture was coming. I swear, sometimes being with Tiernan was like dating a college professor. A really old college professor.

Tiernan was way older than any human professor alive and also way smarter, which could be way more exhausting. I kept trying to get his age out of him but he still refused to tell me. I think he thinks I'll take it badly. He should know that my imagination is probably much worse than the truth. In my head, I placed his birth around the same time as Christ's.

"Seren," he started and I nearly groaned. "The dragon courts are volatile vortexes of violence."

"Sheesh," I rolled my eyes as I took the seat beside him. "Alliteration much?"

"Sometimes I feel like I have to rhyme my warnings so that they'll stick in your memory," he smirked.

"I'm gonna stick something in your memory, Lord Hunter," I growled.

"Seriously," he took my hand. "You need to be prepared for extreme acts of violence. The dragons are eternally snapping at each other and not in a verbal way. You saw how Raza behaved when he was in dragon form."

"Yeah," I whispered, thinking back to the destruction Raza wrought before I talked him down... several times.

"These dragons are much worse," Tiernan said grimly. "They are full-blooded water dragons which makes them both feisty and unpredictable. They turn like the tide and they may not breathe fire but they have other ways of making you sorry you're alive."

"Well now I'm really excited," I said sarcastically.

"I don't mean to scare you," he leaned forward and kissed me quickly. "We'll handle it together. I just don't want you thinking that this is going to be a vacation. You'll have to be very careful of what you say to them or even around them. Dragons aren't afraid of the Sluagh. They'll kill a fairy royal without batting a reptilian eye."

"That's why my dad is so upset," I sighed.

King Keir Bloodthorn, First King of Twilight, had been pissed when I'd announced that his brother had coerced me into joining him in the underwater Court of the Nine Sons. He'd nearly started a fight right in the middle of a party that was meant to be a meet and greet between us and the newly discovered witches. A royal argument was not appropriate to the setting.

So Keir had postponed it. He'd fought with Uisdean over it later but thankfully, it hadn't escalated to blows or magic. Uisdean had finally convinced Keir that he was well within his rights to ask me to act in my role of Ambassador. It was my job to mediate a meeting between him and the dragons. Keir had given in but he was still really mad. You couldn't really blame him for being suspicious of his brother; Uisdean *had* tried to kill me... twice.

Uisdean had vowed that he was over the whole wanting me dead thing, especially since he couldn't kill me now without bringing the Sluagh down on his head. The Sluagh were the monsters of Fairy and one of their main jobs was to kill anyone who tried to murder a fairy royal. When I had accepted the crown, Uisdean had to accept that I was here to stay.

Except now it looked as if he may have found a loophole.

"Do you think Uisdean is counting on a dragon killing me?" I asked Tiernan.

"It has crossed my mind," Tiernan grimaced. "And your father's."

"Why didn't I think of that?" I scowled.

"Because you're starting to let Danu influence your perceptions," Tiernan smiled gently. "She loves all of her children and she wants you to love them as well but Danu can afford to love us all, she's a goddess. You however, may be immortal but you are not indestructible and you must be more careful of whom you trust."

"I never said I trusted Uisdean," I squished up my face.

"No, but you're doing as Danu asked and are opening your heart to him," Tiernan sighed. "It's good that you're listening to her and really, we shouldn't ignore Danu's wishes but perhaps you should remember what else she said to you."

"To watch my step," I nodded. "I'll go one better and watch my back too."

"That's what you have me for," Tiernan grinned. "And I don't care what Uisdean says, he had no right to ask you to leave your personal guard behind. You may be acting in your capacity as Ambassador but you're also a fairy princess and you're allowed to bring your Star's Guard with you wherever you go... even and especially into the dragon courts."

"But don't you think he'll just make me leave them behind?"

"Then you threaten to stay behind with them," Tiernan shrugged. "They go with us or we don't go at all."

"I like that," I smirked. "Either way works for me."

"I'd hope for being left behind," Tiernan grimaced, "but there's not a chance of that happening. Uisdean will allow the Star's Guard to accompany you. He needs you too much."

"I don't see what my presence is going to do for him," I grumbled.

"At the very least, it will give him cannon fodder to throw at the dragons as he runs for his life," Tiernan rolled his eyes.

"You're joking, right?" I asked but he remained silent. "Tell me you're joking, Tiernan!"

"I'm joking," he said but it wasn't at all convincing.

About the Author

Amy Sumida lives on an island in the Pacific Ocean where gods can still be found, though there are very few fairies. She sleeps in a fairy bed, high in the air, with two gravity-defying felines and upon waking, she writes down everything the voices in her head tell her to. She aspires to someday become a crazy cat lady, rocking on her front porch and guarding her precious kitties with a shotgun loaded with rock salt. She bellydances and paints pictures on her walls but is happiest with her nose stuck in a book, her mind in a different world than this one, filled with fantastical men who unfortunately don't exist in our mundane reality. Thank the gods for fantasy.

You can find her on facebook at:

https://www.facebook.com/pages/The-Godhunter-Series/323778160998617?ref=hl

On Twitter under @Ashstarte

On Goodreads:

https://www.goodreads.com/author/show/7200339.Amy_Sumida

On her website:

https://sites.google.com/site/authoramysumida/home?pli=1

And you can find her entire collection of books, along with some personal recommendations, at her Amazon store:

https://sites.google.com/site/authoramysumida/home?pli=1

CPSIA information can be obtained
at www.ICGtesting.com
Printed in the USA
LVHW05s2359041018
592495LV00008B/309/P